CAUGHT

CAUGHT

JAMI ALDEN

BRAVA

KENSINGTON BOOKS
http://www.kensingtonbooks.com

BRAVA BOOKS are published by

Kensington Publishing Corp.
850 Third Avenue
New York, NY 10022

All Kensington Titles, Imprints, and Distributed Lines are available at special quantity discounts for bulk purchases for sales promotions, premiums, fund-raising, and educational or institutional use.

Special book excerpts or customized printings can also be created to fit specific needs. For details, write or phone the office of the Kensington special sales manager: Kensington Publishing Corp., 850 Third Avenue, New York, NY 10022, attn: Special Sales Department, Phone: 1-800-221-2647.

ISBN-13: 978-0-7582-2546-7
ISBN-10: 0-7582-2546-6

First Trade Paperback Printing: October 2008

10 9 8 7 6 5 4 3 2 1

Printed in the United States of America

To my boys, Gajus, Luke, and Myko,
who love me even when I'm a stressed-out head case.
You guys make my dreams come true every day.

Acknowledgments

I am fortunate to have some amazing women in my life, without whom this book would not have been possible. First, I need to thank my editor, Hilary Sares, for giving me a shot at my dream. Thanks for beating me up over e-mail and with sticky notes until my hero and heroine finally came to life.

To the Fog City Divas, but especially to Monica McCarty, who provided endless hours of therapy, and to Bella Andre, my biggest cheerleader, who read more drafts of this book than anyone should have to.

To Anne Mallory and Barbara Freethy, who, along with Bella formed the Starbucks crew and listened to me stress and moan and complain with more patience than I deserved.

To Karin Tabke, Poppy Reiffen, and Virna dePaul, who saved me from plotting myself into a dead end way, way back when.

To Svaja, my amazing, wonderful mother-in-law, who showed up when the new baby was six weeks old so I could get back to work. To Karen, who provides wonderful daycare to my boys and makes it easier for me to go off and write, knowing they're in such capable, loving hands.

CHAPTER 1

*P*AIN. IT SCORCHED *through his arm and across his chest. He was afraid to look down, afraid to see the extent of the damage. He could barely see. He lifted his hand to wipe the blood out of his eyes and bit back a scream. His shoulder felt like it had been torn out of its socket, and he was pretty sure his elbow was shattered. Definitely some broken ribs.*

The twisted wreckage of their plane lay in a heap several yards away. The last thing Ethan remembered was smacking his head into the steering column as he'd piled into the smoothest stretch of land he could find between two knife-edged mountain peaks. He didn't know how long he'd been lying here, shivering in the frigid mountain air. Could have been minutes, could have been hours.

He pushed himself up on his still functional right arm and looked around for his copilot, Huck Finnegan, swallowing back his gorge when he saw the tall, lanky form crumpled next to the wreckage. Like Ethan, Huck had somehow managed to unclip himself from his harness and extricate himself from the wreck, but he hadn't made it very far. Even in the dim light Ethan could see the dark stain spreading under his friend's prone form.

He called out for his friend, Huck's name dissolving into

a groan of agony when that simple movement sent a spear of pain driving between his ribs. His friend didn't so much as twitch. Ethan squinted up at the mountains, taking stock of their situation, dread deepening as he realized how vulnerable they were. Him wounded, Huck possibly dead, sitting ducks in this one flat spot for several square miles with enemy forces running around the area like a bunch of fucking mountain goats.

The emergency beacon would have been set off by the wreck, but there was no guarantee the cavalry would arrive in time to save their asses. Though his legs seemed fine, he didn't dare get up and walk. Nothing said "come and shoot me" like a six-foot-plus white guy in the middle of Al Quaeda country. Ethan rolled onto his belly and cursed silently as he executed a slow, excruciating belly crawl over to his copilot. Thick, dark blood oozed from a wound in Huck's abdomen, and from the amount already seeping into the parched ground, it was likely his friend was already dead.

Ethan reached out his hand, closing his eyes in relief when he felt a pulse at his throat, thready but there. But not for long if he didn't get help soon. Ethan unzipped his flight suit and stripped off his T-shirt, nearly passing out as he dragged it off his fucked-up left arm. He balled up the cotton and pressed it firmly against the wound.

Huck let out a harsh groan. Ethan took it as a good sign that he still had it in him to respond to pain. "Take it easy, buddy. We're gonna get out of this."

Huck coughed, staining his lips and chin with dark blood. "I'm pretty fucked up, man."

"It's not that bad." Ethan pressed harder against the wound. He wasn't about to let his friend bleed out on this cold, barren mountain.

Off in the distance, he heard a noise—faint, pulsing, growing closer. Helicopter blades. It might as well have been angels singing.

"Cavalry's here. We're going to be fine." He prayed it was true, but Huck's color, which hadn't been good to begin with, had bleached out until he was as gray as the granite peaks surrounding them.

A sharp crack, and the dirt next to him exploded.

Ethan wrapped his good arm around Huck and launched himself for the meager cover of the plane in an adrenaline-fueled rush. The chopper peppered the area with gunfire, covering him as they came in for a landing about fifteen yards away.

It felt like fifteen miles as Ethan got his legs up under him, slung Huck over his shoulder in a fireman's hold, and ran for it. He heard a meaty thunk and felt the deep burn as his leg took a hit, the bullet ripping a hole through his left quad. He staggered, hearing his friend groan, felt the sticky warmth of Huck's blood seeping through his own clothing. He refused to go down, willing his leg not to buckle as he gunned it for the chopper. The metallic stench of blood coated his nose, and dust flew into his face, the thunder of the blades and pepper of gunshots deafening as he staggered those last desperate steps . . .

Ethan jerked awake, clawing away the sweat-soaked sheets as his breath came in heavy pants. He struggled toward wakefulness, swallowing back the rising panic as he registered a dark room and unfamiliar surroundings. As he shook off the last dregs of sleep, his eyes slowly made out the dim shapes of furniture and his body registered that he was lying on a comfortable king-size bed and not the hard floor of a Blackhawk helicopter. And the low thrum he heard wasn't the sound of helicopter blades slicing through the frigid air of the mountains south of Kabul.

It was coming from the bathroom. It took him a moment, but Ethan finally recognized the steady hum as the jets on the Jacuzzi tub. Which meant someone was taking a bath.

Gillian.

At least, he was pretty sure that was her name. A sexy blonde in a tastefully slinky red dress, a dress that was now flung across the back of a chair on the other side of the sizable master suite. She'd been a guest at the political fundraiser he'd attended last night. But while she had paid five thousand dollars for her plate of rubbery chicken, Ethan had been on the job, running security for the event.

Like it or not, he was the pretty boy of Gemini Security and Investigations, the firm he ran with his brothers, Derek and Danny. That meant that any time a client wanted low-profile security—someone who could blend with the crowd and make conversation with the guests while ensuring the safety of all involved—youngest brother Ethan was the one they trotted out.

So he'd dragged out his tux and dusted off his social graces. At the end of the night, sexy, sophisticated Gillian had taken him home like a party favor.

He shook off the dust of his nightmare until all that was left was the buzz of adrenaline pumping through his veins. He was keyed up, strung out, and he knew the perfect way to work off the tension the dream had elicited. When he got like this, the only way to get him down was either a long run or a lusty fuck, and he sure as hell wasn't going to go home and lace up his running shoes when there was an attractive and ever-so-willing woman just a few yards away.

He slid from the bed and padded naked across the room, the humming of the jets growing louder as he got closer to the bathroom. Gillian reclined in the tub, her eyes opened into lusty slits. She'd lit about five hundred candles, and their warm light and thick scent permeated the steamy air. After their earlier energetic screw, she apparently wanted to go all romantic for round two. Whatever. He'd go along with whatever mood she chose to create. When it came to the women he slept with, he was nothing if not accommodating.

At least he would be until she started talking about relation-ships or commitment of any kind. Ethan Taggart didn't do relationships, or, God forbid, the self-destructive emotion otherwise known as love.

"Hey there, lover," Gillian said, stretching luxuriously, arching her back so her full, unnaturally perky breasts broke the surface of the water.

He felt his cock stir in interest as she lazily circled her water-slicked breast with her fingers. And she noticed, bit-ing her lip in anticipation as her gaze drifted down his naked body, coming to rest on his thickening erection. She was exactly his type. A sunny blonde who kept her body well maintained and her mind unconcerned with anything too serious. The type of woman who wanted little more out of life than a good time and knew he was a man to give it to her.

He smiled, knelt down next to the tub, and picked up the sponge that rested on the edge. He dipped it under the sur-face and ran the sponge up the smooth skin of her thigh. Her knees parted, inviting him to drop the sponge and con-tinue the path with his bare hand. He closed his eyes, savor-ing the slick smooth skin under his fingers.

This was what he needed. Not commitment, not obliga-tion—maybe, if he was honest, not even sex. It was the touch, the feel of a woman's skin under his hand, a moment of warmth that wouldn't last past his next orgasm. Then the cold would slowly take over until, after a few days, a few weeks at most, he would find another woman, another body to share her heat, if only for a night.

He slid his hand up to Gillian's hot core, dipped his head to kiss her warm lips. She wasn't the most beautiful woman he'd ever been with, or the most interesting but, for tonight at least, she was perfect.

Surveillance work sucked. In the course of her relatively new career as a private investigator, Toni Crawford tried to avoid it at all costs. Especially when it pertained to a cheating spouse.

Yet here she was at three o'clock on a Saturday morning, her nearly six-foot-tall frame folded up in the the driver's seat of her Honda, which felt less roomy as the hours passed while she waited for Phil Barrett to emerge from the Sheraton Palo Alto with his girlfriend on his arm. She'd already given his wife, Christine, all the proof she needed, gathered the way Toni preferred—electronically. It had been child's play to hack into Phil's e-mail account and find incriminating messages that included such pertinent information as names and dates of rendezvous as well as references to specific acts performed on said dates.

Swallowing back her distaste, Toni had printed out the messages and bound them neatly in a folder to deliver to his wife, Toni's client. That was the part Toni hated the most. Watching her client's face crumple when she found out that her suspicions were indeed true. That the man she'd promised her life to had chosen to find his entertainment elsewhere. No matter what was going on in a marriage, no matter how far apart a couple grew, Toni knew firsthand how devastating the proof of a loved one's infidelity could be.

Just once, Toni wanted to be able to go to a client and tell her that she was wrong. That she'd misread the signs, that all Toni had been able to dig up was work-related e-mails and legitimate business dinners.

It never worked out that way. The women were always right.

And so had been the case with Christine. But knowing how it was going to end up didn't make Toni's job any easier. When Christine's face blanched and her throat convulsed, Toni had resisted the urge to wrap her arm around the woman's shoulders. She didn't offer comforting words or tell the woman she knew exactly what she was going through. This was work, after all, and the woman was her client, nothing more, nothing less. The only reason she was in this business was to get paid, not to make friends.

Which was the only reason she was out in the thick dark of this balmy July night, because Christine Barrett was paying her. Even after all the proof Toni had unearthed in the bowels of Phil's computer, his wife still clung to the thread of hope that it was all a big misunderstanding. Really, it could have all been mere talk, a not-so-innocent flirtation between coworkers. There was still no proof that they'd actually done anything.

Toni sighed, took off her glasses, rubbed her gritty eyes, and marveled at womankind's particular talent for self-delusion.

But that self-delusion would pay her rent for another month. So Toni had agreed to follow Phil around to see if she could catch hubby in the act and produce photographic proof of his affair. Toni was in for a sizable bonus if she produced such proof.

And if it still felt wrong to take money to find a nail for the coffin of another marriage, Toni was sure she'd get used to it. Eventually.

After more than a week of tailing him straight home every night, tonight Toni finally hit pay dirt. Earlier in the evening, Toni had tailed him from the office to a bar in Palo Alto, where he'd met up with the coworker. After a couple of hours, the couple emerged and walked a few short blocks to the Sheraton, located right off the main downtown business district. Now it was the wee hours of the morning and the couple had yet to emerge.

Toni hefted her digital camera and once again tested the range on her telephoto lens. From her vantage point, with this lens, Toni would be able to capture the stubble on Phil's chin and the whisker burn on his girlfriend's cheek. With the camera cradled in readiness in her lap, she once again settled in to wait.

* * *

Ethan rubbed his eyes and gulped down the last of his fifth cup of coffee as he pulled up to Jerry Kramer's driveway. He'd been about to collapse into bed after his early-morning return from Gillian's house when the call had come in.

Jerry Kramer, Gemini Securities' most recent high-profile client, had called to inform Ethan that his seventeen-year-old daughter, Kara, was missing.

Now, Ethan could think of a lot of things a seventeen-year-old girl could be up to, none of them life threatening. But Kramer was worried. He'd hired Gemini to handle his family's security after his company, GeneCor, had recently come under fire by activist groups for its new product forays into stem cell research. So when Kara wasn't in her bed when the housekeeper had gone to wake her this morning, Kramer had raised the alarm.

And since Kramer was exactly the kind of client Gemini liked—deep pockets and a willingness to spread the word about Gemini among his peers—Ethan had no choice but to respond. So he had jumped into a cold shower and sucked down a vat of coffee in an effort to revive his groggy brain before heading over to Kramer's.

At this hour it took only ten minutes to drive from his place in Palo Alto to Kramer's plush estate. Though the entire neighborhood was decidedly affluent—not even a teardown shack could be found for less than one and a half million—the Kramers' mansion was beyond even the usual extravagance. Sitting well back from the street, it hinted at nothing of its luxury to passersby. A wrought iron fence surrounded the nearly two-acre property, and half a dozen oak trees not only offered shade but almost completely obscured the house from view.

The house itself sat at the end of a long, circular driveway. As he turned into the drive, Ethan frowned to see the massive wrought iron gate standing wide open. His shoulder muscles tensed under his sport coat. He'd just completed a comprehensive security evaluation for the family last week, culminating in the installation of a state-of-the-art security system that included keyless coded entry, motion detectors, and, as an obvious first line of defense, a front gate that unlocked only when the correct combination was entered into the keypad.

But what the hell was the sense of spending tens of thousands of dollars on security work if they were going to leave the fucking front gate wide open?

He bit back his irritation as he drove several hundred yards to the main house.

The acre surrounding the house was meticulously landscaped, the lawn a perfect green carpct that would have done a golf course groundskeeper proud. Brightly flowering bushes were clipped into submission, not a single leaf out of place. Beyond the lawn, the landscape was allowed to stay in its wild state until it blended in with the surrounding woods.

To the right of the house was a four-car garage. The housekeeper's Saturn was parked in front of the leftmost door, and a black-and-white police cruiser emblazoned with the Atherton Police Department shield was parked beside it.

As he approached the mahogany double doors at the house's entrance, he couldn't help but shake his head at such excess. The house was a massive English manor–style home, designed as a monument to the owner's wealth. Over ten thousand square feet for one resident. Well, three if you counted the time Kara and her younger brother spent here.

Not that Ethan had the right to judge. The house he and his brothers had grown up in hadn't been exactly modest. Their father, Joe Taggart, had made his fortune in investment banking in the late eighties, and Ethan had grown up in a world where money was no object.

Only stints in the military had kept him and his brothers from becoming the type of entitled dickheads that this town seemed to breed.

Ethan rang the doorbell and was gratified to hear the beeping of the keypad in the front entryway. At least they were keeping the house alarm on, per his instructions.

The door swung open to reveal Manuela, Kramer's housekeeper. A petite woman in her early forties, Manuela greeted Ethan with a shy smile. "Everyone is in the kitchen," she said and motioned Ethan to follow her.

The hard soles of his shoes echoed on the marble floor of the foyer before it gave way to hardwood in the hallway that led to the kitchen. He could hear a man speaking in a low voice that echoed off the high ceiling, followed by another voice, more strident. "I don't see what the hell that has to do with anything."

Kramer, operating with his usual subtlety. Ethan often wondered how someone so lacking in tact had managed to become so successful in business. Then again, Kramer was the development guru at his biotech company, working behind the scenes to develop new and innovative products. When Ethan had researched Kramer before taking him on as a client, he hadn't been surprised to read that although Kramer had founded GeneCor six years ago, when the company went public, investors had brought in a new CEO to be the public, polished face of the company.

In the kitchen were two uniformed policemen who quickly identified themselves as officers Hayes and Torres. "Ethan, thank God you're here." Jerry Kramer was a heavyset man of medium height. When he was angry or upset, as he was now, his scalp burned red under his thinning blond hair and a thick vein pulsed across his forehead. "I don't think these clowns know what they're doing."

"And who are you exactly, Mr. Taggart?" Officer Hayes asked. The cop looked like he was straight out of a cornfield somewhere, blond and beefy, and almost a match for Ethan's height of six foot three. His mouth was tight, his blue eyes hot as he obviously struggled with his patience.

Ethan offered his most engaging "Can you believe this guy?" smile, hoping he could salvage the situation before Kramer permanently pissed off the entire police department.

He handed Hayes a card. "My company handles Mr. Kramer's security. He called this morning when he discovered his daughter was missing."

Hayes nodded. "We arrived a few minutes ago and have been asking Mr. Kramer some questions."

"None of which are relevant," Kramer said.

Ethan hid a wince and wished he could simply backhand Kramer across the mouth. "Would you excuse us a moment?" he asked and grabbed Kramer by the arm before the cops could answer. He steered Jerry into the hall.

"Jerry, you're not going to do anyone any good if you piss off the cops."

"But they're not doing anything. Why aren't they out looking for her instead of standing in my kitchen asking irrelevant questions?"

"They said they just got here. They have standard procedure to follow."

"But we're wasting time when we should be out looking."

Ethan gave Jerry's arm a warning squeeze. "The best thing we can do right now is to answer all of their questions and give them all the information we can to help them find Kara."

Jerry took a deep breath and nodded tightly.

As they turned back to the kitchen, Ethan could hear the low murmur of conversation between Manuela and the police. He strained to overhear but their discussion stopped as soon as they heard Ethan and Jerry's approach.

The officers motioned Jerry to have a seat at the kitchen island. If he balked at the idea of being invited to sit in his own home, for once Jerry had the grace to keep his mouth shut.

Officer Torres flipped open his notepad. "Now, Mr. Kramer, you said you got home late last night."

Jerry nodded.

"How late?"

"One AM," Jerry said.

"And you don't make it a habit to check on your children when you get home?"

"No," he said defensively. "That's why their rooms are in another wing. I'm out late quite often, and I don't want to disturb them."

More like you don't want to actually have to interact with them for more than the time it takes you all to pose for the family holiday card. But it wasn't Ethan's job to criticize Jerry Kramer's style of parenting. It was all too common in families like this for kids to be foisted off on a series of nannies, tutors, and coaches while parents committed themselves to high-powered careers and equally demanding social lives.

Ethan should know. He and his brothers had experienced it firsthand.

"And your son is where again?" Officer Torres asked.

Jerry gave a frustrated shrug and looked pointedly at Manuela.

"Kyle is at baseball camp," Manuela said in softly accented English. "He'll be back next week."

Officer Hayes pursed his lips before asking, "Any chance your daughter might also have plans to be away that might have slipped your mind?"

Ethan gave Jerry a warning look. He had no doubt officers Hayes and Torres would relish the opportunity to cuff and stuff a jackass like Kramer for assaulting an officer.

Manuela chimed up again. "Oh no, sir. Kara is home for the summer until Mr. Kramer takes the children to the Lake Tahoe house the first week of August."

"Could she be at a friend's house?" Officer Hayes asked.

"Is it possible she's spending the night and just forgot to check in?"

Before Jerry could answer, the front doorbell rang insistently. Manuela's relief was palpable as she hurried out of the kitchen, the soles of her rubber sandals squeaking along the marble floor.

Ethan heard the murmur of female voices. Moments later, the squeaking approached again, soon drowned out by the clacking of a woman's high heels. A bone-thin blonde of medium height burst into the kitchen, followed by an impressively tall woman with dark hair that angled sharply to her jaw.

"Jerry, what's going on? Where is Kara?" The woman's blue eyes were hollow and bloodshot, her cheekbones sharp and drawn as if she'd gone too long without a good meal or a decent night's sleep.

"Jesus, what is she doing here?" Jerry said to the room at large.

"I called her," Manuela offered softly, then cringed as though bracing herself for a blow.

Jerry's cheeks flushed red and he opened his mouth. Ethan caught his eye and sent him a hard look, reminding him of their audience. Jerry swallowed hard and thought better of his tirade. "Everything is fine, Marcy." He shot a glare at Manuela that promised later retribution. "There was no reason to call Mrs. Kramer."

Marcy Kramer braced her thin shoulders and squared off against her ex-husband. "Don't get angry at Manuela for calling to check if Kara was at my house. You should have called me." Her mouth pulled into a bitter line. "But you were probably too busy boning your little twenty-year-old to even notice."

"I'm surprised you weren't too high on your happy pills to find the phone."

Ethan inserted himself between Marcy and Jerry as gracefully as possible and painted on his most sincere, can't-we-all-just-get-along-here smile. The cops didn't make a move, happy to have Ethan defuse the situation. "Mrs. Kramer, let me introduce myself. I'm Ethan Taggart. Your husband hired us to handle his security concerns."

Marcy frowned and stepped back as though caught off guard, then blinked again as her gaze froze on Ethan's face. She stared for a few minutes, unspeaking. Ethan was used to that. Not that he was especially vain, but if enough women tell you how gorgeous you are, you start believing them. Personally, he didn't pay too much attention to his looks other than to keep himself clean shaven and to make sure his hair was cut short enough to subdue its natural wave, but he'd learned early in life that his good looks could be used to his advantage, especially when it came to women. In the navy, his looks and luck with women had earned him the dubiously flattering moniker Lancelot. Though he still didn't like being compared to a man who slept with his best friend's wife, he wasn't above exploiting the edge his looks provided.

Marcy nodded absently before turning her attention to the police. "I don't understand why you're not out looking for her."

Officer Torres stepped forward. "We're still gathering information, ma'am. The more we know, the better we'll know where to begin our search."

The tall woman, who still hadn't introduced herself, leaned with one hip against the granite island, arms folded across her chest. Low-slung jeans clung to her narrow hips and long, lean legs. A clingy black T-shirt with a picture of a red-and-green dragon rode over high, tight breasts and showed off toned, pale arms. Hazel eyes stared shrewdly through dark-framed glasses, her attention was focused solely on Ethan. With her no-nonsense look and unwavering gaze, she reminded him of his third grade teacher. Not that his third grade teacher had legs that appeared to sprout directly from her armpits or a wide, red mouth that no amount of pursing could make look prim. In fact, Miss Humphrey had been ancient—at least to his third grade mind—while this woman couldn't have been older than her late twenties, early thirties tops. But Miss Humphrey had given him that same look, one that said, "You can smile all you want, young man. But I know exactly what you're up to."

Still, Ethan had yet to encounter a woman he couldn't charm. Even Miss Humphrey had relented after the first semester.

He focused the full force of his smile on her tight-lipped face. "We haven't met. I'm Ethan Taggart, Gemini Securities."

She reluctantly took his hand. Hers was slender and fine-boned, all but swallowed up by his broad palm and long fingers. But her handshake was firm and her face remained impassive, her smile a mere tightening of the lips, a narrowing of the eyes. "Toni Crawford." Her hand slid from his grip, and he felt the trace of her fingers all the way down to his groin.

"This is going to sound rude, but I don't understand what you're doing here," Ethan prodded when she offered no additional information about herself.

"She's with me," Marcy said. "I hired Toni several months ago to do some work for me"—she looked pointedly at Jerry—"before I filed for divorce."

"You're her attorney?" He scanned her outfit skeptically.

Toni shook her head. "I do a little investigative work myself."

Jerry's head whipped around and his gaze narrowed on the woman's face. "So you're the one who cost me an extra ten million." He tried to make it sound like a joke but Ethan could hear the menace in every syllable. "Those pictures really did me in."

Toni straightened to her full height, which was a good two inches over Jerry's. "Mr. Kramer, I only reported your activities back to my client. If you didn't want to get caught, perhaps you should have thought better of your behavior."

Ethan smothered a chuckle. Cool as a cucumber. Not a bit rattled, she stared Jerry down. She should have looked cold and intimidating but Ethan found her inexplicably sexy.

He'd already noticed her impossibly long legs. As subtly as possible, he moved his gaze higher to check out the firm curve of her ass. Nice. Not too big, not too small, nicely rounded against the fabric of her jeans. It was a perfect match for her breasts. Firm and round and high.

Her hair was thick and shiny, cut at a sharp angle that framed her features. And those heavy, librarian glasses did nothing to disguise the sculpted lines of her cheeks and jaw. With her pale skin, full red mouth, and almost-black hair, she was like Snow White in jeans and Converse All Stars. *Yeah, if Snow White looked like she wanted to reach out and snatch your balls off.* Still, Ethan felt his groin stir in appreciation.

Okay, so she was hot in a dark, serious sort of way, but his swift physical reaction didn't make any sense. She was the exact opposite of what he usually went for. His mind flashed back to Gillian, whom he'd left only a few short hours ago in a tanned, blond, well-satisfied heap.

Yet here he was, working on a healthy hard-on for Toni.

Who didn't like to be checked out, if the pursing of her luscious mouth was anything to go by. Unlike good-time Gillian, Toni looked like she hadn't laughed in years and wouldn't know a good time if it bit her in the ass.

Then again, if nipping her in her firmly curved rear was what it took to put a smile on her face, Ethan was game.

But now was neither the time nor the place for Ethan to

fantasize about the many different ways he could make Toni Crawford smile.

Toni was oblivious to his lust, her face impassive as she turned her attention to Officer Torres. "Sorry we interrupted. What have you found out so far?"

"We wanted to know if Kara could be at a friend's house, could have gone out and forgotten to check in?"

"Kara's very responsible," Jerry said. "She would never forget to call." He shot a meaningful look at the housekeeper.

"I check all the messages," Manuela said softly, "and Kara always calls to let me know she'll be out."

Jerry crossed his arms and shot the cops a look as though to say "so there."

"Teenagers sneak out," Hayes said, "go to parties, meet friends, do all kinds of things they won't tell their parents about."

"Kara's a good girl," Jerry said adamantly. "No drinking, no drugs. She gets straight A's."

"Jerry's right. Kara's never been in any trouble." Marcy interjected. "She's even part of the Promise Club."

"Promise Club?" Ethan asked.

For the first time that morning, Marcy's face displayed something resembling happiness. "It's a group of girls who have pledged to save their virginity until marriage. They even started an online support group to encourage other kids to do the same. I know lots of kids Kara's age are into drinking and going to parties, but Kara's just not part of that crowd."

Ethan's eyes narrowed as a look passed between Toni and Manuela. Manuela made herself very busy scrubbing at an invisible spot on the spotless breakfast bar.

The ring of a cell phone echoed off the granite countertops. Jerry snatched it up, his jaw tightening when he saw the number. "I have to take this. It's very important." And very private, if the speed at which Jerry was retreating down the hall was any indication.

Marcy's gaze followed his retreating back, a look of disgust suffusing his face. "Our daughter is missing, and he still can't ignore that damn phone."

Toni reached out and squeezed Marcy's thin arm. "Manuela, is there something you're not telling us?"

Officer Hayes spoke before Manuela could. "A little over two weeks ago we busted a party over on Selby," he said, referring to a street a few blocks away. "Kara was there. She was drunk, said her friends ditched her."

Marcy's face blanched. "It was a mistake. It wasn't her."

Hayes shook his head. "I checked her ID and gave her a ride to this address, ma'am. I—" He broke off as Jerry entered the kitchen, looking even more worried than before.

Whatever illusions Jerry and Marcy had about their "perfect" daughter were about to be shattered. "Kara's been sneaking out, Jerry," Ethan said, not bothering to sugarcoat it.

Surprisingly, Jerry didn't voice a protest. "I don't exactly keep a close eye on her while she's staying here. It never occurred to me that she would sneak out."

Ethan nodded. "The security system keeps a log of all entries and exits. It will be easy enough to see when she left, so let's start there." Flipping open his phone, Ethan quickly dialed his brother Derek's cell. He had no doubt that his older-by-six-minutes twin would already be showered, dressed, and logged in to Gemini's private network, weekend or no.

Derek answered on the first ring. "What's her name?"

"Who?" Ethan asked. Still, his gaze strayed to Toni, who had taken a red BlackBerry from her pocket. Her thumbs flew over the keypad as she said something to Marcy in a voice too low for him to hear.

"The only reason for you to call me before ten on a Saturday is because you're doing the drive of shame home from some woman's house."

He tried to recall Gillian's face but right now all he could see was black, silky hair and plump red lips, tart and juicy. "An hour ago you would have had me. I'm at Kramer's house. I need you to log in to their security system."

A few seconds of silence, then, "Done. What do you need?"

"I need all entries and exits in the last twelve hours."

"We have an entry at six forty-two p.m., exit at eight thirty p.m., an entry at one-oh-nine a.m., and another exit at two thirty-two a.m. "

Ethan hung up and relayed the information to the others.

"Any idea who she hooked up with?" Officer Hayes asked.

Jerry shook his head.

"I haven't seen her much in the past month," Marcy said, her voice tight. "Kara and I haven't been getting along so we decided she should come stay with her dad." She sat down at the breakfast bar and hid her face in her hands. "I have no idea what's going on in my daughter's life. I'm a terrible mother." She started to sob.

"Great, here we go," Jerry muttered, glaring at his ex-wife's heaving back.

Toni's death glare echoed Ethan's own reaction. The woman was distraught. The least the guy could do was cut her a little slack.

Toni put her hand on Marcy's shoulder and gave it an awkward squeeze. "She's fine, Marcy. Probably just at a friend's house."

"She has a boyfriend," Manuela offered softly. "She meets him sometimes. But she always comes back before sunrise."

Jerry whirled on the woman, the vein on his head throbbing back to prominence. "You knew my daughter was sneaking out and you didn't say anything?"

"Don't blame her!" Marcy yelled, her head popping up from the cradle of her skeletal hands. "It's not her fault you can't keep track of our children."

"Maybe if you hadn't kicked her out, she wouldn't be sneaking out and going to parties."

Marcy gasped and clutched her chest as though she'd taken a spear through it. "I did not kick her out."

Time to shut this thing down before Ethan was refereeing a battle of the exes worthy of *The Jerry Springer Show.* Bringing his fingers to his lips, he let out a piercing whistle that broke through the escalating volume of their voices. "Yelling at each other isn't going to help us figure out where Kara is and who she's likely to be with. Let's try to focus so we don't waste any more of the officers' time."

Or mine, he thought wearily, suddenly bone-tired and wishing Kara would pull herself out of whatever bed she'd passed out in and haul her happy ass home.

He rubbed his eyes wearily and looked up to see Toni staring at him as though she knew exactly what he was thinking.

"Do you have someplace more important to be?" she said, one dark brow arched over the frame of her glasses. "Perhaps debugging your fancy security system so Kara can't sneak in and out without anyone being the wiser?" A smirk pulled at her lips. He wanted to kiss it off her face and spend the rest of the morning showing her who was boss.

Too bad he didn't have time. But he wasn't about to stand around and let her take potshots at him in front of a client. He pasted on a dazzling smile worthy of a toothpaste commercial and affected a deferential tone.

"Thanks for pointing that out. Now, I appreciate your coming all the way over here to assist us, but between the police and Gemini, we have it handled." He pulled his gaze away from Toni's face, her pale skin flushed with irritation.

"Marcy, I promise I'll keep you apprised of any new information."

Marcy began to protest but Toni silenced her with a lift of her hand and approached Ethan with slow, deliberate steps. "Listen, Ethan," she said, perfectly mimicking his placating tone, "let's get something straight. I'm not here to assist you. I work for Marcy and her daughter. If you want to run your little investigation, that's fine, but stay out of my way."

CHAPTER 2

WE *APPRECIATE YOUR coming all this way to assist us.* Arrogant bastard, she thought as the police continued their questioning about Kara's recent behavior. One glance from those turquoise eyes and Ethan no doubt thought she'd puddle at his feet and let Ethan Taggart, Gemini Securities, take over the show. Not a chance.

Okay, maybe she had gone a little weak-kneed—not that she'd ever in a million years admit that to anyone else. With his dark, gold-shot hair, laser-sharp blue eyes, and features that looked like they'd been chiseled in granite, he was gorgeous in a way that called to every feminine instinct she possessed. And what healthy heterosexual girl wouldn't get a few butterflies in her stomach at the way his full mouth stretched into a heartbreaker of a smile?

And to up the ante even further, he was tall, at least a few inches over six feet, all of it solidly muscled, if the way his shoulders filled his jacket was any indication. Big and strong enough to make even Toni feel something close to delicate.

Ethan's focus strayed from the policeman's questions to Toni's face. A hot flush erupted in her cheeks when he caught her staring. God, talk about an inappropriate time for her libido to decide to come out of hibernation. What kind of person was she, drooling over some guy when Kara was missing?

The anxious knot in her stomach tightened another notch, silencing the butterflies. Toni had gotten to know Kara over the past year that she'd been working for Marcy. As her parents said, Kara was a nice kid, a good kid, keeping her head down and focusing on school, trying to hold it together despite the ugliness her parents were heaping on each other.

Toni and Kara had struck up a friendship, one of the few occasions Toni broke her "no emotional involvement" rule when it came to her clients. Toni had stayed in touch with Kara via e-mails and text messages, as well as the occasional coffee date.

Kara never told her much about her friends or her social life, mostly just vented about her parents, while Toni offered what guidance she could about surviving your parents' divorce. Toni had seen so much of herself in Kara, in the way she tried so hard not to make waves. Unlike Toni, whose drive had been self-induced, Kara strove to live up to the demands of her exacting parents, trying to live up to Jerry's image of Kara as the perfect daughter who never got into any kind of trouble. Whether it meant staying up all night to study for her SATs or taking a vow of virginity, Kara would do anything to win her father's approval.

But Toni could sense the cracks forming in the facade. Striving for that level of perfection was exhausting, especially when you were dealing with an emotionally disengaged father and a borderline-unstable mother with an increasing reliance on prescription pills to get her through the day.

No surprise then that there was a lot more going on with Kara than Toni or her parents knew. Toni'd hoped that by offering herself as a non-judgy adult to talk to, she could help Kara survive the shitstorm her parents created.

It hadn't been nearly enough, even when they'd been communicating regularly, and Toni felt another stab of guilt that she hadn't pushed harder to keep in contact over the past few months. Kara had stopped responding to Toni's messages, and Toni had let it slide. Now she cursed herself. How hard would it have been to send a freaking text? It would have let Kara know she was still there, still cared. *Don't get ahead of yourself. Sneaking out to party and running away are two completely different things. So far, sneaking out to see her boyfriend is the extent of Kara's bad behavior.*

She ripped her gaze from Ethan's knowing look and listened intently as Jerry and Marcy answered the police's questions.

"Try her friend Laurie," Marcy was saying. "Laurie Friedland. She and Kara have been best friends since the fourth grade. And she was close with some of the girls on her volleyball team."

"What about the boyfriend?"

Marcy shook her head, her thin shoulders hunching. "I didn't even know about him. We haven't really seen much of each other since school ended and she decided to come stay with her father."

Toni frowned. She'd last heard from Kara a couple of weeks ago, and she hadn't mentioned moving out. Then again, Kara hadn't mentioned the boyfriend, either.

Jerry shook his head and shrugged. "I didn't know about the boyfriend, either," he snapped.

"His name is Sean, I think," Manuela offered. "And he drives a white car. That's all I know."

"Do you think he took her?" Marcy asked in a thin voice.

Officer Hayes shook his head. "More likely they met for a date. Honestly, folks, I know you're worried, but there's a good chance she'll turn up on her own." He flipped his notepad shut and nodded to his partner.

Toni's shoulders tensed under the thin fabric of her T-shirt as she remembered another girl, another missing girl no one took seriously. Until it was too late.

She forced the morbid thoughts from her mind. Kara was nothing like Toni's younger sister, Michelle, Toni reminded herself. Unlike Michelle, Kara *was* a good kid, for all that she might have started acting out. Toni's sister had practically had "bad kid" tattooed on her forehead. When Michelle had gone missing, no one, not even Toni, had questioned the idea that she'd run away. After all, she'd done it before, and she had always come back, whenever she got sick of her boyfriend or needed money.

Until that last time, when she didn't come back.

"That's it?" Marcy asked, pulling Toni's attention away from her morbid memories. "You're going to do nothing while we sit around and wait for her to come home?"

He held up a placating hand. "Ma'am, that's not what I said. But situations like this tend to resolve on their own. For now, we'll file a report and open an investigation." He took down a description, a list of Kara's closest friends, and requested a recent photo.

All very standard operating procedure, Toni thought, as the knot of anxiety in her stomach grew. She knew the police would do what they could, but without any sign of foul play, they weren't likely to put a whole lot of resources into the search. Still, the police promised to follow up with Laurie and the girls from the volleyball team. Manuela retrieved a recent picture of Kara, and the officers left, promising to provide an update as soon as they had any additional information.

Jerry wheeled on Marcy as soon as the police followed Manuela out of the kitchen. "This is your fault," he said, raising an accusing finger. "You never want to discipline her, never want to do anything to piss her off. Who's the parent here, anyway?" His face was purple, and a vein appeared in his forehead, throbbing with such force Toni was afraid he was going to have an aneurysm.

"Not you!" Marcy raged right back. "How dare you

make accusations, as though you know what's going on in this house or with your children. Since the divorce, you've hardly spent any time with them. It's all been up to me."

"Yeah, and you're doing such a great job Kara moved out and now she's sneaking out at all hours to meet some idiot."

Toni's head began to pound, and suddenly she was sixteen again, and she and her little sister sat on the couch, staring straight ahead at the TV, pretending indifference to the barbs slinging back and forth between their parents. She wanted scream at them that this was not the time or the place to go twenty rounds of "who is the worse parent," but she held her tongue.

I should never have answered Marcy's call this morning, she thought, then immediately felt like a jerk. She'd promised Kara she could count on her, and she meant it, even if it meant putting up with her parents. Toni straightened to her full height and stepped between Marcy and Jerry. "Look, you can work all this out in your next family therapy session, but right now we need to focus on finding out where Kara is and making sure she's safe."

Marcy looked appropriately shamefaced, while Jerry had to get in the last word. "I don't need you to tell me to be worried about my daughter."

"Good," she snapped back. "Because you should be." She turned and caught Ethan's gaze. His mouth was quirked up in a sexy half smile and there was a glint of open admiration in his eyes. Toni cursed her pale complexion as she felt telltale heat bloom in her cheeks for a second time.

Her skin prickled with awareness and she was overcome with the need to escape from the vitriol spilling from Jerry's and Marcy's pores. And from the walking testosterone bomb that was Ethan Taggart.

"I'm going to go look around her room," Toni said abruptly.

She ignored Jerry's protests as she asked Manuela for directions, feeling the heat of Ethan's gaze on her retreating back.

Toni marveled at the over-the-top opulence of Kramer's house as her sneakers squeaked on the marble steps of the massive staircase. She was used to working with wealthy clients—women like Marcy accounted for the majority of her income—but Kramer's house, with its vaulted ceilings, marble floors, and handmade rugs that probably cost more than her car was beyond anything she'd ever seen firsthand.

But the blatant display of wealth gave the place the vibe of a museum, not a happy home. Growing up, watching her mom struggle, Toni always thought that if they had more money, they would be happy. But in the brief time she'd worked as a private investigator, she'd learned that people could be unhappy no matter how much money they had. Immense wealth couldn't buy perfect children or faithful husbands—in fact, it often made things worse. Recently, Toni had started to feel like she was operating in a toxic cloud, like she had picked up the scent of rot pervading these seemingly perfect lives and now couldn't get it out of her nostrils.

Now, after an ugly divorce rife with infidelity and hidden assets, the Kramer family was being sucked deeper into the cesspool.

She followed the hallway to the door Manuela had indicated. She pushed it open. *Jesus, this is bigger than my apartment.* Not that Kara's room in Marcy's townhouse was exactly a dump, but this was ridiculous. In addition to a queen-size four-poster bed, the room was spacious enough for a sitting area complete with a small couch and a low coffee table. Mounted on the wall was a forty-inch LCD television with a satellite-TV hookup and DVR. Pushed up against the wall was a mini fridge, and a small espresso machine sat on top.

Kara practically had her own efficiency apartment. Completely tricked out so she wouldn't need to leave her room for days if she didn't want to. Toni scanned the room for her prey.

"Find anything interesting?"

The voice was so close she felt his breath across her neck. She spun around and found her nose butting up against a hard wall of chest. For a moment she stood there, her face buried in the open throat of his button-front shirt, inhaling the intoxicating scents of fresh aftershave, laundry soap, and warm, musky man skin.

Okay, the guy might be an arrogant asshole, but the mere smell of him was enough to curl her toes inside her sneakers.

She took a hasty step back before she did something stupid like flick her tongue out for a taste. This guy was so far out of her league it wasn't even funny.

"What do you want?" she asked, hoping her imperious tone and matching expression would mask the fact that her insides were fluttering madly at the heat radiating off him.

"Just wondering where you'd hurried off to." His oh-so-charming smile was cracking around the corners.

Good. Her manufactured hostility was working.

"I wanted to see if I could find her computer."

"Why?" He looked genuinely confused.

"How else were you planning on tracking her down?"

He looked at her as though she were an idiot. "Canvassing the neighborhood, calling her friends. You know, basic investigation stuff."

She shook her head impatiently. What, was he an idiot? "Kara spends a lot of time online."

"Right. The online virgin support group. I'm sure they'll be a lot of help finding her boyfriend."

Toni sucked in her cheeks and bit the inside of her lip. "That's probably just the tip of the iceberg, Ace. And finding out who she's talking to online will get me a lot further than talking to neighbors who probably don't even know her name."

Ethan smirked. "Just because you spend all your time on *Lord of the Rings* message boards doesn't mean Kara does. Talking to real live friends will be a lot more useful than worrying about what Web pages she visited."

She shot him a look of disdain. "*Lord of the Rings* is so 2005." These days, Toni spent more of her time on gaming sites, but she wasn't about to correct Ethan.

He did a leisurely tour of the room, pausing to pick up a framed picture off Kara's desk. Toni tried not to stare at him but couldn't seem to stop herself. The man had hit the genetic jackpot, that was for sure. Taking advantage of his distraction, she studied him more closely, trying to pick out some imperfection that would remind her that he was a mere mortal, just like her.

He'd missed a spot shaving, she noticed with a tug of satisfaction. And the strong line of his nose skewed slightly to the left. That and the bump on the bridge told her he'd broken it at least once and hadn't bothered to get it fixed.

Somehow that made him even hotter.

There were dark smudges under his heavily lashed eyes, as though he hadn't gotten much sleep.

Not that she should talk, since thanks to her recent late stakeouts, the only thing keeping her from looking like an Ultimate Fighting Champ contender was her industrial-strength concealer. Her gaze strayed back to the little patch of stubble, next to his right ear. It would rasp against her fingertips if she touched it, contrasting with the peachy softness of his earlobe.

There was something on his earlobe, she noticed, frowning. Almost like a smudge of blood, but as she moved to take a closer look, she realized it was too pink to be blood. Almost like—

"Is that lipstick?"

He looked up, his left eyebrow arching up his forehead.

"On your ear," Toni clarified.

He pinched his left earlobe between his thumb and fore-finger. "Maybe." His tone was casual, but Toni could see the dark stain smudging across his tanned cheeks.

"Other one." Toni said, folding her arms across her chest.

He rubbed at the other earlobe with his fingers. "Did I get it?"

The dark pink smudge was still there. "Your girlfriend must wear that extended wear stuff," she said, wincing at how snide that sounded.

"Not my girlfriend," he said.

All the more reason to kill the attraction that was sucking her in like a tractor beam. She so did not need to get hung up on a man who spent long nights getting smudged with long-wearing lipstick by women who were not his girlfriend.

"Boyfriend?" She brushed past him and continued her circuit of the room.

He shot her a droll look. "So where is it?"

So he'd noticed that minor detail, too. Kara's MacBook was nowhere to be seen. "Not where I thought it would be."

"Oh, so you can admit you were wrong."

Toni tipped her chin up to glare at him. He was stand-ing way too close for her comfort. He seemed to loom over her, the sheer size and force of him threatening to over-whelm her.

Not that she felt threatened, exactly, but while she was only a few inches shy of him in height, he had at least eighty pounds on her, all of it rock-solid muscle. And the way he held his body in an almost predatory manner hinted at a dangerous core under his charming facade.

She wasn't about to let him see that she noticed. "What is that supposed to mean?"

His eyes narrowed and his nostrils flared as he glared down at her. "Just that you seem like the type who would think she's right most of the time."

He inched so close she was afraid he'd feel the hard points of her nipples poking through her shirt. God, she was desperate. Kara's immense room shrank in size as Ethan's huge frame seemed to suck up all the space. "That's because I am," she quipped. Without waiting for his reply, she brushed past him and headed back to the kitchen, sure that she heard Ethan chuckling. She could hear Jerry and Marcy sniping at each other all the way from the stairs.

"Maybe if you weren't so busy nailing that adolescent who works for you, you might have noticed she was gone."

"I can't find Kara's computer," Toni said, raising her voice to be heard over Marcy's shrill commentary on Jerry's choice of bed partners.

"And if you weren't drinking yourself to sleep every night, Kara would have stayed with you," Jerry retorted before turning his attention to Toni. "What do you need with her computer? I don't want you taking anything from this house." He punctuated his words with a mean look aimed at Marcy.

Toni bit back her temper. "I was hoping to get a look at her recent e-mails, chat logs, stuff like that. Since she's not answering her phone, it's our best way to find out if she made plans to meet someone last night." She took off her glasses and pinched the bridge of her nose as fatigue washed over her. She'd been on that stakeout until almost three a.m. and had barely clocked four hours of sleep before Marcy called. She wasn't in any shape to fight Jerry Kramer every step of the way.

Time for a different approach. She turned to Marcy. "Speaking of her phone, did you sign her up for the chaperone service I recommended?"

Marcy looked at her blankly, and Toni had a bad feeling that that conversation had been sucked into the boozy haze Marcy lived in these days.

"My phone," Toni explained, "Remember how I told you it has a GPS unit embedded inside. As long as my phone is turned on, my location can be tracked." She turned to Ethan and Jerry. "I recommend that all my clients with kids sign them up. Makes situations like this much easier to resolve."

"I completely forgot," Marcy said, thin shoulders collapsing.

"It's okay," Toni said tightly. Of course this couldn't be that easy. "It doesn't work if her phone is off, anyway."

Marcy's face crumpled into sobs. "I'm sorry," she gasped, burying her face in her hands. "I should have been on her more, but she was always telling me to leave her alone. I thought I was giving her what she wanted by giving her space."

It was a familiar refrain, one Toni had heard too many times. Parents who cared more about being their kids' best friends than acting as authority figures. That's why they hired Toni to snoop on them, because they couldn't figure out how to just sit down and talk with their children. It was frustrating to watch, but Toni took satisfaction in the knowledge that in some cases she'd saved kids from potentially dangerous situations.

Despite her frustration with both of Kara's parents, she felt a wave of sympathy when she took in Marcy's haggard appearance. When Marcy had first hired Toni over a year ago to find out if Jerry was sleeping around and hiding his assets, she'd been the epitome of the well-preserved, affluent housewife. Now, after a bitter divorce, lines of grief and stress were etched into her face. Her formerly trim body now bordered on emaciated, and she stood with her arms wrapped around herself like she was trying to keep herself from flying apart. Yes, Marcy could be a pain in the ass, but Toni knew firsthand how scared she must be.

"I promise I'll find her," Toni said, as Ethan pulled Jerry aside.

Marcy sniffled and wiped her eyes with fingers that shook. She shot a look at Jerry and Ethan, who had moved to the opposite side of the kitchen. Ethan's dark head was cocked down to listen as Jerry spoke in a voice too low for Toni to hear.

Marcy's mouth tightened into a flat line. "I want you to keep an eye on him."

"Jerry?" Toni asked. Jesus, it had been a year since they separated. Well past time for Marcy to let it go already. But she strove for tact when she said, "Don't you think it's more important for me to focus on Kara than to spy on your *ex*-husband?"

"Not him," she snapped. "Ethan. I want you to find out everything he knows, as soon as he knows it."

Great. She wanted to get *away* from Ethan Taggart and forget the way one look was enough to send her libido into overdrive. Now she was supposed to follow him around and somehow get him to divulge any information he collected.

"I don't think that's necessary."

Marcy's tears suddenly dried. Gone was the grief-stricken mother. In her place was the bitter, vindictive ex-spouse who was never far from the surface. "I don't trust Jerry. He keeps things from me, always has. He wasn't even going to call me this morning to tell me my daughter was missing."

Toni held up a quieting hand. "I'll do my best. But right now I need to start following up on what we know so far."

She checked her phone for the dozenth time as she walked to the front door. It was still on, set to vibrate. She hadn't missed a reply to the text she sent Kara after Marcy first called her. Wherever Kara was, she wasn't answering her messages yet.

Heavy footsteps approached. She didn't have to turn around to know it was Ethan. She recognized him from the way every skin cell suddenly went on high alert.

"I know you're worried," Ethan said, reaching out to rub her bare upper arm. She knew it was a calculated move, but it didn't stop her from feeling like sparks were shooting through her fingertips. "But we both know the truth. She's out with her boyfriend, and she'll be home as soon as the hangover wears off." Though the words were cavalier, the sympathy riding his tone was sincere. And she couldn't fault his logic.

But she couldn't escape the sick feeling in her gut that told her it wasn't that simple.

Kara Kramer awoke to suffocating darkness. Fear wrapped her chest in its steely grip, making breathing almost impossible. She blinked her eyes hard, praying the room would come into focus, but she saw nothing but black.

This is a bad dream, she tried to tell herself, struggling to recall the last few hours, searching her panic-riddled brain for some clue as to where she was. Her brain throbbed against her skull and her mouth was dry. Had she passed out after too much vodka? She'd been planning to go to a party with Toby. She remembered that much. But she couldn't remember making it there.

Had someone slipped something in her drink? It had happened before, and like now, she'd woken up with no idea where she was and no memory of how she'd gotten there.

It had been horrible, terrifying, but right now, it would be a welcome explanation. She feared that the reality was much, much worse.

Gooseflesh prickled on her arms, left bare by the flimsy cami she'd donned earlier in the evening. Wherever she was, it was cold. Too cold, considering how hot it had been lately. And musty. It smelled like the crawl space under her dad's house. Swallowing convulsively, she tried to wrap her arms around herself to coax warmth back into her icy skin, only to discover that her wrists were tied.

A spike of adrenaline crashed through her, and sweat bloomed on her skin in spite of the chill air. She scrambled to her knees and surged to her feet, running though she couldn't see even an inch in front of her.

She barely got two steps before she was jerked off her feet by a line of rope securing her bound wrists to the wall. Her knees hit the hard floor with bruising force and her startled cry broke the dead silence of the room.

Sobbing now, she yanked against the rope. The cord binding her wrists bit into the tender flesh, dug against delicate bones. Warm liquid trickled down her arm and she knew she was bleeding. Defeated, she lay on the floor, struggling not to throw up as the throbbing in her head threatened to split her skull.

After several moments, Kara struggled back to her feet and followed the line of rope to where it secured her to the wall. She fumbled at the knot with clumsy, cold fingers.

"You can't escape, so you may as well stop trying."

Kara's whole body jerked as she searched frantically, futilely, for the source of the low, raspy voice.

"Who's there? What do you want?" The words struggled past her dry lips, intensified the throbbing in her skull.

The disembodied laugh made her stomach pitch with dread. "Cooperation," he said finally. "And as long as I get it, you and I will get along just fine."

CHAPTER 3

ETHAN WATCHED TONI'S little Honda pull out of the driveway, half tempted to follow her. And not just because Jerry had told him he expected Ethan to keep tabs on Toni Crawford and any information she uncovered. His interest in Toni had already crossed the line from professional curiosity to personal interest, and his brain was cooking up scenarios where Toni slipped off those nerd-chic glasses while Ethan skimmed her tight jeans off her tight ass.

But finding a missing teen—even one who had probably just overslept after spending the night with her boyfriend— pulled rank over chasing tail. He flipped open his phone and dialed Derek as he pulled out of Kramer's driveway.

"What's the sitch?" Derek asked, not bothering with a greeting.

"Kramer's daughter snuck out last night and hasn't come back yet."

"That's why you needed the logs? I figured they had a break-in."

"Nope. More like a breakout staged by a pissed-off seventeen-year-old."

"And they needed you? Why not do a calldown on her friends?"

"No kidding. But the parents say she's a good kid, never does this kind of thing."

"Every parent thinks their kids are good kids," Derek interjected. "For fuck's sake, Dad thought we were good kids. Shit, he thought *Danny* was a good kid."

"Speaking of, is he at the office today?"

"On a Saturday? That lazy sack?"

"Right." At this hour, Danny was no doubt clocking twenty or so miles, a typical training run for the psycho ultra-marathons he liked to do.

"I need you to pull some info and text it to me." He rattled off the names of several of Kara's friends and told Derek to see if he could find a last name for Sean the boyfriend. And before he thought better of it, "And find out everything you can about Toni Crawford."

"I bet I already know. Blond hair, spray-on tan? Head the size of an orange and double D's out to here?"

"C'mon, their heads are always at least the size of grapefruits. Seriously though, this isn't someone I'm sleeping with." *Yet.*

"Good, 'cause you know I don't like to use our resources to stalk your fuck buddies."

"I don't either, but sometimes it's necessary. Remember Amber? She was wanted in Idaho for setting her boyfriend's pubes on fire." His brush with genital assault still made his boys shrivel up and duck for cover.

"If you didn't bang everything that moved, you wouldn't have close encounters of the psycho kind."

"Thanks for the advice, but unlike you I want to get laid this decade." He wasn't *that* indiscriminate. Then he remembered going home with Gillian the night before, for no good reason other than that he wanted a warm body next to him for a few hours. Maybe his brother had a point.

Speaking of warm bodies . . . Toni's image popped into

his brain. Warm, shit. He sensed in Toni a kind of dark intensity that would set him on fire.

But he had his work cut out for him there, if the look she gave him when he said the lipstick on his ear wasn't his girlfriend's was anything to go by. He didn't know why he'd bothered to explain, but he wanted her to know he was single. But instead of looking interested, Toni's plump red mouth had puckered in disapproval as if she'd been sucking on underripe lemons.

"Toni's another investigator." He filled Derek in on Toni's involvement with Marcy. "I want to know who I'm dealing with."

He hung up on Derek and spent the next few hours canvassing the neighborhood. *Finding out who she's talking to online will get me a lot further than talking to neighbors who probably don't even know her name.* It galled him to admit Toni was right.

Neighborhood life in the twenty-first century.

Maybe Laurie Friedland would provide him with something useful. Hell, maybe he'd find Kara sacked out on her friend's couch. He pulled into the driveway, not surprised to see a green Honda Accord already parked there.

Kara's friend Laurie lived about half a mile from the Kramer estate in a large ranch-style home that looked like it had been given a recent face-lift. He rang the bell and a harried woman answered. Over her shoulder, he could see Toni standing in the foyer, her brows knit into a frustrated frown behind her heavy glasses.

"Oh great, *you're* here," Toni muttered.

He flashed her a cocky grin, purely to piss her off, and turned to the woman he assumed was Laurie's mother. A brunette in what he guessed to be her late forties, but it was impossible to tell for sure. With her straight, shoulder-length brown hair and an outfit that concealed the beginnings of middle-age spread, she would have been attractive if she'd left her face alone. He knew that women—especially women in this area—worried about aging, but he didn't get why they thought hacking up their faces until they looked like the Joker was an improvement. "Mrs. Friedland?"

She nodded, her gaze momentarily freezing on his face. Ethan widened his friendly smile for good measure. "Ethan Taggart," he said, holding out a hand, which she blindly grasped with her manicured fingers. "I work for Kara Kramer's father, and I was hoping I could ask your daughter a few questions."

"Is she a friend of yours?" She shot an annoyed glance at Toni. At least Ethan thought she was annoyed. Hard to tell, since her face didn't move much. "What was your name again?" she snapped. Toni repeated her name. "Yes, Tory also wants to talk to Laurie about Kara, but we're about to get mani-pedis at LaBelle, and we really don't—"

"Mrs. Friedland, did Toni explain why we need to talk to your daughter?" Ethan asked, using his larger frame to subtly back her into the house.

"You can call me Joyce," she said, her wide smile made a little creepy by the fact that nothing moved above her cheeks.

"I didn't get a chance yet," Toni snapped.

Joyce's smile disappeared as she turned her attention on Toni. "No, you just barged in here, demanding to talk to Laurie."

"Joyce," Ethan said, placing his hand gently on her bare forearm and looking deep into her brown eyes, "I can assure you we're here for a very good reason, if you'll just let us explain."

She blinked slowly, as though coming out of a trance. "Okay, Ethan, was it? Why don't you follow me to the kitchen and we can discuss it over a cup of coffee."

Toni made a noise that sounded like a gag and followed them down the hallway. Though the house was not nearly as large or as ostentatious as the Kramers', the Friedlands weren't exactly hurting for money. The house was professionally decorated, with expensively upholstered furniture in the living room and dining room and all that knick-knacky crap that women liked to put on every available surface.

"Can you tell me what this is about?" Joyce asked. "We really are in a hurry. Mai gets booked up weeks in advance, and I don't trust anyone else to touch my feet."

"As I tried to explain," Toni said, her voice so tight she sounded like she had lockjaw, "We're hoping Laurie might have some information about Kara Kramer."

Joyce barely spared a glance at Toni as she strode down the hallway. "What kind of information?"

"Kara Kramer didn't come home last night," Ethan said as they entered the kitchen. Laurie sat at a farmhouse-style kitchen table, her thumbs moving rapidly over the keypad of her phone. "Have you heard from her at all?"

After a few more seconds of flying digits, Laurie finally looked up. A pretty girl, lanky, with pin-straight dark hair and light brown eyes that stood out from her summer-tan skin.

"I haven't really talked to Kara in a while," she said, a little wary.

Ethan nodded, accepted Mrs. Friedland's offer of a cup of coffee, and sat down at the kitchen table across from Laurie. He watched as Joyce offered Toni a cup, too, almost as an afterthought. Unlike Ethan, Toni remained standing, leaning against the counter as she sipped her coffee. A stray bead of liquid caught on her lush bottom lip, and he watched, mesmerized, as her tongue came out to flick it away. His cock jerked to attention, and he could almost feel that hot, pink tongue flicking along his skin. He had the unwelcome urge to forget this interview and grab her by the back of the neck and see how she tasted, hot, sweet, and bitter from the coffee.

He closed his eyes, gave himself a mental shake. He never had trouble keeping a lid on his sexual urges, and now was not the time to get distracted by a pair of mile-long legs and a mouth that would have done a porn star proud.

"How long since you've talked to her?" Toni asked. "It's extremely important that you tell us anything you know."

"Are you the police?" Laurie asked, sounding taken aback by Toni's aggressive tone.

Ethan sighed. Sexy or not, Toni had all the subtlety and patience of a bull in a china shop. He shot a look at Toni. *Let me handle the talking.* She seemed to get his message because a muscle throbbed in her jaw, but she kept her mouth shut.

"No, we're not the police," he said. "We're private investigators, hired by her parents to help find Kara."

"Was she kidnapped?" Joyce asked, sounding appalled.

"Right now all we know is that Kara left the house sometime around two this morning and she hasn't come back yet. We were hoping you had seen or heard from her," Ethan said, choosing his words carefully. "We hope she's just at a friend's house and will come home on her own. But in the meantime, we can't rule out the possibility that she's in some trouble."

"Why would her parents hire you?" asked Joyce. "Why not let the police handle it?"

"They are. We're simply picking up some slack." He turned his attention back to Laurie. "So, have you seen or spoken to Kara recently?"

"Laurie's been in France for a month," Joyce interjected. "She got into a very prestigious language immersion program."

"Did you keep in touch with Kara while you were gone?"

"Ah, no," Laurie replied with such deliberation that there was no doubt as to the state of their relationship.

"Wait." Toni pushed off the counter with her hip and walked to the table. "Kara's mom said you two have been close for a long time.

Laurie gave her heavy, straight hair a toss. "Yeah, that was true until this year."

Joyce leaned in and put a hand on Ethan's arm. "Laurie and Kara had a bit of a falling-out. But she won't tell me what it's about." She sighed and shook her head.

"I told you, Mom, we just grew apart or something," Laurie said, her tone full of the sharp exasperation teens had spent centuries perfecting. "Let it go already."

"I don't understand how you can be friends one week and not the next, especially after all this time." She turned to Ethan. "They used to do everything together—dance classes, summer camp, everything. They even made the Promise pact together. Then—poof."

Laurie remained silent. "Fine," Joyce said, throwing her manicured hands up. "Don't tell me. I'm just your mother." She pushed away from the table and walked out of the kitchen, leaving Laurie alone for the moment with Ethan and Toni.

Laurie craned her neck, listening as her mother's footsteps faded down the hall. "Toward the end of the school year, Kara got into some things that weren't exactly my scene."

"Your mom said you made this Promise pledge with her," Ethan said. "Was the fact that she had a boyfriend the problem?"

"We can still date guys," she said, leveling a look at him that would have slain him had he been under the age of twenty-one. "We just don't have intercourse."

Ethan shifted in his seat. Discussing sex with a teenager

in front of a woman you wanted was not a situation he was comfortable with.

"Kara's mom mentioned an online community."

"The V-Club," Laurie said, nodding. "We created a network on FacePlace so we could meet other girls who had taken the pledge and were saving themselves for marriage."

"Girls like you and Kara."

"Yeah. At least I thought so, anyway. But then Kara's parents split up and it really messed her up. She got really angry at her dad. He was always all over her to stay straight, get good grades, all that stuff. And here he was, having an affair and trying to hide money from the family. She said it didn't matter what you really did, as long as you only let people see what they wanted to see."

"Her parents didn't notice any difference."

Another eye roll. "Her dad isn't home very often, and her mom, even when she's there, she's not 'there,' know what I mean?"

"Okay, so tell us more about this weird behavior," Toni said.

"I don't know, she wasn't herself. We'd make plans and she'd flake, come up with lame excuses. Like my mom said, we used to do everything together, and all of a sudden she's never around. A couple of times I caught her in a lie about where she'd been. Finally I confronted her about it, and she told me she'd started hanging out with some new people and didn't want to hurt my feelings. But she invited me to a party right before I left for France. And after that I didn't really even want to hang out anymore."

"Some bad stuff go down?" Ethan prompted. It was hard to imagine what could happen at high school party that would produce the look of disgust on Laurie's face. Then again, she was a twenty-first-century avowed virgin till marriage, so her sensibilities were more easily offended than his.

"Like I said, not my scene. It wasn't a high school crowd. A lot of drunk frat boys and girls jumping into the pool naked. Kara was on something and kept telling me not to be such an uptight bitch, so I left. I didn't want to say anything to my mom because I knew she would freak out."

Ethan absorbed the new information, lined it up with what he already knew about Kara. "What about Sean? Was he at that party?"

"Sean?" Laurie let out a short laugh. "She dumped Sean on his ass after she got back from spring break."

Toni's eyes met Ethan's across the table. "Manuela said Kara had been sneaking out to meet him," she said.

She moved closer to the table until she was standing just to Ethan's left. This close, he could smell the subtle scent of her perfume, fresh and floral. And underneath, a soft, sexy smell that was pure Toni. He snuck a look at her out of the corner of his eye.

And immediately wished he hadn't. With the early-July heat wave blazing outside, the Friedlands had the A/C cranked to eleven. Toni's nipples rose in tight points against her T-shirt, daring him to yank down the scooped neckline and pop one into his mouth. Unbidden, his cock thickened against the fly of his pants, and he almost swore aloud. What the fuck was wrong with him, pitching a tent like some junior high kid? He never let sexual attraction get the better of him.

But something about Toni Crawford and the sexy-librarian fantasies she inspired threatened his normally ironclad control.

Laurie shook her head. "If she's sneaking out, it's not to meet Sean. I think the guy she's seeing is older. I never met him, though."

"So the party was the last time you talked to her?"

"In person. She still posts on the V-Club network, but I don't know why she bothers."

Toni motioned to the laptop that sat closed next to Laurie on the kitchen table. "Would you mind pulling the site up for us?"

Laurie sighed and looked at her watch. "My mom and I are already late."

Toni's stare was cold, hard, unwavering. "Your friend is missing. Your nails can wait."

"She's probably passed out somewhere," Laurie said, but she opened her laptop and clicked on the page. Laurie gestured at the screen. "I told you she's fine—she posted a message this morning."

Toni moved around the table until she was standing behind Laurie, who had navigated her browser to a page emblazoned with a banner that read "V-Club. Virgins of the World, Unite!"

Kara had mentioned the social network to Toni, and Toni had even tried to visit. But to visit, you had to be invited, and Kara hadn't offered an invitation. Toni could easily have posed as a teenager seeking support for her sexual choices, but she didn't feel right about lurking without Kara's knowledge.

Now she wondered if she was just as stupid as the parents she mocked who thought it was important to give their kids "space."

Posted near the top of the most recent messages was a picture of Kara, in all of her blond, fresh-faced glory.

"What does it say?" Ethan pushed out of his chair and moved to stand behind her, his tall, broad body somehow managing to move gracefully in spite of its size. Now why couldn't she master that sort of athletic ease? She'd never quite recovered from shooting up to her current height at the ripe old age of fourteen. Though she dressed to flatter her lean frame and tried to use her height as an advantage, underneath she still felt like an awkward, clumsy teenager who could barely control her unexpectedly long limbs.

Next to Ethan, who seemed to have perfect control over every rippling muscle in his body, she once again felt like the girl her classmates so sweetly dubbed "Stork Legs" after she'd made the mistake of wearing shorts to gym class. Joyce and Laurie didn't help, with their tiny figures that barely topped five foot three. They both looked like little brunette dolls, perfectly sized to fit in the palms of Ethan's big, broad hands.

She could feel the heat of his body permeating her thin shirt as he leaned in to read over her shoulder. As subtly as possible, she tried to move forward but found herself pinned between the back of Laurie's chair and the massive wall of Ethan's chest. She resisted the urge to shove an elbow back under his ribs as her body temperature rose another five degrees. Which had nothing to do with the ridiculously masculine pheromones Ethan was giving off, and everything to do with the fact that after a lifetime in the Pacific Northwest, Toni still hadn't become acclimated to the Bay Area's sun-drenched summers.

She refused to acknowledge the low hum of the air conditioner and the fact that it kept the house at roughly sixty-five degrees.

A trickle of sweat rolled down Toni's neck, and she shifted uncomfortably, careful to keep herself from erasing the millimeter of air Ethan had left between them. Hadn't the guy ever heard of personal space?

His breath wafted over her ear as he read Kara's posting aloud. "Just dropping by to say hi. Nothing new to report. More later."

"She posted that at eleven thirty-eight this morning," Toni said. Almost an hour after she'd left the Kramers.

"That's good news, right?" Joyce said as she came back into the kitchen. On her arm was a handbag roughly the size of Canada. "If she's posting on the Internet she can't be in too much trouble."

Toni nodded absently. She thought of Kara's computer,

missing from her room. Could be Kara took it and really had posted the message. But there was always a darker possibility Toni couldn't avoid.

"It wouldn't be hard for someone to use her computer or hijack her account," Ethan said, echoing her thoughts.

Okay, she had to concede points for his being more than prime eye candy. "Mind if I post something really quick?"

Joyce closed her eyes in exasperation. "Fine, but then I'm afraid we really have to go."

Toni leaned over the table and used Laurie's account to post a quick message:

This is Toni, looking for Kara. Call or text me ASAP. Your folks are worried and so am I.

She straightened up, only to finder herself flush against Ethan, her back to his front. She shot him a glare as her butt made contact with his thighs.

"Sorry." For a split second, something gleamed in his eyes, a mischievous spark that told her he was messing with her, that he enjoyed making her uncomfortable. But it was gone in an instant, replaced by a perfectly bland and deferential look.

"Thanks for your help, ladies," Ethan said, turning to Joyce as he stepped out of Toni's way.

In her hurry to get away from him, Toni took another step to the side, mortification bursting in her stomach as she stumbled over her own feet. At least she was wearing sneakers and was able to catch herself before she fell on her ass.

Joyce Friedland spared a glance for Toni, barely masking her scorn, then refocused one hundred percent of her energy on Ethan. "You're so welcome, Ethan," her tone almost breathless as she placed an earnest hand on his arm and stuck out her ample cleavage. It took a Herculean effort for Toni not to roll her eyes. But she couldn't help sneaking a glance at Laurie to see if she was as embarrassed as she should be to see her mother blatantly flirting with Ethan.

If anything, Laurie looked even more enthralled with Ethan's square jaw and buff body than her mother did. *And to think we give men a hard time for being blinded by big boobs and a pretty face.*

"If there's anything we can do, please don't hesitate to call me," Joyce continued. "And I mean anything."

Okay, this was getting ridiculous. Toni stepped bodily between Ethan and Joyce and stuck out her hand, which Joyce shook reluctantly. She dug a couple of business cards from her pocket and handed one to Joyce and one to Laurie. "If you can think of any other information, anyone else she might be with, call or text me anytime. Or e-mail me. I'm always online."

"No surprise there," she heard Ethan mutter as she showed herself to the door. She could hear the muffled sounds of Joyce's laughter and Ethan's answering chuckle and had no doubt that by the time he left Ethan would have another job offer—investigating the contents of Joyce's pants.

Before she could get in her car, she heard Ethan call over, "Hey, Toni, wait up a sec."

Her spine stiffened, every instinct urging her to get away from this man, and fast. Then she reminded herself of Marcy Kramer's order to keep an eye on him. Like it or not, until Kara was safe at home, she needed to resign herself to spending a lot more time with or near a man she couldn't stop imagining naked. And wondering how it would feel to have him naked beside her.

On top of her.

Under her.

She was going to melt like a Popsicle before he reached the car.

"Was there something you needed?" Toni asked, keeping her tone cold even if her body was radiating more heat than the asphalt.

It didn't deter him one bit. If anything, his grin widened

as he strode toward her. She kept her gaze pinned firmly in the middle of his face, forbidding herself to stare at the way his trousers pulled against his strong thighs as he moved.

I really need to get out more if this is the way I'm going to react to the first remotely hot guy I see. Okay, to be fair, Ethan is more than remotely lot. He is yummy male hotness, the likes of which you rarely see, so appreciate it for what it's worth for the next five seconds and then focus on the task at hand. Five, four, three . . .

"I'm thinking this will go a lot more smoothly if we work together." he said.

She pulled her mind away from wondering whether he had a four-pack, six-pack, or full-fledged eight-pack under the cotton brocade of his shirtfront and replied, "Oh really, how so?"

"No offense, but I noticed you weren't exactly making friends in there." He jerked his head in the direction of the Friedlands' house, his lips still quirked in amusement.

Her eyebrows shot up to her hairline. "Making friends isn't part of my job description."

"Are you always this standoffish?"

She folded her arms across her chest and jerked her chin up. "Just because I'm a professional and don't hit on every member of the opposite sex I come into contact with doesn't make me standoffish."

He had the gall to look mildly offended. "I wasn't hitting on Joyce Friedland."

"Oh, please, like you didn't notice the way she was practically pouring her boobs out onto your arm."

He gave an arrogant shrug. "Women like me."

"Not all women," she lied and went to climb in her car, but stopped when he wrapped a big, long-fingered hand around her upper arm.

"Don't you know it's rude to walk away when someone's talking to you?" he said.

"You want to tell me more about the legions of women falling at your feet?"

He gave her another smile, one that made the lines around his eyes crinkle. "We got off on the wrong foot. There's no reason we can't help each other out." He leaned one hand on her car, just to the right of her shoulder, almost but not quite boxing her in. It wasn't exactly intimidating, but the way he made her tilt her head back a notch to look up at him was his way of establishing authority. He was good at this, taking command with his size and his charm, so subtly that most people probably didn't even notice he was doing it.

"Yeah? How so?"

"I don't know who you've worked with before, but people in this area are used to a certain amount of ass-kissing."

"At which you obviously excel," she muttered.

His blue eyes turned steely, and for the first time she got a glimpse of a hardness that matched his tightly honed exterior. "When necessary, yeah. Especially if it helps me find out the information I need. Now, you do ninety percent of your investigating at your keyboard. Am I right?"

She shrugged and nodded. Jeez, the way he put it, it made her sound like some little troll slaving away in her cave. She thought of her dark, cramped home office and conceded that he wasn't too far off the mark.

"Come on," he said. "Let me finish interviewing Kara's friends while you find out what you can, and we can meet up later to compare notes." His smile changed, suddenly saturated with sexual intent. "Let me take you to dinner so we can get to know each other better."

Toni swallowed hard. God, he was good. Even knowing that his hot look was calculated to make her melt and manipulate her into doing whatever he wanted, she was tempted to say yes.

To dinner, to Ethan, to the amazing, headboard-knocking sex that would no doubt come after. That she was so sorely tempted was enough reason to turn tail and run, even if Marcy had told her to keep an eye on him.

"I'm sorry, Ethan, but as you've probably already guessed, I work much better alone."

Before he could stop her, she slid into her car and closed the door, not caring if his fingers made it to safety or not. As she drove away, she could see him staring after her through the rearview mirror, his expression one of amusement mixed with annoyance. God, she hated that he always seemed on the verge of laughing at her. Reminding herself that she didn't give a crap about Ethan Taggart and what he thought of her, she stuck her hand out the window for a final wave before she pulled out onto the street.

CHAPTER 4

TONI SIGHED AND took a gulp from the glass of ice water next to her laptop. She squirmed in her seat as a bead of sweat trickled down her rib cage. Her air-conditioning had been on the fritz for the past week, and Mrs. Arroyo said it would be at least another week until it would be repaired. There was nothing to do but suffer through it. For the rent she was paying, Toni was lucky to have A/C at all, and she figured if her tiny Filipino building manager and four children could survive the heat of their cramped apartment, so could Toni. At least she had a fan to move the hot air from one end of the room to the other.

What she wouldn't give for a cool Seattle summer rain. She thought wistfully back to the adorable flat she'd had in an old Victorian in Seattle's Queen Anne neighborhood. She remembered how she'd love to curl up on the window seat of the big bay window in her living room and sip a cup of coffee while admiring the view of the Cascades.

Instead, she was spending yet another sweltering afternoon in her home office, such as it was. It was Sunday afternoon, and Kara was still gone. The multiple text messages Toni had sent had gone unanswered, and Marcy hadn't heard anything, either.

Toni had spent most of yesterday and this morning poring over the messages posted to the V-Club, the online community Kara and her friends had set up on FacePlace. Though it offered some insight into the pressures teenage girls faced when it came to sex, as far as giving any clues as to where Kara was, it was a bust. There had been a few responses to Toni's message, but no real information. And so far, Toni could find no evidence of the double life Laurie Friedland had alluded to.

The only bright note was that Kara had posted again late last night. The message was as vague as the last, assuring everyone she was fine but containing no details.

Toni had checked the source IP address. The last two messages had been posted from Kara's computer. So why was her spidey-sense on high alert, sensing something off about the last two messages? Why couldn't she buy the notion that Kara was holed up somewhere with a friend and posting messages to let everyone know she was okay?

Toni contacted several members of the V-Club individually. With over three hundred members, many of them living out of state, Toni had focused on the most active members who lived closest to Northern California. None of whom knew anything.

Toni looked at the phone sitting on her desk, willing it to play a snippet from "Wish You Were Here," signifying the arrival of a text message from Kara.

Nothing.

For now, Toni was stuck slogging through a long debate among V-Club members about whether a girl who'd had anal sex could still be a member of the V-Club. There were a lot of strong opinions.

You're just trying to make excuses for acting like a whore. Laurie Friedland added her two cents. "Letting a guy fuck your ass is the same thing as your pussy. You're exactly like Kstar90, trying to give in on a technicality. Either you're a virgin or you're not. No middle ground."

Intrigued, Toni did a search on Kstar90. She'd been added as a friend by Kara several months ago but banned from the group a month later. After a quick scan through her messages, Toni understood why. Kstar90 was all about technical virginity, full of all kinds of advice about how to get yourself and your boyfriend off without giving up the goods.

Toni's mind fairly boggled at the possibilities.

Kstar90 had engaged in several flame wars with the other members before finally being kicked out of the group. Kara had come to her defense and tried to talk the other girls out of banning her but had been overruled by the cybermob.

As she read through Kstar90's posts and Kara's, Toni started to get a tight feeling in the pit of her stomach. She clicked on Kstar90's member page. According to her profile she was eighteen and lived in nearby Menlo Park. Her photo showed only a woman's topless torso, her hands cupped playfully over her breasts, her face cast in deep shadow, unrecognizable.

She was about to click the link to additional photos when a sharp knock interrupted her. She peeked through the peephole, frowning when she saw Ethan Taggart standing outside her door.

Kstar90's comments careered through her head, and her brain filled with images of herself, naked, doing all the things Kstar90 recommended for keeping your man satisfied without having actual sex. God, she could tie Ethan to the bed and keep herself busy for days.

Don't even go there, she thought, purging her brain of the lust-inducing images. She considered pretending she wasn't home, but Ethan quickly nipped that plan in the bud.

"I heard you walk to the door, Toni. Open up."

Not for the first time, Toni cursed the thin walls of her cheaply built apartment building.

She slid open the chain and reluctantly opened the door. "What do you want?"

He stepped inside without an invitation, his tall, broad-shouldered body seeming to suck up the space in her postage-stamp-size apartment.

He gave her a quick once-over, taking in her threadbare T-shirt and khaki shorts that had seen much better days. His sharp turquoise gaze lingered for a moment on her bare legs, and Toni felt a lick of heat low in her belly, followed by a surge of embarrassment to be found looking like such a slob.

His full lips cocked into a half smile. "Nice outfit."

"I've been working," she snapped, turning on her bare heel with as much dignity as she could muster.

She felt the heat radiating from his chest as he walked up behind her. "Jesus, no wonder you're so angry all the time, spending so much time in a place like this," he said.

She didn't have to follow his gaze to know exactly what he was seeing. He didn't miss a detail of the kitchen, with its cheap Formica counters, faux oak–finish cabinets, and ugly linoleum. Instead of the hardwood floors of the old Victorian, her boxy one-bedroom apartment had cheap, industrial carpet in the living room and bedroom. The only view from the minuscule patio was of the parking lot. Still, that didn't stop her hackles from rising at his reaction.

"I'm not angry all the time," she huffed.

"Okay then, generally pissed off at the world."

"How would you even know? You've known me for less than twenty-four hours!"

"Living in this dump would make anyone depressed." He walked into the tiny living room. "Even if you're not making any money with your investigations, surely you can afford to upgrade."

"When's the last time you looked at housing prices?" It

was on the tip of her tongue to jump to her own defense and blurt out that it wasn't her fault her savings had been depleted to the point where she was stuck in this dump until she could save enough to move back home. Her mom's short but valiant battle with ovarian cancer had wiped out her own and Toni's savings. And her ex-boyfriend John deciding to dump her while she was still struggling to get her investigation business off the ground hadn't helped.

Still, she couldn't hold John entirely responsible for the emotional and financial disasters she'd suffered recently. She was the one who'd been itching for a change, who yearned for a life outside her cubicle. And when he had offered her an escape to a new life in sunny California, Toni had jumped at the chance. Her knight in shining Prius.

She should have learned from her mother's experience that depending on a man for anything was a recipe for misery. She'd always been so careful not to leave herself vulnerable. In work and in love, she'd always been careful and cautious, always choosing the safest route, ignoring the little voices inside her that clamored for more passion and excitement.

Until the one time she'd taken a chance in her boring, rule-following life, and look where it got her. Nearly broke in a crummy apartment that looked even worse as she saw it through Ethan's eyes.

But she hardly needed to justify her living situation to him, especially when he was the one who had barged in on her. Speaking of which, "How did you know where I live, anyway? My information is unlisted."

He turned and smiled, the hard angles of his face thrown into stark relief by the fluorescent lights of her kitchen. "Toni, I'm a private investigator. How do you think I found out?"

Anger settled like a hot weight in her chest. Toni was by nature an intensely private person, not prone to sharing her personal information or—God forbid—feelings with someone she barely knew. She wasn't hiding any big skeletons, but the thought of anyone, especially Ethan Taggart, snooping into her business pissed her off.

"How much do you know?" she demanded.

"Worried that I came across some deep, dark secret?" he taunted.

"How much?" she repeated, her hand itching to smack the self-satisfied smirk off his face.

"For a woman who makes a living digging into other people's lives, you sure are defensive."

"The irony is not lost on me," she snapped.

"Relax, Toni, I only have the information available on a standard background check. I wanted to see who I was getting into bed with," he said with a wink.

"I didn't have you checked out," she said, though she saw his point.

"Maybe you should have," he shot back. "So, you want to tell me what you've found out so far?"

Ethan could see Toni trying to keep a rein on her temper. He'd caught her off guard, and she didn't like it. He'd given her a hard time about her casual-bordering-on-sloppy attire, but he found it almost as sexy as if she'd opened the door wearing something from Victoria's Secret.

Her outfit revealed nothing and everything. Her T-shirt was gray, worn thin from hundreds of washings. It clung to the high, round curves of her breasts in a way that made his palms itch.

He forced his eyes away from the perfectly cuppable curves emblazoned with the slogan "Property of the MIT Computer Science Department" and his eyes slid lower as she walked into the minuscule kitchen off the entryway and reached into a cabinet for two glasses. His mouth went dry as he recognized his mistake. He'd noticed her legs immediately, and they looked even better bare. Sleek with firm, muscled calves and nicely defined thighs. Thighs he could almost feel clamped around his hips as he rode her long and hard. Her skin was smooth, pale, tempting him to run his tongue along every inch.

Even her feet were nice, narrow and slender, toes painted a surprising hot pink with a little white flower design. Who would have pegged Toni as a fancy-pedicure type? Heat flooded his groin as he imagined propping her feet on his shoulders, sucking her toes into his mouth as he pumped her hard.

He shifted on his feet, willing his cock down before she turned around and noticed the pup tent that was forming at the fly of his pants. As casually as possible, he crossed his hands in front of himself.

"You go first," she demanded, filling the glasses with ice and water.

"Not much," he admitted. "Most of Kara's friends are out of town, away at summer camps or on vacation. The ones I did manage to connect with claim they haven't hung out with Kara in quite some time."

"Did you look at Kara's FacePlace page?"

"A little. Didn't find much to go on. But who knew there were so many degrees of virginity?"

Toni didn't acknowledge the comment, but he could see the flush of color creeping up her neck.

"I always thought it was cut-and-dried," he goaded. "Insert tab A into slot B."

"I don't want to discuss your thoughts on sex or virginity," she said. But he could tell from the deepening pink of her cheeks that she sure as shit was thinking about it, and thinking about it with him. "Anyway, it's not funny. Girls talking like that attract all kinds of creeps and pervs."

Toni's mouth was tight with concern. For whatever reason, Ethan was compelled to ease her fears. "I noticed she posted again. That's good news."

"Maybe." But she didn't seem to share his optimism.

"What makes you think differently?"

"I don't know," she said, shrugging him off. "The posts were both made from her computer, but . . ." she trailed off.

"What?"

"I don't know. It doesn't sound like her."

"How can you tell? They're two sentences each."

She shook her head. "Maybe I'm just being paranoid. Anyway, I found something right before you got here. I don't know if it's anything yet."

He let her change the subject. For now. "Show me."

She motioned him over to the corner of her living room that apparently served as her office.

Piled in the small space were a desk, printer/fax combo, and of course her computer. Papers littered the desk in semi-cohesive piles. More papers peeked out of the drawers of an overstuffed file cabinet and out of the tops of boxes.

Ethan thought of his own spacious office with its giant desk and state-of-the-art computer system and couldn't help but wince. "This is how you work?"

Her shoulders tensed. "Not all of us can afford fancy office space. Besides, I have everything I need right here."

He held his hands up in a supplicating gesture, snagged one of the two rickety wooden chairs from her kitchen table, pulled it over to the desk, and settled in next to her.

As he leaned over her shoulder to see the monitor, he caught her scent in the sultry air. A mix of shampoo, laundry soap, and pure female hit him like a ton of bricks. Sexier than any perfume, it had heat pooling low in his belly.

She popped open a window on her browser. "I went back a few months in the archives and came across this girl."

Ethan took in the naked torso, bare breasts barely covered by the girl's own hands, and shifted his gaze away. Sure, her profile said she was eighteen, but he still felt like a dirty old man looking at her.

"She was a member of the V-Club," Toni continued, "invited by Kara, but she got kicked out after a month."

"She doesn't look like their typical member. Guess I don't have to ask why they kicked her out."

"The girls were cool at first, but then"—Toni's blush, which had barely subsided when they sat down, returned in full force—"Kstar90 started giving the other girls tips."

"Tips?" He arched a brow, waiting for her to continue.

He didn't think it was possible for her face to go any redder, but her flush deepened from dark pink to full-out magenta. "Tips on how to keep their boyfriends happy while staying technically intact."

"Really, like what?" He felt a grin tugging at his cheeks even as heat gathered in his groin. Damn, he loved watching her squirm in her seat.

Her withering glare lost its impact under all that pink. "I'm sure you would know better than I," she said, presenting him with her profile as she turned back to her screen.

Damn straight. "I'd be happy to demonstrate any and all of them."

Her mouth gaped as she gave him a disbelieving look. "Are you seriously hitting on me while we're talking about the sexual habits of teenage girls? Could you be any more inappropriate?"

He held up his hands. "The offer was made purely out of professional courtesy."

She shot him a glare. Licked her lips. Shifted in her seat. Yeah, for all her offense, she was thinking about it.

"All right, so Kstar90 got kicked out of the virgin club for being too skanky," he said, letting Toni off the hook for the moment. "Besides the V-Club, what do you think her tie is to Kara?"

Toni clicked on a link to additional photos. Ethan sucked air through his teeth. He thought the picture of Kstar90 on her home page was bad, but these had crossed the line from racy to lewd. There were half a dozen, showcasing Kstar90 in various states of undress, every body part displayed for anyone with a Web browser to see.

All except her face, which had been painstakingly blurred out.

Toni's mouth got tighter and her jaw took on a hard set as she clicked on one of the photos and called up another program. A separate window popped up with a grid full of data and a smaller version of the picture. But this time the subject's face was clear.

Kstar90 wasn't *connected* to Kara. Kstar90 *was* Kara.

"Fuck," Toni swore, echoing his own curse.

She quickly clicked through the remaining photos and ran them through the same program.

"That's an EXIF viewer?" Ethan asked.

Toni looked shocked that he had any clue what she was doing but nodded.

"My brother Derek is more up on digital forensics than I am, but I try to stay current. What program are you using?"

"It's my own program," she said, clicking back over to Kara's main page.

Ethan was grateful. He liked a naked woman as much as the next guy—hell, probably more. But looking at nude pictures of his client's teenage daughter with Toni less than six inches away made him feel all kinds of dirty.

Toni sat back in her chair, worrying her bottom lip with her teeth. "These files have been altered and compressed, so I can't get all of the information about the original pictures."

Ethan didn't have in-depth knowledge of digital photo forensics but he knew that depending on the file size and type, you could find out everything about a picture, including whose camera shot it when, and, if you had a camera that recorded GPS information, where on the globe it was taken. You could also, without much effort, extract unretouched thumbnails of pictures that had been altered.

Toni propped her elbows on the desk and put her head in her hands. "I told her to be careful about what she puts out there. And she goes and posts naked pictures of herself."

Ethan didn't say anything as Toni scrolled down the page through Kara's most recent messages.

"She hasn't posted to this page," she said, voice vibrating with concern.

"Why would she? Her parents wouldn't know to look here. She's probably fine. I know this looks bad, but it doesn't change the likelihood that she's just holing up with a friend."

"I want to believe that. But I never thought she'd do anything this stupid," she said, gesturing at the screen.

"Teens aren't famous for thinking things through. Even smart kids like Kara. Doesn't mean she's in trouble." Ethan knew all about kids making dumb moves, especially kids whose home life was falling apart. When he was sixteen, he'd disappeared for a week to see if his dad would emerge from his black hole of obsession to come looking for him. In the end, his older brother Danny had found him, crashing in a rundown youth hostel in San Francisco.

He focused his attention back on the screen, where he saw the last message from Kara, dated Friday evening.

Can't wait to see my honey tonite. He's still pissed, but I'm hoping he'll give me another chance.

He felt the hackles rise on the back of his neck.

"Who's pissed?" Toni muttered, echoing his thoughts.

Ethan frowned as he read a message a the bottom of the page, dated last Wednesday. *I'll give you one last chance to make it up to me. Meet me this weekend and show me how sorry you are.* This from someone with the charming moniker "T-Bone."

His cell phone buzzed, interrupting whatever Toni was about to say. He swore when he saw his brother Derek's number on the caller ID. "What's up?"

"Just wanted to let you know we're heading over to Dad's in the next twenty minutes. He said he had something important to talk to us about, so don't be late." Tension dug into Ethan's neck like bony fingers. He'd forgotten all about their weekly dinner with his dad. He'd managed to avoid the last two weeks, as he'd been working. But this week he had no excuse to blow it off.

"I wonder what new theory he's come up with this time." He sighed. And how much money he's going to waste chasing after it, he thought. "I'll see you there."

Toni spared him a glance over her shoulder as she clicked through to T-Bone's FacePlace page.

"That was my brother calling to remind me of another standing obligation." He was reluctant to leave, and not only because he wanted to follow the trail to T-Bone and what he might know about Kara Kramer's disappearance. He liked it here in Toni's dark, sweltering apartment, working beside her.

"It's cool," she said without looking up. "I'll let you know whatever I find out." Her fingertip stroked idly over her mouse, as if she were fondling a patch of skin.

Okay, clearly he needed to get laid if watching Toni navigate cyberspace was enough to get him excited. He stood quickly. "I'll be back in a few hours."

Toni watched the retreat of his wide, muscled back with a combination of regret and relief. As much as she didn't want to admit it, she was starting to crush on him. Not only was he hot, he was smarter than she'd first given him credit for. Not many people knew what EXIF data was, much less how it could be used for an investigation, but Ethan must do his homework.

And he had an odd knack for sensing when she was about to head down the dark road of fear and let anxiety override all logic. Using humor or short, pointed questions and remarks, he gently guided her back on track, keeping her from fixating on the worst-case scenario.

But she was grateful to see him go. The lustful undercurrents pulsing between them were far too distracting. Someone she cared about was missing, and she could barely concentrate because she couldn't stop thinking about stripping Ethan Taggart naked. Better he was gone so she could really focus.

From T-Bone's profile page she clicked on a link to T-Bone's Treasure Chest.

Speaking of naked.

"Kara, what the hell have you gotten yourself into?"

Kara huddled on the thin pad and tried to figure out how long she'd been sitting here in the dark. A day? Two?

She had no idea. Her body shook with a combination of cold and fear. She sat with her knees curled up to her chin, her bound wrists looped over her legs in an attempt to hold in whatever body heat she had left.

Her eyes were wide open in spite of the dark, her ears tuned to every slight sound as she waited for the man to come back. Despite her grogginess from whatever drug was working through her, she hadn't slept since the man left hours ago. After his brief greeting, all the more terrifying for how casual he'd sounded, he'd left and hadn't come back.

Hazy details were starting to surface. She'd never made it to the party. She had a vague memory of a dark SUV, a rough hand on her arm.

And then the dark.

And then the man.

Who still hadn't come back. Neither had anyone else.

Not to give her water, or food, or to take her to the bathroom or even give her a bucket to pee in. She'd been forced to scoot to the end of her rope and awkwardly push her pants down, trying not to lose her balance as she squatted in the dark with tears running down her face. She winced as she inhaled, the smell of her urine sharp in the damp, cold air.

Adding to her humiliation, she hadn't been able to pull her pants back up with her hands tied, and they were stuck halfway down her butt.

She had a horrible, awful feeling she would be naked in front of the man soon enough.

He said he wanted cooperation. And though her brain tried to reject the idea, she knew with bone-tingling dread what his idea of cooperation would entail.

As she waited in darkness, panicky thoughts ricocheted through her brain. Why? Why her?

But she was afraid she knew damn well why.

This was all her fault, posing for the pictures. Talking herself into it, getting off on the idea of doing it behind her parents' backs, her own secret life, proving—to herself anyway—that she wasn't the perfect little girl everyone thought she was.

No one else was ever supposed to find out. Toby had promised.

But now someone—some scary-ass creep who kept girls in his basement—knew.

Her stomach cramped as a dozen scenarios, each one more horrifying than the last, raced through her mind.

The panic that had subsided as hours passed with no further contact exploded once again to the surface. "Please, help me, somebody help me," she whispered, starting to cry. She closed her eyes, as though that could shut out the stifling dark, the stomach-churning fear. "Please, please, help me." The whisper grew louder, turning into a high-pitched wail.

"Help me!" The wail became a scream, absorbed by the darkness. Some part of her knew no one would hear, but she couldn't stop, the scream roaring from the deep pit of fear lodged in her gut.

Suddenly a door banged open and the room flooded with light. The brightness blinded her, piercing through her brain like a knife through her eyes. She huddled against the wall, desperately trying to blink the room into focus.

Her mouth opened, but this time her scream lodged in her throat as the large, blurred outline of a man came toward her.

The blade of a knife glittered in his hand; terror clawed at her chest as it came closer. But all he did was cut the rope securing her to the wall.

He jerked at the rope. Fresh pain erupted in the wounds of her wrists. Her elbow and shoulder joints protested as he yanked her to her feet.

What was going to happen to her? Where was he taking her? That and a thousand other questions skittered across her brain. But when she opened her mouth to ask, the fear switch flipped in her brain and another scream barreled its way up her throat, past her lips, as she staggered up a short flight of stairs.

The man was impervious to her fear, not sparing her so much as a look as he dragged her screaming, struggling form down a short hallway. Her scream gave way to harsh, panting breaths, coming so fast she was afraid she was going to pass out. In her hyperfearful state, odd details penetrated her consciousness. The wood paneling on the walls, the heavy furniture in the rooms she passed.

Through the windows she glimpsed the trunks of huge redwood trees, the kind that grew in the coastal mountains close to where she lived. They hadn't taken her far.

Small comfort that was as the man jerked hard on the rope again and sent her stumbling to her knees. She fumbled to catch herself with her hands, missed, and smacked her chin on the hardwood floor. Blood flooded her mouth as her teeth pierced the tender flesh of her inner lip.

She started crying then, tears and snot pouring down her face as she was jerked once again to her feet and dragged the last few feet down the hall. She stumbled into a room, and the man who had come for her dropped the rope and left, slamming the door behind him.

A man sat at a huge mahogany desk, observing her. His hair was dark blond mixed with gray, slicked back from his forehead. He didn't look like a psycho kidnapper. With his carefully combed hair and green polo shirt he looked like one of her dad's golf buddies. Or someone who would show up at one of the dinner parties her mother was always hosting before her parents split, someone who would ask her lame questions like where she was applying to college and what subject she liked best.

He looked . . . normal.

The observation wasn't at all comforting.

Deep-set, muddy green eyes raked her from head to toe, and his mouth stretched in a smile that made her legs shake and her blood chill.

"You're even prettier than your pictures."

He was the one who had first come to her in the dark. The one who wanted her cooperation. Sick dread knotted and pinched at her intestines, and she was afraid she was going to throw up, or worse. "My father," she managed to grunt out. "My father has lots of money." Her lips were numb, her tongue as thick as if she'd done five quick shots of Absolut. She licked her lips and tried again. "He'll pay you. If you don't hurt me he'll pay you—"

He held up a hand, silencing her. "I know all about your father." His voice was deep with a faint accent that sounded almost British but not quite. "And it is my hope, as it should be yours, that he will cooperate."

He rose from the desk and approached her, and Kara backpedaled until her knees hit something, a table. He caught her before she could fall, pulling her up, pulling her close until her nose was flooded with the cloying smell of aftershave and hair gel, until she could feel his faintly sour breath on her cheek.

His hand was soft and manicured against the skin of her forearm, but his grip was bruising as he easily subdued her exhausted struggles. He extracted a handkerchief from a pocket with his other hand and wiped her face in rough swipes.

"Yes, much prettier than the pictures you post for the world to see."

Her skin crawled. "What pictures?" she asked. Maybe if she played dumb they'd think they had the wrong girl. How could he even know? Toby always blurred her face out, promised her no one would ever know it was her. Their little secret.

But she couldn't trust Toby to keep his dick in his pants. Why should she trust him not to out her online?

The man brushed off her question, his hand trailing down her throat like a snake, coming to rest on the pendant that hung just below the hollow of her throat.

"You have a treasure," he said, closing his fingers around the small silver charm. It was a stylized V, with three tiny diamonds, one at each end, one at the point. Laurie Friedland's mother had given the charms to Kara and Laurie two years ago at homecoming.

Right after they'd established the V-Club on FacePlace.

Where Kara often posted pictures of herself along with her almost daily messages.

He hadn't seen the other pictures. A faint flutter of relief started to unwind her nerves.

But her relief was short-lived as his fingers tightened on

the pendant. She shrank from his reptilian gaze as it raked her up and down, lingering on her breasts and between her legs.

"This treasure you value so very much," the man said. "Let's hope your father values it as well."

CHAPTER 5

DREAD BUILT SLOWLY and steadily as Ethan drove to his father's house. He wasn't looking forward to hearing all about whatever crazy lead Dad was chasing this time. Tension and fatigue joined forces and started a dull throbbing at the base of his skull.

By the time he got to his father's house fifteen minutes later, the tension had erupted into a full-blown headache, pounding in his temples with the rhythm of his heartbeat. His father still lived in the house Ethan had grown up in, a sprawling ranch-style home that sat on a full acre of land in the middle of wealthy Atherton.

But unlike the showpieces that lined the oak-studded street, the Taggart house showed its age. The paint on the trim was starting to chip, and as he walked up the driveway to the front door, Ethan noticed that the asphalt had buckled and cracked in several places. When Ethan was growing up, even one of these small defects would have driven his father insane. Though he'd given up his military career to pursue one in finance, Joe Taggart had still expected everything in his life to be spit-polished to a high shine. The lawn was always neatly mowed, the hedges precisely trimmed. The house got a new coat of paint every five years without fail, and he would never have allowed the oak tree roots to spread under the driveway until it became a cracked mess.

But that was before Joe's wife had disappeared without a trace, and the father Ethan had always regarded with equal measures of love and awe had disappeared along with her.

Ethan had memories from when he was a little kid, before they moved to California. Memories of his parents laughing, his mother jumping into his father's arms and kissing him passionately the moment Joe Taggart walked in the door. Then his father had retired from the army, which was supposed to mean more money, more stability, since they wouldn't have to move every few years. Instead, Joe's success in the investment banking world meant long hours in the office, weekends spent at work, and vacations canceled so deals could be closed.

Ethan didn't know when his mom had checked out. He didn't remember the first few years being so bad. His dad wasn't around much, but he didn't remember his mom has sling Joe about his long hours and frequent trips out of town.

But when his mother's face swam into his memory, Ethan didn't see a happy woman. Without her husband around to shower her with affection, she'd wilted like a flower in the desert, and even her three growing boys weren't enough to make up for a husband who was never around.

If Joe noticed his wife's increasing dissatisfaction with their marriage, he didn't show it. He sure as shit didn't do anything to fix it, still working just as hard if not harder. In the end, Anne Taggart had descended into a depression-induced fog of booze, pills, and who knew what else. She'd disappeared emotionally long before she'd disappeared physically.

Joe hadn't meant to ignore her, Ethan knew. He'd been focused on his career, convinced he was doing the best for his family by making as much money as he could, as quickly as possible. He'd ignored her complaints, convinced she would thank him later for every day that she sat in her multimillion-dollar home, dressed in designer clothes from the most expensive boutiques. Unfortunately, Joe hadn't recognized the depth of her unhappiness until it was too late. Anne had already left, without a backward look, leaving no clue as to where she'd gone.

Now, though Joe still did financial consulting on the side, his top priority was finding his wife. He'd spent the past eighteen years chasing every lead, no matter how far-fetched, no matter how unreliable the source. If he'd spent only one-tenth of the time with his wife when she was around as he did searching for her now, Ethan knew she never would have left. The irony wasn't lost on Ethan. Only after she disappeared did Anne truly become the center of Joe's life.

Ethan let himself in the front door, trying to stave off the wave of sorrow he felt every time he saw the house he grew up in. The inside wasn't in any better shape than the outside. While it was kept clean by the housekeeper's twice-weekly visits, the hardwood floor was scuffed and the upholstery on the furniture was worn. His father always kept the heavy drapes closed, giving the house a dark, suffocating feel even on a bright summer day like today. Upstairs, the bedrooms were the same as they'd been since Danny, Ethan, and Derek had left home. Danny had gone to West Point, followed two years later by Derek, while Ethan had opted for Annapolis and navy flight school.

And though he never went in there anymore, he knew his father kept the master bedroom exactly the same as it had been on the day their mother had disappeared. None of her clothing had been removed, none of the personal items she'd left behind in her hurry to disappear had been put away. As though any day now she was going to walk through the front door and start life right back where she'd left it.

On the front table was a pile of mail that no one had bothered to go through in what looked like weeks. Catalogs and bills were piled haphazardly, threatening to spill onto the floor. Ethan reached out to straighten it, freezing when he saw his mother's name on the address label on a catalog.

He snatched it up and crumpled the thick paper in his fist, slamming it into a wastebasket as he stalked down the hall. He found his father and his older-by-six-minutes twin brother Derek in the dining room, looking at a map spread over the scratched surface of the cherrywood table.

"A woman matching her description was at the Champlung Hotel in Ubud," Joe said, indicating the city in Central Bali with his forefinger.

Ethan and Derek exchanged a speaking look over their father's head. *Can you believe he's doing this again?* Derek's look said. *Another lead. Another dead end. Another chunk of change out of Dad's bank account.* Ethan didn't have to utter a word to make himself understood.

Though they weren't identical, they'd always had that weird twin bond. If anyone ever asked either of them about it point-blank they would have denied it, neither of them being big believers in any kind of sixth-sense, touchy-feely crap. Nevertheless, when Ethan's plane had gone down over Afghanistan four years ago, Derek had contacted Ethan's commanding officer to find out his brother's status before the crash had even been reported.

But it didn't take special twin juju to know what Derek was thinking as he listened to Joe.

"She was in Ubud last week, but she's heading south to Sanur," Joe said, as though her presence in Bali were a given.

Derek's shoulders were slumped, his jaw pulled into grim lines. His light brown, close-cropped hair was sticking up on top where he'd run frustrated fingers through it.

Ethan was sure he looked the same, but he did his best to

hide his exasperation. He'd learned a long time ago that it did no good to try to dissuade his father when he'd caught the scent, however elusive, of their missing mother. It did no good to tell him it was a waste of time, that someone was yet again scamming him for the reward money he put up. "So you really think she's in Indonesia, Dad?" Ethan asked, not bothering to point out that the woman he remembered had had a deathly fear of bugs and had hated the humidity because of what it did to her hair. Unless she'd changed dramatically, Southeast Asia wouldn't exactly be Anne Taggart's scene.

Joe pulled a small notepad out of his breast pocket and squinted over the rims of his reading glasses. "Yes. My source said he saw a woman fitting her description just five days ago. So you can see why I have to move fast."

"Dad, the picture you have is almost twenty years old," Ethan said, struggling to keep the impatience from his tone.

In Joe's head she was still a thirty-eight-year-old California blond, whose age and years of increasingly harder drinking had just begun to catch up with her.

Who knew if she looked remotely the same, or if she was even alive?

Didn't matter to their father, though. Send him a blurry picture of an attractive blond over forty and he was off and running. Ethan had long ago stopped trying to talk him out if it.

Their older brother, Danny, had no such qualms about poking holes in their dad's cockeyed theory. "This is fucking bullshit, Dad," he said, slamming an empty pot into the sink and filling it with water. "Like every other bullshit lead you've followed for the past eighteen fucking years. She left us. She's not coming back. She never wanted to be found. Move on."

Joe Taggart went very still, his finger frozen to a point on the map. Very slowly he straightened up and pinned his eldest son with a steely glare. For a moment, Ethan caught a glimpse of the man his father had once been. A man who commanded the room with his very presence, a man whose word was law. A man who brooked no disrespect from anyone, especially not his own sons. "Do I have to remind you that we're talking about your mother and my wife? If I have to spend the rest of my life and every last penny of my fortune to find her—dead or alive—you bet your goddamn ass I will."

Joe folded up the map and strode from the room, shoulders straight like the soldier he once was. Danny swore under his breath and turned back to the pot of sauce he was stirring for the spaghetti. Christ, Ethan thought, wondering how he'd ended up here. He should be out on a date, not having a spaghetti dinner with a heaping side of family drama.

But when he thought about having dinner with a beautiful woman, the only face that came to mind had catlike hazel eyes, heavy-framed glasses, and full red lips pursed as she focused on the screen of her computer monitor. Not his usual evening companion by a long shot.

"Why do you two humor him?" Danny said from the kitchen. "We should declare her dead and put Dad out of his fuckin' misery already." A spoon clattered into the stainless steel sink as Danny hurled it down. His big muscle-bound body looked out of place in the kitchen, but Ethan knew from experience that Danny's hard-bitten exterior hid a master chef in the making. He cooked the way he did everything—aggressively, no holds barred, throwing every bit of his considerable passion into the process.

It didn't make for a particularly neat process, and anger didn't help, Ethan reflected as he watched Danny pick up a spice jar and wrench the top off with unnecessary force. He poured some of the contents into the palm of his hand, then flung it in the direction of the pan. Most of it went in. "I'm so fucking sick of these lowlifes taking his money, and watching him waste his life chasing after a woman who didn't give a shit about us."

"What else are we supposed to do? It's not like we can change his mind," Ethan said. As usual, Derek remained silent, letting Ethan and Danny battle it out. "Besides, if he'd just let her get a divorce like she wanted, she wouldn't have had to leave." It sounded lame even as the words left his mouth, but it's what he'd been telling himself for the past eighteen years. That his father had forced his mother's hand. If Joe hadn't ignored their marriage for so long, she wouldn't have become so depressed. And if he'd let her out when she'd wanted, she wouldn't have felt so trapped.

Danny threw down the wooden spoon, sending a spray of sauce arcing like blood across the backsplash. He threw his hands up. "Oh, here we go again, defending poor Mom, whose life was so fucking hard she had to run away from it."

Ethan didn't say anything. Rationally, he knew Danny was right. Their mother—a woman who had abandoned her husband and children without a single look back—didn't deserve his defense. But inside of him still lurked that little boy who had spent years doing everything he could to put a smile on her face. Who thought that if he had tried hard enough, the happy, fun-loving woman he remembered would reappear.

He didn't dare admit any of this to his brothers. Danny, in particular, would bitch-slap him into next week and tell him to stop being a whiny mama's boy.

Even so, Ethan never accepted Danny's black-and-white version of how things went down—that their mother was weak and shallow and couldn't handle real life, so she'd cut her losses and found herself a new life.

"None of this helps the situation we're dealing with right

now," Derek said, always the voice of calm rationality. "Who's going with Dad to Indonesia?"

"I don't see why we have to hold his hand," Danny said, stirring spaghetti into the pot with such vigor that boiling water splashed across his wrist. "Fuck," he roared and thrust his hand under cold water. Clenching his teeth against the pain he said, "He wants to go on another wild goose chase, let him go on his own."

Derek and Ethan exchanged a look. *It's all bluster.* They all knew none of them, including Danny, would send their father alone into a situation like this. It wasn't that their father was particularly stupid or naïve, just that he had a huge blind spot when it came to tracking down a lead on his wife. It had led him to deal with shady, unscrupulous characters from every dark corner of the globe. Men who would rob him blind and cut his throat if someone wasn't there to watch his back.

"Not me," Ethan said, not bothering to hide his relief. "I'm on duty till we find out where Kara Kramer has gotten herself."

Derek shook his head. "I have three consultations this week, plus a seminar on corporate espionage. Danny, since you just wrapped up that corporate job in South City, I'm afraid it's got to be you."

"Son of a bitch! I need another trip to Southeast Asia like I need a hole in my fuckin' head," Danny said. "Ethan, why don't you let me take over the Kramer case," he said, his tone suddenly wheedling. "You speak better Bahasa than I do, anyway, and since you and Dad actually get along—"

"No way in hell," Ethan held up his hands. He wouldn't be charmed or bullied into covering for his brother. "I'm the one who had to go to Russia with him, last year, remember?" The memory was enough to make Ethan shudder. And not just from the remembered cold, though it had been a bone-chilling twenty below in the Siberian city of Novosibirsk. No, it was the memory of how his father had nearly gotten a bullet in his head when his search for a woman matching Anne's description landed him face-to-face with a couple of Mafiya thugs in the middle of an arms deal. Fortunately, Ethan had been a lot more sober and a lot faster with his fists than the thugs and had been able to get them both out of there.

"Maybe you can talk him out of it," Derek offered.

Though they knew it was hopeless, the brothers spent most of their meal attempting to do exactly that. "Dad, why don't you let me dig a little deeper on these guys," Danny said. "Get someone to corroborate their story before we spend the time and money to fly all the way over there."

"We?" Joe said, affronted. "I don't know where you boys got the idea that I need a keeper."

The brothers' eyes met across the table. Ethan's near-debacle in Siberia had hardly been the first time their dad ended up in danger. Though none voiced it, they all were remembering the numerous occasions when they'd pulled Joe out of potentially deadly situations.

"Going alone is out of the question," Danny said. "And I don't understand the urgency."

"I don't care if you understand or not, Daniel," Joe replied, his voice gone scary-quiet, with an undercurrent of steel. It was a tone Ethan remembered all too well from childhood, the tone Joe used to remind his sons that the Taggart household was by no means a democracy. Joe Taggart was in charge, and his word was law. "I'm leaving tomorrow for Denpasar and that's final."

For several tense seconds, Danny's steel-gray stare met Joe's identical one. But even at age thirty-four, and standing six foot five and weighing over two hundred pounds, former Special Ops badass Danny couldn't stare down Joe Taggart. Danny dropped his gaze to his plate, muttering under his breath as he mopped up a blob of red sauce with a hunk of bread.

Ethan stirred his spaghetti around his plate, his appetite killed by the knot in his stomach. He wished he could be anywhere but here, partaking of this sad parody of family bonding.

He knew how perfect they looked on the outside. His father, still handsome and fit at the age of sixty-three, a silver-haired, more craggy-featured version of his oldest son, Daniel. He and his brothers, strong and square-jawed with their all-American good looks. Nobody looking at them would know they were broken inside, their lives forever altered by the selfish actions of one sad, weak woman.

Ethan took a slug of beer, wondering where the hell that burst of self-pity had come from. Broken? They weren't broken. Hell, he and his brothers were all good-looking, had successful military careers behind them, and had built a rapidly growing business. Okay, so their mom had left them high and dry and sent their dad off the deep end, but they'd all done absolutely fine in spite of it. They'd survived as a family, remained close.

Closer, in fact, than most siblings he knew. Rather than let tragedy rip them apart, their bond had grown more fierce after their mother had disappeared. With their mother gone and their father lost to his obsession, they'd realized they needed to take care of themselves and each other, because no one else would. When they'd all found their military careers ending at roughly the same time, Danny had suggested starting their own security firm, leveraging their combined experience in military intelligence. None of them had hesitated to go into business together. There was no one Ethan trusted more than his brothers to have his back, and he knew Derek and Ethan felt the same way.

But tonight all the family togetherness threatened to smother him. Nights like tonight, his father's relentless, delusional search for their mother made him want to make a run for it.

Plus, Toni had zeroed in on their one and only lead on Kara, and he was anxious to get back to her.

For professional reasons only, of course.

As though reading his mind—which he probably was—Derek asked, "So do you have any leads on the Kramer girl?"

Everyone breathed a silent sigh, relieved at the change of subject.

"We found another online profile for Kara. Not exactly the good girl she's been showing the rest of the world." He quickly filled them in on the photos Toni had uncovered. "But the good news is she updated her other Web page again."

"You'd think she'd call her folks."

Ethan pulled a face. "Yeah, but she might love that she's making her parents squirm." He felt a twinge of guilt even as the words left his mouth, remembering the way worry had etched deep lines into Toni's face.

"You think the nude pictures have anything to do with it?" Danny said.

"Hard to tell. But they sure as hell complicate things," Ethan said, taking a pull on his beer. "Toni's convinced she's in danger."

"But you aren't." Danny said.

Ethan shrugged. "She's been gone for nearly two days. I have to take that seriously."

"So what's she like, the other investigator?" Derek asked. "She looked sort of cute from her driver's license photo."

"If you like the nerdy, I-just-got-home-from-band-camp look." Danny snorted.

Derek shrugged. "Not everyone goes for Pam Anderson clones."

Ethan paused, beer halfway to his lips, considering his words carefully. He didn't know exactly how to explain

Toni. "She's cute enough, I suppose," which was an understatement. She was beautiful behind those big nerdy frames, and with a little makeup and something sexier than jeans and a T-shirt, she'd give the silicone set a run for their money. "And really fucking smart. And a complete pain in the ass." But even as he said it, a reluctant smile crept a across his lips.

Derek shot Danny a look. "Wednesday."

Danny shook his head. "Tuesday, max."

"What?" Ethan asked.

"You'll do her by Tuesday," Danny said.

Ethan shook his head. "I don't think so. She's not my type."

"Oh, please, like that's ever stopped you. Besides, when you talk about her, you get that look." Derek said.

"What look?" Ethan said. "I don't have a look."

"Yes, you do," Danny said around a mouthful of pasta. "It's that look you get when you get a whiff of fresh pussy, and you won't stop until you're nose-deep."

"Jesus, not in front of Dad," Ethan said, the back of his neck on fire. Ridiculous that at this stage in his life he could still be so easily embarrassed. But if anyone had the power to reduce his thirty-two-year-old adult self to an awkward teenager, it was his brothers. Fortunately, Dad seemed to be paying no attention, his mind on his upcoming trip.

"I still say Wednesday," Derek said. "If she's as smart as we think, it'll take awhile for her to fall for Ethan's usual game. He'll have to be more creative."

"No way." Danny shook his head. "The nerdy ones are the fastest to fall. They're not used to the same attention the bar bunnies get, so she'll be all flattered to have a guy like Ethan sniffing around."

Ethan shook his head. Little did they know that despite the attraction Ethan sensed, Toni was throwing up barriers left and right. Ethan suspected Derek was right, that Toni wasn't about to fall for Ethan's regular tricks. It would take Ethan more than a few days to get her where he wanted her.

But he didn't want to talk about Toni, not even with his brothers.

It was stupid, really. Usually he had no problem indulging in a little locker-room talk with them. It wasn't like he gave detailed play-by-plays about his dates, but they were guys, and guys talked.

But he didn't want them talking that way about Toni, even in jest.

Nevertheless, their comments summoned up a whole host of raunchy images of her. Naked on top of him. Naked underneath him. Naked on her knees in front of him, staring seductively up through those sexy-librarian glasses at him as she took his cock between those luscious lips. He shifted in his chair, mentally cursing Derek and Danny for getting him all riled up.

His cell phone rang, and as though he'd summoned her, Toni's number flashed on the display.

"I found out who T-Bone is," she said without preamble. "His name is Toby Frankel, and from what I've been able to dig up, I'm afraid he has Kara into some bad shit."

"I'll be right over." He hung up and met his brothers' curious stares. "Speaking of Toni, I need to get back to her place. Make sure you wear your watch when you leave tomorrow, and make sure Dad has his."

Danny gave him a "duh" look and flashed his wrist where his watch was securely fastened. All three of the brothers and their father had tiny tracking devices in their watches so they could keep track of each other's locations at all times. After what happened with their mother, they were a little anal about keeping tabs. But Danny had an annoying habit of taking off into the mountains for "private time" and leaving his watch at home.

"You don't forget your rubbers," Danny shot back.

"She's a colleague. Nothing else."

Danny's eyebrows wiggled lasciviously, and he pulled his wallet out of the back pocket of his cargo shorts. "Fuck Tuesday, my money's on tonight."

Derek was still mulling over his bet when Ethan flashed them the finger and walked out the front door.

CHAPTER 6

TONI OPENED THE door before he had time to knock. She felt Ethan give her a quick once-over and was glad she'd taken the time to change her clothes. Even so, his intense blue gaze scorched through the thin material of her T-shirt. His lips pulled up at the corner as he took in the cartoon girl and the caption "Little Miss Sunshine."

"Cute," he said. She prayed he couldn't see the way her nipples jumped to attention under his stare.

There was something seriously wrong with her that she could have such a strong physical reaction under these circumstances.

"So tell me about T-Bone," he said, brushing against her as he walked into her entryway. He'd changed clothes, too, trading in his businesslike sportcoat and dress shirt for a black T-shirt and cargo pants. The shirt wasn't one of those metro-fabulous clingy things, but the sturdy cotton outlined the taut muscles of his back and shoulders, and the dark olive cargo pants did mouthwatering things for his butt.

Ogling Ethan's clothed butt reminded her of the bare ones she'd been looking at, bringing her focus back to the task at hand. "T-Bone is the alter ego of Toby Frankel," she said, following him as he walked into the living room. "He'll be a senior at Stanford this fall. He's twenty-two years old, a member of the Sigma Delta fraternity."

She followed Ethan over to her desk, where he was looking at the Web site Toni had left up on the screen. "He's also runs his own porn site."

"Please tell me that's not Kara," he said, looking at a picture of a girl on her knees in front of a guy, about to perform oral sex. Both faces were blurred out.

"Fortunately, no," Toni said, embarrassed heat raising beads of sweat on her neck. She'd seen a lot worse than this on the Net, but sitting here in her apartment with Ethan, looking at porn, sent her usual businesslike cool straight out the window. She strained for equilibrium, reminding herself this was just a case, and Ethan was just a colleague. "There are a few pictures of Kara on the site. You can find them under the 'horny virgin' heading." God, just saying it turned her stomach. She'd known Kara was having a rough time keeping her shit together, but Toni had never thought she'd do something like this. And after reading Kara's comments, Toni had serious doubts about whether she still qualified for the virgin classification.

The small silver lining was that if Kara was having sex of any kind, there wasn't any photographic evidence on the Net, at least not that Toni could find.

And she'd looked a lot in the few hours Ethan was gone, downloading and analyzing all of the JPEG files on Toby's site until she was satisfied that none of the explicitly sexual photos were of Kara. "Her pictures definitely weren't the worst of it. Some topless shots, a few with another girl doing some light lesbian action, but her face was blurred out in all of them."

"But easy enough for you to decrypt." Ethan said.

Toni nodded. "Yeah, me and anyone else with a little extra time and some shareware."

"Looks like he runs it out of his dorm room," Ethan said.

"Yeah, it's strictly low-budget amateur hour," Toni said, feeling her lip curl as she tried to shove the images out of her mind. "I mean, it all looks consensual, but . . . yuck. I'm sure you want to take a look yourself."

Ethan huffed out a chuckle. "No thanks. I'll take your word for it."

"Seriously? A man who doesn't take the opportunity to look at naked women, especially when he can say it was for purely professional reasons?"

He straightened and turned his back on the computer, biceps flexing as he folded his arms across his chest. "Let's put aside the fact that one of the girls is the teenage daughter of my client—not something I need to see. But if I'm looking at a naked woman, ideally it's because I'm in the room with her and I'm about to show her a really good time."

Toni felt her mouth go dry and her body go wet as her mind took that scenario and ran with it. Her—naked, waiting, watching—as Ethan stripped off his shirt and moved over her with that predatory grace. She swallowed hard and pushed her glasses up her nose. "In that case, we might as well go see him." Grateful for the excuse to get out of her apartment before she did something really stupid, she handed him her BlackBerry, where she'd keyed in Toby's address on the nearby Stanford campus.

On the short drive, Toni told him everything else she'd discovered about Toby Frankel, T-Bone. "In addition to his amateur porn ventures, Toby also has had several scrapes with the law. Minor drug stuff, mostly, public intoxication—all of it when he was a minor, and nothing ever really stuck. Then last year, he got busted for allegedly supplying most of the drugs to the local junior high and high-schoolers. It went to trial, but they couldn't get the charges to stick."

"Good lawyers?" Ethan asked.

"The best," Toni said. "He was represented by Goodly and Shipman."

Ethan knew that Mark Goodly took on only the highest-profile cases. "So our boy Toby comes from some major cash."

Toni nodded and scrolled through the rest of her notes. "His father is the managing partner for a hedge fund back east. And it looks like he's spent a fair portion of his multimillion-dollar bonuses keeping his son out of jail. In fact, that's why Toby's taking classes this summer. Funny how a criminal trial will mess with your academic schedule."

Ethan pulled into the parking lot of the luxurious-looking apartment building where Toby was spending his summer. "Wow. Student housing has changed a lot since I went to school," marveled Toni.

"Lots of rich alumni, showing the school a little love," Ethan said.

A young woman was unlocking the front door as they approached. To the right of the entry was an intercom system that allowed tenants to buzz visitors in.

But they didn't need to bother paging Toby. The student looked over her shoulder, took one look at Ethan, and held the door open wide.

Ethan murmured his thanks and motioned for Toni to precede him into the building. They joined the girl in the elevator, Ethan smiling and chatting politely as the girl somehow managed to ask a hundred questions in the course of riding up three floors.

"Maybe I'll see you around," she said, peeking up under her lashes and wiggling her fingers in an impish little wave. Toni watched the doors close behind the girl's nubile twenty-year-old butt. She clenched her jaw, feeling about a hundred years old and as sexy as concrete. She generally didn't indulge in insecurity over her appearance, didn't obsess over how she stacked up against other women. Toni never had been and never would be a sex kitten. She'd never be like that girl—cute and petite with lots of luscious curves. She'd faced reality long ago and never let it bother her. But Ethan's oh-so-easy banter and the girl's receptive smile set her off.

"Do you ever pass up an opportunity to flirt?" she asked, immediately regretting the question.

"I was merely making conversation with a friendly girl," he said. "And besides, she could have had valuable information."

"Yeah, like her apartment number and a hand-engraved invitation into her panties." Toni clamped her lips shut, wishing she could call the words back, and pissed because she'd been in danger of issuing a similar invitation back at her apartment. She would not be the first to melt in the face of Ethan's effortless charm, and she would be far from the last. She really needed to remember that, especially when her body sent out urgent reminders every time he so much as looked at her that she hadn't had sex in over a year.

Ethan laughed as the doors slid open on Toby's floor.

Ethan knocked on his door, which was opened by a guy Toni assumed was Toby's roommate. He was a little shorter than she was, with shaggy brown hair and skinny legs that stuck out from the bottom of his ragged khaki shorts.

"Is Toby here?" Ethan asked. "We need to ask him some questions."

"Who wants to know?" the kid asked. He wore a sleepy, smart-ass smile, his eyes bloodshot and narrowed into tell-tale slits. She sniffed the air. Yep, Toby's roommate was high as a kite.

Gone was the flirty charmer from the elevator. Suddenly Ethan was all steely, square-jawed authority.

The kid blanched. "Toby's not here." The door started to

close, and Toni realized they weren't going to get anywhere with Stoner Boy if Ethan went all *Law & Order* on him.

"Really," Toni said, affecting the sweetest, widest-eyed look she could manage. "I'm sure he told me to meet him here tonight."

The kid squinted at her through red-rimmed eyes. "Are you here for a shoot?"

"Yeah," she said, pushing her way past the roommate and into the apartment. Her nose twitched at the mingled odors of pot, dirty laundry, and stale Doritos. "Is there someplace I should change? I'm Toni, by the way." She stuck out her hand at the kid who shambled after her, trying to keep up.

Ethan had no such trouble, eyeing her as though waiting to see how far she'd take this.

Not that far, Ace.

"I'm Dave," the roommate said. "Toby's not here right now."

Toni feigned a look at her watch. "Really? I swear he said nine o'clock." She looked at Ethan. "Didn't he say nine o'clock, honey?"

Ethan's teeth flashed as he grinned. "That's what he said, baby."

"Wow, you're really tall," Dave said, blinking dazedly as he looked at Toni.

"Thanks. My dad was six four. So when will Toby be back?"

"I dunno." Dave shrugged. Toni strained to keep her smile fixed as he took a long, hard look at her, his gaze seeming to stick somewhere around her boobs. "You're not like the regular girls. No offense, you're hot and all, but aren't you a little . . . old?"

Toni faked a laugh. "I'm a graduate student, doing research on the way pornography and its prevalence on the Internet are influencing portrayals of feminine sexuality in mainstream media. I feel like the only way I can really understand what drives the average girl to want to be the next Jenna Jameson is to experience it for myself. Anonymously, of course. Toby promised he'd blur out my face."

Dave nodded soberly. "I help him edit the photos sometimes. I'll make sure no one knows it's you."

She walked across the messy sitting room and pushed open the door to a bedroom. She switched on the light and looked inside. She recognized the blue bedspread from numerous pictures. A tripod sat empty across from the bed. Wherever Toby was, he'd taken his camera with him. "Is this where he'll set up?"

Dave nodded and shot a nervous look at Ethan. "What's with the big dude?"

"Ethan's my boyfriend. He's very jealous," she said, speaking in a stage whisper.

Her stomach muscles clenched as Ethan's hand slid around her waist. "I wasn't about to let her do this alone." He drew her back against him, until she could feel the hard outline of every muscle in his chest against her back. "She says it's all for her dissertation, but I want to be here in case Toby tries anything."

Toni laid her hand across his forearm in the guise of affection but dug in her nails in warning. Ethan retaliated by pulling her even tighter against him, until she could feel an unmistakable firmness nudging at the small of her back. "Actually, I'm hoping to talk him into a couple's shoot. Do you think Toby would do that?"

Ethan must have been giving him the death stare, because Dave swallowed hard and looked anywhere but at Toni. "Maybe. Listen, should I have him call you when he gets back?"

"Any idea when that will be?" Ethan asked. "We've got a packed schedule and I want to get this over with."

"He took off yesterday for Vegas."

"That's right," Toni said, slapping her forehead. "My friend Kara said something about that. Do you know if she ended up going with him?"

"Kara?" Dave said, clueless.

"She's Toby's girlfriend."

"Toby has lots of girlfriends."

Toni pulled up Kara's picture on her cell phone. "You have to have seen her. She's been seeing Toby for a couple of months now," Toni said, though she had no idea how long they'd known each other or how close they were.

Dave stared at Kara's picture for a full thirty seconds, opening his bloodshot eyes wide as he struggled to focus. Then, as though a circuit finally connected in his brain, he grabbed the picture, pointing eagerly. "Yeah, yeah! I've seen her. Toby started hanging out with her at the beginning of the summer," Dave said. "But she hasn't been around lately. I think they had a fight."

"Huh. She never mentioned it," Toni said, as Ethan slid a possessive arm around Toni's shoulders.

Only the prospect of finding out where Kara was kept Toni from turning and nuzzling her face into Ethan's chest.

"A couple weeks ago she came by and found him in bed with another chick. She went apeshit and flushed his stash of Ex. He got really pissed."

"That's weird, because I'm sure she said she was going to see him this weekend," Toni said, trying to jar a memory out of Dave's pot-laden brain cells.

Dave shrugged and plopped down on the couch in a heap of gangly limbs. "Maybe they made up. You'll have to ask her."

"We'd better go," Ethan said, guiding her to the door with his arm around her shoulders. "We'll see you around."

As soon as the door shut Toni extricated herself from his grip. "You can stop feeling me up now." She stepped into the elevator and moved to the opposite corner, as far from him as possible.

"A couple's shoot?"

"Hey, it got him talking, better than you scaring the crap out of him would have," she said with a chuckle.

He shrugged and pulled a face as though mulling it over. "I've always been a door-closed kinda guy, but I'd be willing—in the interest of our investigation, of course." His naughty smile made her feel hot all over.

"Do not get any ideas," she said, laughing, then trailed off as guilt and worry surged back to the forefront. "This isn't funny. Kara's involved with this scumbag, and I'm laughing about it."

"Kara's almost eighteen," he pointed out. "In a couple of months she'll be able to show her tits to everyone with a Web browser and there's nothing we can do."

"Don't talk about her like that. She's not eighteen yet, and Toby Frankel is exploiting a minor."

The elevator doors slid open and Toni hurried out.

"Still, you're taking this way more personally than you should."

She whipped around to face him. "And maybe you should take it a little more personally. As far as I can tell, Kara's nothing to you but a paycheck. You don't care if we find her in a Dumpster, as long as you get paid." She threw open the front door and stalked across the parking lot.

He caught her in three strides, his grip firm on her upper arm. "That's not fair, and you know it. Of course I care what happens to her. I want to find her and make sure she's okay as much as you do. But you have to remember that Kara's not the innocent kid you thought she was, and she may be off having a great fucking time with her boyfriend while you beat yourself up worrying about her."

She could see his point but had to get in one last jab. "Or her pissed-off ex-boyfriend could have kidnapped her."

"Which is why we're going to track down Toby and find out. But it's probably just like the police said. She's going to stroll into her house in the next couple of days and won't give a shit that she left a lot of people worried sick."

"Smile for the camera."

Kara pressed herself harder into the mattress, trying to disappear into the firm bulk. Smile? Her mouth was shaking uncontrollably as her chest heaved with hysterical breath.

Her parents had never taken her and her brother to church, but now she couldn't stop praying. *Pleasegodpleasegodplease. Let me get out of here. Please don't let them hurt me.*

So far her prayers had been answered. She hadn't been hurt beyond the pain in her wrists where she'd been bound.

But that didn't stop the clawing fear that kept a death grip on her heart.

After her conversation with the man, they'd put her in a shower, fully clothed, and told her to clean herself up or else.

She didn't even wait for the threat of "or else" to start scrubbing herself clean.

Another man stood guard in the bathroom while she showered, a stocky blond guy who watched her through the beveled-glass door in a way that made her want to throw up.

They won't rape me. They want me to be a virgin. It was the only shred of hope she could cling to through her panic.

Her skin crawled when she remembered the way the man had talked about her "treasure."

And now they were taking pictures of her. Pictures of her on a big, white bed, wearing a ruffled white nightgown, the kind an eight-year-old might wear. It was unbuttoned at the throat and pushed up her legs to show the white cotton panties they'd told her to put on.

It was way more clothes than she'd ever worn when Toby took pictures of her for his Web site. But she'd never felt filthier, knowing some gross old man was going to look at these pictures and fantasize about popping her cherry.

"Make them good," the blond man said, watching from

the foot of the bed as the bigger, stockier man aimed the lens at Kara.

"Relax," the bigger man said in a thick European accent. "The camera is brand-new. The salesman said it was top of the line."

"I want our buyers to have a clear image of what they're getting."

The camera clicked, flashing in her face. She focused on the spots, blocking out the faces of the men at the foot of the bed, fighting back nausea as they positioned her legs, spreading her knees wider, before the flash popped again.

Her father would cooperate. He wouldn't let them go through with this. He would give them whatever they wanted to get her back.

But what if he'd found out the truth? That she wasn't his perfect little girl? Would he still do anything and everything to get her back?

No, she couldn't think that way. Her father was a good guy, and Kara knew he loved her even if he wasn't good at showing it. He wouldn't let anyone hurt her.

In the meantime, she would cooperate, do what they told her, keep herself from getting hurt.

CHAPTER 7

ETHAN WAS RARELY surprised by anyone anymore. He'd always been good at reading people, and he thought he had Toni nailed. Serious, thought she knew everything because most of the time she did. The smart girl in the back of the class who kept quiet, rolling her eyes until she finally condescended to raise her hand and enlighten everyone. The girl who thought she knew the score and tapped her foot impatiently for everyone to catch up.

After watching her deal with Joyce and Laurie Friedland earlier, he'd expected her to try to run roughshod over the pothead roommate. Hell, Ethan had been all geared up to do the bad-cop routine and beat it out of the little punk.

Metaphorically speaking, of course.

But Toni had thrown him, morphing in front of him from reserved computer nerd to cyber sex goddess, sassing her way into the apartment and filling Dave's head with visions of Toni in all kinds of provocative poses. Poor kid had been toast from the moment she puckered that lush mouth and batted those big hazel eyes.

Toni, who had been staring out the window, turned at his involuntary chuckle. "What?" she said.

"Porn and feminine sexuality in mainstream media?" He laughed again, taking his attention from the road long enough to see her sly, pleased smile illuminated by the passing streetlights.

"It was the first thing that popped into my head. My friend Megan actually wrote a paper on that for a feminist studies class."

"Research must have been interesting."

"That's one way to describe it." They pulled into Toni's parking lot and she let herself out of the car. She led him up the stairs, and Ethan took a second to appreciate the way her jeans outlined the subtle flex of her butt muscles as she climbed. Those folks at Lucky Brand really knew their business.

"The stuff she saw was enough to make Kara's pictures look like they were taken for a Girl Scout recruiting brochure," Toni said as she unlocked her door.

The mention of Kara quickly sobered him up. Right. They had a spoiled punk amateur pornographer at large, possibly with the teenage daughter of his client in tow. Not the time to be ogling a woman's ass, no matter how tempting.

Toni flipped on the kitchen light and went to the refrigerator and grabbed two beers, twisting the cap off one before offering it to him. She carried her own to her desk and turned on her computer. "I don't get it," she said as she waited for her system to boot. "Why would a kid like Toby, with all that money, everything handed to him, bother selling drugs and porn? It's not like he needs it to make student loan payments."

"Never underestimate the boredom of a kid who has everything."

She looked up from her screen. "And you have experience with this?"

"I grew up less than half a mile from Kara Kramer." He took a sip of his beer as he waited for that to sink in.

Her fingers froze over the keyboard. "Your parents are rich?"

Ethan sank down on her couch and pulled out his phone. "Yeah, my dad was an investment banker in San Francisco."

She swiveled around her her chair to face him, one dark eyebrow cocked over the frames of her glasses. "So did you sell drugs, too? Make your dad pay off the cops?"

He gave a short laugh. "No. We were pretty good." He paused. "Well, mostly. And if we weren't, nobody knew about it."

She turned back to her screen and typed in a series of commands. "We? How many of you are there?"

"Three. There's Derek—he and I are twins—and Danny, our older brother. We formed Gemini together three years ago."

"You must be close if you manage to stay in business together."

He shrugged. "We have our moments, like all brothers do. How about you? Any brothers or sisters?"

She opened her mouth and paused, as though not sure how to answer the question. Something dark passed in her gaze before she shook her head.

Something had happened there, something that hadn't come up in the brief background check Derek had run. Ethan knew it would be relatively easy to find out, but he wanted her to tell him herself. An impulse he didn't want to examine too closely—when was the last time he wanted a woman to share her secrets? In his experience, that was only asking for trouble.

"So why do you? Work, I mean?" she asked, obviously eager to steer the conversation back to him.

"Because we'd all be bored shitless if we didn't," he said. "Besides, my father set it up so that we don't come into our money until we're fifty. I'm not saying we haven't had help. Dad gave us the seed money to start our business."

"Generous of him," Tony said.

Ethan nodded. Yes, it was generous, but it also meant

they got roped in every time Dad went hieing off after some phantom lead.

"Why not just give it to you?" Toni asked.

"Because he's smart and doesn't want the guarantee of a pile of money to turn us all into shiftless assholes."

"Oh, so it's not the money, you managed to turn into an asshole all by yourself?" Toni said with a teasing smile.

Her comment cracked the tension building inside him. He laughed, wondering when he'd ever laughed at a woman calling him an asshole.

And why did he find the one woman who did so goddamn entertaining?

"Okay, I have Toby's car," she said. "It's a black 2006 Yukon, California license plate XJY 424," she read off.

Attention riveted on her screen, she paid no attention to him. She was so fucking pretty and seemed to get better-looking every time he looked at her. Even now, seeing her frown at her screen as she looked up Toby's recent credit card activity, Ethan couldn't stop wondering how she'd react if he went up and bit her on the neck, on that tender spot right below her ear.

He closed his eyes and sipped his beer, hoping it would ease the restless, itchy feeling he'd been fighting all night, as if his skin had suddenly shrunk one size too small. But the second his lids dropped, all he could think of was Toni, the way she'd felt when he'd pressed up against her while playing the part of her jealous boyfriend.

He opened his eyes again and studied her. She was working hard to keep that wall up, to pretend she wasn't interested. But with his arm around her waist, palm flattened on her stomach, he'd felt her catch her breath, seen the pulse in her neck pick up speed when she'd felt the pressure of his thickening cock snugged up against the small of her back.

He couldn't stop wondering if it had gotten her hot. If her thighs had subtly clenched and unclenched inside her jeans. When they got into the elevator, he'd wanted nothing more than to press the emergency override and pin her up against the wall, to slide his hand up between her thighs, slip his fingers down the front of her pants and see if her pussy was as silky-wet as he imagined.

Now wasn't the time or the place for the full-court press, but as soon as this case was wrapped up—

"Aha, got him!" Toni crowed, her fist punching the air in triumph. Ethan casually crossed his ankle over his knee and tugged at the fly of his pants, praying she wouldn't notice the way his cock was straining against his zipper. Either he was regressing to adolescence or he seriously needed to get laid.

He struggled to get a grip on his libido, reminding himself harshly of the seriousness of the situation. A girl was missing, for Christ's sake, and all he could think about was fucking Toni so good and hard she wouldn't be able to move for a week.

"He used a Visa to buy gas in Barstow, and at seven fifty-three yesterday, he used that same Visa to check into the Wynn Las Vegas Hotel."

Ethan quickly dialed Jerry, eager to relay the information and have something to take his mind off sex. Or more specifically, sex with Toni.

While he left Jerry the information in a voice mail, Toni called Marcy and did the same.

"Jerry didn't answer either?" Toni asked, walking over to the couch and plopping down beside him. "If my kid were missing, I'd have the phone glued to my ear. Where the hell are they, and why the hell aren't they answering their phones?"

At the moment, Ethan didn't particularly care, because he was all too aware of how close Toni was sitting. Her arm was only inches away, and he wanted to reach out, trace the inner curve with his fingers and see if the skin was as baby smooth as it looked.

"I should have known something was going on," Toni

said. The deep worry in her voice pulled him momentarily out of his lust-filled musings. "I knew she was having a hard time . . ." Toni's voice trailed off. She took another sip of her beer and stared into space.

"You said that before. Her own parents didn't know what she was up to."

"I know, but I should have been looking out for her, checking up on her." Toni shook her head. "If I'd known about this whole Kstar90 thing, we could have gotten on this before anything bad happened."

"We still don't know that anything bad has happened."

"Nude photos of an underage girl all over the Internet isn't enough?"

He held his hands up. "Point taken. But that doesn't mean she isn't hanging out with him willingly, having a great time. Did Marcy hire you to check up on her kids?"

"No."

"Then how is Kara your responsibility?"

"She's my friend. Don't give me that look." She frowned at his apparent surprise. "My parents split up when I was sixteen and I knew what she was going through."

"And you didn't want to spy on your friend?"

Toni slumped back against the lumpy sofa cushion. "I promised Kara I wouldn't do anything behind her back," Toni said. "I wanted her to trust me."

Ethan placed his hand on the smooth skin of her forearm. "You kept your word to her. You shouldn't feel guilty for that. You did what you could."

"No, I didn't," she said, her voice tight. "The last time I talked to her I blew her off. She talked about wanting to get away, how her mom was a mess and her dad expected her to be perfect all the time. I told her she just needed to stick it out, she'd be off to college soon enough, blah, blah, blah." She took a sip of beer and let out a disgusted sigh.

"Good advice."

She shook her head and snatched her arm out from under his hand. "No—lame, parental, smile-and-nod advice. She needed someone to listen to her and I wasn't listening. And now she's gone, and I'm not going to just leave her out there like—"

She cut herself off, shifted her gaze away, and started to get off the couch.

"Like what?"

She sighed and closed her eyes, as though carefully weighing her response. "When I was seventeen, my sister Michelle ran away. We found her three months later. She'd been raped and strangled. She was fifteen."

Her tone was even, careful to conceal any hint of emotion. Still, the blunt words hit Ethan like a blow. "That must have been awful for you. I'm sorry," he said, his words sounding incredibly lame as they left his mouth.

"After my parents got divorced, she got into all kinds of trouble. You name it, she did it—drugs, sex, everything. I ignored her, kept my head down and focused on being the smart kid who didn't cause any trouble."

He could easily imagine her, dark-haired and somber, trying to keep her world together as everyone around her fell apart. He could relate.

"I'm sure Kara's fine."

"Yeah, that's what they said about Michelle. 'She's run away several times, ma'am. She'll come back when she's ready, ma'am.' And we were so tired of dealing with her by then we didn't even bother looking for her."

"Toni, you were just a kid yourself—"

"I was her big sister. I should have looked after her."

He set his beer down and slid his arms around her shoulders. She stiffened slightly but didn't move away. "Kara's not like your sister. She's not—"

"Not a drug-addicted juvenile delinquent? Maybe not yet, but she's not exactly trending in the right direction."

"Yeah, I know, but she's never run away before, and she's only been missing for two days. Even if she's with Toby, she's probably fine." He felt like a broken record, but he wanted to ease the guilt and pain shadowing her eyes.

She looked up at him, her mouth pulled tight with strain, eyes dark and troubled. A heartbeat passed. Two. In his efforts to comfort her he'd gotten closer, close enough that her thigh was pressed against his. Close enough to smell the sweet woman-scent of her skin.

His hand slid from her shoulder to her neck. His fingers slid up, tangling in silky black hair as his thumb brushed back and forth over the creamy skin of her throat.

The itchy, tight-skinned feeling was getting worse as every cell went on high alert, every nerve screaming at him to cover her mouth with his own, slide his tongue between those plump, rosy lips, kiss away the sadness and guilt.

Not the time or the place, Taggart. But his body was beyond listening. What the fuck was wrong with him? He never had a problem shutting down his libido. Sure, his brothers liked to tease him about being oversexed, but truth was he was always in control.

Until now.

Her eyes widened behind the lenses of her glasses as he leaned forward, but she didn't try to move away or avoid his mouth as it came down and covered hers. His palm spread against her back and he pulled her close like he'd been dying to do since he'd first seen her in Jerry's kitchen.

Her hands came up, curling over his shoulders, resting there, as if she wasn't quite sure what to do.

He figured he'd give her a little hint, and slid his tongue into her mouth for a taste. She was hot and salty-sweet. A shaky breath spilled into his mouth and her lips parted wider, sucking him inside as she leaned in to the kiss, as eager for it as he. For all that she'd been throwing up a brick wall, there was no doubt she was feeling the same insane chemistry he was. Her hands clutched at his back, twisting the fabric of his shirt, and the hungry little sounds she was making in the back of her throat were driving him insane.

What had started as a comforting gesture quickly spun out of control. Any thoughts of work, of the case, flew out the window as the taste and feel and smell of her coursed through his veins. Ethan cupped his hand around the back of her head, holding her in place as his mouth moved greedily over hers. Tongues tangling, lips sucking. Ethan tried to remember the last time he'd gotten hard as a spike from just a kiss, and couldn't.

His free hand slid down the front of her shirt, closing over the soft weight of her breast. Her nipple was bullet hard, pushing eagerly against his palm, and he tasted her startled gasp when he pinched it gently through the stretchy fabric. A gasp turned into a whimper as his fingers plucked and teased the hard tip, until her back was arching away from the couch as she sought closer contact.

His lips slid from her mouth, across her jaw, and down the length of her neck. Her skin was salty with sweat and arousal, the smell of her subtle perfume growing heavier in the sultry air of the summer night. His hand slid down one side of her waist, catching the hem of her T-shirt in his fingers on the way back up. He heard something rip as he tugged her shirt up over her breasts, and he cautioned himself to slow down. But sometime between meeting her yesterday and right this second, the skilled, always-in-control lover Ethan prided himself on being had disappeared.

Taking his place was a lust-crazed, out-of-control hedonist who wanted nothing more than to tear off Toni's panties, shove his cock in her as deep as he could get, pumping and thrusting until he came so hard he couldn't move. He tugged her shirt up over her head and flung it somewhere over the back of the couch.

He paused for a moment to enjoy the view and nearly came in his pants at the sight that greeted him. Toni was half reclining against the cushions of the couch, clad in tight jeans, and nothing on top but a creamy satin-and-lace bra that barely covered even creamier skin.

He tugged the cups down and covered her left breast in his hand, the plump, succulent flesh looking all the more delicious contrasted against his big, tanned hands. Her nipple was a rosy-pink, tight little bud peeking over his fingers, making his mouth water as he anticipated sucking it hard between his lips.

He'd been with more-well-endowed women over the years, but hands down, Toni Crawford had the prettiest tits he'd ever seen. Creamy white with tight, pink nipples that begged to be sucked. His breath exhaled on a groan as he bent down for a taste, meaning to tease her with his tongue, but instead losing all technique and finesse as he sucked her hard into his mouth. Her fingers twisted into his hair, and the little shock of pain was enough to make his cock harden another inch.

He shoved her back onto the couch and used his knees to spread her legs, and even through her jeans he could feel her heat as his stomach pressed against the sweet spot between her thighs. The smell of perfume and aroused woman filled his head. He wanted to move his hands and his mouth lower so he could explore the blossoming heat at her core. But he couldn't get enough of her breasts. He sucked greedily at one while his hand played with the other, stroking the smooth skin, pinching the tight tip in his fingers.

Toni's breath was coming in short, hot pants, her hips lifting and grinding against him. Ethan adjusted himself until his fly was perfectly aligned with her sex. The heat of her seared through the fabric barrier of his trousers as he began a slow, circling counterrhythm guaranteed to drive them both insane. He closed his eyes, savoring the taste and feel of her nipples against his tongue, the sound of her breathy gasps as he rubbed his cock against her, bringing her closer and closer to the edge. Her legs trembled faintly against his, her fingers gripped at the muscles of his ass.

God, she was hot, purely responsive, with no pretense or calculated moves. He could feel her body stiffening, every sinew going tight in preparation for the impending explosion. When she came, it was going to be so hard, so good. And when she came down off that high he was going to strip off their clothes and start the process all over again.

A shrill noise cut through the sounds of heavy breathing and smacking lips, accompanied by a vibrating sensation next to his balls. Ethan jumped like a cat and tumbled to the floor, groping at his pants as his sex-fogged brain realized that both the noise and the vibration were coming from his pocket.

He pulled out his BlackBerry, recognizing Kramer's number as Toni pushed herself upright and pulled her bra cups back into place. She stared at him, dazed, as though she wasn't sure where she was or what she was doing.

"Ethan Taggart," he answered the phone, his voice only moderately more raspy than usual. He glanced up at Toni, silently cursing at Kramer's unbelievably shitty timing. Her face was flushed pink, her pulse still thrummed in her throat. Her lips were swollen and parted as her breath came out in shaky gasps, and all Ethan wanted to do was throw the goddamn phone across the room and relieve the sexual frustration coursing through both their bodies.

But duty called. "Got your message," Kramer said curtly. "You're sure she's in Vegas?"

Ethan stood up and turned his back on Toni, to give her a chance to compose herself and also because the sight of her, clothes half off and primed for one of the biggest female orgasms of the century, was playing way too much havoc with his concentration. "It's the best lead we have so far. I was about to follow up with the detective assigned to Kara's case when you called." It was only a partial lie. But he didn't think Jerry would appreciate the truth that Ethan was going to get back on the case only after he'd fucked Toni every which way he could think of.

Which was messed up. Ethan had never let sex interfere with work and he wasn't about to start now. As much as his aching cock would argue differently, Kramer's call was a blessing. He didn't want to do Toni in some fast, furtive fuck on her couch. He wanted the time and the room to explore her at his leisure and find out what she liked. There would be time enough after they brought Kara home to explore chemistry that snapped, crackled, and popped every time he was in the same room with her.

"I don't want to leave it to the police or anyone else. You go to Vegas. You get her back."

Ethan stifled a sigh and took a look at his watch. It was already after ten. If he moved fast, he could be in Vegas by one a.m. "I'll call you when I get there," he said and hung up.

Toni hurried by, T-shirt clutched to her chest. He heard a door close behind him and water running as he willed his cock back into a semirelaxed state. What a fucked-up night. Two minutes ago, he was on his way to spending several hot, sweaty hours with a woman he wasn't even sure liked him, and now he was flying to Vegas.

The fan hummed, stirring the hot air of the apartment. Ethan could detect the faint aroma of sex breezing by on its way out the window. Desire twisted in his belly, and despite all of his rationalizations, he wondered if he could possibly talk Toni into a quickie up against the wall before he had to go.

She emerged from the bathroom, shirt tucked tightly into her jeans, hair brushed into a sleek curtain. And judging from the grim set of her mouth and her tightly folded arms, hell would freeze over before she indulged in his up against-the-wall fantasy.

The wall was back in place, every brick cemented tight as she brushed past him to go to the kitchen.

"That was Jerry," he said. "He wants me to go to Vegas tonight."

Her head whipped around. "You're going tonight?"

"As soon as I get the plane ready."

Her eyes widened behind her glasses. "You have a plane."

He nodded. "My father keeps it for business travel." Not entirely true, but he wasn't about to tell Toni that his father leased a jet so he could follow up leads about Ethan's missing mother. Toni might have been ready to spill her deep, dark secrets, but he wasn't up for revealing his.

Toni looked like she wanted to ask something but Ethan stared pointedly at his watch. "I have to get going."

She went over to her desk and started shutting down her laptop. "Give me five minutes to get my stuff together." She flipped her laptop closed, shoved it into a backpack, and carried the bag down the hall to her bedroom.

Drawers were open, and she was shoving clothes into her bag. His mouth went dry as his gaze caught on a scrap of pink lace dangling from a drawer. "You don't need to go with me." Seriously, five more minutes in close proximity to Toni and her Victoria's Secret stash and he couldn't be held responsible for anything he did. He grabbed her wrist to stay her hand as she reached for a brush. "I'll call you as soon as I find anything out."

She snatched her wrist from his grasp. "Are you kidding me?"

He looked at her determined face, knew she wouldn't back down. Thinking about what she'd revealed about her sister, he couldn't blame her. And he couldn't do that to her—ditch her here, leave her to twist while he went after Kara alone.

"Fine. But bring something more appropriate for going out than what you've got on."

She looked down at her T-shirt, dark jeans, and black Converse All Star sneakers. "What's wrong with what I've got on?"

"Toby's at one of the hottest hotels in Vegas. They won't let you into any of the clubs looking like that."

She rolled her eyes but rummaged through her closet, emerging with a fistful of silvery fabric and a pair of shiny shoes, both of which she stuffed into her backpack. "What about you, Ace? You're pretty cute, but I doubt you're what the bouncers are looking for."

He gave her a tight grin. "We'll stop by my place on the way to the airport. Looks like we're going to Vegas, baby."

Toni took a deep breath and sank deeper into the buttery-soft leather of the copilot's chair of the twin-engine private jet. Frustrated desire still simmered in her core, and every nerve ending was on high alert as Ethan checked the instruments and communicated with the flight tower. Her skin was hot and too sensitive for the fabric of her shirt. Her satin bra felt like sandpaper against her nipples. And the idea of his piloting the plane was so ridiculously sexy, it made her squirm in her seat as she tried to keep her mind off the scorching feel of his lips and hands running over her naked skin.

If only they'd been able to finish what they started. *No, bad idea, don't even go there,* she told herself harshly. Kara was missing, possibly in danger, and she was so busy lusting after Ethan she could barely keep her brain in gear. What was wrong with her? In the time she'd broken up with John, she'd met plenty of guys she could have been attracted to if she'd allowed herself. But she didn't have time for a guy, a relationship, any of that bullshit. She needed to keep herself focused, first on finding Kara, then on getting herself moved back to Seattle and forgetting this entire unfortunate detour her life had taken after her mom died.

But Ethan had been so sweet, comforting her, a look in his blue eyes that said he understood what she was talking about when she'd told him about Michelle. His strong arms and big hands had felt so good, she'd just wanted to sink into him and stay wrapped up against his chest for a couple of weeks.

Ugh. So did every woman with a pulse. Like the bearer of the dark pink lipstick that had found its way onto Ethan's ear.

That's the kind of man you're dealing with, Toni. A guy who gets lipstick all over him and is kissing someone else two days later.

She should have pushed him away the second he'd put his arm around her, and definitely when he'd leaned in. But he'd smelled so good and tasted even better. And the way he'd kissed her. So hungry, like he was starving for the taste of her. And his hands, rough but tender as they'd cupped and squeezed her breasts. Her nipples tightened at the memory.

And, she admitted to herself, feeling lame and weak and girly as she did, it felt so good to feel wanted. Especially by a man who looked the way he did.

It galled her to admit it, but she knew if Kramer hadn't called, she would have been naked, on the couch, on the bed, hell, the kitchen table if that's what Ethan wanted, legs spread wide as she eagerly took him inside her body.

Between her legs, her sex fluttered as though mourning for the climaxes that would never be. She crossed her legs, willing her libido out of hyperdrive.

Ethan had no trouble shutting it down, she thought, glaring into his back. She was a mess, but from the moment Kramer called he'd flipped like a switch, all business all the time, as if he hadn't just had his lips on her breast and his hips between her legs, rocking her to heaven on her second-hand couch.

The man was dangerous.

But as she watched him adjust his headset and go through a final instrument check, she wondered if maybe some bed rocking, wall banging, no strings attached might be exactly what she needed. She'd never been one for one-night stands, but her body's enthusiastic response to Ethan told her she'd missed sex a lot more than she'd realized. As long as she kept firmly in mind what sex with Ethan would and would not mean, maybe it wasn't a bad idea to give big stud over there a ride.

"What?" Ethan asked as they started to taxi down the runway. "Why are you staring at me like that?"

She was grateful that the dark hid her flush as she scrambled for a reply. "I was thinking how cool it is that you can fly. I don't think I've ever met a pilot."

"I was pilot in the navy for eight years. Fighter jets."

"You were in the navy?" She couldn't keep the incredulous tone out of her voice. Still, she was impressed. "You don't strike me as a military type."

Somehow, she couldn't see Ethan, with his charming smile and devil-may-care swagger, fitting in with a rigid disciplinary structure. However, she could easily imagine how hot he must have looked in his flight suit.

"I did okay," he said with a smile. "My brothers were, too."

Now that was interesting. Several of her high school classmates had gone into the military as a way to afford college, but since when did the sons of *über*-wealthy businessmen voluntarily join the military?

As though he had read her mind, Ethan said, "We're the fifth generation of Taggart men to serve our country."

"And you were all in the navy?"

"Nope, just me. Derek and Danny both went to West Point and joined the army. Danny eventually went into the special forces, and Derek was a sniper. But I always wanted to fly."

A family of warriors, she thought with a delicious little shiver. Somehow, the idea that Ethan wanted to go fast and fly planes didn't surprise her. "So you wanted to be like Tom Cruise in *Top Gun*?"

His eyes creased at the corners as he grinned. "Something like that, but taller and not jumping off Oprah's couch."

Toni laughed and slanted him a sly look. "And I bet you enjoyed having a different woman in every port."

"I was on an aircraft carrier in the Persian Gulf for eight months at a pop. I had to find my fun somewhere."

She could only imagine what kind of fun he found. Her mouth went dry as the kiss they both seemed determined to forget blazed through her consciousness. She swallowed hard and steered the subject away from Ethan's undoubtedly vast experience with women around the world.

"So I suppose you big, tough ex-military types focus more on the personal protection side of security in your business."

He nodded. "We do plenty of that. But we keep up on the high-tech stuff. Especially Derek."

"A sniper turned computer genius. Sounds interesting. You said he's your twin?"

"Yeah, fraternal. But I guess we look alike."

She didn't know what made her say what she said next, but he was so sexually confident, and she was so at sea, she wanted to see if she could get under his skin. "Maybe you could fix us up."

Ethan turned his attention away from the instrument panel, and even in the dim light of the plane she could feel the impact of his stare. The small space was charged with energy and heat.

"I don't think so," he said, in a tone that told her she'd scored a direct hit. He turned back to face the windshield.

He was silent for several minutes. Toni leaned back against the headrest and looked out into the darkness. There was almost no ambient light, only the occasional bright dot of a small town illuminating the desert darkness. Ethan's voice startled her out of her trancelike state.

"So how did a computer genius like you go from having a lucrative job in high tech to working as a PI?"

How did he—? Oh yeah. Her job at SafeTech must have come up on her background check.

Toni shrugged. "Kind of happened by accident. I used to work in network security, and after I moved down here, a friend of a friend wanted me to do some family Internet security."

He cocked a curious eyebrow. "I haven't heard that term."

She laughed self-consciously. "It mostly involves spying on their kids. It's really scary when you see how many sleazebags are out there, trolling the Net and targeting young kids, and it's hard for parents to keep on top of it." She gave a shudder. "Through that first client I got several referrals. I also do some financial tracking, help people find assets their spouses might have moved to offshore accounts."

"And cheating spouses?" Ethan asked.

She wrinkled her nose in distaste. "Not too much, but definitely more than I'd like to. It's bad enough when I have to show women the e-mails their husbands are sending to their girlfriends, but sometimes even that's not enough proof. Like last Friday I was out until three, waiting outside the Sheraton to take a picture of my client's husband."

"Hell of a way to spend a Friday."

Toni remembered the lipstick. While she'd been folded up in the front seat of her Honda, Ethan had been folded up around another woman.

She wondered if the plane came equipped with air sickness bags. "All I know is that even the most devoted husband will screw around if he thinks he can get away with it." And she'd certainly been proven right in her own love life.

"What about the wives? Haven't you caught any of Marcy's friends with their pool boys and their trainers?"

She heard the harsh edge creep into his voice. "I'm sure it happens," she finally said, "but so far I've only been hired by the wives."

He looked like he was about to argue but let the subject drop as the lights of the Las Vegas strip came into view.

Jerry picked up the phone on the second ring as the fifty-year-old Macallan he'd just swallowed turned to battery acid in his stomach.

"Are you alone?"

"Yes." He'd sent Manuela home, closed and locked the door to his study just to be safe. Taggart and that bitch Marcy had hired were on their way to Vegas, of all places, after finding a link to some guy they thought was Kara's boyfriend.

Kara's boyfriend, the amateur pornographer. Jerry had never thought he'd see the day when he'd prefer his daughter be in the company of a wannabe porn king, but even that would be better than where she really was. He'd been going crazy for the past day and a half, knowing Connors had her. Wondering what he was doing to her.

"Is Kara okay?"

"She's fine. Would you like to speak to her?"

There was the muffled sound of the phone being passed. Then, "Daddy? Are you there?"

His heart raced in relief as his gut twisted in guilt. "I'm here, Kara. Are you okay? Has he hurt you?"

"Not really," she sniffled. "But I want to come home. You have to get me out of—"

"As I said," Connors cold, clipped voice came back on the line. "She is perfectly safe for the time being. But if you want her to remain so, you will turn over the prototype without further delay."

"It's not ready yet." Cold sweat bloomed between Jerry's shoulder blades as the lie spilled from his lips. His conscience ate at him. What kind of man equivocated when his daughter's life was on the line?

But he couldn't give up the prototype. Not before he made a few more modifications. "You have to give me more time to run some more tests. The buyers won't be happy if it doesn't work."

"You let me worry about my customers." Connors's voice went even colder, if that was possible. "You have other, more important concerns."

"You'll have it in a few days. Just let Kara go. We can forget this ever happened. I'll turn over the prototype as soon as it's fully functional."

"Your daughter is very, very beautiful, Jerry. I'm sure you know that."

Bile burned at the back of his throat at the unmistakable tone in Connors's voice. "Don't you touch her, you sick fuck." It was a possibility he hadn't allowed himself to entertain for the past day and a half, ever since he realized that Connors had Kara. He'd calmed himself with the fact that this was a business transaction. Connors was pissed that Jerry was waffling on delivering the BioChip prototype, so he was using the best leverage he could find. It made perfect business sense, in a fucked-up criminal sort of way.

He didn't allow himself to dwell on the possibility that his daughter might be raped because of his mistakes.

"Don't worry, Jerry. Beautiful as she is, I have enough self-restraint not to sully the merchandise."

"Merchandise?"

"I wasn't always in high-tech. Prostitution used to be a lucrative part of my business. But nowadays, women—even beautiful, seemingly unattainable women—are willing to flash their tits at the camera, fuck anyone who asks. It hardly makes it worth paying for anymore. Whores have become a commodity. Which is why I moved into the technology business," he said, as though explaining his résumé during a job interview.

"But there is one thing men will still pay for, Jerry, because it has become so very rare. Innocence."

Jerry's blood froze in his veins.

"Though I personally prefer a more experienced woman, I can understand the appeal. There are men who will pay—and pay well—to have first crack at a young woman. Like your daughter, for example. She is so pretty, so fresh. She will generate a great deal of interest."

Jerry tried to speak, but all that came out was a garbled sound of horror and rage.

"Don't worry. I won't sell her to just anyone. The group I deal with is very exclusive. Wealthy men, much like yourself, who crave a taste of innocence. In the event that you do not deliver the prototype on time, I'm sure they will pay more than enough to allow me to pay my customers back."

"I can pay you back!" Jerry sputtered, finally finding his voice. "I'll give you back my cut, plus whatever they paid you. I'll double it, whatever you want, just let Kara go."

Connors's laugh cracked over the phone line, sharp as a gunshot. "Now Jerry, what kind of learning experience would I be providing if I allowed you to buy your way out of this? Besides, Kara is so beautiful, her virginity so unusual at a comparatively advanced age, who knows what price she'll fetch? I may make enough off her to earn a profit."

He spoke of selling Jerry's daughter's body with the same emotion as if it were a used car.

"You sick, perverted fuck. If you harm one hair on her

head . . ." Jerry let the threat linger, though he had no clue what he would do if Connors hurt Kara. He had Jerry over a barrel and he knew it.

"Turn over the prototype and you will no longer have reason to worry."

Jerry ran a hand over his face, wishing he could wake up from this nightmare he had created for himself.

A nightmare in which he had to make a choice: hand over a technology that would spawn the next generation of biological weapons, resulting in the deaths of millions, or allow his daughter to be raped by some disgusting old man who got off on fucking virgins.

"The latest version didn't work." It wasn't entirely a lie. In the last test, the prototype didn't work perfectly, but with a slight modification to the sample preparation, it produced results beyond anything they'd ever seen. If he'd continued to run his experiment, he would have eventually ended up with a measles virus immune to any vaccines or drug therapies.

"Yes, as you mentioned. For that reason, I will speak to my customers and tell them there will be a slight delay. But do not wait too long. My customers are eager to see a demonstration."

A shaky, hopeful breath billowed from his lungs. He could still modify the chip. Once he had Kara back, he'd grab her and Kyle, move all of his money to an offshore account, and go so deep into hiding no one would ever find him. Maybe he'd even fake their deaths, just to be sure. A plane crash—

"You are lucky that the delay works in my favor. It will give me time to settle negotiations for Kara's fate in case something should go wrong." Connors's voice cut like a blade through Jerry's wild imaginings.

"Nothing will go wrong," Jerry bit out.

"I hope not. But I've taken some lovely photos just in case. Marketing material, if you will. You'll see them if you check your e-mail."

The scotch bubbled sourly in Jerry's throat as he pulled up Kara's computer. He'd hidden it from everyone, used it to communicate with Connors so there would be no evidence of their communication on his own computer. He logged in to his free Web mail address and clicked on the message. His extremities went numb with shock as he took in the image of his daughter. She lay on a bed, in a white nightshirt, her face a mask of fear as she stared at the camera.

She knew what would happen to her if Jerry didn't deliver.

God, none of this was supposed to happen. It had all seemed like such a great idea when Connors—at least that's what he called himself; Jerry didn't believe for a second it was his real name—had contacted Jerry.

Jerry had seen it as a way to stick it to the fucking board of GeneCor, who thought they could push Jerry aside, after he'd spent six fucking years of his blood, his sweat, his goddamned money, turning his innovative idea for biological chips into a real product, a real company.

But then the company had gone public, and the investors decided that Jerry was too brash, too volatile, too lacking in focus and discipline to run the company. So they'd hired that fucking automaton and shoved Jerry into the proverbial basement to tinker with his toys. Oh, sure, to the outside world, Executive Vice President of Technology Innovation sounded prestigious.

But everyone in the company, every board member, all of the men and women Jerry had made rich with his ideas and his products, knew it was all a load of shit. At first he'd tried to take it seriously. For a whole fucking year, he had actually spent time and energy developing new product prototypes based on the existing platform.

They'd given him the equivalent of a pat on the head and told him to keep up the good work. When Jerry had complained to the chairman of the board, a man he'd always considered a good friend and trusted adviser, he'd been told that if he wasn't happy, maybe it was time for him to move on. GeneCor had netted Jerry hundreds of millions of dollars, making him financially free to do anything he chose, including starting a new company on his own, where he could develop whatever new products he wished.

Provided he paid GeneCor appropriate licensing fees.

A carefully worded, oh-so-professional way of telling Jerry not to let the door hit him in the ass on the way out. Several days later Connors had contacted Jerry. He had well-placed sources everywhere, and somehow he'd gotten wind of what Jerry was working on. At the time, it had seemed like destiny. Divine justice for those who had tried to screw him over.

Connors's voice ripped him back to the present. There was no time to wallow in regret. What was done was done, and now it was up to Jerry to get himself out of the shithole he'd dug for himself.

"This isn't the first time I've procured girls for this group. And nowadays the Internet makes them so easy to find. Girls just like Kara, proselytizing the merits of saving themselves," Connors said, as though Jerry hadn't spoken. "Did I mention that they videotape the girl's first time? They've sent me some of the footage for my own enjoyment—I've built up quite a collection. There's nothing that compares with the expression on the girl's face the first time she feels a cock shoving inside her untried hole."

Jerry scrambled off the couch, barely making it to the garbage can before the scotch came boiling back up.

"I could send you copies, if you like."

Jerry slumped back on the couch, sick and scared. His little girl. And Jerry had delivered her into the hands of a monster. "I'll be ready. Just tell me where and when."

"I'll let you know the details of the exchange as the time gets closer. In the meantime, you will continue to keep the police uninvolved?"

"Yes. I've already posted to Kara's Web site."

"Good. And this investigator you were stupid enough to hire?"

"I've got him under control. The woman, too. Right now they're off looking for Kara in Vegas."

"As soon as they get back, you need to fire them. The more they dig around, the more the potential complications. I don't want to clean up any more messes than necessary."

"How can I justify firing Taggart if Kara's still gone?" He was already walking a tightrope with Taggart and the police, encouraging them to look under every rock while he planted clues that implied Kara was just another kid who'd gotten pissed at her parents and was blowing off steam at a friend's house for a few days. If he suddenly backed off now, Taggart would smell it a mile away.

And if he didn't, the Crawford woman definitely would. Jerry was already afraid she suspected something, with her too-knowing stare burning from behind the lenses of her glasses.

"Leave it to me. You concentrate on getting the prototype and appropriate literature ready for delivery."

The connection broke before Jerry could ask what that meant. Cryptic bastard.

He poured himself another scotch, enough to dull the rough edges but not enough to impair his ability to drive. Adrenaline pumped through his veins as he drove to GeneCor headquarters. He wouldn't sleep tonight, not with the images of what waited for Kara careening off his skull. But he would put the long, dark hours to good use.

He wanted to get this over with as soon as possible, but

he couldn't deliver the prototype without making the necessary changes. Jerry knew he'd doomed himself to hell for many reasons, but he still had a chance to make sure that handing over the foundation for the world's most terrifying biological weapons program wasn't one of them.

CHAPTER 8

HALF AN HOUR after they landed, Toni followed Ethan through the front doors of the Wynn Las Vegas Hotel and Casino. Toni took her backpack and and ducked into the lobby bathroom to exchange her jeans and T-shirt for a dress and heels. She did a quick application of black eyeliner, a double coat of mascara, and a slick of slut-red lipstick across her mouth, careful not to look at her reflection below her neck.

She knew if she did, she'd chicken out.

She exited the bathroom and quickly found Ethan. He'd also changed his clothes, from cargo pants and the form-fitting black T-shirt to black pants and a striped button-front shirt that was fitted enough to show the contours of his broad chest and trim waist. He scanned the crowd, looking for her, and she took a few seconds to take him in while before he noticed her. He fit in perfectly, with his understated but expensive clothes, perfectly tailored to fit his big, muscular body, his strong, sculpted features that attracted the attention of every female who walked by.

One of the beautiful people, perfectly suited for this glamorous setting. But If you looked closely you could tell he wasn't in Vegas to party. He had an aura of alertness, an icy intensity in his blue gaze as he scanned the crowd, tension in his body as if he were ready to pounce.

Suddenly that icy gaze slid past her, caught, slid back again.

The look in his eyes went from icy to hot enough to melt her flimsy silver dress to her skin.

She met his gaze dead-on, cocked her hip with a bravado she didn't feel. She'd pulled the dress from the back of her closet on impulse. A tiny confection of silver satin and chain link, she'd bought it on a whim after her friend Megan told her it made her look like a Bond Girl from the Sean Connery days.

She'd never had the nerve to wear it out of the house.

But when Ethan had given her outfit a scathing once-over and recommended that she find something to wear, his look saying he expected her to pull out a sack and some combat boots, she couldn't resist.

Now his eyes ran all the way from the manicured tips of her toes peeking out of silver peep-toe platforms, up her bare legs to her hooker-red mouth, all the way back down, and all the way back up again. He looked as if someone had punched him in the face.

He walked over to her, his stride purposeful and intent. The dazed look was gone, replaced with one that said he was thinking of tugging the flimsy straps off her shoulders and picking up where he'd left off back at her apartment.

He stopped just short of her, close enough for her to feel the heat of him through their clothes, close enough that she could feel his slightly accelerated breath stir her hair.

Her lips slid into an involuntary smirk. It wasn't often she got to knock a guy as hot as Ethan on his ass.

She tipped her chin up. In her heels, she was almost as tall as he was and could look him straight in the eye. His were heavy-lidded, molten-hot blue flame, promising things she'd never even thought of.

His hand slid around her bare forearm, the heat from his

palm licking up her skin and making her nipples tighten in hard points against the insubstantial satin of her dress. He leaned in, and for a minute she thought he was going to kiss her.

"Nice dress," he said, his breath hot against her cheek. She could hear the underlying amusement and frustration in his voice. "Now let's go find Kara."

Just like that, the moment was gone, and Toni was snapped back to reality. She was no hot girl in Vegas to party with her hot guy. She had a job to do, a friend to find, and she needed to keep that in mind and not get distracted by a sexy ex–navy pilot who looked at her like he wanted to dip her in cream and lick her all over.

But she couldn't stop herself from ogling his firm, tight ass as he walked a few feet in front of her across the casino floor. Her fingers tingled at the remembered feel of it, so hard and resilient as she'd gripped it. The way the muscles bunched and flexed as he ground against her.

"Here's the place," Ethan said, stopping in front of the club where Toni had tracked Toby's most recent credit card transaction. "Now we just have to find him."

The doorman gave them a quick once-over before nodding them inside. They scanned the bar, looking for a face that resembled the picture Toni had downloaded from Toby's FacePlace profile, but the low light and dark furnishings made it nearly impossible to pick a face out of a crowd.

A waitress walked toward them, looking through Toni as she made a beeline for the bar. Ethan flashed the woman a smile and she halted, changed her course, and walked right over to Ethan as though pulled in by a tractor beam.

"What can I get you?" she asked, gazing up at him from under lashes that she could barely lift, with their thick coating of mascara. Her short, clingy cocktail dress showed off acres of deeply tanned skin, which contrasted nicely with her almost white-blond hair.

Hair was fake. Boobs were questionable, she thought sourly as she watched Ethan grace her with one of his slow, heart-stopping smiles and lean in a little closer.

The waitress's smile widened, and Toni knew exactly what she was feeling. Mesmerized by the intense focus in Ethan's teal blue eyes. A little dizzy, off center. Like she'd just been whacked upside the head.

That was a good analogy: Ethan's charm = head injury. Best to be avoided if at all possible. And, she reminded herself, she had much more important things to worry about than who Ethan was flirting with and why.

"I'm wondering if you can help us out," Ethan said to the waitress.

"I'll do whatever I can," she said.

Yeah, I just bet you will.

"We're looking for a friend of ours," Ethan said, holding up his BlackBerry with Toby's picture on the screen. "Have you seen him?"

The waitress studied the screen and gave a short laugh. "Yeah. He's up in the VIP section." She pointed to the back of the club where a staircase snaked its way up to the second level. "Holding court." She quirked a bleached eyebrow at Ethan. "He offered to make me a movie star, if you can believe it."

Ethan's eyes crinkled as he smiled. "Is that so?"

The woman leaned in, all but propping her enhanced cleavage on her tray and serving it up to him. "Yeah, but he told me I'd have to get naked, and I told him I only do that under the right circumstances."

Toni rolled her eyes and elbowed Ethan in the ribs.

"Thanks. We really appreciate your help."

The waitress placed a tanned, French-manicured hand on Ethan's sleeve. "I'm off at three."

Toni curled her hand around Ethan's bicep and insinuated herself between him and the waitress. The woman looked up, startled, into Toni's face. "He'll be busy."

Toni could almost hear the waitress's sigh of longing over the pulsing beat of the music as they made their way across the club.

"Getting territorial?" Ethan asked, yelling over the din of the music and the crowd.

"Just trying to keep you on task," she snapped before preceding him up the wide metal staircase to the VIP level.

The bouncer moved to stop them, and Toni smiled and batted her heavily lined eyes. "We're supposed to meet a friend up here. He told us it would be okay."

"Who's your friend?"

"Toby Frankel. But you might also know him as T-Bone."

The bouncer gave her an assessing look. Evidently he liked what he saw, because he unhooked the velvet rope and motioned Toni and Ethan past.

It was quieter up here, the music and noise muted, the air tinged with the scent of expensive booze and cigarette smoke. Rail-thin, expensively dressed women lounged on velvet-upholstered banquettes while beautiful men with professionally tousled hair pretended to be interested in every word that came from their heavily glossed lips.

As they moved through the crowd, Toni could feel eyes on them, assessing, wondering who they were, why they were here, were they worth knowing.

They spotted Toby, holding court on an overstuffed red velvet sofa in the back. His table was full of vodka and champagne bottles and he was surrounded by five girls in various stages of inebriation, all vying for Toby's attention.

Her stomach sank as she saw that Kara wasn't among them.

Toni didn't see the appeal of his shaggy hair, youthful gawkiness, and scraggly goatee. "No accounting for taste," she muttered. In three long strides she was at his table, leaning down to say hello.

But before she could get a word out she was grabbed from behind, pulled hard against a beefy male chest, muscle covered with a thick layer of padding. "What do you want, woman?"

Toni jerked against his hold, but though the guy was heavy, he was strong, his grip tight on her upper arms.

She had the impression of space moving, striped fabric, and suddenly she was free. Silence ripped through Toby's corner of the club and Toni turned to see the guy who had grabbed her, a big white gangsta wannabe, wearing baggy jeans, a football jersey, backward cap, and chains.

Ethan had him pinned to the wall, one big hand fisted in the guy's shirt as he held him several inches off the floor.

"You don't touch her, ever," Ethan said, his look and his tone promising severe injury. "Got that?"

An utterly inappropriate, purely feminine thrill pulsed through her at the sight of Ethan acting the cold, hard protector on her behalf.

Toby and his feminine entourage stared, wide-eyed. Toni looked behind her and saw the bouncer making his way over. Time to rein in her champion before they caused a scene. She slid a hand over his shoulder. "It's okay." Ethan gave the guy one last look of warning before releasing him.

"Shit, man, I'm just watchin' out for my bro."

Toni rolled her eyes and turned back to Toby, who slouched arrogantly against the sofa cushions. His lanky frame was draped in an oversize polo shirt, his left wrist adorned with a Rolex that cost twice as much as Toni's car. Two girls snuggled up to him, one on each side. Toni had no doubt that their pictures would be front and center on T-Bone's Treasure Chest come morning.

"Sorry about that," Toni said, making eyes at Toby and his would-be bodyguard. "I'm a friend of a friend and wanted to come over and introduce myself." She leaned over the table, far enough to make sure Toby got a good, thorough look down the front of her dress. "I'm Toni."

He shot her a boozy smile. "Why don't you lose the guy, Toni, and pull up a chair?"

She forced a smile. "Do you think we could go somewhere a little quieter?"

Toby shook his head. "Can't leave my own party."

Ethan came over then and leaned down to whisper something in Toby's ear. Toby shot a wide-eyed look at his faux gangsta friend, who held up both hands as if to say, "Not me, man."

The girls shot each other uneasy looks, and Ethan smiled. "You don't mind if we catch up a little, do you?"

The girls warily shook their heads as Ethan pulled Toby to his feet. If you weren't looking too hard, it looked like Ethan had a friendly hand on Toby's shoulder, but from the lines etched on Toby's face and the limpness of his right arm, Toni could tell that Ethan had him in some kind of Vulcan death grip.

Ethan steered Toby through the crowded club, across the flash and trash of the casino to the bank of elevators leading to the guest rooms.

"What floor?"

"Uh, twelfth," he said, and swallowed hard. "What's this all about, man? Whatever it is, I'm sure we can work it out." He reached for his wallet but was stayed by Ethan's hand.

"We have some things to discuss," Ethan said. "It's best we wait until we have some privacy."

Toby shoved his hands in his pockets, his shoulders slouched. He tried to look all cool and calm, but under the odor of liquor oozing from his pores, Toni could smell something else. Fear? Guilt? Christ, what if he really had hurt Kara? What if they were too late?

A bead of sweat rolled down Toby's face, but his mouth

was still set in that smug sneer. "If I owe you money, bro, I'm good for it. Or if there's something else you need, I'm sure I can get it."

Ethan didn't reply, just pinned Toby with that razor-sharp stare until Toby started to squirm like a little kid about to wet his pants.

They got out on the twelfth floor and followed Toby to the end of the hall. Using his keycard, he opened the door to—hands down—the nicest hotel suite Toni had ever seen. Already trashed by Toby and his friends, of course, but still.

"Is there anyone else here?" Toni asked, praying Kara would walk out of one the suite's bedrooms.

"No," Toby said. "We were all down at the club."

Toni did a quick sweep of the suite just in case. No sign of Kara, or anyone else for that matter.

Her shoulders slumped as she walked back into the sitting room. Toby was sprawled in a lounge chair where Ethan had evidently pushed him and was now looming menacingly, fists clenched.

"I'm only going to ask you once," Ethan said. "Where the fuck is Kara Kramer?"

"Kara? Is this what this is about? Shit, I thought you were one of Shorty's guys—" he broke off as Ethan shot him a warning look. "I haven't seen Kara for weeks. Not since she caught me in bed with the chick from my calc class."

Toni folded her arms across her chest and widened her stance, as menacing as a micromini and platform heels would allow.

Ethan's mouth went dry as the shimmery fabric pulled tight against her legs.

"We know you planned to meet her on Friday."

Toby shifted his gaze between Ethan and Toni, looking for the friendlier face, coming up short. "Yeah? So?" Toby started to get out of the chair.

Ethan stopped him with a flat hand to the center of his chest. The kid bounced off the back of the upholstered armchair. "So she left her house at about two on Saturday morning and hasn't been seen since. We think you might know something."

"Are you the cops?"

"We hear she flushed your stash when she found you in bed with that girl," Ethan pushed. "You were pissed. Maybe you wanted to hurt her, teach her a lesson."

The kid's face went pale. "I swear I don't know anything."

"Was she dealing for you?" Toni asked, coming to stand beside Ethan. "She cost you money—maybe you wanted to get even."

Toby shook his head. "I don't even deal anymore. You can't prove anything."

"Or maybe she was going to rat you out for posting nude pictures of underage girls on your Web site."

"Kara's eighteen."

"Not until September she isn't."

"She told me she was. I took her word for it." Toby sat back in his chair, lip curled in a sneer. "Besides, you can't be sure it's her, not with her face blocked out."

Toni cocked her head and gave Toby an almost pitying look. "Here's a tip. Almost nothing you do online is anonymous anymore. Remember that when you're luring drunk girls to your room and promising to make them stars."

Toby swallowed hard and looked up at them. "Kara was into everything. She tries to act like a good girl, but she's into all kinds of shit. She wanted to do those pictures. She liked the idea of doing it behind everyone's back. Especially her dad. Did you know he bought her a Mercedes after she signed the pledge? She loves driving around in that car, still getting away with everything she can."

"Too bad the courts won't care about any of that when you're charged with statutory rape," Toni said.

Toby snorted. "Can't get me there. I never even fucked her."

Now it was Ethan's turn to snort. "You expect us to believe that?"

"It's true, man. She had this whole virgin thing going, like she was some good girl."

"Yet she let you post nude pictures of her for everyone in the world to see?" Toni's voice dripped with skepticism.

Toby shook his head. "Don't ask me. Who knows what bitches have going on upstairs, you know?" He risked a conspiratorial look at Ethan.

Ethan didn't so much as blink.

Toby's eyes scuttled away. "Anyway, she liked the idea of everyone thinking she was all straight, while she was out partying and posing for the pictures and stuff. But I never used her face, I promised I wouldn't and I never did."

He gave Toni and Ethan a self-righteous look, as if somehow that made him honorable.

Ethan backed up a few steps, a headache creeping up his neck as all the crap of the day finally caught up with him. "So you didn't meet her the other night?" But he already knew the answer.

Toby shook his head. "I was a little late and I thought she'd already gone back inside or taken off without me. She didn't answer any of my texts, so I figured she was being pissy and blowing me off."

"Do you have any idea where she would go, who she might be with?" Toni asked.

Toby shook his head. "No clue, man. I swear on my life."

Another fucking dead end.

They'd been chasing their tails for two days now, missing something, he just didn't know what.

Now they were five hundred miles from home, no closer to finding Kara. Fucking great.

Toby stood up from his chair, but before he could move for the door, Toni stepped in front of him.

In her heels, she towered over him by nearly half a foot. In that dress, she looked like some kind of avenging Amazon straight out of *The Matrix*.

"Remember what I said about not being anonymous, Toby," she said, her voice laced with menace. "I'll be keeping an eye on you."

She turned and strode for the door, all swaying hips and long, lean legs.

Ethan felt his irritation start to drain away as he found himself mesmerized by the shiny, clingy nothing of her dress. Two scraps of silver fabric that left most of her body bare. Held together in the middle by a few links of silver chain. Held up over her breasts by straps about as wide as a human hair.

Every smooth inch of skin, every soft curve and lean muscle was on display. Nothing was left to the imagination. Not the soft curves of her breasts. She couldn't be wearing a bra.

He looked at her ass, at the material of her skirt—fuck, might as well have been a belt, as it barely covered her—as it shifted and clung. No lines, no bulges.

No evidence of panties whatsoever.

He was rock hard, raring to go, just as he had been from the second she walked out of the bathroom.

She stepped inside the elevator, pushed the down button, and leaned back against the far wall. Her arms were folded across her chest, one knee bent as she braced her foot against the wall. He wondered if she had any idea what she was doing to him with all that bare, silky skin, smoky, made-up eyes, and her mouth. Her mouth was killing him, lush, painted red, giving him all kinds of visions about what it would look like sliding over the head of his cock.

Those red lips parted, said something his lust-fogged brain didn't quite catch. "What?" He said, shaking his brain back into focus.

"I said I really thought I knew her," Toni said. "But the

more I find out, the more I realize I have no clue what's going on in her life."

"You knew her. You said yourself, she trusted you—"

She cut him off with a shake of her head. "God, I'm so naïve, thinking I could help her. Just another clueless adult, trying to get into her business." She laughed humorlessly. "So now I guess we go back home and start all over," she said, as the elevator doors slid open. "Or hell, who knows. Maybe everyone is right and she's back home already."

He took in the defeated slump of her shoulders and the tired eyes that mirrored his own.

"We can't leave tonight," he said, starting for the registration desk as he felt her tension ratchet up about fifty notches.

"We're spending the night? But I need to get home."

He turned to look at her. She shifted her weight from one foot to the other and licked her lips. Her gaze flicked nervously over his body, his face, snagging on his mouth. She licked her lips again.

He wondered if she was thinking what he was thinking. About the way her lips had parted so easily under his. About the way her nipples had gone rock hard against his tongue. His gaze slid down her chest, saw the firm peaks beaded against the bodice of her dress.

No fucking way was that the air-conditioning.

"I'm too tired to fly. It wouldn't be safe, even if we could get the plane ready to go this late. We'll crash here and leave in the morning. It'll be fine." Said the spider to the fly.

He ignored her sputtered protests as he walked up to the registration desk. She was a ball of nervous energy, about to start pinging around the room in her shiny heels. Fine. He'd give her one last chance for an out. He smiled at the desk clerk. "Two rooms, just for tonight please."

"I can't afford a room here," Toni whispered through clenched teeth.

"Jerry's paying. And if he doesn't I've got it. But I can't fly when I'm this tired." Not to mention that he needed more blood in his brain than her dress would allow.

The desk clerk affected a disappointed look. "I'm sorry, sir, but we have only one room available."

And the gods of getting laid smiled down on Ethan from heaven.

Toni's breath caught and held.

"It's a suite, though," the woman behind the desk said. "There should be plenty of room for both of you."

Toni's posture was ramrod stiff as they retrieved their bags from the bell station and rode the elevator up to the suite. The walls were slamming into place, her guard going up as clear to him as though she were girding herself for battle.

He unlocked the door, ushered her inside. She tossed her backpack on the couch and took a leisurely tour of the room. "You can have the bedroom," she said, "since you're paying." She stopped in front of the suite's massive window and stared down at the lights of the strip. But he could tell from the tension in her muscles, the way she fingered her skirt, that she wasn't taking in the view.

"Why are you so nervous?" Like he didn't know. But it was fun playing with her.

He tried to remember the last time he'd had to chase a woman, and couldn't. His world had been full of lots of women like Gillian. Beautiful women. Bold, sexually confident, not afraid to go after what they wanted. And a lot of them wanted him.

But he'd never met anyone like Toni, with her brainy beauty and stealth sexiness. A sex goddess in a computer nerd's clothing.

He liked her, a lot more than he'd liked a woman in a while. The way she gave him shit, her brash confidence and unexpected vulnerability.

Like now, sneaking nervous glances at him when she thought he wasn't looking. Something tight gripped his chest, a sudden urge to pull her in his arms and tell her everything would be okay, that he'd never let anyone or anything hurt her.

He shoved the thought away. He was no woman's hero, no knight in shining armor. Not in this lifetime.

"Did you know there are nearly fifteen thousand miles of neon tubing that make up the lights in downtown Vegas?" she said and looked at him over one bare shoulder.

He moved next to her, not looking at her as his hand curved around her waist. His palm slid over smooth skin and metal warmed by the heat of her body. The unfamiliar protective instincts melted away in the face of lust. Ethan seized on it. Lust was good. Desire, he could deal with. This was his territory. Sex and lust and bodies coming together in mutual satisfaction.

It shouldn't be any different with Toni, even if he wanted her with an intensity that danced a little too close to the edge of need.

Her body was stiff as he pulled her to him, but she didn't resist as he turned her to face him and tilted her chin up. Her cheek was baby soft as he cupped it, her cherry-red lips soft and hot as he closed his mouth over hers. That first taste, and he went right over the edge, needing her, feeling like he would die if he didn't kiss her, touch her, taste her, get inside her.

It was too much, too strong, too soon, but he couldn't stop the floodgates now that they'd been opened. Toni Crawford did something to him, made him feel things he wasn't supposed to feel.

But he wasn't about to pull over now and examine the reasons why.

His tongue slid into her mouth, tangling with hers as he drank in her soft sighs, her rich taste. Turning her, he used his body weight to pin her against the cool glass of the window. He bent his knees so his cock was aligned with the V of her thighs and rubbed against her, leaving no question about how much he wanted her.

His fingers tangled in her hair, tugging until she was at just the angle he wanted. He could feel her shaking as her lips sucked at his tongue, the pounding of her heart as he slid his hand over her rib cage, down the side of her dress. His mouth opened wide over hers, taking it in hot, hungry open-mouthed kisses, and he molded his hand over the curve of her hip. It was a short trip to find the hem of her skirt and tug it up to reveal the sweet curve of her ass.

He filled his hands with the firm, smooth cheeks, his thumbs brushing against a silky scrap of fabric riding the upper curve. "You *are* wearing underwear," he whispered, grinning.

"Barely." Her voice was a breathless whisper. "But no bra."

"Yeah, I noticed." And he sure as hell noticed now when her tight little nipples were burning holes into his chest. He wanted to feel her, skin on skin. He fumbled with the buttons of his shirt, heard a few ping against the window as he ripped it open so he could feel her, silky and hot and barely dressed, against his naked chest.

"This dress has been driving me insane all night." He hooked a thumb in the strap of her thong, pulling it tight until she gasped. He wanted her naked. Now. Wanted to feel every inch of her long, sleek body against his. His hand went to the straps holding her dress up and pushed them off her shoulders. Silvery fabric pooled at her waist, and he felt the soft weight of her tits nuzzle against his chest.

His palms came up to cup her breasts and he slid his mouth down her throat as his thumbs teased the bullet-hard peaks. He nipped a path across her shoulders and chest, reveling in the soft gasps and moans that came with every pinch and roll of his fingers.

He felt her shift, wriggle, and the dress slid off her hips, down her thighs to pool at her feet. Ethan stepped back and looked at her, all long legs and soft curves, naked except for a pair of four-inch heels and thong panties that barely covered the sweet mound of her pussy.

He was so gone, any control he might have had was shot to hell as he pulled her against him, yanking off his shirt and fumbling with his pants so he could be naked, too, breaking off here and there to kiss her and stroke her because he couldn't keep his hands off her for another second. Finally he was down to his boxers. He slid his hand down her thigh and hitched it over her hip. Her heels—those sanity-killing, lust-inducing heels—made her almost as tall as he was, the exact right position to cradle his cock against her hot core.

He was shaking, running hot, trying to cling to the control he took for granted. Failing.

Toni could barely think, barely breathe in the face of Ethan's onslaught. It was like before, when he'd kissed her, but more. More raw. More out of control. And as much as she knew she'd regret it as soon as it was over, more irresistible. She couldn't get enough of the taste, the feel of him. She'd never been this close to a man as beautiful as Ethan. Probably never would be again.

He was gorgeous, true, but that didn't account for the total loss of common sense. There was the chemistry that popped and crackled like dry wood on a flame. There was something about Ethan, indefinable, that called to the wild, impulsive part of her that she kept so well hidden. The part of her that urged her to cast aside the rules and to do something for the pure pleasure of it, good, well-thought-out decision making be damned.

He was pressed hard against her, taking away all logic and coordination as his hands teased and pinched at her nipples in a way that had her wet, pulsing, craving the feel of him inside her. The hard ridge of his cock rode between her thighs, making her throb and clench with the need to feel him thick and hard inside her.

Common sense urged her to push him away, warning her that getting involved with Ethan was dangerous. But she wasn't looking to get involved, she reminded herself. Why not indulge her craving for what he offered? Mindless hot sex, guaranteed to blot out the stress and worry and bad memories she could never run away from.

Her hands gripped his hips, one reaching down to trace the outline of his erection through his boxers. Marveling at the size, the raging heat, she pressed her palm against him and stroked him through the soft cotton of his underwear.

Ethan groaned, a harsh, almost plaintive noise as he stepped back. "Don't," he said, stumbling a little as he lifted a shaky hand and raked it through his thick, dark hair. Toni's mouth went dry, as for the first time she got to see his nearly naked body. His chest was thick with muscle, nearly twice as wide as hers. Smooth, tanned skin stretched tight over the muscles of his shoulders and arms. Her eyes eagerly devoured every inch of bared flesh, raking down his six-pack abs and lower.

Her breath caught at the sight of his cock, rock hard and tenting out the front of his boxers. She swallowed hard, nearly overcome with the urge to tug his boxers down his leg and suck him deep into her throat.

"You keep looking at me like that, and in about five seconds you're gonna find yourself pinned up against the wall with me buried ten inches inside you."

She drew back, startled. Intimidated. "Ten inches?"

His wicked grin made everything inside her go buttery soft. "Give or take a millimeter."

She laughed as he lifted her thighs and wrapped them around his waist so he could carry her into the bedroom. Toni could feel the hard press of his cock against her behind, and swallowed hard. Christ, he might not be exaggerating. Then she didn't care as the hard ridge of his abs rubbed against her silk-clad cleft, making her squirm and moan and ache.

She'd never felt like this with a man. Nervous and carefree, wanting to laugh and cry and beg him to make her come. Out of control. Exhilarated. Terrified.

He flipped on the bedside lamp. Smooth cotton met her back as he lay her down on the bed and gently removed her glasses and placed them on the bedside table. He shoved his boxers down his hips and his erection bobbed, long and thick as it reared up from between his legs as he peeled her thong down her legs. Even without her glasses, she could see the thick vein pulse its length, the smooth head engorged and slick with pearls of pre-come. She wanted to reach out, stroke its length, but before she could make a move, he came down over her and clamped his mouth hard over her nipple. She squirmed on the mattress, low, animal sounds she didn't recognize emerging from her throat. His hand dipped between her legs, fingers parting her and finding her embarrassingly wet.

"God, you're hot," he whispered, sucking harder at her nipple as first one thick finger, then two stretched her open. His thumb whisked across her clit, circling and teasing as Toni arched harder up into his hand. He groaned into her mouth, sucking hard on her tongue as his fingers pressed deeper, harder.

Toni cried out in protest as he suddenly jerked away and fumbled through the overnight bag on the chair next to the bed. A pile of foil packets scattered across the bedside table. She heard a ripping sound and then he was rolling on a condom and kneeing her legs apart. His breath hissed through his teeth as he dragged the broad head up and down her slit, rubbing her clit, spreading her wetness around until her hips were bucking off the bed and her hands were digging into his ass to coax him inside before she completely lost her mind.

He was huge, thick and pulsing as he stretched her wide, forcing her body to yield inch by agonizing inch at his slow, inexorable invasion. He began to move in smooth, deliberate strokes, seeming to know the exact rhythm, the exact angle she needed.

God, he was good at this.

And why wouldn't he be, with all the practice he's had?

She tried to force the thought from her mind, not wanting to imagine the legions of lovers he must have had up to this point, and how she might compare. But as he gazed down at her, his eyes narrowing into fierce turquoise slits, Toni couldn't get the unpleasant image out of her head.

This was a man she'd met less than two days ago. A man who, when she'd met him, had just come from another woman's bed. Still had her lipstick on his ear.

Once that thought barreled into her head, she couldn't get it out. Ethan with another woman. Ethan with dozens of other women, women who were sexier, more confident, and more advanced in bedroom Olympics.

Women who didn't care if he went and slept with someone else after this was over.

Her orgasm, so close only a few seconds before, evaporated under the onslaught of insecurity. A lump settled in her throat and she was horrified to realize she was on the verge of tears.

Ethan sensed her change in mood, and his hips stopped their steady pumping. He leaned back on his knees, chest heaving as he struggled for control. God, he was so gorgeous, his body gleaming with sweat, a freaking sex god the likes of which she had never even seen, much less touched, and her stupid, overactive brain wouldn't give her body a break. Why couldn't she just go with the flow?

Because she was the computer nerd, and he was the captain of the football team, and deep down she knew they didn't belong together, and never would. And that shouldn't matter if all she wanted was sex.

"What is it?" he said.

She opened her mouth but was afraid she'd start crying if she said anything. After a few seconds she said, "Nothing, everything's fine." A minute ago she'd been running hot and fast, headlong into sexual oblivion. And now she'd turned it all awkward and uncomfortable, all because she couldn't get out of her damn head long enough to enjoy it.

At least he was still having a good time, if the strength and size of the erection inside her was any indication. No reason for him to stop, just because she'd fallen off the orgasm train. "Don't stop," she urged, hoping it sounded more convincing than it felt. "It's fine."

His mouth set in a tight line. Great. If he hadn't already decided she was a bad lay, this would certainly seal the deal.

"I'm sorry," he said. He leaned down until his forehead rested against hers and kissed her softly. He pushed himself all the way inside her, holding himself still as his mouth teased hers with soft sucking kisses. "I'm going too fast," he panted.

She wanted to reassure him that it wasn't him, it was her, but his tongue sliding into her mouth proved too much of a distraction.

"I just want you too much," he whispered, "Once I touch you, all bets are off and I can't keep it together."

He wanted her too much? The very idea was enough to make her tighten around him, making him groan as the walls of her body clamped hard around his cock. He bent his head to her breast, licking and sucking the sensitive flesh, thrusting into her with tiny movements of his hips, stirring her up, sending her nerve endings back into overdrive.

Then he slid out, her body clinging and protesting every

inch of the way. She moaned in protest. "Don't stop." This time the plea was lustily sincere.

"Let's slow down. Let me make this good for you," he said. She wanted to argue that what he was doing was once again plenty good for her, but she couldn't even form words as his hands and lips coursed down her belly and lower. He grasped the backs of her thighs and hooked her knees over his shoulders, opening her wide to his gaze and his touch. Toni's hands clawed at the sheets as his tongue burrowed into her folds, circling her clit with firm strokes as his fingers teased the opening of her body.

She moaned, arching her hips, trying to urge his fingers deeper. "That's it," he whispered against her throbbing flesh, "make some noise. Show me what you like. Show me what's good for you."

"Deeper," she said. "I want your fingers deeper."

He slid two fingers in as far as they could go at the same moment his lips clamped over her clit. He was relentless, his lips sucking, tongue lashing, as his fingers pressed high and hard within her. Toni's legs and arms stiffened as all the energy in her body centered in a knot between her legs, a knot that pulled tighter and tighter until finally her orgasm exploded, sending wave upon wave of searing pleasure through every nerve and sinew until even the tips of her fingers and toes tingled with it.

Ethan almost cried with relief when he felt the first rippling shudder course through Toni's body. He didn't know how he'd done it, but he'd somehow managed to drag himself back from the edge, managed to regain some measure of the sexual control he'd always taken for granted. He had no idea what had gotten into him, what it was about Toni that made him completely lose his mind.

Thank God he'd somehow managed to sense her withdrawal, even through the all-consuming pleasure he'd felt at being buried deep inside her. He couldn't blame her for pulling back. He was big on foreplay, liked to linger and search out all the secret places that gave pleasure. But with Toni, he was like an animal, driven to mate, get inside her, fuck her hard and deep until he found the kind of white-hot oblivion he'd never gotten close to. Poor Toni—once he saw her naked, all he was good for was a quick paw, a couple of nipple twists, and he'd been shoving inside her like a madman.

But he'd made up for it, he thought with maybe the slightest touch of arrogance. Christ, she tasted good, sweet and salty and hot against his mouth. He couldn't resist sliding his tongue inside her for one last, lingering taste. The last quivers of her orgasm fluttered against his mouth, and he groaned, unable to stop himself from grinding his hips in response. Fuck, he needed to get back inside her before he pulled some amateur move like coming against the sheets.

She was relaxed, boneless with pleasure as he reared up over her and positioned himself at the entrance to her sex. He could feel his orgasm building the second he began the first slow, deep slide. She was so slick, so tight, like a hot, wet fist clamping around his cock with every stroke. He pumped her hard, shaking the bed and making her tits bounce with every thrust.

God, she was so pretty, so responsive as her postorgasmic languor instantaneously morphed into sexual urgency. Her cheeks were flushed, lips deep red and swollen, eliciting all kinds of fantasies of having them wrapped around the thick head of his cock. Her chest was flushed, too, the creamy flesh of her tits rosy-pink as he drove her higher. The smooth skin of her inner thighs slid against his hips as she wrapped those long legs around him, urging him deeper, faster, as her hips rocked up to meet every pounding thrust.

God, she was close, if he could only hold off a few more seconds. He wanted to watch her, see her face as she broke into a million pieces. His thumb delved between her legs, bumping her firm clit in time with his strokes.

His back arched and he moaned as he felt her body clamp down hard around him, milking, kneading his cock as her second climax hit. The sharp sting of her nails digging into his ass sent him hurtling over the edge. He came in a body-melting rush, in pulses so fierce he felt like he was going to burst out of his skin.

He collapsed on top of her, savoring the scent of her as he gulped oxygen into his lungs. After a few moments, he came to enough to realize he was probably crushing her and summoned up the strength to roll to the side.

He stared up at the ceiling, stunned by what had just happened. He closed his eyes and pulled her against him, determined to ignore the voice in his gut that was telling him that Toni Crawford was going to absolutely wreck him.

CHAPTER 9

THE LAST WAVES of pleasure faded as Ethan rolled to Toni's side, and she braced herself for the wave of regret. Waited for her brain to scream at her, *What are you doing? Having sex with a guy you met yesterday?? You didn't seriously believe that line he fed you, did you . . .* I want you so much, I can't stop myself . . . *Seriously, you don't think he says that to every woman he's with?*

Yeah, that was about right. But then Ethan pulled her against his naked body, cupped her cheek, and kissed her. Not a sexy, I-want-to-do-you kiss, but a soft kiss, so sweet and affectionate it almost felt like a thank-you for giving him such great pleasure. A loving kiss.

Warning bells started clanging in a corner of her mind not saturated with postorgasmic hormones.

Why couldn't Ethan be one of those guys who did the come-and-snore routine? Or better yet, come and flee the scene of the crime? Why did he have to pull her against his long, warm body and tangle his legs with hers in a way that made her want to curl up against him and hibernate through the winter?

This was the dangerous part, she realized. Not the sex. This kind of snuggling, the stroking of his hands up her back, the soft kisses pressed to her forehead and cheeks. That could give a girl all kinds of ideas.

Even a girl like Toni, who didn't allow herself to get ideas about men anymore.

He rolled to his side, and she tried to shift away, but he caught her and tucked her against him, her back to his front. *Oh, God, not the spooning*, she thought as a shiver of contentment fluttered through her.

She dozed off, the heat of his body pressed against her and the slow, steady cadence of his breathing lulling her to sleep.

A few hours later her eyes snapped open. She felt the unfamiliar heat and weight of a male body next to her, took in the blurred outline of the lavish furninshings of the suite illuminated by the light of the bedside lamp. Reality hit her with crushing force.

Kara was missing, and she was in a hotel room with Ethan Taggart, her body still humming from the aftermath of sex. She looked at the clock. Four forty-one a.m. She should go back to sleep, but her brain cranked into overdrive the way it only can at four in the morning when the rest of the world is asleep and all you can do is worry.

Worries about Kara pinged off thoughts of Ethan and what she thought she was doing sleeping with him. Visions of her nearly empty bank account and the impossible dream of moving back to Seattle slammed into memories of Michelle, memories she tried to keep concealed but that forced their way forward at this time of night.

Why had she shared that with Ethan? She never talked about Michelle to anyone. Hadn't even shared the details with John, her ex. All he'd known was that Michelle had died and Toni didn't like to talk about it.

Then again, her not talking about it was always what John brought up when he complained about Toni's intimacy issues. But for whatever fucked-up reason, she'd been compelled to share it with Ethan, explain why she related to Kara, wanted to give him some sort of explanation.

Bad enough that she let him into her pants, but letting him into her head was even more foolish.

The masculine weight next to her shifted and Toni stiffened as a sleep-warmed hand curled around her hip and drew her close.

"You're thinking too loud," he murmured and slid his hand over her stomach, up her rib cage to cup her breast.

Her thoughts dissolved into wisps of smoke as his thumb lazily circled her nipple. "Sorry if I woke you up."

He responded with a grunt and shifted until she could feel the hot weight of his erection pressed against her ass. "I won't complain if you promise to help me get back to sleep."

Toni smiled in the dark. His mouth was hot and wet on her neck, her shoulders, his teeth nipping at her earlobes. She shifted, trying to roll to face him, but he held her firm.

"This way," he whispered, the erotic intent in his voice enough to make desire pool and pulse between her legs.

One touch and her body was already eager for more. Already conditioned to want him with the slightest encouragement. Toni didn't want to think about the ramifications, so she closed her eyes and gave in.

Strong arms wrapped around her and his big, long-fingered hands rubbed and pinched her nipples, probed the drenched folds of her sex.

"Your pussy is so tight," he whispered, parting her legs with his knee as is fingers entered her from behind. "I just want to sink my cock inside you and stay there for a week."

A shuddering moan bubbled from her throat. She'd never been with a man who talked about sex so frankly. It embarrassed her. But it turned her on even more.

And he knew it, too, felt her body clench around his fingers as he stroked and pumped. He groaned in response, rubbed his cock against the bare flesh of her thigh. His fingers slipped out, pulling a rush of moisture in their wake. She reached between her legs and grasped his cock in her hand, stroking and rubbing him against the slippery surface of her inner thigh.

"That's right, so perfect," he whispered and pulled her back against him. He pushed her leg down, closing her thighs over his bare, throbbing cock and adjusted his position so his shaft nestled against her cleft.

He'd never felt anything like this. The slickness of Toni's pussy as he stroked against her. The tight fist of her hand, stroking and pumping the head of his cock as he thrust against her. Jesus. He was rubbing against her, not even fucking her, and it felt better than being inside any other woman.

Being with Toni in any way felt better than being inside another woman.

He shoved that panic-inducing thought aside and reached his hand down to stroke her clit, get her in the game, keep her flowing hot and wet. She moaned and tightened her thighs around his shaft, and he shifted till he was riding even more firmly against her dripping slit.

He wished he could fuck her without a condom, something he hadn't done since he was young and stupid and could use that as an excuse not to know any better. Nowadays he didn't mind using protection, even appreciated that condoms lessened his pleasure enough that he was never in danger of losing control.

Not with Toni. Shit, he couldn't keep control even when he had a condom on. Who knew what would happen if he ever got inside her without one?

Fucking nuclear fission.

She was gearing up for her own explosion. Her free hand— the one that wasn't squeezing the head of his cock in a way that made his balls tingle and tighten with every pump of his hips—was fisting in her pillow. Hungry, needy sounds clawed their way out of her throat. Sweat bloomed on her shoulders, and he licked a bead away with his tongue.

He left it, reluctantly, just long enough to reach for a condom. He pried her legs open and rolled it on in record time and thrust inside her even faster.

She gasped, her back arching as her body stretched and struggled to accommodate him. She was soft and supple from their earlier fucking, but he was big, and she was tight. Tighter than any woman he'd ever been with, gloving him and gripping him with every thrust and withdrawal.

His fingers slipped between her thighs and found the hard bud of her clit. Taking it carefully between his thumb and forefinger, he milked her, gently stroking as he thrust into her from behind. She went rigid, her thigh muscles flexing against his as she moaned, almost sobbing now.

He could feel her grasping him, her cunt rippling along his cock as her orgasm built and he stilled his thrusts. He wanted to wait, wanted to make it last. But was too late. Toni covered his hand with hers, pushed his fingers more firmly against her clit as she rocked against him in quick, desperate thrusts of her hips.

"Oh, God," she moaned. "Please. I can't—" her voice broke on a low moan and her pussy clamped down hard, her body pulling him deeper, ripping his own orgasm from him whether he was ready or not.

His eyes squeezed shut and he came so hard he almost blacked out. He pulled her to him. She was breathing hard, shaking, and he wondered if she felt the way he did. Like she'd been ripped apart and put back together. Like she didn't know whether to push him away and take off running or yank him close and never let him go.

Tonight, for him, holding her close won out. He tucked her long body against him, kissed the damp skin of her neck, and wondered how terror and contentment could co-exist inside one man's skin.

The second time Toni woke up in Ethan's arms she didn't waste any time getting out of bed and away from him be-fore she did something foolish. Like have sex with him a third time. She was already in danger of reading way too much into the fact that he had sex with her twice in the space of six hours. He wasn't anything like the experienced, polished lover she'd imagined him to be. Instead he was all raw sex and uncontrolled desire.

As if she really drove him crazy. And if she let herself be-lieve that, she was in for a world of hurt.

She slipped out of bed, taking a moment to indulge in this scene, burn it into her memory. Ethan lay on his stom-ach, head turned to the side, his dark hair tousled and spiked. The sheet was twisted around his waist, and the long, rippling muscles of his back were relaxed, shifting under skin she knew would be hot and smooth under her fingers. Her hands clenched into fists as she retreated into the suite's sitting room.

She dug through her backpack and pulled on her bra, underwear, T-shirt, and jeans like they were armor and flipped on her computer, mostly for something to do. She checked her phone to see if by some miracle Kara had texted or called and somehow she hadn't heard her phone ring, but of course she hadn't. She checked her e-mail, too, but no luck there, either. She checked both of Kara's FacePlace pages to see if she'd posted any new messages.

Nothing.

Toni stared mindlessly out of the suite's window, her brain touching on what Toby said about Kara like a tongue ex-ploring a sore tooth.

She tries to act like a good girl, but she's into all kinds of shit. She wanted to do those pictures. Liked the idea of doing it behind everyone's back. Especially her dad. Did you know he bought her a Mercedes after she signed the pledge? She loves driving around in that car, still getting away with everything she can.

Toni blew out a sigh. She hadn't known about Jerry's bribe, just knew Kara had a nicer car than Toni could ever hope to afford. She hadn't known about a lot of stuff Kara was doing. But the image of the spoiled-brat Internet Lolita didn't jibe with the Kara Toni knew.

Regardless, Toni refused to believe the pictures were Kara's idea. Toni wasn't so far from seventeen that she couldn't remember the dumb stuff she'd done, hoping a boy would like her. And Toby had that slick, smug, manipulative thing going that told Toni he got off on using people, getting them to do what he wanted, using money, drugs, whatever he could as leverage.

He reminded her too much of another rich, spoiled asshole. Another who got away with murder, since his A-list defense attorney was able to convince the jury that a wealthy kid from a good family would never have to resort to raping a drug-using slut like Michelle. And he would certainly not have it in him to strangle her when he was through.

Toni shoved the memory away. Kara was not Michelle, and it was unlikely she was going to turn up in a Dumpster. She was a confused kid going through a hard time who had decided to go AWOL for a few days.

She didn't really believe it, not one hundred percent, but if she didn't think positively right now she was going to drive herself crazy.

The lights of the Las Vegas strip flashed and pulsed against the sky as dawn broke over the desert. Toni was startled from her reverie by the sound of the bedroom door opening and closing. Ethan had donned his pants but foregone a shirt, and he looked rumpled and male in the red-gold light pouring into the suite.

A little thrill pulsed through Toni's lower half as she admired the muscular beauty of his chest, arms, and abs. Now that she wasn't blinded by a haze of lust, she noticed several scars decorating his torso. She wondered what it would be like to trace the marks with her tongue. Her stomach flipped at his lazy, sleepy smile.

She steeled herself against it. No matter how great the sex was, she couldn't let herself get sucked in further.

"Morning," he said, his voice sexy and sleep graveled. He turned to look out the window, his back and shoulders rippling as he yawned and stretched. Toni stared at his bare back, fighting the urge to press her lips against the acres of warm, tanned skin. How could he be so casual when she was so keyed up?

He turned and walked over to her. She held her breath as he dropped a kiss to her forehead. "Last night was amazing, Toni."

She held herself stiff, willing herself not to melt into his kiss, hating herself for the disappointment that surged when he walked away without doing anything else. She didn't want him to pull her into his arms, hold her against his chest, and kiss her the way he had last night. Like she was the only woman in the universe he'd ever wanted to kiss. "Yeah, I bet you say that to all the girls," she said, hating how snappish she sounded to her own ears.

Ethan chuckled and gave her shoulder an affectionate squeeze. The kind he'd give his sister if he had one. "Not *all* of them," he said, with a wink that made her jaw clench.

His eyes had none of the intensity or awareness of last night. He smiled without really smiling, his gaze slid by her as if he didn't really see her.

He was on autopilot, his typical morning-after routine.

She was too smart, too much of a realist for this to hurt as much as it did.

"I'm going to order us some coffee," he said when she

didn't smile back. "Then I'll call the airport and see about getting the plane ready."

"Great idea," she said and headed for the escape of the shower. Once the hot spray hit her, the events of the last twenty-four hours came crashing down. She leaned against the wall. With the spray of the shower, she could almost convince herself there were no tears running down her face.

God, she was an idiot. There was a reason she didn't do casual sex. She'd had a single one-night stand in her entire life, and it had left her feeling exactly like this—disappointed and empty.

Scratch that. This felt worse. She'd opened up to him, told him things she didn't share with anyone. And the sex had been . . . Mind-blowing didn't even begin to describe it. Like something inside her had finally ventured out to make a tentative connection with another person.

She suspected that Ethan found a similar connection with anyone in possession of a vagina. She scrubbed hard at her skin, trying to get the smell of sex, the smell of him, off her. But it did no good. While he could apparently dismiss her as easily as a passing acquaintance, it was as if the scent of him, the feel of him, had been permanently branded into the reptilian part of Toni's brain.

She lathered her hair and closed her eyes. No doubt Ethan was bracing himself for her to hit him with a bunch of expectations, to read too much into their one night of sex. She would show him he had nothing to worry about. She was as capable as he was of putting the sex behind them and working beside him until they found Kara and got her back home.

Ethan hung up the phone as Toni walked out of the bathroom. "The plane will be ready to fly in an hour," he said, hoping his voice revealed none of the tension and frustration roiling right below the surface. Her eyes met his in an unblinking stare, slightly puffy from behind the lenses of her glasses. Exhaustion gave her fine features a sort of blurred look, but it didn't stop him from wanting to slide the glasses down her nose and kiss her into oblivion.

She was dressed once again in her jeans, T-shirt, and sneakers, the silver Bond Girl dress a long-forgotten memory. Her hair was brushed straight, angling to the clean line of her jaw. His fingers twitched with the need to rake his hands through the black, silky strands the way he had last night.

In an effort to distract himself, he grabbed the carafe of coffee and poured her a cup. She took it with a polite nod, and he felt a shot of heat straight to his groin as he imagined pulling her down on the couch and stroking her until the tension that tightened every line of her body disappeared beneath his fingers.

She was having none of his usual morning-after routine. His gee-that-was-great-maybe-we-can-fuck-again-sometime routine that had done just fine for him in the past. Trust Toni to see right through it. Then again, he wasn't exactly at the top of his game.

He was restless, jumpy, and, frankly, hornier than he had a right to be after last night. Usually so confident, so sure of his next move, now he didn't know what to do, wasn't sure if he wanted to shove her back into the bedroom and damn the consequences or get as far away from her as possible.

Last night, in the dark, buried inside her, it had all gotten a little too real for him to handle. And he didn't know what to do except act the way he always did the morning after. But he supposed that only worked when he actually *felt* the way he usually did.

He should be feeling the relaxed satiation he normally experienced after a night of sex, but what he'd shared with Toni wasn't ordinary sex, and she wasn't an ordinary woman. She made him feel things too much, too intensely.

And the way she looked at him, staring at him with that im-
placable hazel stare, like she could see straight through the
wall of bullshit he'd built so thick it had become like a second skin.

As if she could see straight down to the core of him, to
the parts he didn't even want to see himself. She could see
his wounds because she was wounded, too.

Let's cool it right there, Dr. Phil. What kind of asinine
shit was that? Toni didn't know him. She was different, but
not that different. Just because he felt sorry for her and
what happened to her family, it didn't make her any different from all the other women who had come before and
who would come after. No more beautiful, no sexier. Her
skin wasn't really smoother and her pussy wasn't any wet-
ter or tighter. No reason for him to be acting like such an
idiot.

His phone buzzed, indicating an incoming text message.
He flipped it open to read a message from Danny.

*Ubud a waste of time. Dad f/up on lead in Australia. Total
f'ing PITA.*

No surprise there.

Another message came in as he finished reading, this one
also from Danny.

WTF R U doing in Vegas?

Ethan laughed.

Tell U when U get back. Keep ur watch on.

Toni had taken her cup of coffee and retreated to the
desk, busily tapping away at her keyboard. Each keystroke
needled at him, pulling the muscles of his shoulders tighter
and tighter as she continued to ignore him.

"Anything new?" he asked.

"Nope."

Another five minutes of dead silence passed as he sipped
his coffee, searching for something to say.

Finally, her fingers stilled over the keyboard and she took

a deep breath as though bracing herself. "Look, we might as well get this out in the open. What happened last night was a really, really bad idea."

The vehemence grated on his already raw nerves. "You didn't seem to think it was such a bad idea when I had my tongue between your legs."

Her face went beet-red as she glared at him over the screen of her laptop. "Be that as it may, it was still a huge mistake, and we can't let it happen again."

She was making this easy, letting him know that she had no expectations, exactly what he liked to hear the morning after. Because when it came to his love life, Ethan Taggart didn't do expectations.

But that didn't stop him from wanting her again, more than he'd ever wanted a woman, and she'd just made it damn clear she had no intention of letting him back in her bed.

Now, if that wasn't waving a red cape in front of a bull, he didn't know what was.

She turned her attention back to her computer, studiously ignoring him as he sauntered up to the desk and rested one palm on the flat surface as he leaned in close. "What's the matter, Toni? Did I not make you come hard enough? Is that what's got you so determined not to give me another go?" He leaned close enough for his bare chest to brush her shoulder, and he caught the slight change in her breathing pattern. Mistake or not, she couldn't hide her reaction, any more than he could keep his cock from hardening from even this slight contact with her. "I mean, maybe three orgasms isn't enough for you. If that's the case—"

His phone rang, interrupting him. He looked at the display and saw Jerry's number. Duty called.

"This is Ethan."

"Ethan, I have great news. Kara sent me a text message. She's absolutely fine."

CHAPTER 10

"I STILL CAN'T BELIEVE that after two days of nothing, she'd just up and text Jerry out of the blue," Toni said. They were on their way back to the Bay Area, streaking over the harsh, desolate landscape of the Mojave Desert.

According to Ethan, Jerry had received a text message from Kara earlier that morning. Jerry hadn't forwarded it to Ethan yet, but the gist of it was that she had gone with a friend to a beach house, and that she'd be back in another couple of days.

"Why didn't she text me back? What friend is she with, anyway?"

Ethan shot her an impatient look. "I didn't know the first hundred times you asked, and I still don't."

Toni stared out the window, watching as parched rocky canyons gave way to the evergreen forest of the mountains. "It doesn't make sense," she said again for the dozenth time since Jerry's phone call. Toni had immediately called Kara, but her call had gone directly into voice mail. A follow-up text had fallen into the same abyss. Marcy hadn't answered her phone, either.

"What doesn't make sense about it? She took off for a few days, finally realized someone might be worried, and decided to get in touch."

"It all seems too easy," Toni said, unable to get away from the gut feeling that all was not right yet. "It's not like Kara to let everyone worry. I've said from the beginning, she wouldn't disappear and let everyone freak out."

"She did update her FacePlace page," Ethan said. "And I think that if we discovered anything in the past couple of days, it's that there's a lot about your friend Kara that you don't know."

He had her there. Still. "I can't helping thinking there's something more going on."

"You know, Toni, sometimes things aren't nearly as complicated as you'd like to make them."

She didn't need her genius IQ to tell her he was talking about more than the situation with Kara. The remembered feel of Ethan's hands on her skin, his tongue between her legs, his long, thick cock sinking into her as he whispered sexy, dirty things in her ear hit her in a hot rush.

Uncomplicated? Maybe for him.

She stayed quiet for the rest of the trip, leaving him to fly in silence while she considered Kara's actions from every angle. Toni was a rational, logical person, sometimes to a fault, but she couldn't get away from the niggling doubt that something was off here. All the evidence pointed to the simplest explanation: Kara took off for a few days and finally deigned to call.

So why couldn't she let it go?

When they landed, Ethan offered to drop her off before he headed to Jerry's.

"Hell, no, I'm going with you."

"Toni—"

She cut him off. "I know Jerry doesn't like me, but I want to talk to him face-to-face."

"Fine." He flipped open his phone and made a call to his brother, telling him to meet them at Jerry's house.

"What's she doing here?" Jerry asked sharply when Toni

followed Ethan into his office. Another man was already there, a man who could only be Ethan's twin brother, Derek. While they weren't identical, the resemblance was strong enough to inspire a twitter of interest. Nothing compared to the raging torrent of hormones unleashed when she got within touching distance of Ethan, but a woman would have to be dead not to find Derek Taggart attractive. He was as big and muscular as his brother, his shoulders nearly spanning the back of the armchair he occupied. His short-cropped hair was lighter than Ethan's, more gold than brown, and his eyes were deep, dark, intent.

Like Ethan, Derek's skin was darkly tanned from time spent outdoors, and his features had that same sculpted-in-granite look. He and Ethan had the same sharp cheekbones, blunt chins, and wide, sensual mouths. But while their looks were similar, their demeanors couldn't have been more different. Where Ethan was all flirty warmth and easy smiles, Derek radiated quiet reserve.

Ethan introduced them, and Derek took her hand in his powerful grip. His smile was nothing more than a slight quirk of his lips, and he studied her with an intensity that made her shift from one sneakered foot to the other.

Toni realized with a sinking feeling that Derek knew exactly what had gone on between her and his brother.

But now was not the moment to wallow in humiliation over what she'd allowed to happen with Ethan.

She turned her attention to Jerry, who glared at her, not bothering to disguise his dislike. "I made Ethan bring me," she said, not backing down from his hooded look. "Since I hauled my ass all the way to Vegas on Kara's behalf, I thought I deserve to see her message myself."

"Fine." Jerry fiddled with the keypad and passed over his phone.

Toni read the message on the display while Ethan read it out loud over her shoulder.

"Dad, sorry I didn't call went to a friend's house at the beach be back in a couple days. Don't worry. Love you."

Toni checked the caller ID, verifying it was sent from Kara's phone. Jerry had probably done that himself, but she wanted to be sure. "What friends of hers have beach houses?" Toni asked.

"I don't know," Jerry said. "In any case, you don't need to worry about it. You saw for yourself, she's fine. There's really no more reason for you to be here."

"But there are things we should discuss," she said, "Kara's recent behavior, the people she's been hanging out with." She couldn't believe a man like Jerry, one who expected such perfect behavior from his children, would let things like the FacePlace profile and photos on Toby Frankel's Web site slide. "We should talk to her, consider installing software that will monitor her online activity."

"How I address Kara's behavior is a private matter," Jerry said. "And if I need help keeping track of her, I'm confident Gemini can assist me."

"But Ethan and I have been working together on this—"

"But I didn't hire you," Jerry said. "My ex-wife did. And if you don't mind, I have some things I need to discuss with Ethan and his brother that are confidential."

"I got a ride with Ethan," Toni said, grasping at straws, but not ready to be shunted off so quickly. Not when she was even more sure than ever that Jerry had something to hide.

"I'll have Manuela give you a ride," Jerry said, already pushing the intercom button.

Toni looked to Ethan for support, only to find him nodding to Jerry.

"Derek and I need to discuss some modifications to the security system," Ethan said. "It's not appropriate for you to listen in."

"But Kara's not even home yet."

"You no longer need to concern yourself with my daughter," Jerry said sharply. "Consider this case closed."

"As you said, you didn't hire me, your wife did. And until she tells me otherwise, I'll consider myself on the clock. I'm sure Ethan feels the same way."

Ethan sank down in a wingback chair next to the one Derek sat in. "Toni, Kara contacted her father saying she's fine. As far as I'm concerned, the investigative part of my job is finished." He turned to say something to Derek, his tone too low for her to overhear.

Just like that, he was blowing her off. Ignoring her as if what she said didn't matter, as if what happened didn't matter.

Derek looked up, locking eyes with Toni. Beneath the intense focus of his gaze, Toni caught a glimpse of something else. Her hand clenched convulsively at her side as she recognized what it was. Pity. Derek felt sorry for her. He knew she'd slept with Ethan and thought she was hung up on his brother, like the legions of women who had come before.

She bit her tongue, resisting the urge to set Derek straight. She might have given in to temptation, but she was too smart to fall for a guy like Ethan.

"Fine," she said and turned to walk out of Jerry's office. Heavy footsteps followed her down the hall.

"Toni, wait."

"Ride's waiting," she said, as she rounded the corner and saw Manuela waiting with her keys and purse. "I need to get my stuff from your car."

He followed her out and unlocked the car. "Toni—"

"Don't worry Ethan, I get it," she said as she removed her laptop case and her overnight bag from the trunk of his BMW. "Case closed, see you later. But I still think Jerry's hiding something, and I'm going to find out what it is, whether you like it or not."

His hand on her arm stopped her as she turned to walk

away. Even that slight contact was enough to send blistering heat through her as she fought back memories of the previous night. He was so close, his woodsy, earthy scent teased her nostrils and she could see the pulse pounding under the skin of his throat. The same skin she'd tasted last night. He opened his mouth to speak.

"Ethan," Derek called from inside the house, "Jerry wants to get started.

"I'll call you," Ethan said, not letting go of her arm.

Toni pulled away from his grip and made a scoffing sound in her throat. "Don't bother."

Toni seethed the entire ride home, where she picked up her car, and all the way to Marcy's. She didn't know what pissed her off the most. That Ethan accepted Kara's text message as the end of the story, or that he dismissed her with a "don't let the door hit you in the ass" after she'd been the one to discover Kara's secret online life and track down Toby Frankel.

Or it could be because last night he'd given her several of the most intense orgasms of her entire life, and now he was treating her as if they'd gone out for pizza.

She pulled into the parking lot of Marcy's townhouse complex, hoping Marcy had heard from Kara, too. If so, Toni would be willing to dismiss her suspicions as a result of being too close to Kara and letting memories of her past make her paranoid. In any case, she needed to talk to Marcy about keeping better tabs on her daughter.

So far, Marcy hadn't returned any of Toni's calls. Not entirely unexpected, since Marcy regularly liked to sleep in, depending on how hard she'd hit the chardonnay the night before. Toni banged on the door for five straight minutes until it finally opened to reveal Marcy's thin face dominated by huge, bloodshot eyes.

"Did you find her? Is she 'kay?"

Toni stepped back and concealed a grimace. Marcy smelled

like she'd been swimming in a wine barrel. "She texted Jerry this morning and said she was with a friend. She didn't call you?"

Marcy shook her head and blinked hard, trying to clear away the cobwebs. "I didn't hear the phone." She turned and hurried up the stairs, her wraith-thin form listing to the right.

Marcy muddled around her living room until she found her phone. She scrolled through the caller ID, squinting and studying each number so closely Toni had to fight to keep from snatching the phone out of her hand. When Marcy shook her head, Toni took the phone from her and checked the call log herself, to be sure.

Toni pulled her own phone out, compulsively checking her messages, confirming that Kara hadn't contacted her either. The niggling feeling that all was not yet right strengthened in force.

"No e-mails, nothing?" Toni asked, grasping at straws, and she knew it. Still, she had Marcy check her messages, just in case.

"I don't understand," Marcy said as she poured herself a cup of coffee. "Kara told Jerry she was fine. Why are you still so worried?"

Toni motioned for Marcy to sit down at the kitchen table before taking the seat across from her. "In the past few days, I found out some stuff about Kara, things she's involved in that none of us had any idea about." She told Marcy about the partying, the photos, her involvement with Toby.

Marcy's already pale skin leached to gray and she raised weary hands to her face. "I should have seen this. So much has happened. The divorce. And we put so much pressure on the kids." Her voice trailed off as she stared off into the space past Toni's shoulder. "I jus' don't know what to do anymore." Her words were still a little soft around the edges. "But do you think she's in trouble, still?"

Even if Kara was partying on the beach somewhere, she was still in trouble as far as Toni was concerned, but she knew what Marcy meant. "Do I think she's in danger, right this second? I don't know," Toni said. "But I can't shake the feeling that we're missing something." Toni got up and poured herself a cup of coffee, trying to figure out how to explain it to Marcy when she couldn't get her own head wrapped around it. "Do you think it's weird that she contacted Jerry and no one else? Not you, not any of her friends, not Manuela, when she usually checks in with her?"

Marcy took another long swallow and visibly tried to focus. "I don't know. I guess. They've had their issues lately, but then, so have she and I," she said with a watery laugh. "Why does it matter?"

Toni shrugged. She didn't really have any idea either, other than the fact that she didn't like the way Jerry didn't meet her eyes the whole time she was at his house. Then again, she'd been the one to confirm his adultery and find that offshore bank account. Toni didn't really blame him for not wanting to be best mates.

Still, it bugged her how this all conveniently wrapped itself up with a neat little bow, and Jerry the only one holding the proof.

But if Kara was still missing, why would Jerry try to cover it up, especially after hiring Ethan?

Maybe Ethan was right. Some things weren't that complicated.

"I wouldn't have any idea what's going on with Jerry and Kara," Marcy continued. "I barely had a clue what was going on when we were married." She gave Toni a sheepish look. "I know what you're thinking. But I didn't drink this much before . . ." her voice trailed off. "But Jerry was always keeping secrets, even before the affair."

The tiny hairs prickled on the back of Toni's neck. "Secrets?"

"He was always having meetings, secret phone calls. At first I thought it was another woman, but that didn't happen till later. And you know that account you found?"

Toni nodded.

Marcy leaned close and spoke in a whisper, even though there was no one around to overhear. "I have no idea where that money came from."

Toni pulled her eyebrows into a frown. "I don't follow."

"I had an accountant go over everything. All of his paychecks, bonuses, stock options, you name it. That money didn't come from GeneCor."

"Then where do you think it came from?"

"Maybe he was moonlighting, maybe he was selling drugs." Marcy barked out a laugh. "You helped me get my cut." She raised an eyebrow and toasted Toni with her coffee mug. "That's all I care about."

"You really think Jerry was doing something illegal?" It was probably nothing. She was definitely being paranoid.

Marcy stiffened, instantly sobering. "You don't think this has anything to do with Kara? She's fine, right? She wrote and said she's fine."

Toni reached out a hesitant hand and laid it over Marcy's. "You're right. I'm sure she's fine."

She wasn't sure about anything, except for the gut-deep feeling that Jerry was up to something.

Luckily, she had all the tools at her disposal to satisfy her curiosity about Jerry Kramer. Within a couple of hours, she knew every cell phone call he'd made and received in the past ninety days. Kara's number was there in black and white, posting a message at seven-oh-three this morning.

And the money. In addition to the offshore account Toni had found when Marcy first hired her, Toni found a new account set up under BioEnterprises, LLC, based in Cyprus. The account had received several deposits in the last six months, totaling nearly five million dollars.

And there were pending transactions as well, from other brokerage and money market accounts. Big transactions, as though Jerry was transferring all of his assets into one single offshore account.

As though Jerry was getting ready to run.

After Toni left, Ethan and Derek finished modifying Jerry's security system so each person now had a personal security code. As Ethan had explained to Jerry, he'd set it up so that whenever Kara or her brother, Kyle, entered or exited the house, Jerry would receive a message on his BlackBerry.

Ethan hadn't bothered to tell Jerry that they'd also rigged the system to alert Ethan whenever *Jerry* came and went, or that Derek had hidden a GPS tracking device in the glove compartment of Jerry's car.

Jerry was definitely hiding something. Even without Toni's planting the seed of suspicion, Ethan had picked up on Jerry's skittish vibe, the way his gaze kept slipping when they asked when Kara was coming back. And when Jerry had protested the new key codes, asking why they were necessary, as far as Ethan was concerned that was the nail in the evidence coffin.

"Your daughter took off without telling you. Don't you want me to try to help you prevent it from happening again?" Ethan had asked, deliberately not looking at Jerry when he answered.

Lots of people could keep a poker face, but few could keep a poker voice. Ethan knew what to listen for, the tones, the inflections, the careful way a person spoke when he was hiding something. Jerry displayed them all.

Ethan didn't know if it had anything to do with Kara's disappearance, but his gut was telling him he'd better find out. He was equally sure Toni was busy sniffing Jerry out, but she hadn't returned any of the calls or texts he'd sent her since she'd left Jerry's pissed as hell and convinced Ethan was blowing her off.

Frustrated that she couldn't get past her personal bullshit to give him a call back, Ethan enlisted Derek to help him work out some of his frustration.

Two hours later, they were still at it, sweating through their T-shirts and gym shorts as they squared off on the mats. All three brothers had trained extensively in hand-to-hand combat and sparred regularly to keep their skills sharp.

"If Danny finds out we're spying on a client, he's going to be pissed," Derek said. The muscles of his torso flexed as he balanced on the balls of his feet, ready to fend off Ethan's charge.

Not to mention they could lose their license if Jerry found out and lodged a complaint. But that wasn't enough to stop Ethan from following his gut, and his gut agreed with Toni. Not that Jerry's behavior had given any weight to his hunch. Twenty minutes after Ethan and Derek had left, they had tracked Jerry to his office building. He hadn't left since.

Ethan feinted right and swung his fist at Derek's midsection. Derek blocked the blow and kneed Ethan in the right thigh. "I have valid concerns about our client's security," Ethan said, ducking to avoid Derek's punch. "In order to assure his safety, I have to know his whereabouts at all times."

"Yeah, but usually our clients know what the hell we're up to."

"Minor detail. Besides, Toni's right. He's up to something."

Derek gave a brief nod and nailed Ethan with a jab to his chest that stole his breath, then sidestepped to the right to avoid Ethan's answering blow. "Speaking of Toni. She's pretty hot, but not your usual type." He grinned and dodged as Ethan's closed fist whizzed past his head. "Hey, we said no faces!"

Ethan flexed his fist and blew a drop of sweat off the tip of his nose.

"I guess this means I owe Danny fifty bucks," Derek continued when Ethan didn't respond.

Ethan pressed his lips into a tight line and brought his hands up. He didn't want to discuss Toni with anyone, including his twin. And they shared everything. Not just the usual sexual-conquest stories that Ethan embellished to try to get a rise out of his straightlaced brother, who, as far as Ethan knew, hadn't seen any action since his last serious relationship had ended a couple of years ago. Unlike Ethan, Derek didn't view sex as a recreational sport. He didn't have sex with a woman until he did a full-blown analysis of the pros and cons of getting involved with the female in question.

Complete with spreadsheets.

Still, Derek and Danny got a vicarious thrill from listening to Ethan recount his exploits, and usually Ethan was happy to oblige them. But not this time. Not this woman.

Derek wouldn't let it go. He knew he had hit a raw nerve and he couldn't resist applying pressure. "Was she like Danny thought? All eager to please in that pent-up, frustrated-librarian kind of way?"

Derek's comment summoned up a flood of images and remembered sensations from the night before. Toni, her pale, smooth skin damp with sweat. The scent of aroused woman flooding his senses. The pebbly hardness of her nipples against his tongue. The salty-sweet taste of her pussy on his lips. The hot, slick grip of her clenching around his cock as she came for the second time, fingers digging into the muscles of his ass as she tried to pull him even deeper.

Despite her tough, take-no-prisoners attitude, she'd been completely vulnerable in bed. Uncertain, even a little awkward. But it hadn't done anything to diminish his pleasure. If anything, it had enhanced it. Instead of a series of practiced moves, sex with Toni was raw, uninhibited, calling up a gut-deep, primitive response that had tested the limits of his control.

Ethan forced the searing images from his mind and slowly circled his brother, trying to get an angle on an attack. Derek threw a right hook and kept himself just out of reach, taunting Ethan with a shit-eating grin.

"It must not have been that good," Derek said. "Toni didn't look too happy with you this morning," he said. "Did you not perform up to your usual standards?"

"Let it go," Ethan said, striking out with a left hook. Derek turned so that he took the blow to the shoulder instead of the head. He didn't want to share any of it with Derek. He didn't know why he couldn't just forget about it and move on, the way he always did. For him, sex was a pleasant way to spend a few hours, but when it came time to get back to business, he'd never been distracted by a woman. He didn't want to think how close he'd come to completely losing control.

"Either that or she's completely hung up on you, like they always are. Which is too bad," Derek continued, "because unlike your usual hookups, Toni actually seems interesting. All that fierce determination. Not to mention those legs. Since you've obviously cut her loose, maybe I'll ask her out."

"Shut the fuck up." Ethan found his opening and drove through. His hands came down over his brother's arms, and his leg drove into Derek's hip as Ethan took him down with a combination of anger and brute force. Ethan sat on Derek's chest with one hand on his throat, the other raised to strike. "Don't even think about asking Toni out. If I so much as catch you looking at her, I will pound your fucking face into the ground." He was shocked at the violence of his response. He was not a jealous person, especially not when it came to women. But the idea of Derek pursuing Toni, of

Derek so much as thinking of Toni in a sexual way, conjured up possessive impulses he didn't even know he had.

Derek looked up at him with a satisfied smirk. "So it's like that, huh?"

Ethan's chest heaved with his exertion. He had no fucking clue what it was like, he only knew Toni got under his skin Why didn't she fucking return his calls?

"It's not like anything, so drop it."

Derek shifted under him, a vein popping out on his forehead as he tried to break Ethan's position. "Then why do you check your phone every ten minutes to see if she called you back?"

His attention wandered to his phone for a nanosecond, all the opening Derek required. His twin heaved up under him and executed a perfect shrimp-escape scissor-sweep combo, drove his knee up into Ethan's leg, and flipped him over onto his back. Now Derek's hand was at Ethan's throat, his elbow cocked back. "Don't lose your focus."

Good advice, and not just for fighting.

Derek rocked back on his heels and stood, offering his hand to pull Ethan up.

"One more round," Ethan said, bringing his hands up to the ready.

Derek put down the empty bottle he'd just chugged dry and raised his hands, reluctance evident in every line of his body. They started to circle again when the electronic trill of a cell phone echoed off the high ceilings of the gym.

Ethan hurried to his phone and frowned when he realized it was Derek's phone ringing and not Toni calling him back. He looked up, saw his brother staring at him with a raised eyebrow, and knew Derek could read his disappointment and the reason for it. His face got hot. What was the fucking world coming to when Ethan Taggart was reduced to waiting by the phone like some teenage girl by a computer nerd who happened to have the best tits he'd ever had the pleasure to suck?

Ethan forced his mind from Toni's rack to his brother's side of the conversation. "Really? When? You're certain? That shouldn't be possible. Someone good. No, I'll handle it. Thanks for calling."

Derek flipped his phone closed. "That was Alex calling from the office. I think I know why your girlfriend hasn't called you back."

Ethan didn't bother protesting Derek's word choice. He shot him a hard look and nodded for him to continue.

"She's been too busy breaking into Gemini's network. She hacked Kramer's security logs."

Toni pulled into Kramer's driveway and checked her watch. Based on the security logs, Kramer had left the house several hours ago. If he worked a normal day, Toni didn't expect him home for another several hours, giving her plenty of time.

She would have been there sooner, she thought with a pull of annoyance, but it had taken her longer than she'd expected to get into Gemini's network so she could make sure Kramer was out of the house when she showed up. Whoever did their security was good.

But Toni was better. It gave her no small satisfaction that only a few hours after Ethan had booted her out to have his "confidential conversation about home security protocols" or whatever bullshit, she now knew all of the modifications as well as every household member's personal PIN.

She slung her oversize purse over her shoulder. It was big enough to hold everything she needed, but not as official looking as her computer bag. She didn't think Manuela would blink twice, but you never knew.

Toni rang the doorbell and rocked back on her heels, fiddling with the shoulder strap of her bag. She wondered what Ethan was doing right now. Probably counting the big pile of money from Jerry while he trolled for another bed partner.

Manuela opened the door, and Toni pasted a smile on her face as she shoved Ethan's brutally gorgeous image from her mind. "Hi, Manuela, I was driving by and wanted to see if Kara was back yet."

Manuela shook her head and regarded Toni with a frown. "Not yet. Mr. Kramer says she's not coming home for a couple more days."

"Really? I could have sworn he said later today," Toni said, feigning confusion. "I wanted to stop by, you know, see for myself that she's okay."

"Maybe she can call you when she gets back?"

"Sure," Toni said and shifted awkwardly from foot to foot. "Umm, is it okay if I use your bathroom?" Toni barged past without waiting for an answer. "It's really an emergency," she called over her shoulder and started down the hall at a fast trot.

She ducked in the powder room across from Jerry's office and opened and closed the door in case Manuela was listening. Toni waited a few seconds and darted across the hall, praying Manuela would keep herself busy on the other side of the house. With luck, Toni could get everything done in the time it would take a reasonable person to use the bathroom.

Luckily for her, Jerry had a separate computer that didn't go with him to work. She needed to get into his work system as soon as possible, but for now she'd settle for finding out what Jerry was up to in his off-hours. Working fast, she pulled an external hard drive out of her bag, along with a CD. Within minutes, she'd copied his files onto her hard drive and installed both keystroke tracking on his computer and network sniffer software. When she got back to her desk, she could monitor all of Jerry's computer and network use.

She shoved the hard drive and CD back in her bag, did a quick check to make sure everything was exactly how she'd found it, and pulled the office door to the exact same partially ajar position.

"Just bring it to my office, Manuela."

Toni felt her blood form ice crystals at the sound of Jerry's voice. She scrambled into the bathroom and quietly shut the door. Heavy footfalls sounded down the hall. Maybe she could wait until he was busy and sneak out. No, he would have seen her car out front. She flushed the toilet, briefly ran the water in the sink, and sucked in a deep breath, preparing herself to brazen it out.

She waited until Jerry's footsteps were almost to the door and stepped out, nearly colliding with his bulky form. His thick eyebrows pulled tight and that vein started going in his forehead.

"What are you doing here?"

Toni pulled her mouth into a tight smile. "I forgot something earlier." She brandished a small notebook she'd pulled out of her purse, praying he hadn't noticed that Toni never wrote anything down but made all of her notes directly into her BlackBerry or laptop. The knot in her stomach loosened slightly when he didn't question it.

"Hope you don't mind that I used the bathroom. I had a Big Gulp on the way over and was headed for a major accident."

Jerry's nostrils flared at Toni's oversharing.

"When do you expect Kara back, again?" Toni asked, watching for any tics, any tells, any indication that he was lying.

"She'll be back in a couple of days. Now, if you'll excuse me . . ."

"Will you have her call me when she gets back?"

"Why? What do you have to discuss?"

"I'll just feel better when I talk to her myself."

Jerry didn't bother with a reply as he stepped into his office and shut the door.

Jerry couldn't stop his hands from shaking as he sat down at his desk and took a thick folder out of his briefcase. After his meeting with Ethan and Derek Taggart, Jerry had gone to the office, working alone in the lab, testing out the modified prototype he planned to pass off to Connors.

He reviewed the data again, praying this would work. It should work. All tests indicated it would. He knew Connors wouldn't blindly take the chip without a demonstration, and Jerry had fashioned this version so the demo would go off without a hitch.

But a slight modification in the manufacturing process meant that in a short time, the valves of soft silicon polymer would lose their airtight seal. Microscopic openings would allow condensation to collect, ruining any future samples, ruining any future experiments.

All Jerry had to do was make it through the demo, get Kara, get Kyle, and get the hell out. His money had already been transferred, he had fake documents prepared for himself and the kids.

He could pull this off, escaping with his children, his life, and the peace of mind that came from knowing he hadn't put the next generation of bioweapons into the hands of the world's terrorists.

As long as nobody fucked it up.

His thoughts strayed from the data to Toni Crawford. He didn't trust the woman, didn't believe for a second that she had come over to retrieve a lost notebook. He surveyed his office, studying it for signs of disturbance. His computer was on as he'd left it, the monitor black as it hibernated. He jiggled the mouse and was prompted, as always, to enter his login and password.

Everything was as it should be, but Jerry couldn't shake the troubling sensation he was being watched. By Toni. By Connors. He logged on, clicked open his computer security software and ran a diagnostic check, weighing the likelihood that Toni could have somehow bugged his computer. Nothing showed up in the log, and Jerry's computer knowledge was too limited to dig any deeper.

He couldn't take any chances, not when his life and his children's lives were at stake. *Should have thought of that six months ago.* Jerry shoved the thought aside. There was no time for regrets or second-guessing. Toni Crawford and her cybersnooping were a problem, one that needed to be dealt with no matter how uncomfortable Jerry was with the idea.

He unlocked his desk drawer and pulled out a phone, a disposable prepaid unit he'd purchased at Target specifically for communicating with Connors. He knew Connors wouldn't be happy to hear from him, and he prayed that Kara didn't suffer for his fuckups. But Connors was better equipped to deal with the situation than he was. Connors wouldn't feel one speck of the nausea and dread Jerry was feeling as he dialed the phone and entered in his key code.

He pressed pound to send the page and sat back to wait for Connors's call. Guilt was already twisting his insides. He didn't like Toni Crawford. She'd caused him endless trouble and cost him millions of dollars in the past year. But he knew she genuinely cared about Kara and that everything she did was with the goal of getting his daughter back safe. She didn't deserve to die.

"Fucking amateur," William Connors, né Wilhelm Ulbricht, barked in German. His brother, Karl, raised his blond eyebrows in inquiry.

"That was Kramer," Connors said. "Whining to me about that Crawford woman. He's afraid she's going to uncover something." He'd wanted to tell Jerry that it didn't matter. Regardless of what the woman discovered, Jerry wouldn't be around to suffer the consequences.

But if she was good enough and dug deep enough, Toni Crawford might be able to connect the dots back to him, and he couldn't have that.

"What do you want me to do?" Karl asked. Unlike Wilhelm's lean, wiry build, Karl's was a beefy five eleven, his complexion florid from too many years of hard drinking. The brawn to his brother Wilhelm's brains. While under the guise of William Connors, entrepreneur and investor, Wilhelm could move among the highest echelons of the corporate landscape, Karl looked like exactly what he was. A thug spawned in the streets of East Berlin.

But he was Wilhelm's only family, and loyal enough to take a bullet for him. Or several, as he had three years ago in Amsterdam. Through the years, Wilhelm had had several identities and several operations of varying profitability. When it was time to go underground, he took his money and left everything and everyone behind. But not Karl.

Karl always stayed with him, moving behind the scenes, taking care of whatever needed to be done.

As he would now. "Take care of it." He printed out Toni's picture and home address and motioned for Karl to take it. "No later than tomorrow. And make sure it looks like an accident."

Karl nodded and left the room. William didn't concern himself with details of who would do it or how it would be done. All he cared about was that the job couldn't be traced back to him.

His fingernails dug into the mahogany surface of his desk as he thought again of Kramer. That man's ham-handed attempts to manipulate him and those stupid investigators

who were now sniffing around threatened to ruin everything William had worked to build in the past three years.

In the years since he and Karl had left Berlin, William had
had his hands in everything from drug running to human
trafficking to arms dealing. He excelled at building partner-
ships, bringing two interested parties together to help them
run their operations more efficiently. He hooked drug
smugglers up with distributors and Russian girls seeking a
better life in Western Europe and America with pimps in
every country. He liked that he earned a hefty cut without
ever getting mired in the details.

Then three years ago he'd seized on the opportunity presented by the innovations that seemed to pour from Northern California's technology companies. A well-paid source,
a calculated phone call to the right person with a big grudge,
and William had brokered technical innovations to various
interested parties, from competitive companies to foreign
organizations who would use the discoveries to make war
on the western world.

He figured it wasn't treason if he had no loyalty.

He'd even made a few legitimate investments of his own,
giving start-up companies seed money, a layer of legitimacy
that allowed him even more access to the products he brokered.

In only three years, he'd tripled his fortunes, and he'd
only scratched the surface. Now Jerry Kramer's stupidity
threatened to bring the whole operation crashing down
around him. He wasn't afraid of getting caught. He'd gotten so good at disappearing over the years it was almost second nature.

But he wasn't ready to close up shop yet, and he wasn't
about to let Jerry threaten his enterprise.

He grinned, thinking about how Jerry must be squirming, sweating, at what lay in wait for his daughter. William
would be sweating, too, if pretty Kara Kramer were his own.

William had ceased dabbling in prostitution years ago, but he still worked for a select few parties with special interests and deep pockets. His job was to get people what they wanted, whether it was virginal bed partners or cutting-edge product prototypes.

It had been a stroke of divine luck that Kara Kramer fit the profile for one of his most discerning customers, precisely when her father was so sorely in need of a lesson.

He picked up a small red phone and dialed. "Did you receive the pictures?" he asked when the man answered on the other end. "Yes, luscious is a perfect way to describe her. Yes, the other two you requested are on their way." He paused, listening. "Five hundred thousand, to this account." He read off the number. "And then another five hundred after delivery."

The man made a half-hearted protest at the fee, but William knew his client, knew the man wouldn't let such a lovely prize slip through his lustful fingers.

"Come, my friend," William said. "You know as well as I anyone can hop a flight to Thailand and fuck a twelve-year-old, but we are talking about something much more special. And for that you and your friends have to pay."

As Jerry Kramer would pay in the last few moments of his life, knowing that in trying to cross William Connors, he'd sentenced his daughter to her fate.

CHAPTER 11

THE POUNDING ON her door shocked Toni from a sound sleep. She pushed herself up on her elbows, disoriented as she came face-to-face with the upholstery of her couch. Voices sounded in the apartment, and it took her a moment to realize they were coming from the TV.

She must have passed out last night when she'd sat down to take a breather and eat something. She'd spent several hours going through Jerry's files before fatigue and hunger had finally taken their toll. So far, the files from his home computer hadn't revealed much, and she'd found herself wondering several times if maybe she was simply letting paranoia get the best of her.

Then she'd remembered how he was siphoning all of his assets off, and she kept slogging through. She'd only meant to take a short break, grab a snack, and get back to it.

But apparently she'd taken about two bites of her peanut butter sandwich before succumbing to the accumulation of stress and sleeplessness. The last thing she remembered was flipping on Conan O'Brien and leaning her head back. She straightened her glasses and looked at her watch. It was already nine-thirty in the morning.

The pounding on her door stopped, and she breathed a

sigh of relief. She was in no shape to talk to anyone yet. Her still-heavy lids drifted closed, just as her BlackBerry began to shriek. Mumbling a curse, she staggered over to her purse where it sat on the kitchen table, but the call went into voice mail before she could get it. As soon as the ringing stopped, the pounding on the door started again.

"Keep your pants on," she muttered and flung the door open. Bright morning light pierced her sleep-graveled eyes as she took in the sight of Ethan Taggart. Sunlight brought out rich highlights in his hair and gave his tanned skin a burnished glow. She imagined it also did a damn good job of emphasizing her own pallor.

"What are you doing here?" she asked, hoping he couldn't hear her heartbeat, which had suddenly doubled its pace, or see the way her nipples jutted under her tank top at the sight of his sensual lips.

Lips that were devoid of his usual charming smile as he replied, "I thought I'd come check on you, see how you're doing, since you won't return my calls."

He shouldered her aside and walked into her apartment as she stood there trying to jump-start her sleep-fogged brain. "I'm fine. Everything's fine. You didn't need to come all the way over here."

"Want to tell my why you hacked into Gemini's servers to get Kramer's security logs?"

Busted.

"How do you know it was me?" *Way to cover, Crawford.* But it was the best she could do without caffeine in her system.

Ethan cocked an eyebrow as if to say, "Are you fucking kidding me?"

"Fine," she said around a yawn. "I wanted to make sure he was gone when I went over there. I left something there yesterday morning."

"Bullshit. You wouldn't have spent the time and effort I know it took to bypass Derek's system—he's very impressed, by the way—just to pick up something. Try again."

She watched as he filled the carafe of her coffeemaker and spooned grounds into a filter as if he owned the place. She pulled off her glasses and rubbed her eyes. "Since when do I have to answer to you?"

"Since you hacked into my company's network and broke into my client's accounts. I could press charges, you know."

She shot him a glare. "You'll never be able to prove it was me."

"You're probably right. If you're good enough to get through our system, you're good enough to cover your tracks. But if you've found out anything about Jerry, I need to know."

"Why? So you can tell your client he needs to watch his back?"

"No. Because I think you're right, and Jerry's hiding something. And if you had returned one of my half dozen messages yesterday, I would have told you that."

The revelation threw her off-kilter like a blow upside the head. "Do you mind? I'm not even close to awake enough to have this conversation."

"Fine," he said. "Take a shower, get dressed. Then we'll talk. If you're not out in ten minutes, I'm coming in after you," he said, with a wink.

A surge of heat washed through her, pooling and concentrating between her thighs. She hurried down the hall to the bathroom, eager to get away from him and the way every erogenous zone in her body seemed to perk up whenever he was around.

Then she caught sight of her reflection. Thanks to her awkward sleeping position, the imprint of the couch upholstery decorated her right cheek, and her hair had fallen mostly out of her haphazard ponytail. In the harsh glare of the fluorescent light, her complexion looked so pale it had a bluish undertone, and her hazel eyes were nicely accented with giant, puffy bags. Yeah, she didn't think there was much risk of Ethan chasing her down in the shower anytime soon.

She jumped under the cold spray, determined to jolt her brain from its muzzy state. Afterward, she swiped on some mascara and a little blush to save herself from looking like a corpse. With Ethan waiting, she didn't want to take the time to blow her hair into its razor-sharp style, so she left it to wave around her face. She slipped on her robe, grimacing at its tattered state and the thought of Ethan seeing her in it, then scolded herself for caring. Having sex with Ethan had been a Very Bad Idea, and the more he saw her as unsexy and unappealing the better.

She opened the door and stopped short as she came face-to-face with the object of her reluctant lust. He leaned against the counter, sipping at a cup of coffee in a casual stance. But his intense stare was anything but casual. Heat scorched her cheeks, and she knew he was thinking about her naked, stretched under him as he parted her thighs to sink his hips between hers. Her nipples puckered against the soft cotton fabric of her robe at the remembered feel of his hard body pressed up against hers, the heat of his mouth sliding over her skin, the wet penetration of his tongue sliding in the folds of her sex.

Toni broke off eye contact, mumbled something about getting dressed, and hurried down the hall. She emerged a few minutes later dressed in skinny dark-wash jeans and a Pink Floyd vintage concert tee. She would have added a hoodie over the ensemble, but she couldn't take it in this heat, no matter how much she needed the feeble armor another layer of clothing would provide.

She took the cup of coffee he offered, then stepped away to put a good three feet of space between them.

"Cream, right?" he asked.

She nodded and took a fortifying sip.

"So what were you doing at Jerry's?"

"What made you realize I was right?" she countered.

"A feeling," he said, shooting her that toe-curling grin as he echoed her words from the day before. His expression grew serious. "Whatever you did, whatever you found out, I'm not going to rat you out to Jerry."

"Really? You'll compromise your client's security based on the word of someone you've known for less than a week?"

His jaw tightened, and Toni could see that he was still struggling with the decision he had made. "Like I said, I think you're right. I think he's up to something. And if it turns out it has nothing to do with Kara's disappearance, then we agree to ignore what we find and let him get on with it. But I'd rather poke around, bend a few rules and be wrong than do nothing and put Kara at risk."

"I like you better all the time, Taggart," Toni said, wondering what made him change his mind. Whatever it was, she was running with it.

She carried her coffee cup over to her desk and rebooted her computer. She held up the external hard drive for Ethan, who gave her a puzzled look. "I copied the files from his home computer here," she clarified. "And I also bugged his computer and his home network."

"And you don't think he'll notice?"

Toni pulled a face. "He caught me while I was leaving yesterday."

Ethan cursed under his breath.

"But even if he suspects something, he'll never be able to tell. I modified the programs myself to be untraceable."

Ethan's lips quirked into a reluctant smile as he pulled up chair and sat down next to her. "All right, Einstein, what have you found out so far?"

"He's been moving his money," she said, pulling up Jerry's bank statements for Ethan.

As he leaned in for a closer look, she could smell the rich scent of coffee on his breath, the warm smell of his skin, and squashed the urge to to fill her nose with a long, lusty inhale. "This account is based in the Caymans," she said, as much for his edification as to get her mind off tearing his shirt from his chest. "KK Securities, LLC, is a holding company I traced back to Jerry before he and Marcy got divorced. Yesterday he moved all of the assets in that account to another offshore account for BioEnterprises, LLC." She pulled up another page. "He also liquidated several million dollars in stocks and moved it to the same account. Over the past several months he's received several large transfers to that account, and I can't reconcile any of them with money he's making from GeneCor."

Ethan studied the screen and stroked his bottom lip thoughtfully. Toni stared, transfixed by the sensuous curve.

"You think he could be getting money together to pay ransom?" Ethan asked, jarring her from her trance.

Toni swallowed hard against the knot of anxiety in her throat. She didn't want to think it was anything that sinister, but she had to consider the possibility. "Or getting ready to take off."

Ethan's eyes narrowed as he leaned back in his chair and folded his arms across his chest. "We're getting ahead of ourselves. There's still nothing here that proves he's not telling the truth about where Kara is."

Toni shot him a harsh look. "You said yourself you think he's lying."

"I know," he said. "I'm just trying to wrap my head around this. I agree he's up to something—you found the proof. But it's still a leap to go from financial malfeasance to having a hand in his daughter's disappearance."

"You told me you believed me. Is that true or not? Or are you just paying me lip service so you can report everything I find back to Jerry? Did he offer you a corporate security contract at GeneCor if you do?"

His big shoulders bunched under his T-shirt. She was pissing him off. Because she'd scored a direct hit, or because he was offended, she wasn't sure. "What have I done to make you so suspicious?"

Toni made a scoffing sound in her throat. "I've only known you for three days. Give me one reason why I should trust you."

His blue eyes narrowed, taking on icy focus that made her feel like he was seeing straight through her. "You have a hard time trusting men, don't you?"

Toni rolled her eyes and pushed off her chair, grabbing her coffee cup off the desk. "Please, spare me the armchair psychoanalysis. I'm suspicious of a man who flagrantly cheated on his wife and tried to hide money from his family. Any trust issues I have are beside the point."

Ethan pivoted in his chair, his lips quirked in a knowing smile. "So you admit you have them."

Toni poured herself another cup of coffee. "Even so, they're none of your business."

"John Braxton must have done a number on you."

Toni's hand froze on the refrigerator as she whipped her head around to face him.

She wanted to smack the knowing look off his face. "How do you know about John?"

"He came up in your background check."

"Yeah, what did you find?"

"You shared a residence with him for the first nine months you lived here. By the look on your face, I'd say he's your ex."

"And the prize for great detective work goes to Ethan Taggart," she said tightly.

"Why did you break up with him?"

"I had my reasons," she said. She wasn't about to share the sordid details about how, mere months after convincing Toni to move to California with him, John had dumped her for an investment banking analyst he'd met on his frequent business trips to the East Coast. Toni's suspicion had driven her to break into his e-mail account. The intimate messages they'd exchanged had confirmed her worst fears. To this day, the humiliation at having been so stupid and gullible felt as raw as the day she'd discovered the truth.

"Did he cheat on you?" Ethan asked, relentless.

Toni threw up her hands in exasperation. "Fine. Yes. He cheated on me. He started banging some woman in New York a few months after we moved down here." She plunked her coffee on the desk and sank into the chair next to him. "Not that I should be surprised."

"What's that supposed to mean?"

"I mean," she said, shooting Ethan a pointed look, "all men will screw around if they think they won't get caught. Hell," she said, "most men will do it even if they know they'll get caught."

"We're not all bad, you know," he said. "You really can trust me."

She snorted in disbelief. "Give me a break. You're the worst kind."

He actually had the nerve to look affronted. "I've never cheated on a girlfriend in my life."

She rolled her eyes. "Right. And you've been in how many long-term committed relationships?"

His lips pressed into a tight line. "I never make promises I don't intend to keep."

"No, but you imply them. You make a woman feel like she's the most amazing woman in the world, like she's the center of your universe. Until you've fucked her, that is, and then it's all 'Hey baby, that was great. Catch you on the flipside.' " It was good to say all of this out loud, as it reminded her of exactly why, no matter how hot the chemistry that had sparked between them, she would be an idiot to let herself fall for Ethan.

His full lips tightened. "This is about what happened the other night. I didn't mean to make you feel—"

"I want to forget it ever happened. Forget I said anything at all."

Ethan sat back, bristling at the way she'd lumped him in with every other man she'd caught screwing around. "Not every man is unfaithful, you know."

She peeled her gaze from the screen. "Yeah? Name one."

"My father. He's so faithful, it's been almost eighteen years and he's never been on a date."

"Your parents split, too?"

That was one way of looking at it. "Yeah. My mom left when I was fifteen, and I'm pretty sure she was the one having the affairs."

Toni's eyes darkened with sympathy. "I'm sorry—I know how that goes. My dad left when I was the same age. I haven't really seen him since. He didn't even come to Michelle's funeral."

"Yeah, well, it's not always the men who leave." He didn't know why he was talking about his mom. He never talked about her with anyone, never wanted to see that pitying look everyone used to give him that first year. *Poor kid, losing his mom like that.* He didn't need anyone's sympathy.

Toni *knew.* Her look was different. Shit, Toni was different, but hell if he understood why. It wasn't her looks. Yeah, she was beautiful, especially when her lips were red and puffy from kissing and her cheeks were flushed from coming her brains out. But Ethan had dated, slept with, women who could have graced the cover of *Sports Illustrated*'s swimsuit issue.

It was something more, something deeper that made him

want to dig down and find out everything there was to know about her.

The hell of it was, she thought he considered her just another piece of ass, another notch, another meaningless lay. Hell if he knew how to convince her otherwise. He was good at the sex but sucked at anything that smacked of a real relationship.

"Are you even listening to me?" Her question snapped him back to her description of the files on Jerry's computer she'd gone through so far.

"Absolutely," he lied.

"There's also a bunch of stuff he deleted that will take me awhile to recover," she said.

Ethan nodded. "And we're tracking his car and we know anytime he leaves the house." He made a mental note to put a man on Jerry. While he still wasn't convinced Kara was anything more than a runaway, Jerry's recent activity left him with a sense of foreboding.

Toni got out of her chair, twined her fingers, and stretched her hands to the ceiling. Her arms dropped wearily to her sides and she rubbed the back of her neck. "Maybe you're right—I can't see how this all links together. Maybe Kara taking off for the beach is just some weird coincidence."

She looked at Ethan. He could see a flicker of something in her expression and he knew she was thinking about her sister.

He got up and went to her, needing to touch her, to comfort her, even knowing she wouldn't welcome it. His hands settled on her shoulders, kneading the tense muscles, sliding in to work on her neck.

Her entire body stiffened and she tried to move away.

"Relax," he said, murmured, tightening his grip on her shoulders. "It's just a neck rub." But what had started out as a comforting gesture morphed into something else the moment he touched her. The smooth skin of her neck heated up against his fingers, and he focused on the tender patch of skin where her neck and shoulder met. He wanted to sweep his tongue across it, close his teeth over it, leave a love bite for her to remember him by. Her muscles quivered against his hands, and she tried again to step away.

"I don't need a neck rub," she said stiffly.

He dug his thumb into a knot at the juncture of her neck and shoulders, and her right knee buckled. "Really?"

"I carry a lot of tension in my shoulders," she conceded, her voice a little breathless, "but I don't need you to help me work it out."

He leaned in closer, inhaling the fresh scent of her shampoo coming from her still-damp hair. Instead of sleek and straight, this morning her hair fell in loose waves that just brushed the delicate line of her jaw. A curl bounced against her cheekbone as she turned to face him.

"Can you stop touching me, please?"

Not on your fucking life. He spread his hands over her shoulders. "I like your hair like this," he said. He could hear her breath speeding up as his thumbs swept over her shoulder blades.

"It does this when I don't have time to dry it."

"It's sexy."

She jerked away from him as though propelled by some unseen force. "Don't do this, okay?" She spun around, eyes accusing behind their heavy frames, a rosy blush slashing across her cheekbones.

"What?" he asked, honestly bewildered.

"Look, I'm a big girl, okay? I know what the other night was, and what it wasn't. But I'm not really good at sleeping with guys and pretending it doesn't mean anything."

His eyes narrowed. "I never said it didn't mean anything."

She cocked her head and shot him an incredulous look. "Please. Don't feed me some bullshit line about my being," she lifted her hands and did air quotes, " 'special.' You don't have to bother convincing me that I'm any different from any other woman. My self-esteem isn't that fragile. I can handle reality."

He could tell from her posture that she believed every word she said. She really believed he'd just been looking for a warm place to stick his dick, and she'd happened to be close. If he was smart, he'd let her believe it. The way she managed to tie him in knots and throw him completely off his game should have been warning enough.

"You want to hear about my reality?" He grabbed her and pulled her to him, wrapping one hand around her upper arm and the other around the back of her neck. "Yeah, I've fucked a lot of women. And you're right. After I leave, I don't spend much time worrying about their feelings or thinking about when I'm going to see them again."

"Such a gentleman," she spat out.

"But I'm honest. I don't feed women lines of bullshit. I don't have to." He pulled her closer, let her feel his thickening cock surge against her firm belly. "I don't like it any more than you do, but you *are* different. And I know because I've been thinking about you nonstop for three days straight, wondering where you are, what you're doing, when I'll see you again. I gave my brother a black eye yesterday for even joking about asking you out. And now that I've fucked you, I can't get the feel of you out of my head, and I think I'm going to go crazy if I don't have you again."

She opened her mouth to speak, but whatever she said was muffled by the hard pressure of his mouth. He took full advantage of her surprise, thrusting his tongue between her parted lips, his fist tightening in her hair when she would have pulled away.

She splayed her palms and pushed against his chest, but he wouldn't give an inch. He knew he was being obnoxious but he couldn't stop himself. With her, he wasn't capable of any disconnected, calculated seduction. He was wild, out of control, driven by the need to prove she was different. By the need to have her.

He caught one of her hands in his and dragged it to the fly of his pants. His cock surged, hard as a spike against the unwilling pressure of her hand. She let out a muffled sound of protest even as her fingers wrapped reflexively around the thick shaft.

He rocked his hips against her hand, already so turned on he was seconds from coming in his pants like a horny teenager. "Feel that?" He nipped at her bottom lip and released her hand, groaning when she kept it firmly pressed against the front of his pants. "I'm like that every time I get within ten feet of you." He thrust again for emphasis. She responded by giving his dick a firm squeeze. He cupped her face in his hands and began to kiss her in earnest, his tongue tracing her lips and probing her mouth. He kissed her the way he wanted to fuck her, sweeping in and out in a slow, hungry rhythm.

Her hands slid down his back and up again, catching the hem of his shirt on the way. He hissed at the feel of her cool fingers on his overheated skin. He yanked the hem of her T-shirt up her chest and dragged it over her head, his dick swelling against his fly when he saw what she was wearing underneath.

Her bra was made of sheer mesh decorated with patches of lace and did nothing to hide the pale skin and dark pink tips. He covered her with both hands, brushing his thumbs over the rock-hard peaks. "Please tell me you're wearing panties that match." He groaned aloud at the thought of tasting her plump pussy lips through the thin veil of see-through mesh.

Gripping her around the waist, he lifted her off the floor and moved the short distance to the kitchen table. He sat her down and stood between her legs, kissing her all the while. He wanted to suck her tits into his mouth, bury his tongue in her cunt, but he couldn't get enough of her sweet, succulent mouth. He loved the way she tasted, the way her tongue chased his back into his mouth, the way her lips sucked at his, the breathy little moans she made in the back of her throat.

She shifted to fit herself more firmly against the hard ridge of his erection. He could feel her heat through the fabric of his pants and hers. He unbuttoned her jeans, and the buzz of her zipper was the most erotic sound he'd ever heard. He slid his hand over her panties. They were drenched, soaked with the evidence that as much as she tried to hold herself back, she was as hot for him as he was for her. "I've been dreaming of fucking you again," he murmured, pressing his fingers against her hot slit. She breathed a shaky sigh into his mouth as his finger barely brushed her clit through the insubstantial fabric of her panties.

"I was thinking I would take it nice and slow." Another brush of her clit and she jerked as though hit with an electric shock. "I want to spend hours sucking on your tits, licking your pussy. Making you nice and soft and ready for me to fuck."

A soft "Oh God" whispered across his cheek.

"You liked when I went down on you, didn't you?" His long, firm stroke teased out another surge of moisture. "You got so wet, just like you are now. I want to taste you again when you come." He held his hand still, pressed against her pulsing sex, keeping her hovering on the edge. Her hips rocked against him imploringly, and his cock answered with a throb so intense it was nearly painful.

He began working his fingers in a slow, circular motion. "I want to go down on you for hours, make you come so much you beg me to stop." She was moaning now, matching the rhythm of his fingers with her hips, hovering on the edge. He slid his hands from her pants, ignoring her shocked noise of protest.

Stepping back, he yanked her pants down her legs and bent his head to her stomach. He knew he wouldn't last long, knew he wouldn't have the willpower to tease her the way he wanted, but he couldn't resist going in for one sweet taste. His lips slid across the sweat-slicked skin of her belly, skittered across her hip bone. He lowered to his knees, hooked her leg over his shoulder, and pressed his mouth against the soaked fabric of her panties.

He hooked his fingers in her waistband and was just about to tug them down her miles of legs when his cell phone played Nine Inch Nails. Derek's ringtone.

"Let it go to voice mail," she pleaded.

He was right there with her. Ignoring the insistent ring, he tugged the panties off her hips, following their progress with soft sucks and nips. The phone went silent. Ethan had licked and sucked his way halfway down Toni's leg when Derek called right back.

He tried to shut it out, but a still-functioning corner of his brain reminded him that his brother wouldn't keep calling if it weren't an emergency.

"Fuck!" He roared, tearing himself away from the perfect creaminess of Toni's thigh. Snatching his phone off the table, he answered it with a curt, if slightly breathless, "This had better be good."

He barely heard his brother's voice as he watched Toni scramble for her clothes. "Don't move," he whispered, holding up a hand as if to stay her. But it was too late. She'd already tugged her pants up her legs and was scooting into a seated position as she yanked her T-shirt back over her head.

Lust was still roaring in his head so loud Derek's words didn't quite register. "What did you say?"

"I just talked to Dad. There's been an accident."

How did this keep happening? Toni thought as she tucked her T-shirt firmly into her waistband. What was it about

Ethan? All he had to do was kiss her and suddenly her clothes were flying off and she was ready to do him on her secondhand kitchen table. She snuck a glance at him as he began pacing in agitation around the room. Whatever the news was, it wasn't good. She took advantage of his distraction to pull herself together, smoothing her shirt and pulling her hair back into a twist. She finger-combed the loose waves, trying not to think of Ethan's husky voice in her ear telling her that her hair was sexy.

Halfway composed, she turned her attention to Ethan, trying to pick out the details of his side of the conversation. His tone was quiet, calm to the point of coldness, even though she could make out words and phrases like "airlift" and "Will he need surgery?"

Her concern deepened when Ethan finally paused in his pacing by the sliding glass patio door. His broad shoulders hung in a defeated slump.

She moved off the couch and over to her desk so she could see and hear him better. His side of the conversation was now limited to murmured "uh-huhs" and monosyllabic responses. The harsh set of his mouth deepened the grooves on his cheeks until he looked older than his thirty-two years.

Finally, he hung up, exhaling on a weary sigh. He stared out at the parking lot with unseeing eyes for several long moments.

She wanted to wrap her arms around him in comfort but couldn't bring herself to approach him. Funny how she'd been ready to screw him on the kitchen table, yet offering a hug felt far too intimate. "Is everything okay?" she asked tentatively.

He started as though he'd forgotten about her presence. For a split second his face was open and unguarded, and she could see what looked like decades of weariness clouding his eyes. But the vulnerability was gone in an instant.

"My father and my older brother got in a car accident while traveling in Indonesia."

"Oh, my God. Are they okay?"

"Danny broke his nose on the steering wheel and dislocated his shoulder. My dad has a few scratches. But they're fine."

"Still, that's so scary, especially when it happened so far away."

He shook his head, brushing off her concern. "Nothing but the usual Taggart family drama. I've gotten used to it by now."

She got up from behind the desk and went to stand beside him. Not brave enough to touch him but wanting to comfort him nonetheless. "Yeah? Like what?"

He studied her for a minute and looked like he was about to say something. Then his stare went blank. "Typical family bullshit. Nothing worth sharing."

Not with you, anyway. He didn't say it, but Toni got the point loud and clear.

Ouch. Not only had she let him see her naked, she'd told him all about what happened to Michelle, a subject she never brought up with anyone. Sure, she'd kept it matter-of-fact and to the point. She didn't tell him that Michelle's death had sent her mother into a depression from which she'd never recovered. To this day, Toni was convinced it was that, and not the cancer, that had killed her. Guilt had ravaged Susan Crawford's body to the point that she didn't even want to fight. She didn't tell Ethan what it had felt like, living with a mother who missed Michelle so much that Toni felt guilty for being alive every time her mother looked at her.

Now, as she looked at Ethan, his face closed up like a black box, she was glad she hadn't shared any of that with him. Glad she hadn't reached out in some ham-handed attempt to offer comfort he didn't want. All that talk about her being "different," but his boundaries were as clearly staked as if he'd put up caution tape.

Intimacy issues. Funny how she should be so hurt by Ethan's reluctance to share, when John had so often accused her of the exact same thing. Served her right. She knew exactly what to expect from a man like Ethan, and it wasn't deep conversations all about sharing emotions and childhood traumas.

"I'm glad everyone is okay, then," she said, retreating behind the security of her computer screen.

"Thanks. If you don't mind, I need to meet with Derek and make some arrangements. I'll call you later."

As she watched the door slam shut behind him, Toni could hardly believe this was the same man who, less than five minutes ago, had been describing in vivid detail how much he enjoyed performing oral sex on her.

She slumped back in her chair, wishing she had it in her to let this go, wishing she didn't have the gut-deep instinct that something was very wrong, wishing she didn't need proof that Kara was safe and sound and on her way home.

As soon as she heard from Kara, she was getting out of town and on with her life. At this point, she didn't care if she had enough money for a security deposit or another job lined up when she got to Seattle. Right now, she needed to get out of here before she did something really stupid. Like fall in love with Ethan Taggart.

CHAPTER 12

KARA LAY ON a twin bed, one wrist handcuffed to the metal bed frame. They'd moved her here right after they'd taken those creepy pictures, and she still wore the same white nightshirt thing and cotton panties they'd posed her in.

So some disgusting man could see what he was getting before he paid someone for her virginity.

Nausea roiled her stomach. She tried not to think about it, reminding herself over and over that this was all about her dad, that the blond guy only threatened to hurt her because he wanted some chip or something from him.

But it had been at least a couple of days, and she was still here. Not in the basement anymore, at least, but in a small wooden building on the property. Kind of like a shack that had been converted to a really crappy guest house. It had electricity and a bathroom, and a set of twin beds. Mostly, Kara had been left alone, except for a few times a day when someone—usually a mean-looking guy with dark hair and bad skin—came to give her food and water and uncuff her long enough to let her go to the bathroom.

What was taking so long? This would be her third night here. At least, Kara thought it was the third, but it was hard to tell how much time had passed since she had no clock or watch, and both windows in the place—one across the room from her, the other in the bathroom—were shaded so completely they blocked out all the light. Not to mention that it prevented anyone from seeing in. But from what Kara could tell while they were moving her to the other building, there weren't any people out here to see. They'd loaded her into a dark SUV and driven her a short distance down a dirt road bordered by dense redwood forest. There wasn't a single other vehicle or person other than the guy driving the car, the same big blond guy who'd taken her pictures while the other guy watched.

She'd been so scared, wondering where they were taking her. She'd cried and begged him to let her go, promised that her dad would pay him whatever he wanted if he just let her go now.

He hadn't even glanced in the rearview mirror, stonily focused on navigating the narrow, bumpy road.

None of her captors tried to hide their faces from her. No one seemed to care that she saw her surroundings.

On TV and in movies, that meant they weren't worried about being identified by their victims. Which usually meant the victims ended up dead.

At the realization, Kara had been hit by wave after wave of panic, followed by periods of fitful sleep as her body recovered from the stress.

Right now, she almost felt numb, lying here in the light of the single lamp. The sandwich that Crater Face had brought her sweated on a plate next to her. She hadn't touched it, or any of the other food they'd brought her. Fear cramped her stomach and killed her appetite, and now the smell of lunch meat made her want to hurl.

Suddenly the door burst open. It was Crater Face, but this time the beefy guy was with him.

Along with two other girls.

Kara barely registered the girls' faces as they were dragged roughly through the shack and shoved into the bathroom. She could hear the girls crying and protesting over orders to strip. The water ran in the shower, muffling their cries. A few minutes later the girls were dragged, naked and shivering, into the main room.

They were both young—younger than Kara. Maybe fifteen or sixteen? One was tall and thin, her dark, wet hair sticking to her shoulders as she tried to cover herself with one arm over her chest and a hand between her legs. The other was blond, shorter and kind of chunky. She was completely freaking out, screaming and crying, "Please let me go, let me go," like a siren, over and over, until Kara was afraid she was going to scream, too.

Crater Face grabbed a canvas bag and fished a bundle out of it, shoving a white garment at each girl. "Shut up and put this on."

The dark-haired one snatched it to her. Her eyes darted over to Kara, then slid away, as if maybe if she didn't look, the girl tied to the bed would disappear. There was something oddly familiar about the girl's face. The girl yanked the nightshirt on—it was white and ruffly, identical to the one Kara wore—and dragged the underwear up her legs.

The blonde was still screaming, backing away with her hands up as Crater Face tried to make her take the shirt.

Suddenly, the blonde made a break for it, busting past both men and running headlong for the door. She hit the door and flung it open, but Crater Face caught her by the hair and dragged her back inside. He grabbed her by the throat and shoved her up against the wall.

The girl's fleshy shoulders heaved and her eyes bugged out as her scream finally stopped, cut off by the thug's meaty grip.

"Shut. The fuck. Up. You hear me." Tears spurted from the girl's eyes and she started to whimper.

Crater Face backhanded her across the face.

"Stop, you are not to mark them," the big guy said in German accented English. "Now we have to do touch-ups!"

Crater Face released the girl, who sank to the ground in a quivering, whimpering mess. The dark-haired girl stood frozen in the center of the room, chest heaving and eyes darting wildly from Kara to the thugs to the chubby blond and back again.

"Get her up," the blond said to Crater Face. "You." He motioned to the dark haired girl. "Come with me." She slid Kara a wide-eyed look and took a reluctant step toward the door, while Crater Face heaved the blond girl to her feet and dragged the white shirt over her head.

"Just do what they say," Kara blurted. "Do what they say and you won't get hurt."

She had no idea if that was true, but so far it had worked for her, and she prayed it would be the same for the other girls.

They were back shortly. The men handcuffed the blond next to Kara on her bed and the dark-haired girl to the other one and left without a word.

Kara mashed herself against the wall to make room for the other girl, who lay on her side, so scared the bed shook with her tremors. The dark-haired girl was statue-still, curled in a ball as she stared at Kara with wide, fear-soaked eyes.

"What are they going to do to us?" the girl said in a high, thin voice.

Kara shook her head and awkwardly patted the blond girl next to her. "I don't know. Maybe nothing."

"Why did they take those pictures of us?"

Kara shook her head, not wanting to freak them out. "They brought me here because they want something from my dad. I think they took those pictures to show our families."

The girl's face pulled in confusion. "Do you think they

want money? We don't have any money." Her voice started to shake. "My dad's a postal worker, he can't pay ransom."

The blond girl started to sob again. "My mom teaches third grade, she hardly makes anything, either."

Kara's mind raced. What could she tell them? That her father was rich and could pay whatever their captors wanted, so too bad for them?

Besides, she couldn't shake the feeling that something really bad was going to happen to her, whether her father gave in to her kidnappers' demands or not.

"It's going to be okay," she said, patting the blond girl's shoulder to try to calm her down.

They were silent for a while, the only sound in the dim room the blond girl's muffled sobs. The dark-haired girl stayed frozen in a ball of skinny limbs.

"What's your name?" the blond girl finally asked with a sniff.

"Kara. What's yours?"

"I'm Emily. That's Jessica."

"Are you from around here?" Maybe they knew where they were, knew if they were close to a road or as far out in the middle of bumfuck nowhere as Kara feared.

Emily's hair brushed Kara's shoulder as she shook her head. "I don't even know where here is," she said. "They knocked me out, and we drove for a long time after I woke up."

"Where are you from, then?"

"Fresno," Emily answered.

"How about you?" Kara asked Jessica. She wasn't even sure if the girl heard her, she was so zoned out.

But Jessica answered, "I'm from Mission Viejo," through lips that barely moved.

Something clicked in her brain and fear crystallized in Kara's stomach, spreading and spreading until even her scalp felt cold. "You're from the V-Club."

EmilyJ from Fresno. JezzC from Mission Viejo.

Both girls had been members of the online community for months, posted regularly, had their pictures all over it. Kara remembered that Emily was fourteen and Jessica fifteen. Kara thought of the explicit posts, the vicious taunts she'd posted under her Kstar90 alias, and felt guilt pile onto the anxiety that already had her stomach in knots. Though it was only a matter of a few years, she felt ages older than these two girls. And ashamed at the way she'd made fun of them, goaded them, laughing because no one realized who she really was.

"Oh my God, you're that Kara," Emily said.

"You think that's part of the reason they took us? Because they want girls who promise to stay virgins?"

"It has to be," Kara said. This was so messed up. How many times had they chatted about meeting face-to-face?

And now here they were.

"I know we're supposed to be careful about what we say," Emily said, her voice cracking. "But who ever thought it would be dangerous to talk about being a virgin?"

She remembered how Toni had cautioned her to be careful about what she did on her FacePlace page. "Don't ever give any details about yourself. Never friend anyone unless you're positive who they are." Kara had rolled her eyes, thinking how she liked Toni and all, but she was way too paranoid from all the snooping around she did.

"We're a bunch of virgins, Toni. No one cares what we have to say."

Of course, Toni had no idea about her other online persona. She had no idea Kara was posting pictures of herself and talking graphically about sex. No one did, except for Toby. Kara loved the rush she got every time she logged on as Kstar90, knowing that no one had any idea who she really was. As far as anyone knew, Kara was the model kid everyone wanted her to be.

She'd never expected that keeping up her image as Daddy's perfect little girl would land her and two other online friends handcuffed to beds in a shack in the middle of nowhere.

She felt Emily shaking next to her, heard the sobs she tried to hold back in her throat. That bad, dark feeling she had when she realized the men weren't hiding their faces came back. "They're going to sell us," Kara said finally. Her friends deserved to know the truth, no matter how horrifying. Emily stiffened next to her. "I heard one of the men— the head guy, I think—tell my dad about it."

Her throat got tight, and panic once again seized her lungs. At the time, she'd been able to keep a grip on her fear, convincing herself it was all bullshit, a ploy to get her dad to cooperate and give up whatever prototype the man was talking about.

Now she was afraid they had no intention of letting her go, no matter what her dad promised.

Toni hadn't heard from Ethan since he left her apartment the previous day. She'd pulled her phone out to call him a dozen times, but each time she'd stopped short of dialing his number. She had nothing new to tell him. Though she still held the faint hope that Kara was just partying at the beach with her friends, she wasn't surprised not to hear from her. She assumed Ethan would have called her if he'd heard anything new.

In the meantime, she was still going through gigabytes of files and archived messages on Jerry's computer and had recovered his deleted files. But she hadn't found anything of particular interest, and it didn't help that she wasn't sure exactly what she should be looking for.

And a lead was the only excuse to call Ethan. No matter how much she wanted to call him, see if he was okay, see if his brother and father were okay, he'd made it clear yesterday he didn't want her sympathy. Didn't want her probing into his personal life.

For the billionth time, she wondered why the hell she cared. It wasn't as if she was looking for a relationship with Ethan or any other man. She was blowing town as soon as possible, getting in her car and taking off for Seattle ASAP.

That was her plan, and she was sticking to it.

She wondered if Ethan spent last night alone.

She wondered what was up with the family baggage he alluded to.

The urge to do an extra-thorough background check was nearly killing her. It would be so easy. Ten minutes, fifteen tops, and she'd know everything about Ethan Taggart from his birth weight to where he'd had dinner last night.

When the urge reached the overwhelming state, she laced up her running shoes and drove to the foothills near the Stanford campus for a run. She loved running here, through the sunbaked hills dotted with twisted old oaks, up to the massive satellite dish with its nose tipped to the sky. And right now, focusing on not passing out from the heat as she pounded up a steep hill that led to the dish was enough to keep her brain occupied for half an hour or so.

On the way home, she made a quick stop at the grocery store to pick up milk, coffee, and cereal. Stalling, since she knew the second she got home she was going to Google Ethan at the very least.

She pulled into her parking space, the afternoon sun hitting her like a blast furnace as she got out of the air-conditioned car. She went around to the back and saw that everything had scattered across her trunk in the course of the short drive home. She bent over to gather up her groceries and heard an engine roar to life somewhere in the parking lot.

Someone needed to get their ass to the Midas Muffler shop, stat.

She shoved everything back into the bag and grabbed the plastic handle, cursing as the handle ripped, sending a carton of milk tumbling back into the corner of her trunk. She reached into the trunk, fumbling around until her hand finally closed around the cool cardboard. As she pulled it out, the rumbling engine grew louder and louder until the sound was almost deafening.

She looked up to see a beat-up sedan barreling right at her. The milk carton slid from her hand. The car was going way too fast to stop before it hit her. She flung herself to the side, landing between her car and the one in the next parking stall a split second before the sedan slammed into the back of her Honda.

She barely had time to catch her breath as the car backed up and came charging at her again. She scrambled toward her driver's side as the car hit hers at an angle, smashing her Honda into the car next to it, leaving only a small space for her near the front bumpers. Panic clawed at her stomach as she heard the engine revving again. Her car lurched at the impact. She was pinned down, trapped between her car, her neighbor's, and the concrete wall at the front of the carport.

She needed to move before she was crushed. The sedan's engine rumbled again as her assailant backed up, and she dived over her neighbor's car, skittering over the hood, hitting the ground running as she heard the car get up to speed. The scream of metal and steel colliding rang across the asphalt. A car door slammed, a male voice cursed, and she kept running for the stairs. Tires squealed and the loud rumble of the engine faded as the crazy hit-and-run driver fled.

In her dazed state, she only wanted to get to the relative safety of her apartment. Her hand shook as she fumbled with the key, but she finally managed to get the door open.

She knew something was wrong the second she walked through the door, but she couldn't put her finger on exactly what. As she squinted into the dimness of her apartment, her breath caught as she saw her desk. It was clean.

Every piece of computer equipment, every scrap of paper, was gone.

In a flash, she realized the hit-and-run downstairs had been no accident. She pulled her cell phone out of her pocket and dialed Ethan's number without thinking.

"This is Ethan."

The mere sound of his voice was enough to comfort her. Yet when she opened her mouth, she found her lips and tongue were so dry she could barely speak.

"Hello? Who's there?" he snapped.

She licked her lips and tried again. "Ethan? It's Toni." Her voice quavered as her entire body began to shake.

"Are you okay? Tell me what's wrong."

"I think someone just tried to kill me."

CHAPTER 13

ETHAN BROKE NEARLY every traffic law on the books in his hurry to get to Toni. He'd been in bad shit before, times he was sure he was toast, but he had never felt the kind of panic he was experiencing now. All his energy was focused on getting to her, making sure she was safe, and hiding her away somewhere so she couldn't be hurt again.

Once she'd described what had happened, and the fact that her computers and files were missing, he knew the hit-and-run wasn't random. Toni was getting too close to finding out something Jerry wanted to keep hidden.

Ethan pulled into the parking lot of her apartment complex. Two squad cars were already on the scene. A paunchy guy was talking to a policeman, gesticulating wildly as he described how the car came out of nowhere and slammed into him as he was backing out of his space.

Ethan spotted Toni across the parking lot, talking to a police officer over by her car. Ethan's gut tightened when he saw the damage to her little green Honda. The back end was completely crushed. Given the extent of the damage, he knew the guy must have been going at least forty miles an hour when he slammed into the car. If she hadn't jumped out of the way, she would have been crushed.

He winced as he saw the raw scrape on her leg, left bare

by her running shorts. Another raw mark decorated her shoulder. Ethan's gut clenched as he took in her wounds. It could have been so much worse, but even the small evidence that someone tried to harm her made protective rage simmer through his veins.

She was remarkably composed as she talked to the officer, but as he got closer he could see the lines of strain around her mouth and the faint trembling of her fingers as she pointed to the entrance of the parking lot.

". . . got louder and louder," she was saying. "By the time I looked up he was practically right on top of me."

"Did you get a look at him?"

Toni's arms crossed around her waist, hugging herself. "He was white, I'm pretty sure. Youngish. But he wore a baseball cap and sunglasses, so I couldn't make anything out."

"And no license number?"

"There wasn't a license plate at all," she said, rocking back on her heels.

Ethan approached her from behind and slipped his arm around her shoulders. She jumped at the contact, but the tension in her shoulders faded by degrees as she let him pull her against his side.

He'd spent the last twenty-four hours trying not to think about her, trying to convince himself that what he felt for her was no big deal. That the urge to spill his guts and share all his deep, dark secrets with her would pass, along with the sexual fascination like nothing he'd ever felt before.

Then he'd gotten her call, heard the fear in her voice, faced the possibility of losing her before he even had her. The fear, anxiety, all that bullshit melted away in a moment of icy clarity. Some deep, primitive part of his brain recognized Toni as *his*. His to protect, to keep safe. And all the other stuff he was still too freaked out to think about.

A warm glow spread through his belly at the way she leaned into him, like she trusted him, like she needed him.

He pulled her all the way into his embrace, loving the way she buried her face against his throat and wrapped her arms around his waist.

"You scared the shit out of me."

Her watery chuckle was muffled against his shirtfront. "You think you were scared? You didn't have a two-ton rust bucket barreling at you going fifty miles an hour."

After a moment she pulled away but kept one arm around him. "I was just telling them that I'm sure the guy was some drunk and got the gas pedal confused with the brake."

Ethan gave her a hard look. Toni's gaze was steady as it warned him not to contradict her.

The patrolman flipped his notepad closed and handed Toni a card. "Call us if you can think of anything else that will help us get this guy. You're lucky you weren't seriously injured or even killed."

Toni nodded, and Ethan's fear mingled with irritation at Toni's determination to play the hero. He hustled her up the stairs to her apartment. The second the door was closed he grabbed her by the shoulders and gave her a little shake. "Why didn't you tell them about Jerry?"

She gave him a look that said she doubted the existence of his frontal lobe. "And what do you expect me to tell them? That I think he's covering up his daughter's disappearance when all the evidence shows that she went to the beach with some friends? Oh, and that the reason I suspect he's up to anything illegal is because I went into his house, copied his computer files without permission, and I'm illegally monitoring his home network? Yeah, that'll go over well. In the meantime, why don't you tell them how you and Derek are following him without his knowledge."

Ethan ran a hand through his hair in irritation. He grabbed Toni by the arm. "I'm taking you someplace safe and then I'm going over to Jerry's. I'm getting to the bottom of this if I have to beat it out of him."

Toni dug in her heels and pulled at his grip on her arm. "Look, Rambo, I know it kills you to sit back and do nothing, but you can't go busting in there and let him know that we're onto him."

"I would say this is a good clue Jerry already knows you're onto him," Ethan snapped.

"But he doesn't know you are. And if he does have something to do with Kara's disappearance, I don't want to take the chance of his panicking and taking off before we find her."

"Even if it means putting your own life at risk?" Ethan moved toward her until they were separated by mere inches. Hands on his hips, he loomed over her, trying to intimidate her.

Of course, it didn't work worth shit. Toni put her hands on her own hips and stuck her chin out even farther. "I can take care of myself. Kara can't."

"That remains to be seen." He looked over at her empty desk. "So they took everything?"

She shook her head. "All they have is my backup computer, my networking equipment, and all the files I had on the desk. I had my laptop with me, and everything else is backed up on a remote server."

His hands closed into fists when he thought of someone in her apartment. "Pack a bag." He wanted nothing more than to get her out of this dark, depressing apartment with its flimsy locks and nonexistent security.

"Where are we going?" she asked, her left eyebrow quirking above the heavy frames of her glasses.

"You'll stay at my place tonight. We'll figure out where to go in the morning."

She froze in the act of putting a cushion back on her couch. "I can't stay at your place."

"You can't stay here, especially once Jerry and whoever he's working with find out you're not dead."

She tossed her keys on the kitchen table. "Take me to a hotel then. You don't have to baby-sit me."

He could have taken the time to explain, to convince her that she would be safest with him, but he was out of patience. "This isn't up for debate," he said. He was hanging on to his control by a thread. Even though she was safe, his brain kept going back to what might have happened. "Pack a fucking bag and get your sweet little ass out to my car."

"Or what?" Was she smiling? Was this a game to her?

"This isn't a fucking joke, Toni. You're coming with me if I have to hog-tie you and carry you out myself."

"I'd like to see you try," she muttered. Then she rolled her eyes. "Fine. Let me get cleaned up first."

She went to the bathroom and he heard the shower run. He fought the urge to burst in uninvited and examine every inch of her to make sure she was really okay. But for all her tough-girl attitude, she was scared, and she didn't need him pawing her all over like a Neanderthal.

Plenty of time for that once they got back to his place.

While he waited for her to pack a bag, he called Derek and filled him in on what had happened. "I want someone on Kramer at all times. If he gets up to take a piss, I want to know." He could kick his own nuts for not doing it sooner, but he'd thought—hoped—Toni was overreacting by connecting Kramer to Kara's disappearance. They still didn't have any hard proof, but the attempt on Toni's life was impossible to ignore.

"You going to explain to Danny why we're tailing Kramer?" Derek asked.

Ethan sighed. "Not until I absolutely have to."

He hung up the phone and moved to stand in Toni's doorway, watching her as she packed some clothes into a carry-on-size rolling suitcase. He tried not to look at the pile of lingerie on top, an explosion of lace, satin, and silk that made his mind boggle with all the possibilities. Looking at her underwear made him think of her *in* her underwear, followed by thoughts of getting her *out* of her underwear, and if he let his thoughts wander too far in that direction, they'd never make it out of here.

Fifteen minutes later he was unlocking the door to his condo. As she walked in, he was hit with a wave of self-consciousness, wondering what she would think of his place. The quintessential bachelor pad. His living room was dominated by a huge flat-screen television and a large leather sectional sofa. Back issues of *The Economist* and *Sports Illustrated* were strewn across the heavy teak coffee table. A woman's touch was nowhere to be found, and he wondered if that was a good thing or not.

Toni's sneakered footsteps squeaked on the hardwood floors as her gaze swept the apartment. "Nice" was her only assessment. The door clicked shut behind them, and the atmosphere around them changed. The air crackled with the knowledge that they were alone in his apartment, and she was going to spend the night. And he wasn't positive, but he was pretty damn sure she was remembering the last time they'd spent the night together.

Pink bloomed in her cheeks as she grew antsy, bouncing a little on the balls of her feet in her All Stars. She pointed to the duffel bag he held in his left hand. "You want to show me where the guest room is so I can get settled?" She started down the hallway off the living room, as though eager to put some space between them.

He caught her before she'd gone more than two steps. That cave man feeling was back, the need to have her that took priority over everything else. He wanted to keep her, protect her, possess her in a way that had everything and nothing to do with sex. He'd been patient back at her place, kept his hands to himself, and let her process what had happened.

But now the need to feel her, naked and aroused and alive in his arms, overpowered everything. "You're kidding, right?" He pinned her up against the wall, lining up his hips with hers and pressing close. "You know exactly where you're spending tonight, and it sure as shit isn't my guest bed."

She swallowed hard and her tongue flicked over her plump bottom lip. He leaned in close enough to taste her breath as she spoke. "I think it's better if we keep this relationship all about business." The lack of conviction in her tone would have been funny under other circumstances.

It was business time all right, he thought as he rocked his hips against her, making sure she felt every long, thick inch of the erection that strained against the fly of his pants. "Too late. It hasn't been about business from the first time I kissed you, and you know it."

"We shouldn't let ourselves get distracted," she whispered feebly.

"Tell me you didn't want me yesterday." He rocked his hips against her, savoring her little gasp and the way she squirmed against him. "Tell me you haven't been wishing we could have finished what we started. You were so wet. I bet you're wet now." He palmed her through her pants, the heat of her scorching him.

He kissed her like a starving man, hungry for the taste of her. His hands started to shake as he realized how close he had been to losing her, how easily that call could have come not from her but from the police, telling him she was dead. If something happened to her, he'd be devastated.

It didn't make any sense. He barely knew her, and yet every instinct in him screamed at him to grab hold of her and not let go.

The confusing mess of emotions he'd been struggling with since he first laid eyes on her converged into a single point of need, driving him to take her, possess her, make her his using any means necessary. He closed his eyes, drinking in the taste of her lips, the slick heat of her tongue sliding against his. Her hands tugged the hem of his shirt out of his pants, and he released her mouth long enough to pull it over his head. Their hands collided as they scrambled to pull her shirt off. He shoved, she tugged, until the stretchy cotton was yanked over her head and thrown to the floor, followed by her flimsy excuse for a bra.

He pressed against her, chest to chest, pausing for a moment to savor the exquisite feel of her skin against his. "God, you feel good," he groaned as her hands skimmed down his back, up his sides, and back down his arms. Her fingers twined with his, and she pulled his hands up to cover her breasts.

"Touch me," she said, and he nearly came in his pants. He kissed her again, the sound of smacking lips and soft sighs bouncing off the walls of his condo as he cupped and caressed the soft weight of her breasts. Her nipples were pebbly hard against his palms. His mouth practically watered to taste them. But he couldn't get enough of her lips, her tongue, the soft panting of her breath against his mouth as he teased her.

He leaned in to her, swallowing her small sound of protest as he crushed her against the wall. Somewhere in his lust-fogged brain he realized it was time for a change of venue. Without releasing her mouth, he held her by the waist and guided her down the hall to his bedroom. With a flick of his fingers he unfastened the button at her waist and shoved her pants down her legs as she kicked off her shoes. His own pants and boxers joined her clothes in a pile on the floor.

He fell back across his king-size bed and pulled her down on top of him. He kissed her again and felt the hard edge of her glasses against his nose. He slipped them off and placed them on the bedside table. The silky skin of her back was hot and slightly damp under his hands. The firm curves of her ass filled his hands perfectly. She still wore her panties, her wetness seeping through. He ground his cock against the mound of her sex, groaning as the wet satin teased achingly sensitive flesh.

She moaned and rocked, sliding and grinding against him until they were both on the verge. He caught her hips, stilling her motions before he lost control. He pulled her up his body until she knelt over his face. He sensed her discomfort in the tightening of her thigh muscles, in the way her abs contracted above the waistband of her wispy panties.

She shifted as though to slide back down. His fingers closed around her thighs in an iron-hard grip. The heat of her, the scent of her, so wet and turned on, was driving him insane. He wasn't about to let her stop him. "Hold on to the headboard," he instructed, licking his lips as he anticipated the first sweet taste.

"I don't think this is going to work," she said, even as she braced her hands on the top of his heavy wooden headboard. "I don't—"

The rest of whatever she was going to say was lost in a gasp as he tugged the crotch of her panties aside and delved his tongue into the drenched folds of her pussy. Salty-sweet honeyed heaven. "You taste so fucking good," he groaned, thrusting inside, taking her with his tongue the way he wanted to take her with his cock. Holding her steady with his hands at her hips, he pulled her forward, sucking her clit into his mouth, licking at her with firm strokes of his tongue.

He could hear the moans pushing past her lips, the occasional "Oh, God," "Oh, please," and his favorite, "Oh, Ethan." Her arousal flowed hot and wet onto his tongue as tension built in her muscles. He knew she was close.

As much as he wanted to taste her orgasm, he wanted to feel it more. He wanted to feel her clenching around his cock when she came this first time. He'd spend the rest of the night making her come in a thousand different ways, but right now he wanted her to feel him planted deep inside her when he pushed her over the edge.

He took one last greedy taste and gripped her hips to move her down his body.

"What are you doing?" she said, her voice high and frantic. Every sinew was taut, trembling as she hovered on the edge of release. He caught the back of her head with one hand and fumbled in his bedside table with the other. Her kiss was wild, all open mouth and thrusting tongue as she spread her knees wide and settled over his hips. She shifted so his cock was cradled against the slick, plump lips of her pussy.

He groaned into her mouth, his fumbling fingers finally closing around the elusive foil packet.

"You feel so good," she murmured, her tongue flicking over his lips as she slid her hot, wet core up and down his shaft.

Reaching between them, he managed to slide the condom on one-handed. He gripped his cock, circling her clit with the thick head until he couldn't stand the wait. Urging her forward with one hand, he worked himself inside. His breath hissed out of his chest as her slick heat closed around him. "God, you're so tight," he murmured, groaning out a curse as she sank her hips to take him deeper.

She gave a funny little laugh. "And you're so big." She rocked forward until only the head of his cock was inside of her, teasing them both as she took him with short, shallow thrusts. Bracing her hands on his chest, she sat up and sank all the way down, until he could feel the sweet press of her ass against his balls.

Her back arched, her beautiful tits with their petal-pink nipples pointing up at the sky, pale skin flushed in pleasure. Her lips parted on a broken sob as she came, her body convulsing around him, squeezing him so tight it was all he could do to hold back his own release. She was so gorgeous, eyes closed, her mouth swollen from his kisses, her inky-dark hair framing her face. He thrust up against her, grinding his cock deep inside, wanting her pleasure to go on and on.

His balls tightened, his cock throbbed, but he held back his orgasm so he could watch hers. Watching her let go, seeing her pleasure and knowing he was responsible made something tight and hot bloom in his chest. Something that was more than mere sex. Protectiveness, possessiveness. Jealousy. Rage. Need.

She brought out every male, territorial, testosterone-fueled instinct he possessed.

Ethan didn't know how to process any of it, so he channeled the intensity the only way he knew how—through sex. He gripped her hips and held her hard against him, rocking against her as she rode her orgasm out. She collapsed against him, her chest heaving against his as she fought to catch her breath.

He tangled his fist in her hair and pulled her mouth to his, letting her know in no uncertain terms that he wasn't even close to finished with her. His hands slid up and down the silky skin of her back and hips as he fought to control himself. She shifted and he froze, struggling not to come when even the slightest movement threatened to send him over the edge. He kissed her again, focusing on how good she tasted, how smooth her hair felt against his fingers until he had regained control.

He flipped her over, keeping his mouth on hers as his hips resumed their rhythm. He sank into her, relentlessly slow and deep. He hooked her knees in his elbows and spread her legs wide, but it wasn't enough. It was as if he couldn't get close enough, couldn't get deep enough inside her.

He gave her one last deep kiss and eased out of her. Her eyes fluttered open, blurry with sexual heat, and she gave a soft sound of protest as his cock slid free. Gently he turned her over onto her stomach, urging her onto her knees. Bracing herself on her elbows, she eagerly arched her back and tilted her hips up in invitation. He gripped his cock in one hand and positioned himself against her slick entrance. She was watching him over her shoulder as he slid inside, her hair falling in her face in an inky tangle. He could make out the dark flush of her skin and the sharp gleam of her gold-green eyes through the dark strands. He held her gaze as he sank into her, pushing until he was once again buried to the hilt.

He began to thrust, his gaze drawn to where they were joined. A primitive sound ripped from his chest as he watched the thick column of his cock sink inside her. The sight of himself, slick with her juices, made him so hard he thought he was going to burst out of his skin. She moaned into the pillows, rocking her hips back against him to take him deeper.

He could feel her tightening, rippling around him, and he knew she was going to come again. This time there was no holding back—he was going with her. He fucked her without restraint, pumping his hips in hard, deep, strokes, pushing as deep inside her as he could possibly go.

She took it all and begged for more, matching him stroke for stroke, her hips meeting his with greedy thrusts until finally she froze, her pussy gripping and kneading his cock, her body shaking as she came on a long, throaty moan.

He didn't even try to hold back this time. His fingers sank into the giving flesh of her hips as his orgasm ripped through him with such intensity that he nearly blacked out. His release radiated out from the base of his spine, working its way through every nerve as his cock twitched and jerked inside her. When it was over, he collapsed on top of her, barely managing to turn them both to their sides to avoid crushing her.

He looped his arm around her waist, hugging her to him as he buried his face in her neck. He held her like that for several minutes savoring the feel of her. She snuggled against him, so relaxed he wondered if she'd fallen asleep. The air was thick and heavy with the scent of sex. Perfect. That was the only word he could think of to describe this moment. Holding her in his arms, still buried deep inside her, he never wanted to move from this place, from this moment.

But he could feel himself softening and knew he had to pull out and get cleaned up before the condom slipped off. Nothing like the realities of birth control to ruin a tender moment. He reluctantly withdrew, his brain already working on how he was going to get back inside her.

He kissed her on the shoulder and went to the bathroom to clean up. When he came back to the bedroom Toni had pulled the sheet over herself and was reclining against the pillows. She'd put her glasses back on and was watched him warily in the late-evening light that spilled through his half-open blinds. His chest tightened at the way she looked at him, like she was steeling herself, waiting for a blow.

He slid under the sheet with her and pulled her against him. Ethan had never been a big fan of sleepovers, especially at his place. On the rare occasion when he brought a woman home, he usually tried to politely herd her out the door as quickly as possible after the deed was done.

But tonight, Toni couldn't go anywhere, and for the first time in his life he didn't mind. He wanted to stay right here, in his bed with her, kissing and touching her until he was ready to have sex again.

Cradling her jaw in his hand, he brushed his lips across her mouth until finally she parted her lips. He kissed her, deep and slow and wet, and to his amazement, his cock rose insistently against her hip.

Her eyes flew open and she broke the kiss. "You've got to be kidding me."

He grinned, sliding his hand down to cover her breast. "I

can't believe it either. I just had the best sex I've ever had in my life, and I already want to go again." The words slipped out before he could stop them, but he realized as he said them they were true. Toni Crawford, with her know-it-all attitude in life and her unbridled enthusiasm in the bedroom, was, bar none, the best lay he'd ever had. And something more, but he wasn't ready to put that into words just yet.

Toni stiffened in his embrace, bracing her hands against his chest as though to push him away.

He held her tighter. "What?"

"Don't," she said impatiently, trying to wriggle from his hold.

"Don't what?" he said, sliding his leg over hers to keep her still.

"Don't feed me a line of bullshit just because you think it's something I need to hear."

"Why do you automatically think everything I say is a line of bullshit?" His voice rose in irritation. "Why is it so hard for you to believe I could be telling the truth?"

"Because look at you. And look at me." She gestured down at her body. "I'd be an idiot if I let myself believe the things that spew out of your mouth."

Fuckin' great. Here he was having a case of the warm fuzzies, and she thought he was full of shit. He cut her off and rolled her onto her back, pinning her there with his legs between hers. When she tried to push him off, he caught her wrists and pinned them to the pillow. "You want the truth? Here it is. I just came so hard I thought the top of my head was going to blow off. And the second I was finished coming, all I could think about was how soon I could fuck you again. Five minutes later I've got a hard-on that could pound nails." He rubbed his cock against her stomach for emphasis. "This hasn't happened to me since I was in high school," he muttered, as much to himself as to her.

He could tell she still didn't quite believe him, but he didn't have words yet to explain what she did to him. Instead, he kissed her, trying to translate the emotions roiling in his chest into his touch. "All I know is that I see you and I want you," he murmured against her mouth. He slid his hips lower until the tip of his cock slipped and slid against her slick folds. "I feel like I could fuck you for the next hundred years and never get enough." He didn't know where the words were coming from, only that he needed to stop them before he said too much.

He slid her glasses off her nose and placed them on the bedside table, lingering there for a moment to retrieve another condom. Quickly sheathing himself, he slid into her without hesitating. Tasting her surprised gasp as he thrust deep, he took her mouth in an open-mouthed kiss, his tongue thrusting in the same rhythm as his cock. He held himself inside her, barely moving as he kissed and caressed her. He came in long heavy spurts as she pulsed around him, and for the first time in his life he thought he knew what it meant to make love.

Toni awoke a couple of hours later to the unfamiliar sensation of smooth cotton sheets against her naked skin. More unnerving was the heavy weight of a hairy, muscular leg thrown over hers. She turned slowly and saw Ethan asleep on the pillow next to her. He was gorgeous even in sleep, his full lips parted, dark stubble dusting his jaw, his long lashes lending a soft touch to his sharp cheekbones.

The events of the afternoon and evening muddled around in her head, creating so much noise that it was impossible for her to roll over and go back to sleep. As if having someone try to kill her weren't enough, Ethan suddenly had to change his game and throw her for a complete loop.

Far from his previous hot–cold routine of winding her up and then shutting her out, tonight he was all hot. Irresistible, with his hungry mouth on hers and big hands that seemed to know exactly how and where to touch her to make her go off like a roman candle.

She hadn't known sex like that existed. Theoretically, maybe, but seriously, headboard-slamming, screaming up-to-the-rafters sex didn't exist anywhere except in fiction.

At least that's what Toni had thought, even after Sunday night. She'd been able to write that off as the result of having gone so long without.

But now she had to face the truth. Sex with Ethan was nothing short of earth-shattering.

She wasn't sure she liked it. While the sex itself was amazing, the aftermath left her shaky and unsure, like her whole world was slowly peeling off its axis.

And then there was the other stuff. The way he'd sped to her rescue, made sure she was safe, and whisked her off to his lair. They made love—no, she reminded herself sternly, guys like Ethan didn't make love. They fucked.

Then he'd *fucked* her with such heart-stopping intensity—twice—that Toni's nerve endings were still dancing hours later.

And then he'd told she was the best sex he'd ever had. She didn't believe him for a second, but the fact that she *wanted* to believe him was a sure sign she was on her way to big trouble. All kinds of fantasies were spinning through her head, of what it would be like to have Ethan at her side, at her back, her own macho, protective superhero.

Yeah, Toni knew better than to go dancing down *that* road again.

Her brain wasn't where it was supposed to be. Someone had tried to kill her earlier, for Christ's sake. Probably someone hired by Jerry, which meant he knew something about Kara that he wasn't telling them, something that was still frustratingly out of reach.

Instead of lying in bed next to Ethan, fantasizing about

hot sex turning into happily ever after, she should be doing everything she could to find Kara.

And if she wasn't doing that, she should be figuring out how the hell to get her life together enough so she could move back to Seattle before the end of the summer.

Ethan stirred as she slipped out of the king-size bed. His hand reached out, curling into the empty space next to him as though searching for her. Toni's stomach tightened, and she told herself not to read too much into his unconscious movement. A T-shirt lay discarded on an armchair across from the bed and she slipped it on as she padded down the hall to his kitchen.

His condo was beautiful, though she preferred her old flat in Seattle with its charm and history to the sleek, modern lines of Ethan's place. But Toni couldn't find fault with its polished hardwood floors and high ceilings. Large windows faced the foothills. In the daytime, light streamed in, making the unit seem larger than it was. The living room was furnished simply, with heavy, comfortable leather furniture and of course a massive TV. Colorful throw rugs saved it from complete sterility, and she wondered if Ethan had picked them out himself. Judging from his clothes, the man had good taste, but throw rugs seemed like something a woman would choose.

She pushed the idea of Ethan's buying home accessories with a girlfriend out of her head. If she let her mind go there, she'd start wondering how many women had graced his bed before her, and how many would come after. The thought made her a little sick. She forbade herself to dwell on it as she unpacked her laptop and switched it on. She looked at her watch. It was just after one in the morning. They'd heard from Derek earlier. They'd tailed Jerry home from work, and so far he hadn't moved. Toni didn't really expect him to be up working in his home office at this late hour, but hell, it was worth checking.

Nothing. He hadn't accessed his computer or gone online since he got home. She clicked open Kara's FacePlace pages, first checking her regular profile, then checking her Kstar90 page. There were no new postings from her on either page. The last message taunted her: *I'm chilling out at the beach.*

Toni had wanted to believe that was true, wished the instinct that told her Jerry Kramer was lying had been wrong. It blew her mind that he'd tried to have her killed. He didn't seem like the kind of guy who would know and be able to contact a hit man on short notice. Maybe it wasn't Jerry but whoever he was working with. He was getting those millions from somewhere.

Any way you looked at it, Jerry was neck-deep in shit. Now, if only she could put all the pieces together to figure out what the hell was going on. Right now she wasn't getting anywhere.

She rubbed her eyes and stretched, wincing as her body protested. Not only were seldom-used muscles tight and strained, now that the adrenaline and endorphins had worn off, Toni realized she was sore from where she'd slammed herself into the pavement to avoid that speeding car.

Maybe a hot shower would soothe her aches and calm her down enough to get back to sleep.

Ethan's bathroom was as gorgeous as the rest of the place, with a huge, glass-enclosed shower with sandstone tiles that went all the way up to the ceiling. Nozzles were mounted at several different angles, in case the showerer was too lazy to actually wash himself or herself by hand. As she adjusted the temperature, she saw that it also had a steam bath feature. Maybe it was worth almost getting killed if it meant she could stay at Ethan's and indulge in his luxurious bathroom amenities for a few days.

Not to mention the other perks of staying with him She slipped off his T-shirt and stepped into the shower. The hot spray hit her body everywhere, blasting tension from her muscles even as it served as a sharp reminder of exactly how she'd spent the last few hours. Her skin was sensitive, stinging in places where he'd rubbed his whiskered chin a little too aggressively or kissed her a little too fiercely.

She squeezed some shampoo into her palm, the scent filling the shower, bringing back memories of the same fragrance emanating from his sweat-dampened hair as he kissed her breasts and stomach. The tender flesh between her legs began to pulse. God, she was in trouble. Even a whiff of Ethan's shampoo was enough to turn her on. Shaking her head, she dipped it under the spray to rinse and reached for the soap.

Though it was her same old body, her skin felt different under her own hands. As her palms ran over her arms, legs, and belly, she found herself lingering, wondering how she'd felt to Ethan. Had he noticed the smooth skin on her inner thigh? Did he notice the patch of stubble on her knee where she'd missed a spot shaving?

Her cheeks heated as she thought of all the places his hands and mouth had been, all the things she'd let him do. She'd never been with a lover like Ethan, so skilled, so passionate. And he brought out a side of her that she barely recognized. Brazen. Uninhibited.

And, as she remembered her moans echoing up to the ceiling, loud.

The sound of a door opening and closing jerked her from her reverie. She couldn't see him through the steam-fogged glass, but from the way her blood sang and every nerve went on high alert, Toni knew Ethan was there.

The shower door opened and steam billowed around him. He wore nothing but a smile as his gaze raked her naked, wet form. Judging from the gleam in his eyes and the truly impressive erection he sported, he very much liked what he saw.

Her mouth went dry as he stepped into the shower, the water running in rivulets down his muscled abs and thighs.

Without a word, he took the soap from her grasp and worked it into a thick, creamy lather. Her mouth practically watered in anticipation as he bent his head to kiss her and ran his soap-slicked hands down her back. Callused palms slid over her hips, paused to cup her buttocks as his tongue tasted hers.

"I woke up and missed you," he said, breaking the kiss. "Everything okay?" His hands slid to her front, closing over her breasts. His thumbs teased her nipples until her knees went watery.

This was wrong, fooling around in the shower when things were so messed up. But he overwhelmed her with his touch, his kiss. His very presence seemed to suck all of the oxygen from the steamy, enclosed space. "I couldn't sleep," she murmured and placed a hot, open-mouthed kiss against the smoothness of his shoulder. "Too much on my mind."

He squeezed her breasts appreciatively. "Guess I have to work harder to tire you out."

Was it so wrong to allow herself a few more moments of pleasure, of distraction, when she knew reality would slam her in the face soon enough?

Not when you were in a hot shower with a hot man sliding wet and naked against you, she decided.

Feeling daring, she skated her hand down his abs and wrapped her fingers around his rock-hard cock. He was so thick, her fingers barely met, and her sex throbbed at the remembered feel of him sinking hard and deep. He throbbed under her fingers, silky-wet skin stretched tight over his hardness.

She slid her hand up and down and rubbed the plump head against the soap-slicked skin of her belly. He groaned and moved eagerly, pulsing against her palm. Another spurt of wetness trickled between her thighs, the knowledge that she was giving him pleasure was a powerful aphrodisiac.

He kissed her hungrily, plundering her mouth with his tongue as she squeezed and stroked his cock. She switched their positions until his back was against the tiles. She could feel the spray of the shower on her back as she slid to her knees, kissing and sucking at his chest and abs as she went.

By the time she was at eye level with his cock, he was strung tight as a bow, holding his breath. A thick, pearly drop of pre-come glistened at the tip. He let out a harsh groan when she used her thumb to spread it around, and she felt his fist knot in her wet hair. But he didn't push her head forward, didn't try to push his way into her mouth.

She glanced up, saw him watching her, his bright turquoise eyes gleaming as he waited for her to make a move. His restraint was visible in the way he held himself, every muscle tight, veins in his forearms and biceps bulging. He was on the verge of losing control. She could feel it in the trembling of his hands, hear it in the rough, tight sound of his breath, feel it in the angry throbbing of his cock against her fingers.

Keeping her eyes locked on his, she flicked out her tongue, holding his gaze as she swirled it around the head, dipped it into the sensitive slit, ran it up and down his considerable length. His lips parted, his eyelids dropped nearly closed, but she knew he was still watching her, enthralled.

She closed her lips over him and sucked him into her mouth as his groans echoed off the tiles. The taste of him flooded her mouth, hot, salty, and male. She drew him deeper, her jaw stretching to accommodate him as he pressed against the back of her throat.

His legs shook, his hands clenched her hair. "God, that's so fucking good," he whispered. "I love the way you touch me."

Ethan urged her on with his whispered praise and throaty groans. His pleasure sparked her own, until it became a sharp ache between her thighs.

As though sensing her need, Ethan cupped her face in his hands. Gently he pushed her head back and slid his cock from her mouth. Hooking his hands under her arms, he pulled her almost roughly to her feet and turned her so her back was once again against the wall.

Pinning her there with his hips, he held her face still for his rough kiss. He broke away abruptly, pressing his forehead against hers as he took several slow, deep, breaths. "You're driving me fucking insane, you know that?"

She wasn't sure if she was supposed to answer that. She hoped not, because at that moment he slid his hand between her legs, his fingers circling and exploring.

"I love that you get so wet." Another flood of moisture surged against his hand as he slid his fingers along her slit. "You liked going down on me, didn't you? It turned you on?"

Embarrassed heat flooded her cheeks. She'd never been with a lover who spoke so frankly about what they were doing.

"Say it, Toni," he murmured. "Tell me you liked sucking my cock."

Her breath hissed out as his thumb skillfully swirled around her sex, and the words tumbled out. "I loved sucking your cock."

He groaned and thrust his hips against hers. "You like it even better when I fuck you, though, don't you, baby? You can't get enough."

"Yes," she whispered, moving her hips eagerly against his palm. She didn't like the way she was letting down her guard. She enjoyed sex, but she'd always kept a certain distance, even during the most intimate acts. But Ethan broke down every last one of her defenses. If she hadn't been so turned on, the realization would have scared the hell out of her.

As it was, she could barely think, her entire being focused on Ethan's hands, Ethan's body, the carnal things he whispered that made her blush even as they pushed her higher and higher.

Her sex quivered in anticipation when she felt his hand reach into the soap dish, heard the ripping of foil.

"And I can't get enough of you," he said, bending his knees until the tip of his cock pressed against her folds. He hitched her leg over his hip. She could feel the large head pushing, stretching her wide. "I wanted you from the moment I laid eyes on you." He pushed in another inch. Her body, sore and swollen from before, struggled to accept his invasion. "And now that I know how you taste"—he kissed her—"how it feels to be inside you"—he pushed in another inch—"I don't think I'll ever get enough."

He hooked her knee over his elbow and pushed in to the hilt. Toni muffled a cry of mingled pleasure and pain against his shoulder.

He immediately froze. "Am I hurting you?"

"Yes, no," she said mindlessly. She was sore, yes, but so hungry for him it would take only a few deep thrusts to bring her to orgasm.

"I'll be gentle," he said against her cheek as he pulled out with mind-bending slowness, "but I don't think I can stop."

"I think if you stop I'll have to kill you," she said, and rose up on the tiptoes of her standing leg, adjusting his angle until his cock slid against her clit as he pumped slowly in and out. "I've never been so glad to be tall," she said inanely as pleasure tightened low in her belly. "We fit."

He stopped, staring hard into her eyes and said,"Yeah, we're just about perfect together."

She felt her whole world flipping as she realized he wasn't speaking in mere physical terms.

But she would worry about that later, because right now all that mattered was the feel of him, thick and hard inside her, as he braced his arms against the wall of the shower and his hips picked up speed.

Soon he was thrusting hard enough to lift her off her standing leg with every thrust. Her earlier tenderness forgotten, she wrapped her other leg around him, urging him on with her hands and lips. His head bent, and he took her nipple between his lips, sucking hard as he buried himself to the hilt. Her orgasm burst through her, pulsing in waves through every fiber and sinew.

Vaguely she heard him shout, felt him stiffen against her, as his arms wrapped around her so tightly she could barely breathe. His cock jerked hard as he came, sending aftershocks through her as she clung to his wet, shaking body. Her leg dropped from around his waist, and for a moment she wondered if her trembling legs could support her weight.

He leaned in to her, chest heaving, his face buried against her neck as he held them both up against the wall. She could feel his cock inside her, still thick, still semihard. Her body involuntarily clenched around him as he slid out, as though protesting the loss.

When he could finally stand up straight, Ethan turned off the shower, dried them both off, and led Toni back to bed. He drew the sheet up over him and pulled her so she was lying half on top of him, her head tucked under his chin. He couldn't seem to stop touching her, running his hands up and down her back, bending his head to press a kiss to her dark head.

She lay silently against him, absently combing her fingers through his chest hair. But within minutes he could hear the gears in her head start to grind, feel the muscles of her back tighten under his stroking fingers.

"What's wrong?" he asked around a yawn.

She shook her head and stayed silent.

He jostled her softly. "I can't sleep with you lying there humming like a mainframe, so you might as well just out with it already."

Her sigh blew hot and soft over his chest. "It feels wrong, that's all."

Ethan's fingers tightened in her hair, echoing the tension knotting in his stomach. In the past, right about now was when a woman tried to get all mushy and tell him how amazing he was, talk about when they could see each other again, all the things that made him want to bolt. And here he was, wishing Toni would say those exact things, and all she could talk about was how "wrong" it felt. Figured.

"Doesn't it feel weird to you?" Toni prodded.

He slid his hand down and squeezed her ass cheek. "Feels pretty damn good to me. I don't see what the problem is."

She rolled over and switched on the bedside lamp, then settled back against him, propped on her elbows so she could peer into his face. She looked cute without her glasses, her eyes a little squinty as she focused in on him. "That's not what I'm talking about. I mean it feels wrong to be fooling around like this when we still don't know where Kara is, what could be happening to her."

He knew guilt was eating at her, not just about Kara but about her sister. "You've been working nonstop since Saturday. We're doing everything we can, following every lead."

"What if it's not enough?" She pushed away and swung her legs over the side of the bed. "I should go check on Jerry again."

He wrapped his arm around her waist and pulled her back down to the bed. She struggled to get out of his hold, but he easily flipped her over onto her back, pinning her there with his hips between hers. "It's the middle of the night, Toni, nothing is happening."

"You don't know that."

"Forget about the sex for a minute. You think it's unreasonable to take time to sleep, get something to eat? It's okay to live your life, Toni." As the words came out of his mouth, he knew he wasn't talking about Kara or even Michelle anymore.

Toni stiffened and rocked her hips, trying to get out from

under him. "You don't know what you're talking about. You don't understand what it's like."

Irritation built in his chest, tightened his jaw as he grabbed Toni's flailing hands and pinned them to the pillow, harder than he needed to. "What? I have no idea what it's like to lose someone? I have no idea what it's like to have my family break apart because of it? Is that what you were going to say?"

Her mouth flattened into a thin line. "If you did, you'd understand."

His fingers tightened around her wrists and pushed them deeper into the pillows. "Now, that's where you're wrong."

She froze, her struggles stopped as her eyes locked on his face. "What do you mean?"

"You know how I told you my parents split?"

She nodded.

"My mom didn't just leave. She disappeared."

Toni's mouth fell open in shock. "I'm so sorry," she whispered. "You haven't seen her in—"

"Eighteen years this October," he bit out. Old, dark anger bubbled like bile from the deep place he kept it hidden. Anger at his mom for taking off, anger at Toni for pulling all of this old shit out of him. Shit he had no interest in discussing with anyone, especially not a woman. "She packed a bag and took off. No foul play and no clue where she'd gone. We never found any trace of her. "

Instead of saying something trite like how hard it must have been, Toni squinted up at him with her big hazel eyes. "You're sure she left on her own?"

He nodded. His fingers relaxed a little on her wrists, but he didn't let her go yet. "I'm surprised you don't know all this. There was a lot of press at the beginning. Someone like you could find it without digging too hard."

Toni's lips pulled into a sad sort of half smile. "I wouldn't let myself do a background check."

"Why's that?"

Her gaze flicked away from his. "Because then I would have had to admit to myself that I wanted to know about you."

Ethan released her wrists and lay down next to her, pulling her in to him again. The story of his mother's disappearance poured out, from God knew where. He told her things he'd never told anyone. Sure, anyone who'd lived in the San Francisco Bay Area at the time remembered the story of the wealthy investment banker's wife gone missing, but Ethan never talked about it, and as far as he knew, his brothers didn't either. "It destroyed my father. He's spent almost twenty years and hundreds of thousands of dollars chasing every half-baked lead in the world. I mean that literally. That car wreck my dad and older brother got into in Indonesia?"

Toni nodded.

"They were there because someone called my dad and said he thought he saw a woman matching my mother's description in central Bali." He combed his fingers through Toni's hair, focusing on the silky smoothness as he tried to send the ancient resentment back down to the hole where it lived.

"I take it that was a dead end?"

"Happens every year or so, someone comes up with information that, to Dad at least, seems halfway credible. So he pays a hefty reward and goes hell-bent for leather chasing after her. By now you'd think he'd have learned his lesson. If a woman is that determined to get away from you, maybe you should stop chasing her."

After several moments of silence, Toni finally asked, "What do you think really happened?"

"I don't know. Danny thinks she took off with her boyfriend—we're pretty sure she was having an affair with someone when she left but were never sure who. Derek thinks she drank herself to death somewhere."

"And you?"

"I don't want to believe either of them. I mean, what's worse? She left us and was so determined never to come back that she'd rather hide than let us know she's okay? Or that she's been dead all this time and we don't even know it? But sometimes I wish we could just find a body and get on with it. I know how awful that sounds."

Toni's hand stroked his cheek, pushing away the cold dark rising inside him. He wanted to purr like a big cat. "I understand," she whispered.

"Yeah, I guess you do." He swallowed past the unfamiliar, unwanted knot of emotion lodged in his throat and leaned down to kiss her. Her lips parted under his, heat surged through him. His cock hardened against the soft skin of her thigh and he ground his hips against her, distracting himself with sex.

Sex was simple. Sex was easy. So much easier than the complicated emotions boiling and swirling like a typhoon inside.

But even this wasn't as uncomplicated as he wanted, not with the way he responded to the tender strokes of her hand, the way her kiss sent heat and light pouring through him. He groaned and slipped his hand between her legs, wishing he could feel the same nothing he had felt for all the other women, wishing he didn't want to rip himself open and spill his guts to her. That the feel of her sex, so soft and warm and slippery-wet from wanting him, didn't make him feel as though giving her pleasure was his higher purpose in life.

She rocked under his hand, threaded her fingers through his hair and kissed him, soft, wet, hungry kisses, hot and sweet, as if she knew exactly what he needed.

His BlackBerry emitted a shrill alarm, jerking him rudely from his sensual haze. He pushed Toni away and sat up. "That's the alarm on Kramer's security system," he said in response to Toni's look of confusion. "He keyed in his access code and is on his way out."

Within seconds his phone rang. It was Alex Novascelic, the Gemini security specialist who'd been assigned to watch Kramer's house. "Kramer's vehicle just exited his driveway," Alex said.

"Stay on him," Ethan said. "No matter what, don't let him know he's got a tail." He made sure Alex could call up the tracking device they'd planted on Kramer's car so he wouldn't have to follow Kramer too closely. "Derek and I are on our way."

"What's going on?" Toni sat up and slid her glasses on.

"Kramer's on the move," he said, walking to the closet. "And at two-thirty on a Wednesday morning, it's a solid bet he's up to no good."

CHAPTER 14

TONI SCRAMBLED INTO her own clothes as Ethan pulled on a black T-shirt and black pants and laced up his black combat boots. Her stomach knotted as she watched him shove a semiautomatic handgun in his waistband and strap a mean-looking knife to his calf.

"You really think you'll need that?"

He gave her a look like she was on crack. "I hope not, but I'm sure as hell not going out there unprepared." He slipped a leather shoulder harness on over his shirt and holstered the pistol he'd removed from a locked gun case. "I don't know how long this will take," he said as he slipped on a lightweight black jacket. "I'll call you and tell you what's going on as soon as I can."

Toni managed to slip on one sneaker and was struggling into the second, hopping on one foot as she chased him down the hall. "Wait a second."

He ignored her, swiping his keys off the console table as he hurried to the door. He punched the access code into the alarm system. "I'm arming the security system. Don't let anyone in, and stay away from the windows just to be safe."

She managed to hook the heavy canvas of her shoe over her heel. "You're not leaving me here."

He gave her a sharp look. "There's no reason for you to go."

"If you think I'm going to sit here doing nothing while I wait for you to call, you're seriously delusional. As soon as you walk out that door, I'm right behind you."

His mouth pulled into a smirk. "You can't unlock the dead-bolt without the access code."

She gave him an oh-please look. "Which I'm sure is accessible somewhere on the Gemini Securities system."

"You don't have a car," he said, opening the door but blocking it with his body so she couldn't slip past him.

"I'll call a cab," she said through gritted teeth. "Now, are you going to waste time arguing or are we going to find Jerry and figure out what the fuck is going on?"

A muscle pulsed in Ethan's jaw as he moved out of the way to let her out of his condo, but before she could take more than one step, he grabbed her and pinned her up against the wall. "You can go on one condition. You do exactly as I say."

"I—"

His big hand smothered her protest, and his laser-sharp blue eyes seemed to glow in the moonlit corridor. "Exactly as I say. I will not put you in danger, even if it means I have to handcuff you and throw you in my trunk. Do you understand?"

She nodded. He took his hand away and leaned down to give her a hard, fast kiss, then grabbed her arm and took off at a jog down the stairs to his parking garage. He handed Toni his BlackBerry so she could monitor the red dot that represented Jerry Kramer's car, currently headed north on Highway 101.

He docked his cell phone and clipped on an earpiece. "Call Derek." His phone dialed, and moments later Derek's low, clipped voice filled the interior of Ethan's BMW. Derek patched in Alex, who was tailing Kramer about five miles ahead.

"He's getting off at the Holly Street exit," Alex said. "I'm about a mile behind him."

Toni watched the dot of Jerry's car head east, toward an industrial park that sat on the bay. He pulled into a building complex and the dot stopped moving.

Ethan instructed Alex and Derek to park in a lot a quarter mile away. "Alex, as soon as you get there, head over to where Jerry is and give us the lay of the land. But don't engage. We're about five minutes behind. After we hang up, radios only."

"Got it," Alex said.

Derek was already waiting as they turned into the dark lot, a shadowy figure pulling gear from the trunk of his car. Ethan's radio crackled. "Kramer's still in his car, hasn't moved yet," Alex said. "I've got two cars approaching the southwest entrance. License plates 6XJS-626 and 8GHC-439. They're turning in now."

Toni keyed the plate numbers into her handheld and watched as Ethan slipped on what looked like night-vision goggles and Derek slipped extra ammunition into a pocket of his cargo pants.

She suddenly felt as though she'd fallen down a rabbit hole and ended up in a scene from *Rambo*.

"I've got an additional seven men exiting the cars. Six are armed."

Toni swallowed hard and felt a trickle of sweat snake down her inner arm. She'd suspected Jerry was into something bad, but she hadn't anticipated this. God only knew what this might mean for Kara.

"Stay in your position," Ethan told Alex. "We're sixty seconds away."

Ethan was so intent on gearing up that he seemed to have forgotten about her. He checked the gun in his waistband one more time, then turned to her. "Stay in the car, activate the alarm, and don't move. If anything happens and you get scared, call nine one one and stay put. The glass is bulletproof, so you should be fine."

He got out of the car, walked over to her side, took her hand, and pressed the keys into her cold, shaking palm. Amazingly, his hand was warm and dry, as if he were heading to the grocery store and not going off to face several armed men. His fingers tightened around her hand and he leaned down. "Don't worry. It's all going to be fine." He brushed a quick kiss on her cheek. Before she could react, he and Derek took off across the dark parking lot, swift and silent, like wolves running through the night.

Ethan and Derek arrived just in time to see Kramer and four other men enter the darkened building through a back entrance next to a Dumpster. The remaining two men pulled the cars around to the side of the building and got back out, circling, watching, waiting to scare off anyone who might stumble across them.

Alex stayed in position to keep an eye on the two outside, while Ethan and Derek slipped around to the front of the building. Through the dark, Ethan could make out a sign that said "Office Space For Lease." The door was locked, armed with a security system that required an electronic key card to enter.

They did a swift assessment of the square, squat building. They could override the security system, but that would take time. More time than they had.

Looking up, Ethan saw a roof-level window, open a few inches.

Pay dirt.

He and Ethan pried the window open enough to slip through and crept along the steel girding in the high ceiling of the warehouselike structure.

A light came from the back, and he and Derek climbed across the metal framing for a closer look. Five men, including Jerry, stood in a glass-walled room at the back of the building. The walls didn't go all the way to the roof, and Ethan and Derek perched in the darkness.

Unlike the rest of the office space, which seemed to have been given up for dead some time ago, the room was a small but fully equipped lab space.

Jerry wiped his hands on the front of his pants before using a pipette to drop liquid on what looked like a microscopic slide. Two of the men, one a medium-built blond with muddy green eyes and the other a tall, hunch-shouldered, hollow-chested guy, hovered close, watching Jerry's every move. Both were in their late forties.

The other two men were muscle, one a big blond guy with a florid face and a thick layer of fat over muscle. The other was shorter, darker, built like a brick wall. That guy made Ethan nervous, the way his thumb traced the butt of his gun in his side holster.

Derek shifted his position for a better view, pulled out his handheld, and snapped a few photos.

"I trust you're prepared for the demonstration, Jerry?" They had no problem hearing the wiry blond guy's faintly accented voice. For all his friendly tone, Jerry shot him a look full of venom.

"Of course," Jerry said. "I'm sure Mr. . . ." he trailed off and looked at the tall, dark-haired man.

"You can call me Meester Smeeth." The man's fleshy lips pulled into a smile. Ethan guessed the accent to be some flavor of Eastern European.

"Right," Jerry said, recognizing the name for the alias it was.

The blond guy and "Smith" exchanged a few words in what sounded like Russian and laughed.

Jerry gave them an uneasy look and moved to where a computer monitor sat atop an unfamiliar-looking piece of machinery. "If you're ready, we can get started."

Ethan's grip tightened on the metal catwalk as he prepared to move in and get this over with. He didn't like it that Toni was sitting alone in the car—he should have called

Danny over to keep her in his condo, by brute force, if necessary.

He eased forward and caught Derek's eye, signaling him to move in. Derek shook his head in a short, sharp motion, motioned for Ethan to back off.

Ethan held himself in check, but barely. Yeah, Derek was probably right. They should figure out what Jerry was up to that had him sneaking into secret labs in the middle of the night accompanied by sketchy foreign characters and their armed bodyguards.

But Kara Kramer was God knew where, and he'd bet his left nut one these men knew. And the woman he lov—*don't even go there, dude*—Toni was alone in a dark parking lot, and one of these men had tried to have her killed yesterday.

Jerry's hands shook slightly as he dropped a small amount of liquid onto what looked like a piece of clear plastic. "You'll see—with a very small sample size, we can synthesize the bacteria and quickly mutate it." He loaded the chip into a casing and slid it into the machine. He typed in a command and the computer screen showed a complex network of channels and valves, separating off different parts of the liquid. At this magnification, you could see the small organisms being partitioned off into the valves.

Smith's smile widened. "Then it's simply a matter of picking the most virulent strain for cultivation."

Jerry's face was marble white. "Yes."

Smith turned to the blond man. "It is as exciting as you promised, William. My colleagues will be most pleased."

Ethan and Derek exchanged a look. Bacteria? Virulent strain?

His stomach flipped at the implications. Biowarfare. And Jerry was putting it into the hands of people who sure as hell weren't representing the interests of the United States and its allies.

Jerry slid the casing from the machine and packed it away.

The blond man, William, motioned for Jerry to pack up the rest of the equipment as he and Smith conversed in Russian.

Jerry handed the case holding the machinery to Smith's bodyguard. "There are ten chips and cartridges included. Enough for . . ." Jerry swallowed hard.

Ethan wanted to bum-rush him and pound his face into the concrete floor. Fucking weasel.

Smith and William shook hands, then Smith and his bodyguard exited the room.

Ethan and Derek froze in the darkness, holding their breath as the men passed directly underneath them.

"I held up my end," Jerry said. "Now you do the same. Where's Kara?"

Every nerve and sinew went on high alert. Ethan sank back into the darkness and whispered to Alex, "Bring one of the cars over. Park on the street. Be ready to tail the Mercedes. These guys are going to lead us to Kara."

"Don't worry," William said, taking Jerry's arm and leading him to the door. "Everything will end as it should."

Fear had a taste. Bitter and metallic, it rose up from the pit of Jerry's stomach, spread into his throat and coated his tongue like a film. *Calm down. You did exactly what they wanted. It's all fine from here.*

Now Connors would release Kara. Jerry would drop her off at Marcy's and head south. He'd be in Mexico by dinnertime.

He'd wanted to take Kara and Kyle with him, had planned on it, but he couldn't do that. He couldn't expect two teenagers to give up their identities and go into hiding with him. He'd left notes explaining his disappearance as best he could and set up hefty trust funds for both of them. They would never need anything.

Connors's hand was like a manacle around his arm. His bodyguard walked behind, close enough so that Jerry could smell the man's body odor. Or maybe that was his own. He'd been bathed in terror-spiked sweat since Connors had first called him four days ago.

Connors pushed Jerry outside into the cool night and directed him around to the side of the building, where Connors's car was parked. He looked around, hoping Kara was already here, or on her way.

All he saw was Connors's bodyguard and another thug, his face in shadow as he leaned against the hood of a silver Mercedes. Jerry yanked his arm from Connors's grip and spun around. "Cut the bullshit," he said, inwardly cringing at the high edge of fear in his voice. "I came through. Now tell me where Kara is."

Connors laughed and shook his head. "Jerry, you didn't seriously think we'd let her go, did you?" His brow was furrowed as he looked at Jerry with the same condescending sympathy one gave the mentally disabled.

Jerry felt as if his insides were being sucked out. "You told me—"

"And you fucked with me." The smile was gone. Connors was hard, cold, emotionless as granite. "Even if I were inclined to honor our agreement, you and your daughter would prove too much of a risk to my operation."

"You sick son of a bitch!" Jerry rushed him. Who cared? He was dead anyway. He took a wild swing at Connors and felt his feet lift into the air as he was grabbed from behind. He slammed into the pavement, the air rushing from his lungs as his head and torso hit the asphalt. He rolled over and pushed himself onto his hands and knees. He was lying on something, he realized. Someone had put down a tarp.

He looked up at Connors, who stood off to the side, smiling, enjoying the way Jerry gasped and retched as he tried to catch his breath.

"Now," Connors said, "I must be going. I have some men waiting to meet three lovely young ladies." He nodded at the dark-haired thug who stood just behind Jerry. "Make sure there is no mess." He slid into the passenger seat of the Mercedes while the big blond guy got in the driver's seat. The car came to life with a low rumble, the discreet German engine barely disturbing the still night.

The sedan began to back away, and Jerry felt the cold press of a gun to his back. "On your knees."

Jerry sank to the ground, feeling like his life, his soul was already pouring out of him. He'd never been a religious man, but prayers to God raced through his head. Not for himself. He didn't bother begging for forgiveness. If there was an afterlife, he knew exactly where he was headed.

Now he prayed for Kara. For someone to rescue his little girl from the horrific fate Connors had planned for her. All Jerry's fault.

He heard the metallic slide of the gun being cocked and closed his eyes, trying to visualize his children's faces. Wetness trickled down his leg as he pissed himself in fear.

He heard the shot that killed him.

But wait. He opened his eyes. There was no bright light. He was staring at the Dumpster. The thug was screaming, clutching his arm to his chest.

"Don't move!"

Jerry held up his hands and watched as Derek and Ethan Taggart rounded the corner of the building.

Ethan skidded to a stop and hauled Jerry to his feet, slamming him against the Dumpster. Jerry's would-be shooter was down for the count, whimpering as he cradled his wounded forearm. Had to hand it to Derek. He was still a crack shot, even without a scope and a sniper rifle. Running full out, taking a shot where there were inches between saving Jerry and killing him, Derek had nailed the shooter right in the forearm, sending his gun flying and the guy to his knees.

Derek was still running, chasing down the Mercedes on

the off chance he could get close enough to take out a tire. But the taillights receded into the night, out of range of the Sig Sauer .45 Derek carried.

"Why aren't you shooting them?" Jerry said, flailing against Ethan's hold. "We have to stop him. He has Kara."

Ethan subdued Jerry with a forearm across his neck. "One of my men is tailing him. You got him, Alex?" he said into the mouthpiece.

"That's affirmative. Heading west on Veterans Boulevard. I've got my lights off and my night-vision goggles on, hanging back enough so he can't see me."

"We're right behind you."

"Tell him to shoot them!" Jerry said. "Connors has her. You have no idea what he's going to do to her!"

Derek's response was bone-dry and matter-of-fact. "If Alex tries to take them out, they'll catch on that they're being followed. You think they'll lead us to Kara then?"

Ethan pulled a pair of plastic cuffs from his pocket and used them to restrain Jerry while Derek did the same to the shooter. Ethan flipped his phone open and dialed Toni's number.

"What the hell is going on?" she demanded, her voice high and harsh. "Did I hear gunshots?"

"I'll explain everything. Get the car over here, now." He hung up on her in midquestion, grabbed Jerry by the arm, and dragged him over to the approaching BMW.

Toni screeched to a halt and flung open the door. "Someone tell me what's going on!"

Derek grabbed the shooter and wrestled him into the backseat. "You got a first aid kit?"

"In the trunk," Ethan said and shoved Jerry through the rear passenger door. "Try not to bleed all over my seat."

The guy gave him a weak "Fuck you."

Derek slid in the back with their prisoners while Toni rode shotgun.

"Alex, what's your position?" Ethan asked, slamming the

car into reverse. The sound of tires squealing and the smell of burning rubber filled the air.

"I'm on them, heading west on Woodside Road, about to cross Alameda."

"Let me know if he gets on 280. I'll get ahead of him and intercept."

He glanced in the rearview mirror and saw Jerry, white as a sheet, pressing himself as far away as possible from the wounded guy, who winced and swore as Derek knotted a bandage around his forearm.

"Gotta be tight to slow the blood flow," Derek said, giving the knot another yank with a grim smile.

"Where is he heading?" Ethan asked the guy. "Where does he have the girl?"

"He has Kara?" Toni said, eyes going wide as she whipped her head around.

"I don't know about any girl," the guy said. "I got a call this morning. Someone has a job for me, tells me where to show up. That's all I know."

Derek wrapped his hand around the guy's wounded arm and squeezed. "You sure about that?"

"Fuck!" The man's voice broke and he half sobbed, half groaned, "Yes! I swear! I don't know nothing about a girl! I was gonna get ten grand for killing and dumping."

Alex's voice broke in through Ethan's headset. "They did not get on the highway. We're still heading west on Woodside Road."

Woodside was part of Highway 84, running all the way from the East Bay across the Dumbarton Bridge, over the mountains, to the coast. Connors was heading up into the hills, where homes were tucked amid dense redwood forests, and narrow, twisty roads offered seclusion and privacy from curious neighbors.

"I bet Jerry knows," Toni spat out. "I knew you had something to do with this, you fucking weasel."

Toni's body coiled as if she was going to launch herself into the backseat and pound Jerry into oblivion. As much as Ethan would have enjoyed watching that, now wasn't the time. "Ease off, Toni."

"I don't know," Jerry said, his voice high, panicked.

"It's fine," Ethan said. "We're on him. We know exactly where he's going." He wished he could stop, dump Toni off somewhere safe and the two stooges with the police, but there wasn't time. Jesus, this night was turning into a fucking circus act.

"We have to hurry," Jerry said, as if Ethan weren't already driving like a bat out of hell. "He's says he's going to sell her."

Ethan was pretty sure he knew what that meant, wished he didn't. "Sell her? To who? White slavers?"

"He says there's a group of men, very wealthy men, who pay to . . . have . . . virgins."

"What?" Toni said, the horror in her voice echoing Ethan's.

"He knew all about Kara from all her stuff on the Internet," Jerry said. "When I balked at handing over the prototype, he took her, said he knew people who would pay a lot of money to . . ." he stopped, unwilling to voice what they were all thinking.

Toni buried her face in her hands. "And knowing all that, you didn't call the police?"

"I had time!" Jerry said. "He said if I delivered the prototype she would be okay!"

"And you think you can trust a guy who sells teenage girls to wealthy perverts?" Toni scoffed. "You knew you'd ruin your career. You put Kara in danger to cover your own ass."

Jerry didn't even try to defend himself.

"I heard Connors say something about three girls. Who are the other two?"

Jerry shook his head. "I don't know, that's the first time I've heard anything."

"As long as we're on the ride, Jerry, why don't you tell us everything you *do* know."

Ethan listened, his hands tightening on the steering wheel as Jerry recounted how William Connors had approached him nearly a year ago with a proposition. Ethan had figured out most of it, but his stomach tightened as Jerry filled in the gaps, describing what his cutting-edge biochip was capable of.

Toni shook her head. "You knew who had her, all this time."

"I had it under control," Jerry said, the streetlights flashing on his pale face as Ethan flew through a yellow light.

"Son of a bitch!" Both Ethan and Derek jumped as Alex's voice crackled over the headset. Alex cursed again, and there was a squeal of a car skidding, the roar of metal twisting and glass smashing as a vehicle hit something with devastating impact.

Then silence.

"Alex? Alex!" Both he and Derek were shouting into their mouthpieces. "Are you okay? What's the situation?"

A low moan, then, "I hit something big. I think it was a deer. Came around a sharp curve and the damn thing jumped right in front of the car. I skidded out and smashed into a tree."

Of all the fucking luck. The woods in that area were thick with wildlife, everything from deer to jackrabbits to the occasional mountain lion. And now Kara's rescue was thwarted by fucking Bambi. "Are you injured?"

"The airbag smashed the NVGs into my face, but other than that I'm okay. Car's smashed to hell, though."

Ethan slammed the heel of his hand into the steering wheel. Alex's car was wrapped around a giant sequoia, and Connors was long gone.

CHAPTER 15

"WHAT ARE WE going to do?" Jerry asked, his panicky voice grating across Toni's nerves like a fork on a plate. She was strung tight, nerves frayed, as she sat in the passenger seat of Ethan's car. The sound of gunshots had made her blood run cold, fear spiking as she imagined Ethan lying in a pool of blood on the asphalt.

She'd almost cried in relief when she heard his voice, strong and firm and sure. The brief rundown of events was mind-boggling. Yeah, she'd been sure Jerry was up to something, but she never imagined this.

Now, once again, she had to fight from jumping into the backseat and pounding his face in for what he'd done to Kara. His very presence revolted her. Part of it was the smell. In other circumstances, she would have been delighted that Jerry had been so scared he'd wet himself, that fear coated him with acrid sweat. But in the close confines of the car, the stench of sweat and piss made her gag.

As if the smell weren't enough, the thought of what might happen to Kara—what might already be happening—sent bile bubbling into the back of her throat. Name her a sexual fetish and Toni could find an online community with hundreds of devoted members. That there were men out there willing to pay to sleep with unwilling virgins didn't surprise her.

She was horrified nonetheless. At what the victims went through. At what happened to them afterward. And what if they discovered Kara wasn't as innocent as they thought? What then?

She pushed the what-ifs aside. She had to focus on gathering every clue, every scrap of information they could get if they wanted to find her in time.

Ethan ignored Jerry's frantic babbling as he instructed Alex to sit tight and call 911. "Don't tell them what you were doing up there," he said. "I don't want to bring the cops into this just yet."

"No cops. Good idea. I'll pay you," Jerry babbled. "If you get us out of this you can name your price."

Toni was appalled. Ethan was silent, and for a long, sickening moment Toni thought he was actually entertaining the proposition.

"You covered up your own daughter's kidnapping, and you tried to have Toni killed," Ethan said finally, his voice so menacing even Toni got chills.

"I didn't," Jerry protested. "It was Connors. I told him she was snooping around, but he's the one—"

"Don't try to logic your way out of this, Jerry. Whether or not you made the call, you instigated it. And if that wasn't enough, my brothers and I have spent a combined twenty-eight years in the military." Ethan stopped at a red light and turned to face Jerry. "Twenty-eight years defending our country against people who want to destroy us. People like that slimebag you sold your technology to. You really think there's enough money in the world that would get me to help someone like you get away with it?"

Toni wanted to kiss him and sing *The Star-Spangled Banner.*

Jerry's swallow was audible.

"Get one thing straight. We're keeping the police out of this for now because I don't want to waste time answering questions. But when Kara's back, safe and sound, I'll see to it that you spend fifty years to life locked up with a big burly-top named Bubba."

"Why are you turning?" Jerry asked when Ethan veered off Woodside and started heading south. "They were going this way."

"We need to get back to the office to regroup. Toni, when we get there I want you to find everything you can dig up on William Connors. Did you run his plates yet?"

She nodded. She'd been able to run them on her Black-Berry while she waited in the car for what had seemed like decades. "The car is registered to a Whitepoint Corporation, and the address is a P.O. box. Once I'm at the office, I can find out if it has a nav system or anything else to track its location."

They pulled up to the Gemini offices. The lights were on and the place was humming even at three in the morning. Toni took a moment to marvel at the contrast between her cramped, makeshift office and Gemini's spacious, modern, beautifully decorated headquarters. Customers would walk in here and know they were dealing with the best of the best.

Ethan's older brother Danny greeted them. The man managed to look intimidating even though he was wearing baggy gym shorts and flip-flops, his left arm still secured by a sling. Even with a broken nose and two black eyes, he was as good-looking as his brothers. But there was something almost menacing about the oldest Taggart. First there was his size. Ethan and Derek were big guys, but Danny had at least two inches of height and twenty pounds of muscle on both of them. And then there were his eyes, steel gray, cold as a glacial river.

Toni swallowed hard and made a mental note to steer clear of scary Danny.

Danny took off with Connors's bodyguard while Ethan pulled Jerry into an empty conference room. Toni and Derek followed. She sat down at the conference table and opened her laptop. "Jerry, how did you communicate with Connors? If you have an e-mail address or a cell phone number, I might be able to trace his location."

Jerry shook his head. "We used those pay-as-you-go phones."

Toni swore. Cell phone calls were getting so easy to track, that the disposable cell phone had become the modern criminal's favorite mode of communication.

"And I deleted all the e-mails, all communication."

Toni shook her head impatiently as she logged in to the secure server where she'd backed up all of Jerry's files. "I was able to recover everything off your computer, every last fragment." People thought they could wipe out their digital tracks the way they wiped away fingerprints. "Just tell me where to look."

"There's nothing on my computer," Jerry said. "I've been using Kara's computer so nothing could be traced back to GeneCor."

"Her computer's at your house?" Ethan said, already heading for the door.

"It's at my office," Jerry said. "Middle desk drawer. You'll need my key card." He grunted as Ethan shoved him forward and dug around in Jerry's back pocket. Card in hand, he headed for the door.

"You're going alone?" Toni said. "Shouldn't Derek or someone go with you, since people were, you know, shooting at you before?"

The look Ethan gave her was pleased, if a little puzzled at her concern. "I'll be fine, babe. Back in a flash."

She bent over the keyboard and risked a glance at Derek to see if he'd noticed the small endearment. "Ethan can take care of himself," Derek said without looking up from his handheld.

Jerry's bound hands left damp marks on the surface of the mahogany table. His leg bounced hard enough to launch him into the stratosphere. "You're just going to sit there?" He looked over at Derek's screen. "What, you're doing e-mail? 'Hey, dude, how's it going?' My fucking daughter is missing and you're e-mailing your friends?"

Derek set down his BlackBerry and leveled Jerry with a look so harsh she expected Jerry to turn to stone. "I'm e-mailing pictures and descriptions of your buddies Connors and Smith to a good friend of mine at the FBI. With any luck, they'll stop him in Customs before he can make off with the means to build a supervirus."

"Oh," Jerry said, chastened. He licked his lips. "It won't work, you know."

Toni raised her eyebrow inquisitively.

"I modified the chips," Jerry said, almost beseechingly. "The seals on some of the valves aren't airtight. Without the proper level of humidity, they can't run their samples. The chips are useless."

"So no supervirus?" Toni said.

Jerry shook his head, looking smug at his ability to cover his ass.

Toni's lips curled into a snarl. "Nice of you to grow a conscience at the eleventh hour, but that doesn't help us pinpoint Kara's location."

She got everything ready, then went to the kitchen and made herself a double latte in the espresso machine in the break room. Ethan still wasn't back. "Show me the deposits from Connors," she said as she called up Jerry's offshore account statements, unwilling just to sit and do nothing while she waited for Ethan to show up.

There were deposits from three different accounts, and Toni and Derek doubled up to try to track the source.

Toni had managed to link one account to a corporation headquartered in Düsseldorf when Ethan arrived with Kara's computer.

She pounced on it like a lion on a gazelle and immediately set to work, hooking it up to her own computer so she could start the data-recovery process. Ethan came over and removed her watch from her wrist. Toni barely spared him a glance. "Did you use a shredder program?" she asked Jerry.

Jerry nodded and gave her the name.

Most shredder programs worked by overwriting data with a pattern of zeros, though more sophisticated utilities used specific overwrite patterns. Fortunately, the program Kramer had used was relatively easy for Toni to work around.

Toni started the data- and media-recovery programs, limiting her search to files that had been deleted in the last thirty days to make the process go faster. She looked over at Ethan, her attention snagging when she saw he'd taken the back off her watch and was poking around inside. "What are you doing?" Her watch was a cheap digital model from Target, but hey, it worked, and she didn't want to buy another one.

"Cool your jets," he said, poised over the watch with a pair of tweezers. "I'm planting a tracking device in here. Don't worry. Your watch will work fine."

"Why do I need a tracking device?"

The look Ethan gave her was hard, exasperated. He held up his own wrist and nodded to Derek. "We all wear them, and with everything that's happening, I'll feel better knowing exactly where you are, okay?"

Toni didn't protest as he buckled the watch back on her wrist, inexplicably warmed by the idea that Ethan wanted to keep tabs on her. "I'm not the one we need to worry about," she reminded him as she turned her attention back to her excavation of Kara's computer.

It seemed to take forever for the program to churn through the gigabytes of data, but finally the photo-recovery program got a hit. Toni clicked to restore the image, then opened it up to view.

Jerry made a small, choked sound as he looked at the screen.

"Connors sent you this photo?" she said, nausea roiling her stomach as she stared at a mockery of a sexy boudoir photo. But that was no lingerie-clad seductress giving the camera a come-hither look.

In the photo, Kara Kramer was dressed in a white, ruffled nightshirt, the hem pushed high enough to allow a glimpse of white cotton panties. Her blond hair spilled across the pillow and her eyes were wide with fear. Toni zoomed in on her face and saw a faint bruise at the corner of Kara's mouth.

Toni saw the terror in Kara's eyes and felt her throat tighten, her eyes sting. God, she was so scared. Had to still be so scared.

Ethan's hand rested on her shoulder, calming, bracing her. Toni pushed Kara's fear aside, disassociated herself, reminding herself it could have been so much worse.

At least, she thought morbidly, if they wanted her to stay a virgin, it's doubtful she'd been raped.

"Can you figure out who took it?" Ethan asked as she ran it through her EXIF viewer.

Toni scanned the data, unable to suppress the triumphant smile pulling at her lips. "I can do better than that. I can tell you exactly where it was taken."

Ethan, Jerry, and Derek all leaned in to see what she was talking about. "I'd love to say it's my brilliance, but it looks like Connors got a fancy new camera and didn't take into account all the special features."

A smile spread across Derek's face as understanding dawned.

"Someone clue me in here," snapped Jerry.

"Certain high-end models like the one Connors used to take this picture have a GPS device built in. Those," she said, pointing to a box on the grid, "are GPS coordinates."

Toni clicked open another Web browser window. And there it was, right there on Google Maps. Located off Skyline Boulevard, the serpentine roadway that wound its way along the ridge of the coastal mountains, the property was situated back from the main road.

Within minutes, Toni had gathered all of the information about the property. "It's a twelve-acre parcel with two main houses and three outbuildings. It was purchased two years ago by the Whitepoint Company, the same owner listed for Connors's Mercedes." She zoomed in on the satellite photo of the property. "The only road access is through the driveway, if you can call a two-and-a-half-mile road a driveway. It's guarded by a security gate, so you'll have trouble getting in. But the property borders open-space preserves on two sides, and you can see where these hiking trails cross the property lines here and here." She indicated with her mouse. She looked at Ethan, who leaned over her shoulder, blue eyes sharply focused as he absorbed every detail on the screen.

"Got it." He turned to Derek. "Let's suit up. Danny, call Moreno. Since he lives up that way, have him do an assessment of the security situation, how many guards there are, what we're up against. And don't let her" he indicated Toni "out of your sight."

Her hackles rose and she pushed herself away from the table to follow Ethan and Derek down the hall. "There's no way I'm staying here."

Ethan ignored her as he and Derek riffled through a utility closet, gathering up enough ammunition to take over a small country.

"Ethan, I'm sick of your trying to leave me behind while you go save the world. Kara's my friend and this is my case, too."

Ethan spun around and caught her by the arm. Toni barely caught a glimpse of Derek's curious look as Ethan dragged her down the hall to his office and yanked her inside before slamming the door shut. He pushed her up against the door, trapping her with his hands on her shoulders and he pinned her with an icy-blue glare.

"Dammit, Toni, this isn't about playing hero or taking all the credit. This is about finding Kara and getting her out in one piece. And I can't focus completely on that if I'm worried about you getting hurt."

"You don't have to worry about me," she insisted. "I can help."

He leaned his head in, pressed his forehead to hers. "You don't get it. If you go with us, I'm going to want to keep an eye on you at all times. It was bad enough when I worried about you alone in the car, thinking someone might find you and you'd be helpless."

"I'm hardly helpless," she said, insulted.

"But you're not trained for something like this, either. Have you ever even held a gun?"

"No," she said sullenly. "But I could help you bypass the security system."

"Derek can do that. Bottom line, Toni, I can't be as effective for Kara if I'm worried about protecting you."

"I don't see why—"

"Because I care about you, Toni," he said, sounding like the words were being ripped from his chest. "A lot. Connors already tried to have you killed. What do you think he'll do if he sees you? The thought of anything else happening to you drives me fucking insane, okay? So let it go. You're staying here where Danny can keep an eye on you."

She laid her palms flat on his chest, pressing against the hard slabs of muscle. "You think it was easy for me, alone in the dark, no idea what's going on? Then I hear gunshots and think maybe you're dead—" her voice started to crack. "I can't just sit here, not knowing what's happening."

"I'll hook you up to the audio feed," he said, his voice gentling. "You and Danny will hear everything that's happening."

She knew he was right. She didn't know how to shoot, had no experience sneaking past guards and staging rescues. But she hated that she wouldn't be there herself, to make sure Kara and the other girls were okay. To make sure nothing happened to Ethan.

Somehow in the past four days he had started to matter to her. Too much. And the thought of him getting hurt or killed was devastating.

He bent his head, his kiss settling over her like her favorite cashmere hoodie. An oasis of warmth, comfort, and safety on this cold, freaky night.

"Trust me," he whispered, sliding his nose against hers before kissing her again. "Let Derek and me do what we're good at, and everything will be fine."

She leaned her face in to his chest, breathing in his warm scent. It had been so long since she'd trusted anyone, depended on anyone for help.

But Ethan and his brothers were tough, determined, strong. If anyone could save Kara from a monster like Connors, they could. "I'll stay with Danny," she said.

He pushed away from her and opened the door, and she caught his arm as he stepped out into the hall. "Be careful."

He shot her that thigh-melting, toe-curling grin. "You're not getting rid of me anytime soon."

It was just getting light as Ethan and Derek made their approach. Coastal fog had settled along the ridge, sending fingers of mist winding through the canyon. Ben Moreno had done a quick assessment of the property. A keycode-accessible gate blocked the driveway entrance from the main road, and another gate, flanked by two men, guarded the main property.

Most of the twelve acres was dense redwood forest, undeveloped, easily accessible by foot. The main grounds were guarded by a state-of-the-art security system. But Ethan and Derek had yet to find a security system they couldn't bypass.

Right now his biggest concern was avoiding any early-morning hikers as he and Derek hoofed it up the trail. Sure, Northern California was known for its weirdos, but two heavily armed men dressed in camouflage running through the woods at five in the morning were bound to attract notice.

"Moreno, give me your position." Ben responded from the woods near the gate guarding the main house. "Take out the guards as quietly as you can," Ethan said, "and see if you can find a way into the main house. We'll enter from the northeast corner."

"Roger that."

They veered off the hiking trail, following a deer path that went up a steep slope. The sun was gaining strength, washing the fog in a yellowish gray light. They needed to hurry. Right now the fog was their friend, concealing them as they moved through the woods. Ethan wanted to get inside before it burned off.

He and Derek skirted the fenceline, picking their way carefully through the woods. There was a clearing several yards ahead. A gate had been installed where the road from the grounds met up with a path leading to the neighboring open-space land. Derek got busy disabling the security system while Ethan stood guard. They slipped through the gate and Moreno's voice crackled over the radio.

"Guards are out. I'm approaching the main house. It looks pretty sealed up." He paused.

"What is it?" Ethan asked as he and Derek jogged up the fire road that took them past a dilapidated riding arena and run-down barn as they approached the main house.

"There's a vehicle approaching. A black Lexus sedan."

Connors slammed his phone down. Fucking amateurs. Was no one capable of doing the job they were paid for anymore? First Metcalfe had failed to take care of Toni Crawford. Now he didn't return any of the calls Karl had placed to confirm he'd taken care of Kramer.

Kramer had to be dead. When they'd left him, Metcalfe had his gun to the man's head.

But with the way this week had gone, Connors wouldn't rest easy till he knew for sure.

And now this. His guests had just called him to inform him there was no one at the gate to let him in. Dodd and Anderson knew he was expecting people this morning, and they'd chosen the same exact moment to go have a piss?

"Karl, go down and let them in. You," he said to Martinez, whose dark eyes glowed, piglike, in his pockmarked face, "go get the girls and bring them up here." A smile stretched his lips. "Tell them their new owners are here."

Kara jumped as the door banged open, and she huddled closer to Emily as weak light filtered through the doorway.

Crater Face came in and unlocked Jessica from her headboard, flipped her over, and cuffed her hands behind her back.

"What's going on?" Kara said as Emily started to whimper. Crater Face didn't answer as he half dragged Jessica out the door. She heard a car door slam and then he came back inside. "Wait! Where are you taking them?" she demanded when he unlocked Emily, cuffed her, and dragged her, kicking and struggling, out the door.

"You're all going," he said, his wet, fleshy lips spreading

over nicotine-stained teeth. "Up to the big house. Your buyers are here."

"No! My dad is coming for me! He won't let this happen."

"Your daddy is dead, you little bitch. That's what happens when you fuck with Mr. Connors. You get a bullet through your brain."

Her father was dead? How? Didn't he give them what they wanted in exchange for getting her back?

Time froze as he reached up to unshackle her wrist from the bed. This was not how it was supposed to go. Kara's dad was going to get her out of here and then she was going to send help for the others. She had it all planned out.

The truth hit her with crushing force. They'd never intended to let her go. She'd seen all of them, including Mr. Connors—seen details of the property. She knew they had taken the other girls. Maybe they'd even planned on killing her dad from the very beginning.

She couldn't let this happen. She'd played along meekly, cooperated this entire time, doing what they said so they wouldn't hurt her. Now she had to fight. She didn't care if she was hurt, even if she was killed. Whatever happened couldn't be much worse than being raped and sold into prostitution, as they planned for her, Jessica, and Emily.

She heard the metallic slide of the handcuff releasing from the metal headboard. She had only a split second to act. Her wrist slid free, and Crater Face moved to flip her on her stomach. But he was careless, had gotten used to her cooperation and wasn't expecting a fight.

Before he could flip her, she brought her knee up, nailing him in the jaw. He swore and fell off the bed. Kara scrambled out the door and over to the SUV parked outside the shack. Emily and Jessica stared wide-eyed out the window. Kara's sweaty fingers slipped on the door handle.

Locked!

She risked a glance over her shoulder, a short, sharp scream bursting from her throat when she saw Crater Face barreling out of the shack. "I'll get help," she promised, praying she could make good on it as she took off at a sprint.

"Get back here, you fucking cunt!"

The ground was damp and cool under her bare feet as she veered over into the brush that bordered the dirt road. If she could make it to the woods, she might be okay. She heard the SUV roar to life and ran harder, stumbling but not slowing her pace when something sharp stabbed the sole of her foot. The car was getting closer. Kara fled through the grassy clearing, and headed for the trees.

"What is taking so long?" Connors smiled at the speaker, who sat in the wingback chair flanking a low coffee table across from his desk. Distinguished-looking with his precisely barbered salt and pepper hair and exquisitely tailored suit, Kenneth Barnes looked like he was attending a high-powered business meeting.

Only the presence of two armed bodyguards gave any indication otherwise.

The man took a leisurely sip of his coffee and gave Connors an inquisitive look as he waited for the girls to arrive. He glanced meaningfully at his watch. "How much longer do you think this will take?"

Connors's cell phone rang.

"The Kramer girl, she got away," Martinez said, breathing fast like he'd been running hard. "Ran into the woods. I'll find her."

Connors didn't let his smile slip as he held the phone away from his face. "Will you excuse me a moment?" He walked into the hall where he could vent his rage in private. "You fucking idiot. How did this happen? No, never mind. Don't tell me. Bring the other two here. I'll send Dodd and

Anderson after her. Do not fuck up again, or I will personally cut off your balls, put them in a blender, and make you drink them through a straw! Are we clear?"

"I'll be right there."

Connors cursed as he dialed Dodd. These fucking amateurs were going to be his downfall.

He couldn't take the car in the woods.

The car stopped but Kara didn't, dodging between the trees, pulling up short as she ran into the six-foot-tall fence surrounding the property. She jumped up, grabbed the top, and tried to pull herself over, but she wasn't strong enough.

Frustrated sobs built in her chest as she tried again, scraping her knees and feet on the rough wood as she tried to scramble up the wall. She lost her grip and fell, tumbling to the ground. Sobbing, she waited for Crater Face to come charging at any second.

She heard the revving of the SUV's engine, then, like a miracle, the sound faded as Crater Face drove away.

Toni paced back and forth in the conference room. Ethan, Derek, and Ben had been silent since witnessing the black Lexus enter the property. Both she and Danny listened intently, but the only noise coming over the radio was the crunching of leaves as the men moved through the woods.

"Ethan, what is going on?" Toni muttered as she poured herself another cup of coffee. She took a sip without really tasting it.

Danny, who stood stock-still behind the leather chair at the head of the table, shot her an annoyed look. But Toni knew he didn't like being left behind any more than she did. She could tell from the way his massive arms tensed and rippled under his skin that he wanted to be out there, in the thick of it, instead of stuck back in the office thanks to his injured shoulder.

Toni sat back down at her computer. Since Ethan and Derek had left, she'd distracted herself by finding out everything she could about William Connors and Whitepoint. So far she'd tied him to three previous aliases in four different countries, all of whom were wanted in connection with drug and human trafficking or money laundering.

He was a slippery fish, always managing to stay two steps ahead of Interpol and the FBI, going underground, consolidating his cash, and cropping up in a new city with a new identity.

As Toni kept her ears tuned to the smallest sound from Ethan, Derek, and Ben, she continued tracing Connors's money trail. She might have been left out of the rescue mission, but at least she could do her best to make sure he didn't have access to his millions. By the time she was through, every law enforcement agency across the globe would have details on every penny she could find, every account would be flagged.

"What's that look for?" Danny asked, his voice harsh in the humming silence of the conference room.

"Just making sure Connors won't have the funds to set up shop again anytime soon."

Danny's gray eyes glittered as he bared his teeth in a nasty smile. "He won't get away." He reached one massive hand up to rub his injured shoulder.

Toni jumped as his phone rang, her heart pounding in her chest. It couldn't be Ethan; she would have heard him on the radio. Still, she unabashedly eavesdropped on his side of the conversation.

"Why don't we wait a few days to see if it pans out," he said. A pause. "Because we didn't find anything in Bali, and Australia is a guaranteed dead end."

It was their father, had to be.

Danny's next words confirmed it. "Dad, this isn't a good time. We're right in the middle of something. Yeah, the Kramer girl. I'll talk to you later."

"Your father?" Toni asked.

Danny flipped his phone closed. "Yeah."

"Sorry about that," Toni said. At Danny's puzzled look she said, "About your mom, I mean, disappearing the way she did." When Danny didn't reply, she licked her dry lips and nervously met his inscrutable look. "I don't know if Ethan told you, but my sister ran away and was murdered. It was a long time before we knew what happened to her. So, um, anyway, I know what that's like."

"I got over it a long time ago," he said finally, but kept staring at her with that hard, metallic stare.

Toni squirmed in her seat and wished she'd stifled the urge to share with Ethan's scary big brother.

"He told you about our mother?" Danny asked a few minutes later. Toni looked up to find him studying her like she was a specimen under a microscope.

Toni nodded. "A couple of days ago. I'm sure it's no big deal," she said, wondering from Danny's reaction if Ethan had broken some brother-bond of silence.

Something resembling a smile pulled at the corners of his full lips. "He never talks to anyone about that. None of us does."

What was that supposed to mean? She could read everything and nothing into that tidbit. She was dying to ask Danny, but he didn't strike her as the type who'd be interested in dishing about what his brother's topics of conversation did or did not signify.

And Toni didn't have any more time to dwell on it herself, as the sound of a crash and a scuffle crackled over the radio.

There was the sound of branches breaking and a female scream cut short.

Toni locked eyes with Danny as her blood froze in her veins.

"Kara," Ethan's voice was low, steady, reassuring. "Kara, it's okay. We're here to help you."

CHAPTER 16

AT FIRST ETHAN had thought it was a deer crashing through the underbrush as he and Derek had skirted the perimeter of the main grounds, staying in the cover of the woods as much as they could as they headed toward the main house.

Then he caught a flash of white, a glimpse of dark hair, as someone darted between the trees. Someone running hard, running scared, snapping branches and crushing needles without a care for the noise.

Derek nodded at Ethan and they separated, moving swiftly and silently through the brush as they flanked the girl. Ethan approached from behind as Derek headed her off from the front. She stopped short when she saw Derek, her bare feet skidding in the leaves that covered the damp earth. Stumbling back, she let out a sobbing scream.

Ethan silenced her with a hand over her mouth. "Kara, it's okay," he whispered as he subdued her panicked struggles. Not an easy feat, even for a man of his size and strength. Kara was a tall girl, strong and athletic, with the added fuel of fear running wild inside her.

He clamped his arm around her waist and pulled her hard against him, murmuring in a low, steady voice, "Kara, it's okay. We're here to to help you."

Derek held his hands up and approached slowly, making shushing sounds. After a few seconds, Kara got it, and her struggles slowed, though she still held herself ramrod stiff against Ethan.

"I'm going to take my hand away," Ethan said, "and it's very important that you don't scream, okay? No one knows we're out here and we don't want to attract any attention."

She nodded against his hand. "Who are you?" she asked when he removed his palm.

He quickly introduced himself and Derek. "Your father hired us."

"Is he dead? The guy, he wants something from my father—a chip or something. There was supposed to be an exchange, but they said he was dead—"

Ethan held up a silencing hand. "Your father is fine," *for now,* "he's safe at our office. But we need to get you out of here."

"You said they're here," Derek said. "Who's here?"

"They're going to sell us," Kara said, her voice breaking. As she talked, Ethan and Derek directed her back toward the gate they had come in through.

Ethan's mouth pulled into a grim line. "Us? You're not the only one?"

"No. They brought two more girls yesterday. We're all part of this online community."

"The V-Club, yeah, we know all about it."

"So you know what they're planning to do to us?" she asked. Derek nodded and caught her arm as she stumbled on a root.

"You have to go back for them," she said. "Jessica and Emily—Emily's only, like, fourteen. We can't leave them."

"No one's leaving anyone," Ethan said. "Moreno," he said, voice sharpening. "Meet us at the northeast gate. I want you to take Kara back to Gemini headquarters. We're going after the other girls."

Within minutes Moreno arrived, appearing out of no-where, seeming to melt out of the woods.

"How many we got up there?" Derek asked.

"Besides the guys at the gate, we have at least one armed bodyguard inside with Connors, and two guys in the Lexus, assume both are armed. One is definitely muscle."

"Crater Face—he's got a gun," Kara said.

Ethan looked at her inquiringly, and she described the guy with the bad skin she'd somehow managed to get by while he was in the process of transporting the girls. "He was chasing me in the car, but then all of the sudden he stopped and turned around."

"He'll be looking for you," Moreno said. "Let's get going." He took Kara gently by the arm and started to lead her away.

"Will they be okay? You won't let anything happen to them, will you?"

"Your friends will be fine, Kara," Ethan promised. "We won't let them be taken. Your father will be waiting for you back at our offices." He addressed Toni and Danny through his mike. "Ben is twenty-five minutes out. Call Marcy and tell her Kara's on her way. Call the police and explain the situation. Derek and I are going in for a closer look."

Moreno and Kara slipped through the gate and down the steep slope as Ethan and Derek took off for the main house. As they got closer they slowed their approach, taking cover where they could. The SUV Kara had mentioned was parked in the drive. The girls were already inside.

They crept around the back of a horse barn whose stalls had been converted into a four-car garage to plan their approach.

"At least three, maybe five armed," Derek mused, checking the magazine in his Sig and flipping the safety off. "Not the worst odds we've seen."

"Not even close," Ethan said. "Besides, we have surprise on our side."

The front door opened and a man hurried down the wide wooden steps of the front porch. About five ten, with a thick neck that bulged over the back of his shirt collar, the man had dark, greasy hair and a dark, acne-scarred complexion.

"Crater Face," Derek mouthed to Ethan.

The thug was hurrying for the beat-up SUV.

Keeping low, Ethan crept along the side of the barn and ducked down next to the SUV, skirting it as Crater Face opened the driver's-side door. As he took a step into the car Ethan came up behind him, locking his arm around the guy's throat and bracing the other hand behind his head. Crater Face struggled, heaving his thick, heavy body against Ethan's hold.

Ethan breathed slowly, calmly, focusing all his energy into the muscles of his arms as he choked away the guy's supply of oxygen. Finally he slumped, a dead weight in Ethan's hold. Ethan and Derek quickly bound his hands and feet, stripped him of his weapons, and heaved him into the backseat of the SUV.

He and Derek sidled along the house, peering in windows until they located Connors and his visitors. They were in a room at the back of the house, and Ethan and Derek had to strain on their toes to see inside.

Here the ground began to slope, then dropped away sharply. The room opened up onto an expansive redwood deck with twenty-foot wood pylons that braced it into the hillside.

Inside, Derek could see Connors seated, talking to another man, a well-dressed business type in his late forties. Next to Connors was the big, beefy guy from earlier, while a slick, dark-haired guy stood in the opposite corner. The way he watched Connors, Ethan made him as Gray Hair's bodyguard.

Ethan studied the other man carefully. The man was decent-enough-looking with his good suit and silk tie. But even through the glass Ethan could pick up the sick glint in his eyes as he walked a slow circle around the two terrified girls, both dressed in white nightshirts similar to the one Kara had been wearing.

What kind of fucked-up psycho got off on kidnapping avowed virgins and raping them?

He looked at Connors's cool, almost reptilian look of satisfaction. What kind of monster tracked the girls down to feed someone's sick fetish for profit?

He looked at Derek and knew from his cold, closed expression that his brother was thinking the exact same thing. "I could go up into that tree," he said, indicating a massive redwood. "I'm pretty sure I could take out all of them."

"Too risky," Ethan shook his head. "You don't have your scope, and the glare of the window could throw you off. You could hit one of the girls."

Gray Hair looked pointedly at his watch, and Connors made a conciliatory gesture and pulled his phone out of his pocket. He punched in a number, frowning as he held the phone up to his ear. He flashed his friend a reassuring smile that was a little tight around the edges. He hung up the phone and said something, made a placating gesture to the other man.

Gray Hair shook his head and said something to his thug, who pushed away from the wall and pulled out his gun, sweeping it in the direction of the girls, who huddled in the center of the room.

Connors dropped his congenial facade and got between the thug and the girls, his face going red as he said something to Gray Hair. The thug raised his gun, pointing it at Connors now as Gray Hair motioned him out of the way.

Connors countered by yanking his own pistol out of his waistband and leveling the muzzle at the thug's nose.

"Guess that answers whether or not he's armed," Derek said.

Through the double-paned glass, Ethan could hear the muffled shrieks of the girls, the shouts of the men. Then, without warning, so fast they barely saw it, Connor's big, beefy bodyguard shoved Connors aside, lifted his Uzi, and sprayed the room with machine-gun fire.

The girls screamed and hit the deck as Gray Hair took one in the chest. His bodyguard managed to squeeze off a round before doubling over, shot in the stomach. Connors grabbed the dark-haired girl by the arm and the blond girl by the hair and dragged them to their feet as he shouted orders at his bodyguard.

Ethan and Derek took off at a dead sprint around the house, guns drawn as they circled, and entered through the open front door. Ethan entered first, moving softly through the front entryway before motioning Derek to follow.

They pressed back into the walls flanking the closed door to the office. It sounded like chaos inside, the girls screaming in spite of admonishments in German and English to shut up. Men groaning while Connors barked at his bodyguard in German.

The door burst open and the girls spilled out first. Without hesitation, Ethan grabbed them and thrust them into a nearby bathroom, then ducked as bullets peppered the wall above his head.

"Run, Wilhelm!"

The bodyguard didn't even see Derek on the other side, didn't see him fire the shot that blew the bodyguard's hand off and sent his Uzi flying.

Screaming in pain and cradling his mangled hand, the man didn't stop. Like a crazed, wounded bear he charged Derek, closing his hands around his throat. Ethan scrambled to get a clean shot as his brother's eyes started to bulge.

But Ethan didn't need to bother. Though his face was rapidly turning purple and a vein throbbed in his forehead,

Derek's hand was absolutely steady as he brought his gun up to the thug's chest and pulled the trigger.

The man's hands slipped from Derek's throat as he fell to his knees, dead. "We need to get Connors. He went out the back."

They stepped over the thug's body like it was a bag of garbage and ran past the other wounded men, through the sliding glass doors that opened onto the deck. They ran to the edge and looked over. There was a break in the ground cover where Connors had landed. Dark footprints led into the dense woods.

"Toni, Danny," he said into his mike, "the girls are safe. Derek and I are fine."

"Speak for yourself." Derek coughed.

"We have two wounded, one dead. Connors got away on foot."

Now would be a good time for the police to show up. As if on cue, he heard the din of approaching sirens. He looked out into the woods, searching for a sign of movement, a sign of Connors, but could see nothing. His fist clenched around the railing of the deck, and he felt like kicking himself. After all this, Connors had still managed to slip away.

Toni watched as Marcy Kramer grabbed Kara and held her to her thin chest, laughing and weeping as she stroked her daughter's hair. Marcy had only just learned the truth about her daughter's disappearance, and Toni had spent the last thirty minutes keeping tabs on her, preventing her from finding the conference room where Jerry was being held. Toni was pretty sure that if Marcy found Jerry, she'd stab him to death with a letter opener or a ballpoint pen.

It was a good distraction, especially when, fifteen minutes ago, an explosion of shouts and gunfire had come over the radio. The auditory assault sent Toni's fear spiking as she listened, helpless, wondering who was wounded? who was dead? Who was having the life choked out of him by someone screaming in German? Who took the shot that was fired so close to one of the brothers it sounded like it was happening inside the conference room?

Marcy had looked on in confusion as Toni stood frozen in fear. Even Danny, big, tough, scary Danny, hadn't been immune, coming over to stand next to Toni and gripping her hand until Ethan's voice had crackled over the radio.

"Toni, Danny, the girls are safe. Derek and I are fine."

Connors had fled on foot but Toni didn't care as long as Ethan was okay. Tears of relief pricked her eyes at the sound of his voice. She tried to brush it off, tell herself she was just as relieved Derek was okay, but she knew that was a lie.

She cared about Ethan. Way too much for someone she'd only known for four days. A scary, deep kind of caring that was bound to leave her with a mile-wide hole in her chest if she wasn't careful.

Then Kara and Ben Moreno arrived, putting aside any opportunity for deep emotional analysis. Marcy hugged and rocked her daughter, sobbing how sorry she was. Kara patted her mother's thin back and buried her head in Marcy's shoulder as if she were seven instead of seventeen.

Toni went over and gently guided Kara to a chair. "Why don't you sit down and take a breather before the police get here to take your statement."

Kara sat down, and Toni knelt beside her chair and slipped her arm around Kara's shoulders. She looked tired, her hair tangled around her face, bruises and scratches marring her legs and arms, but otherwise okay, considering. Still, Toni wanted to make sure. "Did they hurt you?"

Kara looked up at her, her lips trembled. In that moment she looked much more like a little girl than a woman. "No, not really. I mean, they didn't rape me or anything." Fat tears rolled from under her lashes. "But I was so scared. Especially when the other girls got there and I realized they weren't going to let any of us go."

"But you managed to get out of there," Toni said.

"Fought off a guy twice her size," said Ben admiringly as he offered Kara a glass of water. Ben was cut from the Gemini mold, tall, dark, and lethal-looking. But his dark eyes were warm as they looked at Kara.

Kara took the water and smiled, hero worship shining in her eyes. "Jessica and Emily are okay, right? Ben says Ethan and Derek found them."

Toni nodded. "The police are up at Connors's place now, and both Jessica's and Emily's parents are on their way up."

Kara's shoulders relaxed and her grip loosened on her water glass. Her eyes turned somber as she looked up at Toni. "Can I see my dad?"

Toni looked at Marcy, who gave a grudging nod. "He's down the hall."

She took Kara's arm and led her down the corridor. "He's in a lot of trouble, isn't he?" Kara said, pausing before the closed door of the conference room.

"He's not the only one," Toni said meaningfully.

Kara did a decent job of feigning confusion.

"I saw the pictures, Kara. I know the V-Club isn't the only thing you've been up to."

Hot color rushed into Kara's face. "Does anyone else know? My dad will kill me."

"Your dad is very happy to have you home safe. Not to mention that he has much bigger things to worry about. But after this is over, you and I are going to have a serious talk."

Kara nodded and grabbed Toni in a fierce hug. "Thanks for looking out for me."

Toni hugged her back as tears burned her eyelids, and she

opened the door to the conference room so Kara could see her father.

Their reunion was cut short by the arrival of the police, and Toni spent the next few hours giving her statement and providing the police with everything she knew about Jerry Kramer, William Connors, their arrangement to sell intellectual property to terrorist organizations, and Connors's twisted plan for revenge when Jerry balked at delivering the goods.

She watched as the cops loaded Jerry into the back of a squad car, knowing he would be on the phone to his lawyer in record time. She had little doubt that his elite legal team would broker a deal and that Jerry would be let off with little more than a slap on the wrist. But the damage to his reputation would be irreparable, and the press would crucify him. There was satisfaction to be had in that.

She only hoped Kara and her younger brother didn't suffer anymore in the aftermath.

Her stomach churned as she downed what had to be her fiftieth cup of coffee, and she wondered how soon they could wrap everything up and go home. She was grungy and exhausted and she wanted to crawl into bed for the next week or so.

Preferably with Ethan.

But there was no sign of him, and they hadn't heard a word since he'd informed them the police had arrived at Connors's compound. He and Derek had turned off their radios, and Toni imagined they were busy smoothing everything over with the cops. No mean feat, since there were three gunshot victims to explain.

Finally, the police were ready to let Kara and Marcy leave. Toni walked them out to Marcy's car and hugged Kara again before she got into the passenger seat of her mother's BMW station wagon.

"I'll come by tomorrow, okay?" Toni said, and Kara nodded.

She turned and found herself locked against Marcy's thin, trembling frame. She placed her hands awkwardly on the smaller woman's shoulders.

"Thank you," Marcy said, her thin arms surprisingly strong as she wrapped them around Toni's waist. "Thank you for looking out for her."

"It's what you hired me for," Toni said, Marcy's emotional display making her more uncomfortable by the second.

"No," Marcy said, pulling away and wiping her eyes. "I've been too caught up in my own problems, not paying attention to what's going on. I believed Jerry when he said she'd be home in a few days. But if you hadn't kept digging . . ." her mouth pulled tight, and Toni knew she was fantasizing about cutting off her ex-husband's balls. "You saved my daughter, Toni, and I won't forget that."

Marcy gave her a last, heartfelt squeeze and climbed into her car. Toni turned to go back into the office. The police needed a few more details about Connors's financial records before she could go.

"Looks like you have a satisfied client."

His voice curled low in her belly and pulled her mouth into a smile as she turned around. Eyes sunken with fatigue, sweat streaking his face and staining his shirt, Ethan was the most glorious sight she'd ever seen.

He reached for her hand and she went to him without hesitation, letting him pull her into his arms. She leaned in to his chest and started to shake, the sound of gunshots ringing in her ears as she relived those short, terrifying moments when she and Danny could hear everything but had no idea if Ethan and Derek were okay. "I was worried," she said. Understatement of the year.

Ethan wrapped his arms tightly around her and she felt

the warm press of his lips on her cheek. She tilted her face up to meet his kiss, needing to feel him, taste him.

"Ethan!" Danny's voice boomed into the parking lot. "When you're done playing grab ass, the cops want to talk to you two."

CHAPTER 17

"COME HOME WITH me." Ethan slipped his arm around Toni's waist and pulled her against him. The police were finished with them for the time being, and now all Ethan wanted was to get Toni alone.

She nodded slightly and finished packing up her laptop, then followed him out as they both studiously ignored Derek's cocked eyebrow, Danny's yell of "Ride 'em, cowboy," and accompanying thumbs up.

"Do you think they'll catch him?" Toni asked as they drove to his place. "Connors, I mean?"

"They've issued an APB and they're watching the airports and borders. It'll be damn hard for him to slip away."

"Even harder without his bottomless money pit," she said with a smug grin that made his cock thicken.

"Remind me never to piss you off. You're evil."

"Only to those who deserve it."

They walked into his condo, the early-evening sun streaming through the windows. It felt odd and surreal that it was only the evening, that the sun was still out. It felt as if a week had passed since they'd followed Kramer to the lab, instead of mere hours.

"I really hope they nail him." She looked at him, her hazel eyes wide, shell-shocked from the events of the past eighteen hours. "I'm just glad you got the girls out before . . ." Her throat convulsed over a swallow.

He threaded his hand through her hair and pressed her face into his neck. "Don't think about that. It's over now." He pulled her tighter against him and buried his face against her hair. He kissed the top of her head and trailed kisses down her cheek.

"It was so awful," she said in a choked whisper. "Hearing the gunshots, not knowing if you were okay."

"Yeah, it kinda sucked for me, too."

She laughed a watery chuckle and lifted her mouth, her lips parted, to brush his. She wove her fingers through his hair and held his face to hers. "You could have died. I was afraid you were going to die." She'd been holding it together, composure never slipping as she'd stayed on task, but now he could feel the tremors coursing through her body as delayed trauma hit her with devastating force.

He clung to her, holding her steady as she kissed him with adrenaline-fueled desperation. He opened his mouth, welcoming the invasion of her tongue. She tugged his shirt up his chest and ran her hands up the hot skin of his back.

Her hand ran up his rib cage, pausing when it came across the bandage on his left side.

"What is this?"

"Nothing," he said, grabbing her hand and pushing it down to his waist.

"You're hurt," she said, her voice catching. She yanked his shirt over his head and leaned in for a closer look.

"It's just a graze," he said, trying to distract her as he felt her fingers go icy against his side.

"I swear to God," she said, her voice trembling, "if you try to tell me it's just a flesh wound I'll punch you."

"It is." He chuckled, wincing as he peeled back the bandage the EMT had put on to reveal the angry-looking furrow. "I didn't even need stitches."

Her fingers traced the outline of the wound before she carefully replaced the bandage. Then her palm slid up to his chest, pausing over his heart, warming over the steady thrum. Her other hand curled around his neck and she pulled him down for a kiss. "I need you," she whispered against his mouth. "I need to feel you inside me."

He slipped off her glasses and tossed them in the direction of the coffee table without breaking contact with her mouth, starving for the taste of her. He knew what she was feeling. After dodging several rounds of gunfire and feeling a bullet graze his side, he felt it, too. The need to connect, to prove he was alive in the most primitive way possible. His cock thickened to full hardness, eager to give her what she needed.

Her shaky fingers fumbled with his belt and tugged at the buttons of his pants. He shoved his pants down his hips, groaning when her hand closed around his erection, stroking, squeezing almost enough to hurt.

"I want this." Her grip tightened in emphasis. "I want you inside me. Now." She kissed and stroked him, panting and almost frantic with desire.

This was a side of Toni he'd never seen, aggressive, hungry, needing him like no woman ever had before. Her hunger stoked his own. His cock swelled in her hand. He felt bigger, harder than he'd ever been in his life. Somehow he got her pants off, shoving them and her panties down in one motion. They had barely hit the floor before she toppled onto the sofa, pulled him down on top of her, and guided him between her thighs.

The sweet heat of her pussy closed around him, so slick and tight he had to use every ounce of restraint not to come right then and there. She shimmied under him, trying to urge him deeper, but they kept sinking into the too-soft cushions of the couch. With a groan of frustration, Ethan caught her legs around his waist and lifted her off the couch and onto the floor.

She moaned and arched her back as his hips surged forward, taking him deep. He tried to slow down, tried to restrain himself from pounding her into the floor the way he wanted to.

Toni's fingers clawed his back. "Don't hold back," she said, shoving her hips against his. "I don't want you to be gentle. I want you to fuck me like you mean it."

He felt her tighten around him, tightening her inner muscles, kneading him from the inside until he saw stars behind his tightly closed lids. "Jesus," he muttered, unable to resist her demands. He thrust without restraint, pumping inside her so hard he had to hold her hips to keep her from sliding up the floor. He was lost in her, every cell focused on her, giving her what she needed, his own pleasure almost too much to stand.

She arched and moaned under him, her hand coming up to caress his face. Her thumb traced his mouth, he caught it and sucked it between his lips.

"Ethan." His name was a broken sigh, her eyes were wide, filled with something like wonder as she gazed up into his face.

His heart swelled like a balloon in his chest, bigger and bigger until he couldn't breathe. She made him feel as powerful as a god, as weak as a child, as she wrapped her legs around him and stared up at him with such open need and and trust. He drove himself impossibly deep inside her, gasped at the slick, tight grip of her sucking him in, sucking out his soul.

He was falling, so hard and fast, the ground coming up to meet him with devastating impact. He hoped he made it out of this alive.

Toni was going to die. She was sure of it. Nothing could feel this good and not kill her. Every nerve in her body was tight as a bowstring, vibrating with pleasure, and she knew that when she came she was going to blow apart into a million little pieces.

She would welcome it, since it meant she got to feel Ethan's huge, amazing cock tunneling inside her again and again. He was amazing. He was magic. Heating her from the inside out, banishing her fear, her guilt, until nothing was left but pure, unadulterated pleasure. She wanted this never to end. She wanted to swallow him up, absorb him into her body and never let him go. She wanted to hold on to him forever so everything could always feel as perfect as it did right now.

Her fingers tensed, her toes curled, and her orgasm bore down on her like a tidal wave, pounding through her in a devastating wash of pleasure. He rode her through it, sliding in and out as her body clenched and pulsed around him.

His thrusts increased in speed and her legs fell open. Suddenly he froze, muscles trembling. "Fuck."

"What is it," she whispered. "Why are you stopping?"

"I didn't put on a condom, I'm safe, I promise." He made a mournful sound, bent his head, and started to pull out.

"Don't," she said, gripping the firm muscles of his ass to keep him in place. "It's okay."

"What about . . ."

Awash in pleasure, she didn't even consider the consequences of what she was about to do. "It's okay. I'm okay. I want you to come inside me."

He rested his weight on his elbows and came down over her, his mouth closing over hers. His tongue slipped inside, taking up a slow, lazy rhythm that matched the movements of his cock inside her. Pleasure curled in her belly until she was again matching him thrust for thrust, moan for moan. His hand came between them, his thumb circling her clit in firm strokes. "I want you to come with me," he murmured into her mouth. He swelled even bigger inside her, filling her completely. His eyes squeezed shut and the muscles of his arms and chest stood out in stark relief. With a final thrust, he let out a harsh cry and came hotly inside her.

Another orgasm rolled through her, jolting in its intensity. When she came down, Ethan was murmuring against her neck, telling her how beautiful she was, how much he wanted her. Then, so muffled against her throat she wasn't sure she heard him right, "Christ, Toni, I think I'm in love with you."

The words were barely out of his mouth before every muscle in his body went rigid. Her eyes flew open. The shock in his blue eyes mirrored her own.

"I . . ." His voice trailed off.

She didn't have any problem completing his thought. "Didn't mean to say that. Don't worry about it." Her throat got tight as she struggled against the urge to say it back.

What kind of idiot fancies herself in love after less than a week?

She pushed at his shoulders and tried to roll out from under him. But he held her there, pinned. "Don't. Don't try to shut me out."

"I'm not shutting you out. I'm letting you off the hook." She shoved harder at his shoulders, and this time he let her go. Avoiding his gaze, she searched the living room for her discarded clothing.

"What if I don't want to be let off the hook? What if I meant it?"

"No one falls in love in less than a week, Ethan," she said, as much for her own benefit as for his. "We had sex. Again. That's all." She hurriedly pulled her panties up over her hips and reached for her T-shirt. He was still on the floor, bare-chested, with his pants below his hips. His penis was still half hard, slick and shiny-wet with the evidence of their passion.

The evidence of her stupidity. Oh, God, what had she done? The damp warmth between her own thighs mocked her, a vivid reminder of how careless she was not only with her heart but also her body. "I need to go," she said, launching herself toward her jeans where they lay crumpled in a corner.

"Toni, you're not leaving until we talk about this." She heard Ethan get up, heard his heavy footsteps approaching. "How are you going to get home, anyway, when you don't have a car?"

And of course he wouldn't give her a ride. Bastard. "I'll call a cab," she snapped. Her phone rang as she slid her jeans up over her hips and she fumbled it out of her pocket, grateful for the distraction.

The caller ID displayed her friend Megan's number. She'd been friends with Megan since high school, when they were the only girls in the computer club. Megan still lived in Seattle and worked for Microsoft.

Toni felt a sharp stab of homesickness at the sound of her friend's voice. At Megan's innocent "How are you?" Toni wanted to lock herself in the bathroom and give her a play-by-play rundown of the events of the last few days, starting with the call from Marcy and ending with her confusing and dangerous reaction to Ethan Taggart. If anyone could talk sense into her, it was Megan.

But Ethan was staring at her, his arms folded across his bare, hard chest as he waited for her to get off the phone. Toni would keep Megan on the phone all night if it meant avoiding the discussion Ethan wanted to have.

Toni offered a semi-sincere "Fine" in response to Megan's greeting.

"You don't sound fine," Megan replied, "but I have excellent news."

"Good, because I need it."

Ethan cocked a dark eyebrow and made a "wrap it up" motion with his hand.

Toni walked over to the window, showing him her back.

She heard his heavy footsteps thud across the hardwood floor, the thump as a kitchen cabinet was opened with unnecessary force.

"Sounds like there's a juicy story there somewhere," Megan replied, and Toni couldn't help but look at Ethan, who was still watching her and obviously eavesdropping. "Too bad I'm about to go into a meeting. But I wanted to tell you—I got the job in Paris!"

Toni made appropriately excited sounds and offered her congratulations. Megan had been trying to get transferred to the Paris office for six months now.

"That's not the only good thing," Megan continued. "I'm only going for a year, so I'm keeping my apartment. I already talked to my landlord, and he's totally cool with you subletting it until I get back. Isn't that great?"

"Yeah, great." Toni's reply sounded lackluster to her own ears. What was wrong with her? This was the solution to all of her problems. Megan's apartment was gorgeous, located only a few blocks from where Toni had lived. Better yet, her landlord was a family friend, so her rent was well below market value. And because Toni wouldn't have to come up with a security deposit, she didn't need to wait to build up her bank account before she could move.

All she had to do was pack up her stuff and head north. Megan's apartment was furnished, and Toni could fit all of her stuff in the trunk of a car.

"Why don't you sound more excited?" Megan asked. "This is the perfect solution to the mess John left you in after he dumped you."

"I know," Toni said, doing her best to brighten her tone. "This is great news." But the reason for her lack of enthusiasm was less than twenty feet away, chugging a glass of water before slamming it down on the granite counter, watching her with an intense blue gaze that made her insides melt like hot fudge. Less than a week ago, Toni would have been jumping for joy at Megan's news. Knowing that she didn't have to wait until the end of the summer to move back to Seattle should have had her over the moon.

But that was before she had met Ethan, before he'd blown through her defenses and shown her exactly how amazing a physical connection between two people could be. But it was more than mere sex. He'd stripped her naked in more ways than one. She'd talked more to him about Michelle and how her sister's death had affected her than she ever had to anyone. He alone seemed to be able to get her to admit to feelings she'd rather keep boxed up and stored away in some deep, dark corner of herself.

He'd told her he loved her.

But she couldn't stake her future on something he said at the height of climax.

Could she?

Even as every logical brain cell warned her he would get bored quickly and move on, something about him tugged at her, pulled her in, until the thought of moving back to Seattle and never seeing him again was enough to make her physically ill.

Didn't she know better than this? Hadn't her experience with John been enough to teach her not to change her plans for any man? She knew exactly what she had to do to be successful, and John had thrown her so far off track she'd been afraid for a time that she'd never get back on. Now she had the chance to get back to her friends and to the life she'd missed so much in the past year. Was she actually contemplating giving it up? And for what? Because she was stupid enough to let a handful of orgasms fool her into believing this was true love?

Really, Toni, what in God's name do you think is going to happen? That he's going to declare his everlasting love for you? Ethan Taggart can have any woman he wants—and most likely already has. Are you seriously dumb enough to fall for the whole taming-the-bad-boy fantasy?

Toni was a lot of things, but stupid wasn't one of them. What she had with Ethan was nothing more than a hot fling, made all the more intense by the crazy circumstances of this case. Now the case was closed, Kara was home, and Toni couldn't let herself be distracted from her plan.

"I can't wait to get back," Toni said, almost convincing herself that she meant it. Ethan's eyebrows shot up, then furrowed slightly. "I've been dying to get out of here for months."

"I can't wait to see you! But I'm leaving for France at the end of August, so you have to get up here before that so we can hang out for a little while before I go."

"I just have to wrap up a few details on a case and pack up my stuff. After that, I'm out of here."

Toni hung up, trying to ignore the imposing male presence now standing about two inches behind her. As if Ethan would ever be ignored.

"Who was that?" he demanded.

"My friend Megan." She told him the news about the apartment. "I'd been planning to move back sometime this fall, as soon as I could get enough money saved up. But now I don't have to wait. Isn't that awesome?"

He looked at her as if she'd just grown two heads. "You're moving back to Seattle?" he asked.

"I've been planning it for the last year. I moved here to be with John," she said, not wanting to go into the details of how, in addition to being cheated on, she'd found herself financially stranded here or else she would have moved back immediately. She didn't want him to see how pathetic she really was. "Since we broke up, there isn't much point in my staying."

"What about us?" he said.

"What 'us' Ethan? We've known each other for four days." Her heart picked up speed, and she tried not to let herself get caught up in wild fantasies of ending happily ever after with Ethan Taggart.

He leaned into her, pressing her up against the wall. "Tell me you don't feel anything. Tell me you don't feel something real here."

"Okay, I can't deny there's something, but it's not enough to base the rest of my life on." He leaned in and kissed her, sliding his tongue against hers in a way that made her want to give in, promise him anything. "People don't fall in love in four days," she repeated, feebly.

"Maybe I have," he said and kissed her again.

CHAPTER 18

ETHAN CUPPED TONI'S face, holding her still as he pinned her against the wall and devoured her mouth. His hands shook with frustration and lust. And, yeah, a little bit of fear.

Okay, a whole fucking lot of fear.

There was a reason he didn't do love, didn't do commitment. He'd seen what love had done to his father, seen how his mother's abandonment had wrecked a strong man. Ethan never wanted to be that weak.

Yet here he was, handing over his heart to a woman too scared to take it. Didn't she realize he was terrified, too? Terrified of getting hurt, opening himself up and letting someone inside?

But after he'd blurted out the love he'd only barely acknowledged, he figured it was up to him to be brave. Or stupid, depending on how you looked at it.

"I love you," he said, the words sounding angry to his own ears.

"Don't," Toni gasped against his mouth, almost crying. "Don't say that."

He nipped her lip in punishment, then slicked his tongue over the sore spot. "Why not?"

Her fingers dug into the bare skin of his back, kneading

the tense muscles. "Because I want to believe you too much, and we both know it's not true."

His cock swelled against the zipper of his pants, insistent, needing. "You can believe me, please believe me." Christ, was he begging? He kissed her throat and sucked at the delicate skin.

"Please don't do this to me," she said, her voice high and breathy. "I don't want to talk right now. It's too much."

She didn't want to talk? Didn't want to hear him say he loved her? "Fine."

He could force himself to be patient.

She brought her hands between them and pressed against his chest. "I need some space. I need to process everything."

"No," he said as he pinned her wrists above her head. "No talking. No thinking, either."

She was running scared, and he wasn't about to let her shut him out.

He yanked her shirt up her chest, releasing her wrists long enough to drag it off. Her feeble protest was cut short when he bent his head to her bare breast, taking her stiff nipple into his mouth and rolling it along the edge of his teeth. He sucked her hard, reveling in the sounds of pleasure burbling from her throat at the little taste of pain.

He ground his erection against her and slid his hand down the front of her pants. "You're mine, Toni," he said, sliding his fingers along the wet folds of her pussy. "You don't want to admit it yet, but you know it's true."

"No," she gasped, and arched her hips up against his hand. She was molten-hot, slick with a combination of his come and her own sweet juice.

His cock stretched another inch at the remembered feel of coming inside her, the feel of her tight, slick pussy closing around him with no barrier to his pleasure. "Yes," he said, shoving her pants down her legs, keeping her arms pinned firmly above her head.

One-handed, he shoved his own pants down his legs. Gripping his cock, he positioned the engorged head against her slit, sliding himself up and down and around her clit until they were both shaking and panting with need. "You feel how much I want you?" he breathed into her mouth, licked inside hers, groaning when she sucked on his tongue the way he wanted her to suck on his cock.

"So I make your dick hard," she said, nipping at his bottom lip before licking away the sting. "I'm not the first woman to do it and I doubt I'll be the last."

Anger mingled with lust at her comment. Even with all the blood rushing to his dick, his brain suffused with a red fog, he knew what she was doing. Bringing up other women to remind herself not to trust him. Grasping at anything to keep herself from falling, too. He hooked his elbow under one knee and hitched her leg over his hip. Thumbing his cock into position, he bent his knees and entered her in one firm thrust.

She arched her back and gasped as her body stretched around him. He held himself inside her, pinning her against the wall as he gripped her chin, forcing her to meet his gaze. He rocked his hips forward, wanting to crawl up inside her, wanting to go so deep she'd never lose the feel of him.

"Believe that if you want to," he said, gritting his teeth, sweat rolling down his chest as her pussy gripped him. "But I could fuck you for a year straight and not get enough. I've never met a woman I couldn't walk away from until you." He pulled out an inch before thrusting back inside.

He looked down to where they were joined, and the sight made his balls ache. Her plump clit was red and ripe, her flushed pussy lips stretched around him. The muscles of her stomach were tense and quivering, and he could feel every shudder like an electric current up his dick.

He bent his head, his mouth closing over the moist skin of her neck as he slid in and out with slow, deliberate strokes.

Making her feel every inch of him. Savoring every inch of her. Pausing with every stroke to swirl and stir and stoke her higher.

Her breath caught, her lips parted on a groan, and he knew she was about to come. God, he loved watching her, the way every trace of her hard shell fell away in an instant.

He didn't change his pace, didn't ease his grip on her wrists or her hip as she started to shake and shudder. Moaning, she buried her face against his throat. He hissed at the feel of her teeth closing over his skin in a punishing love bite. He focused on her pleasure, drawing out every last ripple of her climax until she collapsed weakly against him.

He released her hands, drew her arms around his shoulders, and gently withdrew, sucking in his breath at the silky drag of her body against his painfully sensitive skin. He wanted to come so bad he could taste it, but he wasn't done with her, not by a long shot. If this was the only way he could get to her, he was going to have her in every way he could think of until she admitted she was his.

He carried her to his bedroom and laid her across his bed, coming down over her and cradling her face in his hands. His kiss was urgent, hungry, as his hands skimmed over the long lines of her body. He parted her legs and slid back inside, never breaking his kiss. His thumb brushed over the velvet-soft skin of her nipple, coaxing it back to hardness as she shifted under him.

"Please," she whispered against his lips. "Give me a break. I can't—"

"Sure you can," he said, flexing his cock inside her, making her gasp.

"It's too much," she said, shifting underneath him, which only served to drive him deeper inside.

"No such thing," he said, reaching between them to dip his fingers between her swollen folds. He circled his thumb around her clit, careful to avoid the sensitive tip.

She clenched around his cock, kissing him frantically as a high, keening sound started in her throat.

He lost count of how many times he made her come before he finally let go, his body shaking and trembling as everything, all the fear, frustration, the love she didn't want to acknowledge ripped through him, pouring out of him in thick hot spurts as he spent himself inside her.

When he could finally breathe again, he rolled to the side and pulled her against him. "I do love you," he whispered and kissed her cheek before falling asleep, still buried inside her.

He made love to her throughout the night, waking up to pull her into the shower to wash them both clean. Spent the next hour or so licking and fingering her to climax after climax. He shouted his pleasure to the ceiling when she took him in her mouth and returned the favor.

Dawn was licking at the sky and he was drifting off to sleep, Toni tucked against his side, when her heard her voice, barely audible, muffled against his shoulder.

"I love you, too," she whispered.

He thought his heart might explode as she nuzzled into his chest. Within seconds they were both sound asleep.

Toni padded out of the bedroom the next afternoon, barefoot, wearing one of Ethan's T-shirts. Delicious smells wafted down the hall, and she followed them to the kitchen, where she was presented with the mouthwatering sight of Ethan cooking in nothing but his boxers.

She was shell-shocked, her body achy, her mind blown by last night. She'd lost count of how many times she'd come. He'd been relentless, not giving her an inch of space, not losing contact with her for a second. He'd held himself inside her, touching her, stroking her, wearing her out and wearing her down until finally "I love you" had forced its way past her lips.

Now, in the brutal light of the summer day, she was forced to acknowledge that her feelings were real. But she still wasn't sure it was enough.

He turned around, his mouth stretching into that sexy, cocky grin that made his eyes crinkle at the corners. He set down the spatula and came over to her, grabbing a handful of the shirt to pull her to him. She closed her eyes, breathed in the musky-clean scent of his skin, and tipped her face up for a kiss.

His lips parted against hers, and even after last night's acrobatics, she could feel a hot stir low in her belly.

"My eggs are going to burn," he murmured against her lips, "but hold that thought." He turned his attention back to the stove.

Toni poured herself a cup of coffee and sat down at the breakfast bar, taking the opportunity to gather her wits. It was hard to keep her common sense when he was looking at her, completely impossible when he was touching her.

She watched him slide an omelet onto a plate, her heart tripping at the way the muscles in his back rippled. He got to her the way no man ever had before. John had hurt her feelings, hurt her pride, when he'd dumped her. And she hadn't felt anything approaching the intensity she felt for Ethan.

The thought sobered her, and her stomach twisted as she looked up and caught Ethan staring at her with a look of guarded expectation.

He put a plate in front of her and she took a bite of the fluffy omelet. "It's delicious." She had no idea what was in it—some kind of exotic cheese and maybe sundried tomatoes? But it tasted amazing.

"Yeah, enjoy it, because it's the sum total of my cooking ability."

She smiled and took another bite, trying not to notice as the silence grew thicker with every passing second. She shoveled in the last bite and looked pointedly at her watch. "I should probably get going." She slid off the bar stool and he grabbed her arm to stay her.

"Where do you have to go?"

"I told Kara I'd stop by today, and I need to go by my apartment."

He took a bite of eggs and washed it down with a sip of coffee. "Speaking of which, I think you should just pack your stuff and move it over here." His tone was casual, but his look was hard, probing.

Her gaze slid away from his. "Ethan, I need time to think about all of this."

"Fine," he said, his muscles tense as he wiped his mouth and stood up. "Let me shower and I'll give you a ride to Kara's."

She shook her head. "I'll get a rental car."

"Why spend the money when I can—"

She held up her hand. "I need some space, okay? Give me some time alone to figure everything out."

He moved closer, backing her into the breakfast bar. "Did you mean it?" he asked softly. "When you said you loved me?"

She closed her eyes, shoulders slumping. She couldn't deal with this, not right now.

"Did you?"

"Yes," she said, barely audible.

He slid his hand up to cup her neck, brushed his thumb across her lips. "Then I don't understand what it is you have to figure out."

He kissed her cheek and she started to melt. God, he was doing it again. In about five seconds she wasn't going to be capable of saying no to anything.

"Stop," she said, proud of how firm she managed to sound. She ducked under his arm and managed to get a few feet of space between them. "Yes, I said it, and yeah, I meant it, but how do we know this is even real? How do we know it's not just sex?"

"You think this is about fucking? Fine. Stay here and I'll not fuck you for as long as you want to prove how I feel about you. I love you, Toni. Don't ruin it just because you're scared."

"People don't fall in love in four days." But the churning in her gut was telling her otherwise.

He slammed his fist into the counter. "I'm so goddamned sick of hearing you say that. How long does it take? A week? A month? A year? How long do you need, Toni?"

She shook her head. She didn't know. She'd known John a lot longer and trusted him, and look where that had gotten her.

"Just know this," he said, his voice somber. "I meant it when I said I love you. And in case you're wondering, I've never said it before, because I've never meant it before. So you may want to take that into consideration before you go running back to Seattle with your tail between your legs."

Her head snapped up. "I'm not running anywhere."

"Not yet." His thick shoulders were bunched with tension.

"I haven't made any decisions yet," she said.

He didn't say anything, just stared at her, disappointment carving deep grooves in his face.

"I should go," she muttered, fleeing for the relative solitude of the shower.

She grudgingly allowed Ethan to drive her to pick up a rental car. She needed to get away from him, from the devastating effect he had on her mind and body, so she could make a good choice.

A smart choice.

A safe choice.

He grabbed her when she started to get out of the car,

capturing her mouth in a hungry, needing kiss. "You're staying with me tonight."

"I'll call you later," she said noncommittally.

His kiss bruised her lips and made her toes curl before he
released her.

Toni's head was pounding by the time she got to her apartment later that evening. She'd stopped by Marcy's to see Kara
and was relieved to see that Kara was doing fine, considering her ordeal.

"Mom says I have to go see a therapist," Kara said,
rolling her eyes. She was trying to act as if being kidnapped
and having her father try to cover it up were no big deal,
but Toni could see the lingering shadows in her eyes.

"I'd say that's a very smart idea," Toni replied. "You may
think you're fine now, but stuff like this can sneak up on
you and mess you up in ways you never realize."

Kara shrugged and settled deeper into the couch cushions. "Yeah, well, I made her a deal. If she'd quit drinking,
I'd go to therapy. So she's checking into rehab next week."

"That's great. Is it an inpatient program?"

Kara nodded and took a sip of her soda, her gaze darting
from Toni's. "My mom wants us to go stay with my aunt,
but she lives in the middle of nowhere up in Oregon. My
brother likes it out there because there's, like, horses and
cattle and stuff. But I hate it up there. I mean, there's seriously nothing to do."

"It's only for a month, right?"

Kara nodded and tucked a strand of hair behind her ear.
"Yeah, well, I was thinking, maybe instead of going to see
my aunt, maybe I could stay with you."

That brought her up short. "Kara, my apartment is a
shithole. Trust me, you don't want to stay there."

Kara's eyes were wide, beseeching. "We could stay here. I
bet my mom won't care. She's, like, ready to give you any-

thing for finding me. Or we could stay at my dad's—there's seven bedrooms."

Toni shook her head. "I don't even know if I'll be here through next week. I'm probably moving back to Seattle-"

"You're moving? But what about me? You're the only one who knows, you know, what I did. You're the only one I can talk to."

Toni rested a hand on Kara's shoulder. "You can talk to your mom. She'll understand. And if you can't talk to your mom, you can talk to the therapist. They have to keep that stuff confidential. You have a lot of people who love you and want to support you."

"Yeah, whatever," Kara said, shrugging off Toni's hand as she stood. "Um, before you leave town, is there anything you can do to, like, make those pictures disappear?"

Toni sighed. "I'll do what I can." She could blow up Toby Frankel's server and get the pictures removed from Kara's FacePlace page, but she couldn't completely obliterate everything. "Just be careful about what you post from now on."

"I will," Kara said. "I shut down the V-Club. Even though that pervert Barnes is in the hospital, there are probably a bunch of other weirdos just like him," she shuddered.

Toni liked to think that millionaires willing to pay hundreds of thousands of dollars to rape virgins were a rare breed, but you never knew. And if the threat kept Kara cautious, all the better.

"I'd better get going," Toni said.

"Yeah, you probably need to start packing for your big move."

"I'm still not sure I'm going yet. And even if I do, we'll keep in touch."

Kara snorted. "Yeah, right, I'm sure you'll be down here every weekend."

Toni rubbed her suddenly aching temples. Up until a week

ago, she'd felt almost completely alone. Now she had two people urging her—practically browbeating her—to stay, even as everything was lining up perfectly for her to move back home. "Look, I'll be at Ethan's later if you need anything. He's only five minutes away."

"Whatever." Kara turned her attention back the the latest issue of *Us Weekly*.

Marcy caught her as she got to the door and handed her an envelope.

"Thanks," Toni said, surprised. She usually had to send Marcy at least two invoices before she got paid. "But I haven't even billed my hours yet."

Marcy shook her head, her eyes watery but clearer than they'd been in a long time. "Send me your bill whenever. This is extra."

Toni opened the envelope. There was a check inside for fifty thousand dollars. "Marcy, you don't have to—"

Marcy held up her hands. "You saved my daughter's life, you and Ethan. It's the least I can do."

Toni walked out to her rental car and drove to her apartment in a daze. Fifty thousand dollars was enough to wipe out the remainder of her debt and give her a solid cushion as she looked for a job. She could afford to move back to Seattle, no problem. It didn't even matter if Michelle's apartment was available or not.

She could even afford to wait and see if things worked out with Ethan.

At the thought of him, she pulled her phone out of her pocket to call him as she'd promised. But as soon as she dialed his number her phone beeped in distress, indicating the death of her battery.

Maybe this was better. This way, she could gather her thoughts, tell him of her decision in person. The thought made her heart pound and her head throb as she went through her apartment, packing up the essentials she needed for the next few days. Her hands shook as she threw a pair of running shoes into her bag.

Could she really do this? Really open herself up and risk her heart with Ethan? Move in with him after only five days, hoping it would turn into forever?

Warmth coursed through her at the thought of his smile, the touch of his hands, his low voice in her ear whispering that he loved her.

Would she ever forgive herself if she didn't? Scary as it was to admit it, she needed him. And if she shoved her fear aside for a minute, she was pretty sure he needed her, too.

None of that stopped her from feeling a little sick as she walked down the stairs of her apartment building, imagining his face when she told him she decided to take him up on his offer. What if, in the time she'd been gone, he'd realized how crazy it all was? Maybe he was sweating bullets, praying she'd packed up and headed for Seattle.

She shoved the thoughts aside, holding an image of him telling her he loved her, asking her to give them a chance. He wouldn't say something like that unless he meant it. She hadn't known him long, but she already knew him well enough to be sure of that.

The tension in her neck began to ease as she loaded her suitcase into the trunk of the rental car. The evening sun drenched the parking lot in golden light, washing the stout brick building in butterscotch. Her blood hummed as she anticipated seeing Ethan.

And saying yes, to whatever he offered.

She heard a small noise behind her and turned slightly, freezing when she felt something hard press against the base of her skull.

"Make one move, and your brains will splatter across this car."

CHAPTER 19

"GET IN THE car," Connors ordered, shoving Toni toward the front of the car, careful to keep his gun trained on her. He saw her eyes dart frantically around the deserted parking lot, could see her calculating the risk of making a run for it. "The safety is off. My finger is on the trigger. I'd advise you not to try."

Anger and fear showed in her eyes as he directed her into the passenger seat and slid in after her. He shoved her over to the driver's side, not releasing his hold on her for an instant. "Start the car."

"Take the car. Take whatever you want," she protested. "I won't even tell anyone you were here." Her voice was high with fear, her eyes wide.

He pressed the gun hard into her ribs. "Start the car," he repeated. Her already porcelain complexion went completely white, and he smiled. He loved the look of fear on a beautiful woman's face. He couldn't wait to see her eyes widen with horror when he held a gun to her head and fucked her. But first things first. He needed her to undo the damage she had caused. If all went to plan, there would be plenty of time to use her before she died.

She backed the car out and drove to the street exit. Before she could make the turn onto the main road he grabbed

her face and forced her to meet his gaze. "Do not try anything stupid. Do not try to attract attention in any way. I
will not hesitate to kill you."

The truth was, he needed her alive, at least for a short
while. But better to make her think her life depended on her
cooperation.

He would kill the bitch in a few hours, after she helped
him regain access to his funds. She was already a loose end,
supposed to be dead two days ago, but somehow she'd
managed to survive. And somehow she'd managed to follow the money trail back to him, just as he'd feared when
Jerry first warned him. Now the authorities were alerted to
his offshore accounts. Holds had already been placed.
There was no way he could get to the money without tip-
ping them off. And if he didn't have access to funds, he was,
as they liked to say, completely fucked.

Twenty-five years. Over twenty-five years he'd been in
business, dealing with the scum of the earth, the most ruth-
less figures in organized crime, and he'd never come close to
being caught. Not by the authorities. Not by those who
wanted him dead. He and Karl had always slipped away,
pockets full, ready for a fresh start.

Now look at him. His entire operation brought down because of a deal gone wrong with an idiot like Kramer. He'd
underestimated Taggart, dismissing him as hired muscle who
would blindly follow Kramer's direction. And Toni was to
have been handled before she could cause any more trouble.

Yet it had all gone completely awry, and here he was, escaping by the skin of his teeth, alone. His gut twisted as he
remembered his brother, loyal to the end, covering him so
he could escape. Now Karl was dead, thanks to this bitch
who had led Karl's killers to their door.

He looked at Toni, her jaw set in tight lines, her knuckles
white against the steering wheel. He would make her pay

for her part in his brother's death. He smiled at the thought of her crying, begging him for her life.

"Get onto highway 101 North," he said.

"I still don't see why you don't just take the car," she said easing up on the gas, hesitating before merging onto the freeway on ramp.

He leveled her with a cold, hard, stare. "The longer you cooperate, the longer you will live. Drive."

"Where are we going?" Toni asked, shooting a nervous glance at the gun William Connors had pointed at her side. He hadn't answered the first half dozen times she'd asked. She didn't expect him to answer now, but was compelled to ask anyway.

They'd been driving north for nearly two hours. After they'd crossed the Golden Gate bridge, Connors had directed her to follow Highway 1 where it split off from the freeway, over to the coast. Her palms sweated as she navigated along the winding coastal road with its sharp curves and steep dropoff.

The sun was barely visible in the horizon, sinking into the Pacific. Soon it would be completely dark. She glanced at her watch. It was almost nine. Was Ethan worried? Had he tried to call her on her cell phone, which was still charging back at her apartment?

She looked at her watch again, trying to calm her racing heart, reminding herself of the tracking device still embedded inside. Connors had no clue that if Ethan wanted to, he could pinpoint her exact location.

But after the way she'd left things this morning, that was a big, fat "if."

And even if he did check up on her location, that was no guarantee he'd come after her. For all he knew, she'd taken the coward's way out and was on her way north to Seattle without a word of goodbye.

If a woman is that determined to get away from you, maybe you should stop chasing her.

His words rang in her ears, haunting her.

Please don't let me go, Ethan.

"Turn up at this intersection," Connors said. Toni did as he said, pulling off the coastal highway onto a side road. Connors directed her to a ramshackle hotel that stood next to a marina. He held her arm and walked her to the lobby. When they reached the door he paused. "Do not try anything," he said, his whisper making the fine hairs stiffen on her neck, "or I will kill her," he said, nodding to the middle-aged woman with long gray hair sitting behind the desk.

"You have high speed Internet access, yes?" Connors asked in his vaguely accented voice.

"Oh yes," the woman, whose name tag read Vera, replied. "Wireless, the whole nine yards. Not that I understand any of that. I'm still marveling at the advent of post-it notes," she said with a hearty laugh.

Toni responded with a weak chuckle, the best she could manage with Connors's gun pressing against the small of her back.

"Good," Connors said with a smile. "My wife has much work to do," he said.

"Get your computer," he said when they left the hotel lobby.

Toni shivered as she walked to the car. The evening was cool, a layer of fog settled over the coast. The streetlights washed the parking lot with milky yellow light. "What are we doing here?" Toni asked as she slung her backpack over her shoulder.

Connors steered her to the stairs leading to the second floor. "You are going to help me get the funds I require." He motioned her to unlock the door and precede him into the room.

Toni shot him a confused look.

"I know you helped the authorities locate my accounts. Now you will help me appropriate them from other sources."

"You want me to help you steal money? It's not that easy, with anti-fraud measures—"

His eyes narrowed and he brought the gun up to her chest. "I know you are very good at what you do. I trust you will find a way."

Her first instinct was to refuse. Connors was going to kill her anyway, so what did it matter. At least this way she would die knowing she hadn't helped a sociopath like Connors.

Ethan could still come for you. It was a long shot. But she still had her watch, and as long as the tiny tracking device emitted a signal, there was a possibility that Ethan could come after her.

Holding onto that shred of hope, she turned on her computer and logged on. "I shouldn't do this from my computer. They'll know it was me."

"By the time anyone realizes, I will be gone." Connors said. "Speaking of which, I need to make a phone call."

He flipped open his phone and dialed, but stayed close so he could watch every move she made. Still, she waited for a moment of distraction so she could send a quick e-mail or instant message—something to let Ethan know what was going on.

But Connors kept his flat green eyes locked on her screen as he spoke on the phone. "One a.m.? No sooner?" He bit out a curse. "That it was short notice is no excuse. The boat should have been ready to go." He cursed again and flipped his phone closed.

That explained why they'd stopped near the marina. Connors was going to slip out in the dead of night, into the open sea. From there he could easily head south to Mexico or South America.

"What exactly do you want me to do here?" Toni asked, holding her fingers stiff over her keyboard.

Connors held his phone out to show her the display.

"That is an account number for Kenneth Barnes, the man your friends shot yesterday morning."

"The man who was going to buy Kara and the other girls," Toni said.

Connors smiled was cold, reptilian. "In a manner of speaking. Barnes is exceedingly wealthy, and can afford to indulge his fetishes. Even if he survives, he won't miss the seven million I want you to transfer."

She turned back to her computer screen, trying to ignore the gun less than an inch from her cheek. "It could take me awhile, depending on the security protocols." How long could she stall? Long enough for Ethan to realize something was up and come find her?

"You have until one a.m."

Toni looked at her watch. She had three and a half hours to break into Barnes's account and transfer the funds. More than enough time.

But if Ethan didn't realize—or care—that she was gone in that time, she had no illusions about what was in store for her. As soon as he got his money, Connors would kill her without a second thought.

She was gone. Without a fucking word. Without even a phone call or even a fucking text message, Toni had taken off.

When she hadn't called or showed up after several hours, he'd been annoyed. When her cell phone had dumped him straight to voice mail, he'd gotten worried. Connors was still out there, after all. Even though Ethan was sure Connors hadn't wasted any time hanging around, he'd wanted Toni dead.

His stomach churning with worry and guilt that he'd let her go off on her own, he'd finally called up her tracking device on his hand held. The little red Toni dot was right there, plain as day. Hauling ass north.

His first impulse had been to jump in the car and drag her back down here, fight back her fears, convince her to stay.

Then he thought of his father, wasting his life chasing after a woman who didn't want to be with him anymore. Who wanted to escape so badly she'd made herself disappear.

If a woman is that determined to get away from you, maybe you should stop chasing her.

He'd give Toni exactly what she wanted.

Anger burned like acid in his stomach as he tracked the dot to Tomales Bay, about eighty miles up the coast, where the dot had stopped about an hour and a half ago. She must be taking the scenic route, he thought bitterly.

Taking all that time she said she needed to get her head together.

He paced the length of his living room, wanting to punch something, to throw something. He called Derek to meet him for a workout, but Derek was busy with a client. Danny was still injured, and Ethan didn't want to have to pull his punches.

He looked at his Blackberry. Toni had accused him of being a player and she was right. He had dozens of women's numbers, and he could have one of them under him in less than an hour.

But the thought of being inside anyone but Toni made his throat tighten and his stomach twist.

How could she just leave without a word? How could he be so stupid to think he was in love with her?

He remembered something his dad had said about falling in love with his mother. "I saw her and it felt like I'd been hit upside the head with a two-by-four."

Smashed in the face by love. Yeah, that about said it all.

He poured himself a tall vodka on the rocks. This bottle was three quarters full and there was a backup in the freezer. He hoped it was enough to take the edge off.

His phone rang as he took the first biting sip. He called himself an idiot at the burst of disappointment when he saw it wasn't Toni, but Marcy Kramer.

Reluctantly he picked up.

"Um, hi," said an uncertain voice. "This is Kara. I was wondering if Toni was there. Her cell's off, so I know you might be having, uh, private time, but I really need to talk to her."

"What makes you think she's here?" he said, more harshly than Kara deserved.

"Because, when I saw her this afternoon she said she'd be at your place tonight."

Ethan barked out a laugh. "Well, she never showed up." He took another sip of the vodka.

Silence. Then, "But she told me she was going to your place right after she stopped by her apartment."

Uneasiness curled in his stomach. "She must have changed her mind, because last time I checked, she was in her car, heading north."

"She left? Without saying goodbye?" Kara's voice cracked on the last word. Ethan pressed his thumb and forefinger against his own burning eyes. "No. Toni wouldn't do that. She's way too anal."

"What do you mean?"

"The last time we met for coffee she texted me three times to confirm, and once while she was on her way to let me know she was running late. She doesn't just turn off her phone and go offline."

The uneasy feeling built and built until it roared in his ears. "I'm sure she's fine." He grabbed his keys and wallet off the counter. He was probably overreacting. Setting himself up to be dumped on his ass when he burst into Toni's hotel room and demanded an explanation. But he'd rather have his heart crushed in person and be sure she was safe. "I'll call you if I talk to her, and you do the same, okay?"

"Okay," Kara said, worry evident in her voice. Then, her voice so soft he could barely hear her, "You don't think that Connors guy has her do you?"

Ethan checked the clip in his gun and shoved it in his waistband. "I sure as hell hope not."

He slammed his car into gear and took off up the highway and prayed Toni was running from him, because the alternative was even worse.

Toni rubbed her bleary eyes and clicked on the "confirm transfer" button. It had taken a clever approach, but she'd finally managed to get into Barnes' account and transfer the funds to Connors's account. All with about fifteen minutes to spare until the boat came.

"It's done," she said finally. Her eyes burned and she swallowed back the lump in her throat. The likelihood of Ethan riding to her rescue was fast dwindling to zero.

"Good," Connors said. She shuddered as he laid his cool, dry palm settling on the bare skin between her neck and her shoulder. She held herself still as marble as his fingers dipped down to trace the neckline of her T-shirt. "Now, how to pass the time until my friends arrive?"

Toni swallowed back bile and tried to subtly shrug off his hand. His fingers bit into her tender skin and he rested his other hand, the one with the gun, on her opposite shoulder.

"You have been so cooperative up until now."

Was this how it was going to end? Raped and murdered in a hotel room?

She bit the inside of her lip, keeping her gaze focused on her computer screen as she struggled to keep it together. His hand slid down her chest to cover her breast and Toni fought not to gag.

"I was thinking," she said as though his hand wasn't squeezing her breast hard enough to leave bruises, "you could use someone like me."

"Exactly my thought," he said, pinching her nipple hard enough to draw tears.

"That's not what I meant," she snapped. "It was easy enough for me to track you down. You need someone to help you cover your tracks better. Someone like me."

His hand stilled.

"I know you're not going to let me go when your boat gets here. I'm guessing you're planning to kill me and dump my body off the side."

"What are you proposing?"

"That you keep me around. I can make myself useful. I can hack into any bank, any corporate network you want. You won't have to deal with people like Jerry to get what you want. I can get all the information you need."

She turned to gauge Connor's reaction, encouraged by the light of greed in his mud colored eyes.

Then her stomach bottomed out as he gave her a regretful smile and shook his head. "An interesting suggestion. Unfortunately, I cannot risk my livelihood working with those I cannot trust."

Toni looked him dead in the eye, struggling to convey confidence she didn't feel. She knew if she panicked Connors would feed off it like an animal. "I can be very loyal if the price is right."

He smiled, thin lips stretching over capped white teeth. "You make me want to believe you."

Toni felt her heart slow a fraction. She'd bought herself some time.

His smile disappeared. "Now show me how cooperative you can be." His hand landed in the middle of her chest and he pushed her back on the bed.

Toni instinctively twisted under him, kicking and squirming as his hands tugged at the hem of her shirt. She forgot about the gun in his hand as she fought to escape the brutal fingers digging into her skin.

He reared up and backhanded her across the face. Stars exploded behind her eyes as his knuckles cracked across her cheekbone. He hit her again in an open-hand slap. Her lip throbbed and her mouth flooded with the metallic taste of blood.

Connors's face was flushed red, a vein throbbing in his forehead. His hand closed around her neck and Toni felt panic rise as he slowly increased the pressure, cutting off her air by degrees as he brought the gun to rest in the middle of her forehead.

Without releasing his hold on her neck, he roughly kneed her legs apart. She almost threw up when she felt the unmistakable bulge of his erection against her inner thigh.

His breathing was labored, his voice laced with menace. "If you want to work for me, you must show your cooperation." His fingers tightened around her throat and she felt the sting of tears as her vision grew dark around the edges.

"Okay," she managed to rasp before she passed out.

His grip slackened enough for her to breathe freely, but he didn't release her throat. The cold metal of the pistol still kissed her forehead. "Now take off your clothes and show me how cooperative you can be. Then we'll talk about letting you live."

Bile burned the back of her throat. Could she really lay back and let him rape her?

Even if she got on that boat, Ethan would be able to find her. And even if he didn't, if she was alive there was a chance for escape.

How much time would giving in buy her? Enough?

Toni grasped the hem of her shirt with shaking fingers, her eyes scanning the room for anything that could be used as a weapon even as the pistol didn't waver. There would be a moment of distraction once he got started. His guard would come down, at least in the moment of . . . oh God, she couldn't go there. She just had to lay back, pretend it was happening to someone else and seize any opportunity to get away from Connors before he got her on that boat.

She didn't so much as flinch when Connors palmed her roughly through the fabric of her jeans.

The bedside lamp would pack a good wallop. If she laid across the bed just so and waited for the opportunity—

Connors bit out a curse as his phone rang. Tears of relief stung her eyes when he released her to answer. She scrambled to pull down her shirt and balled herself into a corner of the bed, her entire body shuddering with revulsion.

"You are early." Connors spoke briefly to someone on the other line, eyes narrowing on Toni as he hung up. "Pack up your computer. We will have plenty of time to pick up where we left off on board."

CHAPTER 20

NINETY MINUTES AFTER he left Palo Alto, Ethan pulled into the parking lot of the Sea Cliff Inn. He took advantage of the lack of traffic and kept his eye on his radar detector as he tested the capacity of the BMW's horsepower.

The hotel was nothing fancy, a shabby, two-story structure next to a small marina. The parking lot was lit by two streetlamps on either end, their light muted by the warm mist draping the light. There were only a handful of cars in the lot, including a Cobalt bearing a sticker from the rental car company where he'd dropped Toni earlier that afternoon.

He got out of his car, his jaw clenching as he wondered what the hell he was doing here. All the way up he'd been tempted to turn around. As the miles passed, his doubt grew. Connors was likely long gone, biding his time while he waited for the next opportunity. What were the chances he'd risk everything by going after Toni?

Paranoia had propelled him to the car, compelled him to drive nearly one hundred miles in the middle of the fucking night, all for a woman who was likely trying to get the hell away from him.

As he drove, arguing with himself about whether to turn around, he felt an unwilling kinship with his father. Was this how his father had felt all these years ago when Ethan's mother had disappeared? The bone-deep need to deny the truth staring him in the face? Guilt came with the realization that, as much as he wanted to find Toni safe and alone, in a sick way he hoped she was kidnapped, because it meant she didn't leave him.

Staring at Toni's car in the thick silence of the parking lot, Ethan vowed to be more supportive of his father's search, no matter how futile.

Now, to find Toni and get this over with. The tracking device allowed him to find locate the hotel, but not the exact room. He called her cell phone, shoulders tightening another notch when he got dumped straight to voice mail yet again. Her phone was still off.

Of course.

He approached the darkened lobby and knocked. Nothing. He pounded harder, peering in the glass to see if he'd managed to rouse a desk clerk.

Shit. Looked like he'd have to go door to door, or wait until morning until Toni came out to her car. Hell. He'd driven all this way, and if he had to wake a few people to find her, so be it.

He started across the parking lot when he heard a door open on the second floor. Through the milky light he could see the the figure of a tall woman emerging. He couldn't make out her features, but every cell in his body knew it was Toni. His jaw tightened and he started forward, freezing when he saw a man appear immediately behind her, slightly shorter than Toni, with a wiry build.

The way he held her , one hand gripping her arm, the other nestled against her back, he knew Connors had a gun pressed to her back.

Fear gripped his guts like a cold fist, along with guilt for having the passing hope Connors had her. Seeing the woman he loved, held at gunpoint, nearly buckled his knees. He would let Toni rip out his heart and eat it in front of him, as long as he got her out of here.

He swallowed back his fear and tried not to think about what might have happened to her in that hotel room.

Ethan sank back into the shadows, measuring the distance, trying to figure out the best way to approach, to get Toni away from Connors. They were down the stairs now, Connors guiding her across the parking lot. If he stuck to the outside and moved fast, he could flank them, maybe tackle Connors from the side.

He cut right and started to move, ducking in between cars, thankful he'd slipped on running shoes that didn't make much noise. He slipped his Beretta from his waistband and checked the clip, and heard the low rumble of a boat approaching.

Connors steered Toni down a small slope toward the Marina.

Through the fog he could see a pinprick of light, and a little gray Zodiac emerged through the fog, its way lit only by a handheld flashlight as it approached the dock.

Connors started moving faster, his grip on Toni's arm never slackening as he pulled her to the boat. There were two men on the boat. If Connors got Toni on that Zodiac, he was fucked.

Christ, why hadn't he brought backup, called the police? Even with Kara's assurances Toni wouldn't just take off, Ethan still hadn't been convinced she was in danger. Anger pummeled him as he thought of all the hours he'd wasted, angry and seething, convinced she'd taken off. And now he might lose her because of it.

His gaze never wavering from Connors and Toni, he took out his phone, dialed 911, and set the phone on the ground. He couldn't risk being heard, but the police would eventually track the open signal.

In the meantime, he had to keep Toni from getting on that boat.

He crept closer, cursing the dim light and fog that interfered with his visibility. Connors and Toni were halfway down the dock. A few more feet, and he was close enough to see the expression on Toni's face.

Even in the dim light, he could see the swelling of her cheek and the skin purpling in a bruise. Her lip was swollen, a smear of blood at the corner. Anger roared through his veins. Goddamn bastard had hit her. Maybe worse. His hands started to shake, his guts curdling at the thought of what Connors might have done to her in the hours he'd had her.

Despite the terror Toni must be feeling, her face was carved in marble. But he could see her eyes darting around the parking lot, looking for any chance, any opportunity to make a run for it.

It was up to Ethan to make sure she had one.

He slowed his breathing, pushing back the anger that made his hands shake with the need to tear Connors apart with his bare hands. He needed to stay cool, keep his focus, not allow his anger or fear to interfere with what he needed to do.

Connors walked another two steps, into a puddle of light. This was it. Ethan wished Derek were here. Even though Ethan was a marksman in his own right, he'd feel a lot better if his brother the sniper were the one taking this shot.

And Ethan knew he had only one shot.

Bracing his legs in a wide stance, he lifted his Beretta and took careful aim.

"Connors!" he shouted.

The other man froze, startled, a nanosecond of distraction.

Toni hurled herself to the dock, giving Ethan the opening he needed.

* * *

Toni thought she was hallucinating when she heard Ethan's voice burst through the dark. Then, almost in slow motion, she felt Connors freeze, felt the pressure of the gun ease a degree, and she threw herself to the damp wood of the dock.

Shots rang out in rapid succession, and she braced herself for impact.

Running footsteps, more shots, and the motor of the Zodiac roared to life.

Strong arms wrapped around her, pulling her to her feet. She caught a glimpse of Connors, lying still on his back, a trickle of blood running from the corner of his slack mouth. A neat bullet hole pierced his forehead.

She ran, pounding down the dock, Ethan behind her, returning the fire of the men on the boat. She heard him curse and stumble.

"Don't stop," he yelled. They were almost to the parking lot.

They veered off into the darkness, and Toni heard the roar of the Zodiac engine as it sped off into the the mist.

Ethan slid to the ground, holding his leg. Blood stained his jeans, spreading from a wound in his left thigh.

"You're hurt!" Toni said, her hands hovering above the wound. She needed something to apply pressure.

"It's okay," he said, his voice tight with pain. "It went straight through the muscle. All meat, no bone," he said with a weak chuckle.

"There's so much blood."

"I'm better off than Connors."

"You came after me," she said, shuffling closer, falling into his chest when he pulled her close.

"At first I thought you left," she could hear the tremor in his voice, feel the tremor in his lips as they pressed against her cheek. "I should have come sooner."

She buried her face in his throat, breathing in his scent

like oxygen, and slid her palm up his chest to rest over his heart, comforting herself with steady beat. "I wouldn't have left like that. I was on my way to your place when Connors grabbed me."

She could feel Ethan's muscles tense as he pulled away slightly. "He hurt you," he said, his mouth pulling tight. Toni winced as Ethan's thumb grazed her throbbing cheekbone.

"It could have been a lot worse." Toni said. She explained what Connors had wanted, how she'd bought herself time. "The boat showed up before he could . . ." Her throat seized in remembered horror.

"I want to kill him all over again for laying a hand on you." His blue eyes shimmered with tears. "I waited too long to come after you, and I never would have forgiven myself if he had—"

She cut him off with a kiss, barely noticing the sting in her split lip as his arms crushed her to him and his mouth moved over hers. "I'm alive," she said when she finally broke away. "That's what matters. I knew I had to stay alive long enough for you to find me." Sirens were approaching in the distance, and a few hotel patrons poked their heads out of their rooms, drawn by gunshots.

The first squad car pulled into the parking lot and screeched to a stop.

Ethan's finger drifted to her chin and tipped her face up to meet his gaze. "It's going to take us awhile to clear all this up, but I want you to know that I love you. Nothing's going to change that. And if that means I have to commute to Seattle to be with you, I will. Whatever it takes."

Toni felt the sting of tears. "I love you too, and I—"

But her assurances that she wasn't going anywhere were cut off by a sharp order of, "Put your hands where I can see them."

CHAPTER 21

"YEAH, I'M SURE. Go ahead and list the apartment on craigslist," Toni said to Megan. It was late the following afternoon, and Ethan was still asleep. After they'd cleared everything with the local police, he'd gone to the ER where they'd stitched him up.

Rather than stay in a hotel, Ethan had insisted on going home. Loaded up with pain pills, he'd slept as Toni drove his car back home, and barely managed to get in the house before collapsing again.

"You're really sure?" Megan asked for the tenth time. "You've been talking about moving back here for a year, and suddenly you're changing your plans because you think you're in love?"

"I don't think. I know," Toni said. And she did, gut deep, where it counted. Yes, she was certifiable, taking a risk like this.

But Ethan had taken a bullet for her. The least she could do was have a little faith.

Ethan emerged from the hallway into the living room, looking tired and sleep-mussed and brutally sexy in his boxers and nothing else. His weight supported by aluminum crutches, a white bandage standing out starkly against the tan skin of his thigh, he thudded into the room and shot her a thigh-melting smile.

"Megan, I have to go," she said and hung up.

"Megan?" he said, a dark brow arched, his expression guarded.

"Yeah," she said, getting up from the couch and walking over to his side. She slid her hands around his waist and pressed a kiss into his bare chest. He held himself still, muscles tense as though bracing himself for a blow. "I told her I didn't want the apartment."

His tension eased and he let a crutch drop as he pulled her closer. "So you're staying?"

"If the offer's still good."

The other crutch dropped and he cupped her face in his hands. "Offer's always good." He bent his head kissing her with such intensity and emotion, it left no room for doubt about how he felt. But just in case, he said, "I love you Toni. I'll make you happy, I promise."

"I love you too," she murmured against his lips. "And we'll make each other happy."

Ethan had never felt anything more right, more perfect than this moment. Knowing she loved him, and no matter what happened, if she loved him half as much as he loved her, the odds were way in their favor.

"You better not break my heart," she whispered in between wet, open-mouthed kisses.

"You better not break mine." He said against her mouth, sinking his tongue into her mouth, drinking in her taste. "This is going to be great. You and me together. We're going to be great."

Their kisses got hotter, deeper, and the throb in his groin soon outmatched the throb in his wounded leg. His hand slid up under her shirt to squeeze and stroke her breasts. "I need you," he whispered. "Need to be inside you."

He felt her nipple peak against his fingers, heard the soft growly sound in the back of her throat. She wanted him just as much. "Your leg," she said, voice laced with regret. "We can't—"

He released her mouth and gave her a gentle shove toward the bedroom. "We'll manage."

He retrieved his crutches and thumped down the hall after her. When he would have stripped off her shirt, she pushed him gently back onto the bed and said, "Uh-uh. If we're doing this, you need to lay back and let me do all the work."

His cock went ramrod stiff, and he groaned as Toni hooked her thumbs in the waistband of his boxers and dragged them down his hips. She pulled them carefully down his thighs, doing her best not to aggravate his injury.

He couldn't stifle a hiss of pain as she inadvertently put pressure on the wound. She froze.

"Maybe we shouldn't do this," she said.

He grabbed her hand and pressed it against his dick. "Trust me, this hurts a lot worse."

She gave a breathy laugh and rose to her feet. He almost came as she undressed in front of him, the afternoon light slanting off her smooth, pale skin, lean curves, endless legs.

All his, for as long as he wanted.

Forever sounded about right.

She knelt over him, her back arching, taking him all the way inside her tight, slick heat. Her hazel eyes sparkled down at him, open, happy, free of shadows.

On second thought, forever might not be long enough.

Don't miss Jami Alden's next book featuring the Gemini Men—here's a sneak peek at KEPT, coming in May 2009 from Brava . . .

DEREK TAGGART. HIS name suited him. Hard and tough with plenty of sharp edges. He was beautiful in a way that reminded her of the harsh granite faces of the Grand Tetons. Rugged and chiseled, with great eyes, square jaw and cheekbones that stood out beneath his skin.

One look at him and she knew he wasn't a guest at the lavish charity gala. Alyssa would have noticed him immediately if he'd been in the crowd. His size alone would have drawn her attention. He wasn't merely tall, he was huge, towering over her, but from what she could tell it was all hard muscle. But it didn't take a psychic to see he wasn't part of this crowd, that he was here to work and he took his job very, very seriously.

She watched him, stationed up on the gallery like a sentry on a battlement. His weight shifted from foot to foot as he surveyed the crowd, looking ready to spring into action at the slightest provocation. The jacket of his suit pulled tight as he folded his massive arms across his chest. His gaze slid back to her, and even from across the room and one story down, she could feel its heat. It unknotted the tension in her neck, slid down her spine, and made a warm glow shimmer down her thighs.

This time he didn't break the stare, and it was she who

reluctantly turned away. She continued to work the room, shilling for silent auction bids on the small fortune in diamonds that adorned her wrists, fingers, and ears. Through it all she could feel him looking at her, his gaze like firm, warm fingers tracing over her skin.

Being stared at wasn't new. She'd lived in a fishbowl her entire life, first, thanks to her mother's, then to her own publicity-attracting antics. Yes, sometimes it chafed, never more than recently, but Alyssa had grown so used to being looked at, watched, and judged that she was almost immune to it.

". . . disgusting. Mindy is sixteen, and because of Alyssa Miles she thinks it's okay to go around dressed like a whore and sleeping with everyone in sight."

The snippet of conversation pierced Alyssa's warm glow. Almost immune.

Alyssa turned and gave the woman a guileless smile as though she hadn't heard a single barb.

She blocked the woman's comments out, instead focusing on him and his stare, sliding over her like a hot flame. He wanted her. She could feel it. That, too, was nothing new. Not because she was extraordinarily beautiful. But she knew she had her appeal and had played up her image as a sultry, playful sexpot in the press. Now it was all but guaranteed that men looked at her and thought of only one thing.

But this was different. Derek was different.

He had no idea who she was.

A delicious thrill had shot through her the moment realization had dawned in the study. When he walked into the room, all of her senses had gone on high alert. Not only was he a strange man, he was an *attractive* strange man. No. Scratch that. A smoking-hot, set-the-skin-of-your-inner-thighs-on-fire man. The last thing she wanted was for him to notice her reaction to his dark, sun-streaked hair, chiseled jaw, and acres of muscles.

So when he'd tried to hustle her back to the party, she'd put on her "don't you know who you're dealing with" act and tried to shoo him away like the insignificant insect she pretended to think he was.

But he wasn't having any of it. He didn't care who she was. Because he didn't know who she was.

He hadn't so much as quivered an eyelash when she told him her name. She couldn't remember the last time that happened.

Derek, who was already a blatant ten, shot up to fifteen on the hotness scale. When he shook her hand her arm felt scorched all the way down to her red-tipped toenails.

And he felt it too. She could see the surge of awareness in his eyes, the blast of desire, quickly shuttered by his dark gaze. But he couldn't hide it. Not completely.

The thrill shot through her again and it was all she could do to keep still as another socialite held Alyssa's arm so the woman's husband could admire the diamond-encrusted cuff on her wrist. He wanted her. And not like other men wanted her. He didn't want the crazy, sexy party girl or the notorious heiress.

He didn't want to fuck her so he could brag to his friends and the media about how he'd nailed Alyssa Miles and it really wasn't all that great after all.

He didn't want to fuck her so she could introduce him to a producer, a director, or a record label executive.

Derek Taggart looked at her and saw a gorgeous girl he met at a party and wanted to get with. As simple as that.

Sure, he probably saw her as a spoiled brat—her initial response pretty much guaranteed that. But a little flirting and a wide smile would go a long way in getting past any bad first impressions. The monster of her public persona was another beast entirely. The image of the fun-loving, ditzy chick whose lifestyle was funded by her father's bottomless bank account wasn't an image she'd purposely cultivated, but once established she used it to her advantage. She had thought she'd made peace with the fact that it would forever taint every interaction she had with another human being.

But the gut-deep thrill she got from knowing a man like Derek wanted her and not the image, made her realize she'd been craving that kind of honest chemistry more than she'd realized.

There was nothing to be done about it, though. As the night wore on, Alyssa didn't have another opportunity to speak to Derek, even though she knew he tracked her every move. She considered sneaking back to the study, just to see if he'd chase her down, but as the silent auction drew to a close she was surrounded by guests who all wanted one last look at Van Weldt Jeweler's exquisite designs.

"I'm going to walk Mother and Daddy out," Kimberly leaned down to speak quietly into Alyssa's ear.

Alyssa nodded. "I can't leave until the auction's over."

"I know," Kimberly replied, her voice lowering so no one else could hear. "But I'm afraid Mother is about to lose it."

Alyssa looked across the ballroom, where Grace clung to Oscar's arm. As Alyssa watched, Grace weaved, barely noticeable to the untrained eye. Her social smile was gone and her mouth was pursed tight. A pang of sympathy tightened Alyssa's stomach as she watched her father struggle to maintain his oblivious smile. She didn't envy him one bit, knowing her stepmother would explode with a vodka-fueled, venomous tirade as soon as the limo door slammed shut.

"I called Bryan," Kimberly said. "He'll pick you up in the back by the servant's entrance so you won't have to deal with the photographers."

Alyssa nodded, grateful her sister had remembered to remind the Van Weldt's regular driver of that detail. In the past six months, as she'd struggled to clean up her image and Alyssa had done a complete one eighty when it came to dealing with the press. No more calls from her assistant to alert the paps she was on her way to shop on Melrose. No more "anonymous" tips that she might show up at the Chateau Marmont with the lead actor from this season's hottest new TV series. Now, unless she was making an official appearance with her family or doing publicity on behalf of the company, she avoided reporters like the plague.

Which only served to make her a hotter target. She knew that along with the hired photographer there were dozens of paparazzi outside the Bancrofts' mansion in Atherton, waiting for a glimpse of Alyssa. No doubt praying she'd do something stupid like slip and fall and lose her top, or show her underwear and give them a money shot to sell to *Us Weekly* or *OK* magazine for six figures.

Finally the auction was over and most of the guests were milling around the front door, waiting for their cars and limos to arrive.

Alyssa did another scan of the room, tamping down her disappointment when she didn't see Derek. *Stupid. What do you think is going to happen?*

She closed her eyes, memorizing his face, taking that memory of desire in his eyes and curling it close.

She retrieved her coat from the coat check and slipped out the back entrance, down the short driveway that let to the street on the side of the house opposite the front door.

And waited. She looked at her watch, shivering at the chilly bite of the October evening. It was still early, not even ten. Before she'd moved from Los Angeles, she wouldn't have even had dinner by now. But the crowd at these charity things always skewed older, and Alyssa figured they all needed to get home and tucked into bed before midnight.

Another ten minutes passed, and the driver from the car

service still wasn't there. Annoyed, she flicked open her cell phone and called.

Bryan's town car had been clipped on the freeway. Another car was en route, but it would be at least half an hour before it arrived.

Alyssa bit back a curse and pulled her coat tighter around her, wishing she'd brought something heavier to wear over her short, backless dress.

"What's up with you going where you're not supposed to?"

The deep gruff voice slid around her, grabbed her, and wouldn't let go. She couldn't have held back her smile if she wanted to.

His eyes were hidden in shadow, but his mouth curved into a half smile. His lips were firm and full and she knew they'd be hot against her skin.

"Do I even want to know why you're hanging out at the servant's entrance looking like you're about to stick your thumb out for a ride?"

"I didn't want to have to deal with the crowd on my way out. And now my driver got into an accident, so it looks like I'm stranded for a while."

He was silent for several moments, and though his eyes were shadowed she could feel him studying her.

Ask me.

"Can I give you a ride home?"

A thrill of pure triumph shot through her and she didn't hesitate for a second. "Sure."

He looked a little surprised at her enthusiasm but quickly hid it, and left without another word to get his car. As she waited she shifted on her sky-high heels, restless, alive with anticipation. After so many months on her best behavior, a reckless urge was pulsing through her. Uncontrollable, unstoppable. She needed to forget the consequences and do something outrageous.

But this time it wouldn't be for publicity or her father's attention. This time it would be all for herself.

A silver Audi rumbled up to the driveway and Alyssa wasted no time sliding into the passenger seat. The leather was cool against her bare thighs, and the interior of the car was full of his cedar and soap scent.

He backed out of the driveway and turned the corner, passing the snarl of limos and guests crowding the circular driveway of the Bancrofts' estate.

"Where to?"

Nerves warred with desire. It had been a long time since she'd had to make the first move. Alyssa rummaged in her bag and dug out her lip gloss, slicking on a coat to give herself something to do.

Derek stopped at a stop sign. "Where are we going?"

She swallowed hard, her throat suddenly bone dry. What she was about to do was crazy. Stupid.

Necessary.

"You know, it's so early," she said, and turned to face him. She kept her eyes locked with his and placed her hand deliberately on his thigh. "And I'm not quite ready to go home."

He stared at her hard for what felt like an eternity. His thick, dark brows drew together in a faint scowl.

Her stomach bottomed out as she realized he was about to turn her down.

"You want to get a drink somewhere?"

The moment of truth. She slid her hand farther up his thigh, delighting in the swells and ripples of rock hard muscle hidden beneath wool gabardine. "I'm not much for crowds. Why don't you cut to the chase and take me back to your place?"

GREAT BOOKS,
GREAT SAVINGS!

When You Visit Our Website:
www.kensingtonbooks.com

You Can Save Money Off The Retail Price
Of Any Book You Purchase!

- **All Your Favorite Kensington Authors**
- **New Releases & Timeless Classics**
- **Overnight Shipping Available**
- **eBooks Available For Many Titles**
- **All Major Credit Cards Accepted**

Visit Us Today To Start Saving!
www.kensingtonbooks.com

All Orders Are Subject To Availability.
Shipping and Handling Charges Apply.
Offers and Prices Subject To Change Without Notice.